MURDER MAY I

GAMES WE PLAY MYSTERIES, BOOK ONE

ENDORSEMENTS

It takes very little arm-twisting to get me to read a mystery. Add a cast of characters that I can't help but fall in love with, along with an engaging plot line, and I'm even more eager to read it. Stories like that are impossible to put down because I just cannot wait to find out what's going to happen! So it was with Cathy Rueter's debut, *Murder May I*. This novel is engrossing, compelling, emotive. It's so much more than a murder mystery. It's a story of what it means to be a family. Readers of Patricia Raybon and Christina Suzann Nelson will enjoy the storytelling of Cathy Rueter.
—**Susie Finkbeiner**, author of *The All-American* and *All Manner of Things*

In her gripping debut novel, Cathy Rueter proves herself an exciting new voice in Christian mystery and suspense. In *Murder May I*, Rueter weaves a twisty mystery that will keep readers on their toes. Her richly drawn characters bring the story to life. Rueter's crisp prose and masterful plotting mark her as an author to watch. Fans of Christian mystery, take note—Cathy Rueter has arrived!
—**Robin Patchen**, *USA Today* bestselling author of *Running to You*

A murder in a fashion house, uniquely gifted twins, and a mama-bear godmother who struggles with her own challenges. With a diverse cast of characters, a gentle faith element, and a sweet romantic arc, *Murder May I* by Cathy Rueter dripped out clues and delivered multiple plot twists that kept me guessing until the end.

—Jayna Breigh, author of *The Hunted Heir*

As someone who writes primarily fantasy and dystopian, I have always admired authors who can write mystery. To be able to keep the reader guessing until the reveal, then show how all the details from the smallest to the largest fit in, astounds me. To be able to achieve this with added finesse and charm is another story. Cathy does just this. Starting with the first twist, this novel gets its hooks in you and doesn't let go until the end, using the fashion industry as a colorful backdrop second only to her cast of characters. This is one book which doesn't disappoint.

—Katelyn Pfeiffer, author of *City of End*, Book 1 in the Provenance Chronicles

I thoroughly enjoyed Cathy's debut novel, beginning with the title. She writes a riveting mystery of murder, stalking, and family secrets. Cathy's cast of flawed but faithful characters, and a few not so faithful, find themselves wrestling with their personal conflicts and secrets from the past—when murder challenges all they believe to be true. Some win their struggles through faith, family, and friends. Others don't. You will love the set of nine-year-old twins and the detectives. If you like a good mystery with twists, turns, and a bit of romance, you will be glad you chose *Murder May I*.

—Donna K. Stearns, author of *The Nazarene's Price* and *Cost & Crown*

Murder May I dropped me right into the story and kept me reading into the night. The book has all you want from a murder mystery—a touch of romance, a lot of drama, and a satisfying ending. The twists and turns kept me intrigued until the end. I can't wait for the next one!

—**Jane Daly**, author of *Lipstick and Gunpowder* and The Broken series

MURDER MAY I

GAMES WE PLAY MYSTERIES, BOOK ONE

CATHY RUETER

A Christian Company
ElkLakePublishingInc.com

COPYRIGHT NOTICE

MURDER MAY I

Cover and Interior Design: Kelly Artieri, Deb Haggerty
Editor(s): Ann Harrison, Cristel Phelps, Deb Haggerty

PUBLISHED BY: Elk Lake Publishing, Inc., 35 Dogwood Drive, Plymouth, MA 02360, 2025

Library Cataloging Data
Names: Rueter, Cathy (Cathy Rueter)
Murder May I—Games We Play Mysteries, Book One / Cathy Rueter
394 p. 23cm × 15cm (9in × 6 in.)
ISBN-13: 9798891342927 (paperback) | 9798891342934 (trade paperback) | 9798891342941 (e-book)
Key Words: Christian mystery romance suspense murder secret; Faith-based murder mystery glamour thriller love; friends to lovers spiritual mystery betrayal; Christian romantic thriller whodunit redemption; Suspense thriller fiction investigation love Jesus; Salvation murder woman danger clean romance; Christian fiction suspense secret past lovers
Library of Congress Control Number: 2025937070 Fiction

DEDICATION

To my mother, Sharon:
My loyal, caring, first fan, and original teacher.
You fostered my affection for words by offering
your lap, reading aloud to me, and, eventually,
sharing your mystery books. Thank you.
Love you, Mom!

ACKNOWLEDGMENTS

"Stitching together stories with a dash of romance and a slash of death" is the tagline for my fashion-based Christian mysteries, but just as there is more to a luxury gown than a model sashaying down the runway, a novel is greater than a pretty cover with words inside—especially one that took years to construct. So many people for whom I am grateful poured into this journey to publication that I can't name them all. Here are but a few:

Elk Lake Publishing, Inc.—Deb Haggerty, Publisher. Thank you for taking a chance on me. The ELPI team, including Cristel Phelps, Managing Editor for Fiction; Ann Harrison, Editor; and Kelly Artieri, Cover Artist. Just as buttons, sequins, and beads make a garment notable, you all enriched this story into a final, beautiful dream come true.

The 1129 Scribes critique group: Joy, Paula, and Deena. Properly fitting a pattern takes patience and learning the tricks of the trade from others. Thank you for lending all of that to me and pushing me along when my doubts threatened to unravel everything.

My wonderful CLeaRly Creative team: Macenzie, Sherri, Paula, Lee, Lotteice, Joy, and Sheila. A warm iron smooths out the wrinkles. You all gently pressed the words, pages, and chapters into a piece I am proud to "wear" as an author.

Cathy's Crew—Many designers require and send up prayers. Thank you for lending me yours. Crystal, Tina, Liz, Lyndie, Sharon, and Joy, you are my small but mighty band of prayer warriors. I appreciate you. And Stacy, who helped brainstorm more than one of these scenes before she went Home.

Additionally, copious amounts of pins, patterns, and basting stitches are never seen. These details were figuratively added by others sharing their writing journeys with me. Thanks to:

- Breathe Christian Writers Conference friends. As my first writing community, you will always have a special place in my heart.
- ACFW Dallas/Fort Worth chapter. You reminded this Midwesterner of my worth when I floundered in a new writing place.
- Lena Nelson Dooley Critique Group. Especially Lena. You opened your home and arms to so many of us over the years. And those who sat around that circle during my time, your encouragement and "red pens" were invaluable.
- Sheila, Amanda, Lee, Joy, Tex, Macenzie, and Pastor Sherri for your special insights which made certain chapters and characters so much better.

A fashion house is nothing without the team that makes it run day-to-day, and mine is the best. Mr. A, Older, and Younger, without you three adding your support, supplying technology, bits of wisdom, willingness to eat a lot of thrown-together meals, and your ever-present encouragement, I couldn't do this writing life. Love you guys!

Finally, to my Heavenly Father. None of this is possible without You. Plain and simple.

Cast all your anxiety on him because he cares for you. 1 Peter 5:7 (NIV)

CHAPTER 1

Such a long week and today was only Tuesday. Jennifer Clark unlocked the showroom doors of Lilac Lane Fashion. Her gaze darted around the reception area of her design house. Murky shadows scurried away from the pale morning glow squinting through the entryway. Flicking on the display lights at the front of her flex-space warehouse, she peered into corners and crevices where trouble might secret itself. A taut breath escaped her lungs. For once these past weeks, nothing seemed amiss.

Later, she swiped a polishing cloth across one of the chrome-colored, faceless mannequins in Lilac's main showroom. She adjusted the train of the blush-pink brocade gown gracing the elegant dress form. "There you go. Picture perfect."

She stepped back and hooked the display ropes back on their stanchions. Sticky, inquisitive fingers didn't mix well with bridal gowns.

Walking the short distance to the reception area, she admired the three Grecian-inspired silver figures. The mannequins scattered around Lilac's display spaces had been a pricey splurge when she opened the shop four years ago, but they appealed to her Dallas, Texas, clientele. She didn't regret a penny.

She trundled the utility cart to a set of statuettes closer to the runway and dusted them. Finished, she picked up her coffee mug and sipped the now cool brew. Rubbing at a pull of tension between her brows, she addressed the middle figurine she'd adorned in a diamond-white satin gown trimmed in ruby-red faux fur. "I think a bouquet of silver pinecones, olive branches, and dusty miller will compliment you nicely."

Music blared over the loudspeakers. The insistent *thrum, thrum, thrum* matched the bass pounding in her head. Why was it so loud?

Sneakers squeaked on the polished concrete floor and a blond-headed blur galloped past her, knocking her elbow. Coffee splashed over the edge of her cup. "Auggie ..."

Heels click-clacked behind the boy. A light floral scent frolicked to Jen's nose right before its owner arrived. "August Isaiah Marshall, you get back here this instant and apologize to your aunt." Caribbean Marshall, Jen's lead model and best friend, shouted after her son.

"Sorry, Engine." He slowed for two seconds. "I gotta tell Reeree sum'n."

"Some*thing*." His mother corrected.

"Yeah, that. It's important." The nine-year-old resumed his gallop in search of his twin.

Cari chuckled. "Always on the go. Thanks for letting me drop January off earlier. Er, Ree, as she prefers to be called now." Her eyes twinkled. "Where my girl is getting this attitude from lately, I just don't know."

Jen's lips twitched but she chose not to comment on her goddaughter's latest expression of confidence. "You know that's never a problem. She's in the office. She must be planning something with our favorite jeweler because she wanted to call Sassafras."

Caribbean's eyes widened. "You didn't let her, did you?"

"She was persistent, but I'm not having Sassy fuss at me the rest of the week. Seven-thirty Seattle time is too early to wake up that night owl, even by one of her favorite kids."

Cari glanced at her watch, a Sassafras Montgomery original, wound around her delicate wrist. The silver band clashed comfortably with multiple homemade wristlets braided by her own daughter. "I'll let Ree call now. I foresee another discussion coming up about Adira, that wonderful, courageous, imaginary lion my girl has been channeling lately." She hooked her keys to her Dooney & Bourke leather bag with a dollar store clip.

"All your fame and designer threads, yet you're still frugal as ever."

"Pfft. And you're not?"

"Touche." Jen chuckled. "Are you and the kids coming over this weekend for the cookout?"

"Who's grilling?"

"I think it's Leo's turn. But since he burned the burgers last time, he may opt out and man the doors instead."

The tip of Cari's tongue stuck out. "Yeesh. You tell Leo, I'll bring him some of those Torino chocolates if he'll take over door duty and let me in your complex early." She winked.

Cari often treated the attendants at both of their buildings with small indulgences. They tended to open the door a little faster for her, paid closer attention to her conversations, and held the paparazzi at bay when needed.

Jen spotted drops from her jostled coffee on the floor and made a mental note to wipe them. She glanced up in time to catch Cari's soured expression. Peering over her shoulder, she saw no one there, but a skitter ran over her scalp.

Annie, the photographer from next door they often hired, appeared in front of them. "Smile. Business chic for this one." Click, pop-flash. She squinted over the top of her camera. "Now something silly. Come on, you two. No serious expressions. This is a fun project."

Jen readjusted her headband to corral her mop of auburn curls and mugged for the camera. Cari bent to bring her face closer to Jen's smaller stature. Pop-flash.

The photographer cackled. "Getting you two to cooperate will be the death of me." She shook her graying bob and headed down the hallway.

"There she goes, in search of her next victim." Jen rubbed her temples.

"Headache?" Concern nestled in Cari's tone. "I'll start some tea. Let me know when you're finished with the music. About twenty?"

Jen nodded. "Thanks."

"Meanwhile, I'll go find my daughter and remind her about Central and Pacific time."

"By the way, how'd Auggie's checkup go?"

"Checkup?" Cari's precisely waxed eyebrows scrunched together.

"You said he had a doctor's appointment."

"Oh, yes ... it was fine." A shadow crossed behind her long-lashed lids. "He seems to be doing well." Cari motioned to Jen's clothes. "Cute outfit."

Dizzyingly embroidered kitten-heeled mules completed an ensemble of skinny jeans and oversized shirtwaist ... nothing unusual for her. Why was Cari not-so-successfully changing the subject?

With that, Caribbean turned and sashayed toward the back room. Her lace sheath toyed with lithe curves under a silk jacket. If it was a thrifted piece, she'd never say. They could both afford, and did, the occasional fashion splurge. But they'd learned early on where to spend their hard-earned money and not to chase the fickle desires of the fashion industry.

Jen bent and swiped at the dribble of coffee.

"Auggie should be more careful."

The throaty voice behind her made her jump. "Daphne." She held her hand to her chest. "Please don't sneak up on people like that."

"I wasn't sneaking. I saw him spill your drink." Lilac's college intern held out a tattered, filthy rag. "I went to get something to wipe it up. Do you need anything else?" Ignoring Jen's outstretched hand, her gaze followed Lilac's lighting tech as he entered the showroom with his head bent toward one of the many models Jen contracted.

"Morning." The coworkers' voices rang in unison. As they passed, Jen caught part of their conversation.

"I can't believe you know Edward Baas. What I wouldn't give to design some special lighting effects for that man."

"I was in a show with him about a year ago," the model explained. "Nice guy. I see him occasionally at events."

"Lucky you. I follow him on social media, but he doesn't give much away." He clasped his chest in a mock swoon. "Can you put in a good word for me?"

"He's very private. Cari was in that show too, sugar. I'm *sure* she knows him. Maybe better than any of us." Her inflection hinted at something deeper. "Until the day she retires, she's got more clout than I ever will. Ask her." Their chatter followed them.

Daphne propped her fist on her hip, heedless of the grime on the rag in her hand. "I don't know what he sees in her."

Time to redirect. "Did you check with Cari regarding the plus-size modeling agencies you asked me about last week?"

"She's so slim, she doesn't understand what it's like to be what everyone calls *fluffy*." Daphne's nose wrinkled. "She won't be able to help."

Jen's shoulders tensed. "We never refer to a model that way at Lilac." She reminded herself the girl was still new to the industry. "She has better modeling connections than I can give you."

"I'll think about it, but I'm building up a nice little list of contacts on my own."

"Good for you. I'd love to talk to you about it on Monday when we discuss your classes for next semester. Remember to bring your final paperwork for me to sign."

She'd have one last heart-to-heart with the girl about fashion, treating the pros with respect, and the business in general, before the model's internship ended. The fashion industry was tough, and they all needed to rely on each other to remain relevant for the long-haul. Burning bridges— or worse, disparaging wise counsel from others—this early in her career wouldn't do.

Note to self ... call the school about next semester's intern.

Daphne had taken earlier advice on how to dress for a design house. The girl no longer appeared as if she'd raided her grandmother's closet—most of the time. Today, her rainbow-streaked hair was slicked back in a chic ponytail. Her woolly red sweater resembled squashed Christmas cactuses blooming a month too early, but she'd redeemed the slouchy look with stylish, wide-legged jeans—NYDJ brand, if Jen were to hazard a guess—and stacked heels. She was trying.

"When will I get to design for you?"

"You'll have to check with your advisor about another internship. First, you get used to how a fashion house runs and learn the industry from the ground up. You'll need more classes before design work."

Light flashed from the backroom. A shiver of anticipation warmed Jen's shoulders. She couldn't wait to see the shots Annie had for their special project.

Daphne leaned toward Jen and lowered her voice. "Do you think Annie would take headshots for my portfolio?"

"I don't know. You'll have to ask her."

"Would you? As our boss?"

"Sorry, I contract her work. She's not my employee."

Daphne's face fell.

"You need to be brave about these things." Jen put a measure of reassurance in her voice. "Why don't you ask her now? If you wait too long, she'll be busy with the holidays, then weddings and senior pictures."

Daphne ducked her head. "Maybe. I'll go see if Rose needs any help sorting supplies. Do you think she'd show me what it's like to be the head seamstress?"

"Remember, we call them sewists now." Jen corrected in as gentle a tone as she could muster. "I'm not sure she'd be able to do that with the one week you have left." Why did the girl always wait until the last minute for everything? "Are you going through the office?" She held out her mug and dust cloth. "Would you mind putting these on my worktable?"

"Sure," Daphne chirped right before a thump of techno beat blasted through the speakers. She grabbed Jen's mug, spilling the last few drops, and blithely meandered down the hall.

"And throw that one in the trash. It's well beyond its usefulness," Jen hollered. She wiped her hand on her jeans in time to cover her mouth for a horrendous sneeze. Ugh. Daphne must be wearing that patchouli stuff again.

Heading farther into the showroom toward the catwalk, Jen focused on the available crew. Boxes, dress forms, and tools were strewn everywhere. A hot mess. But her setup team was topnotch. Scurrying around like ants, they'd have everything under control before Cari's charity fashion show.

Reaching the heartbeat of Lilac's events, the mahogany booth housing the soundboard, Jen's ears vibrated when the music boomed through the system again. She waited for a momentary lull in the noise and caught Lilac's sound engineer, Richard Kearne's, attention. "Can you turn the bass down? It's really loud today." Winding her nape curls in a knot, she fanned the heat rising from her tense shoulders.

He shoved levers and poked buttons, uncharacteristic for the quiet, gentle giant. With the music finally silenced, he frowned at the equipment. "Sorry. Someone messed with the board before I got here."

Jen stamped her foot. "Not again. First the lighting rig, and then the knitting machine. What else?" They had a maintenance schedule in place—nevertheless, machinery mishaps could be age related. "The board's brand new. Isn't it?" She eyed the laid-back tech genius, with them for less than a year. What did she really know about him?

"It worked perfectly when I left last night." He massaged the back of his neck. "Are any of the other kids here?"

"Stan's boys are, until their mom can get off work and pick them up. No water or something at their school. Why?"

"All the faders were out of place when I got in. The controls were messed up and ... well, I wondered."

"Auggie's the only one allowed back here. This is his domain, after you."

Despite the worry over the strange mishaps of past weeks, she smiled with thoughts of the kids. Surprisingly, the little imp wasn't in his chair beside Richard. He loved learning under the specialist's tutelage and already exhibited a mastery over the technology. And January, or Reeree to her brother—dubbed so early on when he couldn't pronounce her name—showed signs as a gifted artist.

Richard chuckled, then turned serious. "It wasn't Auggie. He would never ruin—" He clamped his lips tight.

"I thought you said a bunch of dials and switches were moved?" Her voice edged higher. "What's broken this time?"

He stuck his thumbs in his pockets and glanced away.

"Out with it." She beckoned the information with an exasperated wave of her fingers.

He shined a flashlight under the shelf. There, nestled in tissues, lay her brand-spanking-new Beta 58A show mic, or what was left of it. She reached out.

"Don't touch it," Richard cautioned. "There might be fingerprints."

She snatched the light and pinpointed the damage. The top mesh was mangled. Lilac Lane's custom purple paint showed signs of someone having taken heavy-grit sandpaper to the finish.

"You've got to be kidding me." Her wail echoed through the booth. "I just got that back. It took weeks to find someone capable enough to coat it without jacking up the working parts." Hurt replaced her anger when the extent of the damage sank in. "This wasn't an accident."

"Not by a longshot. You couldn't do this much destruction if you dropped it from the stage."

Her eyes stung. "Did you call the police?"

"I wanted to talk to you first."

A flash popped in front of them. Annie smiled.

Jen worked to pull any annoyance from her face. "Hey, hon, can you get the rest of the crew for now? We've got a situation here." She heaved a sigh. "Wait. Take a couple photos of that, will you?" She pointed.

Annie kneeled. "Whoa. Nasty." She snapped several. "I'll get these to you later today." She trotted off.

Yanking the sleeve of her shirt, Jen became all business. "A police report is next. There's probably not much they can do about this either, but ..." She chewed her thumbnail. "Who could get in and out of this building without you, me, or—"

A shriek erupted from backstage. Cari.

"Dear God, please." Jen directed her muttered plea—both prayer and petition—skyward. "All I ask is a little extra dose of your strength and grace today." She'd need it. Cari, in one of her moods, was a force to be reckoned with. Best friend or not, sometimes her lead model could be high maintenance.

Richard didn't seem concerned. The staff was used to Cari. Making her mad was easy. But she soon got over her slights and forgave readily, often contrite.

Moments later, the shrill terror-filled scream of a young girl ripped the air.

January!

Headache and microphone forgotten, Jen sprinted toward backstage.

CHAPTER 2

Jen skidded across the threshold of the lead model's dressing room, Richard colliding into her back. Her attention riveted to Cari sprawled on the floor.

She fainted ... that's all ... right? Playing the damsel in distress? But she was so still.

Richard shoved past Jen to kneel next to Caribbean. After pressing his fingers to the side of her neck, his chin slumped to his chest. A moment later, he looked up, his mouth a thin, grim line, and shook his head.

Icy-hot electricity poured through Jen's veins. Raw noises clawed at her ears. Rose gasped. Daphne groaned. Brian, the lighting tech, uttered a sharp cry. Someone behind them swore under their breath. Richard rose and returned to Jen's side.

Snippets of details crashed on her brain like stills from a camera to form ghoulish illustrations at the back of her mind. The blood. Dress. Mask. Their Lilac family. She gulped for air that wouldn't come. Someone guided her to Cari's dressing table. She sank onto the stool.

Her best friend lay in a heap on the soft carpet. Gorgeous, even in lifeless repose. Nothing about Cari spoke of life. Not the vital fluid winding its way through the lacy needlework of her dress, nor the droplets splashed over the nubs of the creamy frieze rug below.

Her eyes stared in horrified confusion. Those beautiful eyes—amethyst ringed by sapphire—never to be seen awake again.

Jen's creative mind, ever used to beauty and elegance, warred with the abhorrent scene before her. Wisps of delicate roses, so much a part of Cari, registered their fragrance somewhere in the back of her imagination.

A different aroma tangled with the scent. Something off. Earthy. Faintly disagreeable. And the blood. That acrid, sharp metallic stench, tainting the floral notes.

Odors roared inward once her eyes adjusted to the scene before her. She retched. Pulling at her long shirttails, she covered her mouth, breathing deeply. Inhale. *One.* Exhale. *Two.*

Cari's spiritless body wasn't causing Jen's nausea. Nor was Ree, standing in the middle of the room—the girl's face devoid of color and shuddering with silent sobs. No, not her either.

Bile rose in Jen's throat, threatening to spill. She blinked, but he was still there. August. Kneeling next to the body of his mother. His usual kinetic energy, now still as marble. Blood on his hands. On the weapon he clutched. Crimson smudged like a macabre grin across the green and black of his favorite Creepers shirt.

Lightheaded, Jen bent over, driving deliberate breaths into her lungs.

One—calm. Thumb to index finger. *Two*—cool. She touched the pad of her middle one. *Three*—collected. Tap the ring finger. She had to take command. Peering through the slit of her eyelashes, the room slowed its dizzying spin.

Fully opening her eyes, she forced herself to sit up. With a final assuring touch to her pinky, she completed the ritual. *Four*—in control.

Focus. She was the head of Lilac Lane. The boss. The business side of her brain cataloged those she could see, as if backstage choreographing a show. There, plastered against the wall, stood Rose, lead sewist, her fist jammed to her mouth. Daphne, close enough to touch, crying into her hands, gooseflesh crawling up her arms. There were others. Sobs, moans, and curses filed through her brain like obedient toy soldiers from different areas of the room and hall.

Eva Corbin, another longtime employee and Lilac Lane model, was now in the room. Sometime during the chaos, she'd kneeled beside Ree and put her arms around the girl.

Jen considered each of them. This was their family. Hers and Cari's. She swiped at her eyes. Could one of them have done this? Who? How?

All eyes were on her. All except Ree and Auggie. Her priority.

Taking a sharp breath, Jen stood. Wobbled. Richard caught her. She patted his fingers. Squaring her shoulders, it was "Big Boss" time. A role they were all familiar with.

"Richard." Her tone sounded reedy. Clearing her throat, she tried again. "Make sure no one leaves the building."

He strode past everyone. Her worry didn't encompass him. He'd been within her sight since he'd arrived.

Daphne moved toward a wedding dress lying on the floor. Cari's final piece in the upcoming charity event. A mock-up only, but what was it doing here? Her hand shot out. "Stop!"

Daphne recoiled.

"Sorry." She lowered her voice. "It'll be okay for now. We'll get it later." She turned to the rest of her employees. "Don't touch anything. Harold, call the police."

He took his cell from his back pocket and limped toward the door, poking at numbers with his bony, aged fingers.

"Annie? I know this is horrible, but please take some photos of the room. Before anyone else moves."

Whir. Pop-flash. Tears trickled down the photographer's cheek.

Jen walked to Auggie. She leaned down, gripped his wrist, and pressed gently until he dropped the weapon. Bewilderment swam in his eyes.

Rose yelped. Laying next to his knee were the ornate, silver dressmaking shears the sewist claimed to be missing last week.

Turning Auggie toward the door, Jen crouched behind him and pulled him as close as she dared. "Everyone except Ree, Auggie, and Eva, go out in the hall and stay there." She softened her tone. "Please." Employees and contractors alike milled around to do her bidding. She mentally check-marked each one as they filed past.

"Will you stay with Ree?" She asked Eva.

The island beauty nodded and half-lifted the girl, guiding her to the edge of the room, all the while cooing in her sing-song Barbadian accent.

Jen placed a kiss on Auggie's mass of blond curls. The scent of roses, as delicate as gossamer wings, wafted up. Cari must have snuggled with him earlier that morning.

I will never smell roses the same way again.

Sirens blared outside Lilac Lane, breaking the painful silence of the dressing room with muffled authority. No screeching tires or brash, big-bellied cops shoving their attitude around like the movies portrayed, but that did little to dispel the surreal atmosphere. Instead, two police officers stood at the door, donning contamination covers, calling orders to others behind them. The only evidence that something was not right. That, and the dead body with the too-familiar face.

Jen shuddered, wishing she could click a remote and turn off the chaos like she did her favorite television shows.

Both men flashed their badges as they strode in the room. The one with the salt-and-peppered dad haircut spoke. "I'm James Henderson. This is Officer Everett Pratt."

"Ma'am." The younger one touched the brim of his cap.

Henderson took a step closer to the body, causing Auggie to rear back against Jen. The officer backed off. The boy's shoulders relaxed, and he wilted in place. Staring at his hands, he turned them over and over. And over.

"A child is involved?" Henderson glanced at his partner. "I don't think dispatch knew that. Sorry, ma'am. I can see this young'un's distressed. We'll get an advocate here as soon as possible."

"I'll call it in." Pratt punched numbers on his cell. He scanned the room, presumably looking for a quiet corner. Walking behind the partially open door, he called, "Sarge."

Henderson turned and let out a weary sigh. There, hidden from their initial view, sat Ree, supported by Eva. The two leaned against a freestanding, ornate bureau. He turned back to Jen and Auggie. "Hey, champ. Is that your sister there?"

Silence.

"Officer, do you mind if I speak for him?"

"You are?"

"Jennifer Clark. The owner of Lilac Lane and the twins' godmother. This is August. He usually goes by Auggie. He has some special needs. When he's stressed, he gets *absorbed*." She hoped the weight of her emphasis carried its import. "He may not answer." She tipped her head toward the girl shattered against Eva. "His twin, January, she goes by Ree, is the opposite. She'll have other issues if you question her. Can I stay with them?"

"Where are their parents?"

Did he mean the ones who stepped in when Cari became pregnant and refused to divulge further details? *That would be me, Mom, and Dad.*

"The father isn't in the picture. Their mother—" Her voice broke. *One*—calm. Cheeks puffed as she exhaled. *Two*— Her usual mantra failed her. She motioned to the body behind her.

"Gracious Lord." He muttered and turned to his partner. "Cancel the advocate. Have them phone Melissa Frazier. Tell her it's an emergency."

"Will do." Pratt spoke in hushed, urgent tones to the person on the other end of the line.

Officer Henderson addressed Jen. "I take it you were close with ..." He pointed to the body.

"Caribbean Marshall."

He noted the information.

"She was my business partner, lead model, and best—" She cleared her throat to dislodge a stab of emotion. "My best friend."

"I'm sorry for your loss, ma'am." He turned, including Eva in his next statement. "We'll have both of you clear out of the room with the kids as soon as we can. We've got a team out there taking statements." He gestured toward the hallway with his pen. "We need to collect evidence."

"I ... didn't know. I thought you'd need everything like we found it. I turned Auggie away from ... so he wouldn't see ..."

"Understandable. We'll take good care of y'all. Especially these two young'uns." He glanced around the room. "Is there someplace private we can take them? We'll have an officer stay with you until our specialist gets here."

"My office. Across the hall."

He requested a nearby colleague to ready the room then turned back to Jen. "If y'all aren't with the kids, Miss Frazier will be. You'll give statements too. If there's anything we can do to minimize their discomfort, short of washing up until evidence is collected, let us know."

Jen's thoughts tumbled and fell in a disjointed heap around her. Closing her eyes, she mentally searched for strength but failed. She'd missed some of what he said.

"—people in and out of this building over the next hours. Miss Frazier should be here in less than ..." Henderson tipped his wrist to look at his watch. "Thirty minutes. We can get this going so it's easier on y'all. First, the evidence collection, at least from you and this fine young man here."

Still no notice from Auggie. *Please Lord, don't let him retreat from us.*

"When Miss Frazier gets here, she'll discuss the next steps. Until then, direct any of your questions or concerns to Officer Pratt or me."

"Can we at least cover Little One?" Eva's Bajan singsong requested. "She's shivering something fierce. There be some blankets in the playroom next door." She pointed toward the wall behind her.

Officer Pratt walked near them, kneeled, and inspected the area.

With her head now nestled in Eva's lap, Ree's lids fluttered open. Her eyes rolled back, with the whites showing. The girl shuttered her lashes, squeezing out the world again.

Jen's heart lurched. She desperately wanted to comfort Ree. But she had to stay near Auggie. Anchor him. Keep him from withdrawing too far into his head. Pure hopefulness.

"She have nothing on her. I made sure before she lay down." Eva's dialect measured heavier than usual. A habit that surfaced, Jen learned early on, when the model was nervous. "She be the one to come here and alert everyone with her screams."

Pratt nodded. "We'll get her up in a minute and collect anything that might help us. Sometimes it can't be seen with our eyes. We'll get a blanket around her as soon as that's done."

Eva offered a grateful smile.

Pratt stood and walked to the door. "Do you think he needs one, Miss Clark?" He gestured toward Auggie. "Or yourself? We'll start with the girl first. Then get the two of you."

She put a gentle hand to Auggie's cheek. "I think he's warm enough. I'm afraid if we put anything around him, he won't take it well."

Pratt asked someone in the hallway to grab the coverings and put them in the office. He turned back to the room. "Once shock sets in, sometimes cold does too."

Jen's knees screamed. Fatigue had lodged there what seemed hours ago but was probably only minutes. She sought the senior officer's attention. "Is it okay if I sit with Auggie in front of me? My knees are killing—" Heat washed through her face.

Henderson hurried to her, seeming to take little notice of her misstep in words. "Let me help you up." He held her elbow while she unhinged from her crouch. His touch remained gentle with Auggie, assisting him as well. Jen was surprised her godson allowed the intrusion into his space.

"We need to clear the room and get photos." Henderson nodded toward the door where a strip of white showed through the space at the doorjamb.

Pratt spoke in hushed tones to the person and opened the door wider for their entrance.

There, a woman stood engulfed in a Tyvek suit. She held a big black box in one hand and an impressive camera setup in the other. Her eyes radiated compassion as lines of sorrow nestled near her mouth. She'd probably seen more death in a week than Jen wanted to witness in a lifetime.

"As each person comes to the door, I'll photo document everything." Her voice held a soothing undertone. "Front. Back. Hands. I've been briefed about the kids. I'll be gentle."

"They're used to Annie taking pictures, if that helps."

"But they're not familiar with me." The forensic photographer gave her a kind smile. "When we get to the two of you, let me snap a few photos without light first. The clicks might make your young man more comfortable. Then I'll turn on the flash."

Pratt brought Eva and Ree forward. The photographer's expression was considerate, her actions quiet. Still, Ree sobbed. Eva administered soft pats as she murmured. The girl clung to Eva's hand as if it were a life raft.

Jen shut her eyes. She took deliberate breaths with each silent count, fingers touching in succession. *Father, please help me protect the twins.*

Auggie stirred.

Cari always seemed to cope when they both needed her at the same time. How had she managed?

How am I going to? Especially without her?

Jen paid close attention to the procedures taking place in front of her. Pratt had left and a younger officer now stood at the entrance. He shone a special light on Eva's and Ree's hands. Ree allowed the process if Eva remained next to her. The moment the officer told the model to step aside, Ree hyperventilated. Jen surged forward. Protocol or not—

Henderson waved her back. He turned to the fresh-faced deputy. "We have their statements. The girl never went near the body. You haven't found anything on her. I think it's okay to let her friend stand next to her," he gently reproved.

"Yes, sir. Trying to be thorough, sir." The officer's peach-fuzzed cheeks turned pink.

Jen caught the hushed baritone as Henderson leaned in toward his young colleague. "That's their mother lying there. And her best friend. They need out of this room, pronto."

"I'm sorry, sir. I didn't know."

Henderson's eyes were kind as he returned to where Jen stood with Auggie and pointed to his underling. "New young pup. Doing a good job proving himself."

His words, no longer hushed, evidently carried to their intended target. The young officer's shoulders squared, and his manner turned solicitous to Eva and Ree as he guided them across the hall.

Now it was her and Auggie's turn. She tried to remember the steps, but her mind seemed as blank as one of her sketch pads before she placed pencil to it.

The photographer still had not entered the room but waited for them by the door. A pristine paper mat was placed directly inside the threshold. She didn't need to watch a lot of CSI to know what it was for.

She guided Auggie over to stand on it. He remained engrossed with his hands, but he tilted his head to brush a glance off the lady in the paper suit. The camera whirred and clicked with no flash. He didn't flinch. *That's a good sign, right?*

White Suit fiddled with her equipment. Click. Flash. The camera did its job.

Another cop stood nearby with paper bags, vials, and other equipment. Jen's chaotic thoughts cleared long enough to register their activity. She glanced at her shirt. A smudge of red ran along the sleeve. Evidence.

Jen readied her stance to hold Auggie still if necessary. An officer took care swabbing blood from his hands. He stiffened but didn't pull away. A miracle.

She recalled a fender bender Cari and the twins had been involved in the previous year. Cari mentioned the only thing stopping her from bashing the drunk driver was keeping Auggie from lashing out at the first responders. He had not handled the intrusion into his world well. Why so different this time?

"We need to remove his clothes. We'll place them in these bags. Yours too, ma'am."

"Is it necessary for me?"

"Sorry. You were holding him. Trace evidence might have transferred to you. Plus, you have blood on you."

"Right. Umm ... what will we wear?"

"We have these outfits you can put on." The officer held a stack of paper garments.

"I'm afraid Auggie won't react well to unusual clothing." Jen fingered his soft Creepers T-shirt. "He has a thing about texture."

Henderson pointed to some dressy children's clothing hanging on a bar on the side of the chifforobe. "I can't allow those out of here."

Jen shook her head. "We have extra sets of clothes in my workroom, behind the office. Can we use those?" At Henderson's questioning glance, she explained. "Set design can be messy. We have special dinners with clients." She ticked down the list. "Or Auggie doesn't like what he's wearing. We never know what the day will bring." She paused. "This room is too small. Only their show clothes are here. Their work and play outfits are in my workroom."

Henderson signaled to an officer in the hallway.

Jen called after her. "Ask Eva. She knows where everything is."

Minutes later, all eyes averted as Jen removed her stained clothes and handed them over. Auggie stood in front of her but never took notice. He shook his hands, more as if to release the blood, than his usual flapping.

One—calm. Finger touch. *Two*—cool. Her normal count floundered. *Get a grip. The sooner you get this over with …* *Three*—collected. She didn't bother with four. There would be no control over this.

She hurried into the long-sleeved shirt and peasant skirt Eva had sent back for her, one of Jen's own designs. An oft-worn favorite. She felt the hug of familiarity and wished she could do the same for her godson.

Auggie flinched when the officer reached for his Creeper top. He pulled back, clutching the game shirt to his chest. "No!"

"It's okay, sweetie. We'll get you another one." Jen promised.

He shook his head in agitated jerks and balled the folds of the garment tighter around his stomach. Crashing to the floor, he hunched forward in a rocking motion.

Officer Henderson moved to the edge of the paper and crouched near him. He spoke quietly. Jen didn't catch his words, but his gentle demeanor appeared to soothe her godson. That and a small, smooth rock the officer took from his pocket and placed in Auggie's hand, curling the boy's fingers around it.

How could she help him? "Sweetie, this lady needs to put your shirt in a bag. Eva sent your orange hoodie for you."

Auggie clutched the neck of the t-shirt. "It's mine. Cari gave it to me."

He hadn't disappeared into his world after all. At least not yet. *Thank you, Jesus.*

The boy turned his head away from the paper-clad officer. "That's itchy."

Henderson gave a rueful smile. "You don't have to wear one of these suits, champ. Only this officer does."

Auggie angled his ear toward the man as if he'd become his emotional ally. He took Henderson's outstretched hand and allowed himself to be hoisted up again, all the while, his fingers smoothed the gifted pebble.

"This lady wears it, so she doesn't bring dirt in here."

"Cari won't like that." Auggie's shoulders slumped.

"I bet not, my friend." Henderson's baritone cracked. "I bet not."

CHAPTER 3

The clock on her desk had to be lying, right? But no, the hour number had only changed once on her digital timepiece. It wasn't even noon yet.

With the initial evidence collection of their persons concluded, Jen collapsed in the overstuffed armchair in her office with Auggie tucked under her arm. The noises and smells coming from across the hall were nauseating. Thoughts of shifting the chair away from the door didn't translate to her muscles moving. Her mind wandered while they all waited on the Frazier woman.

Jen licked her parched lips and thought of scattered tea leaves. They'd never even had a chance to share a moment this morning—when Cari offered tea earlier. And they never would again. Regret slammed through her chest.

Her own favorite blend, Cari's specialty, existed in beautiful tins at home and on a shelf in the workroom. Cari even kept one in her lower-left vanity drawer, always. Jen often stopped by the private dressing room for a quiet moment. The model's favorite sparkling water—glass bottles only, thank you very much—could be found in Jen's office fridge, standing ready for when Cari floated in. They took care of each other. They always had.

Show weeks would never be the same. Jen both loved and lamented her office located across the hallway from Cari's Kingdom, the name given only half in jest by a former model. From her usual vantage point at her desk, Jen could see the cozy little room's door. It was book-ended by a sizable fitting area for other models on one side, and a large playroom for the staff's kids and grandchildren on the other. There followed spacious storage off the long hallway.

Being this close meant she could scoot over to see if Cari or any of the other models needed wardrobe repairs or fitting assistance before shows. Diminutive stature aside, Jen's staff jokingly referred to her as *Big Boss*, the reason for the executive sign on her desk. She calmed frayed nerves, doused creative tempers, and got their tushes in gear when necessary. Usually a mixed blessing, today the nearness of the Kingdom clawed at her nerves.

Eva sat behind Jen's desk, with Ree wrapped in a blanket curled on her lap. "You be okay?"

"Why is this taking so long? I need to get them home." Would she even be allowed to take the kids? A question she didn't dare voice yet. Jen moved to get up, to stretch.

Auggie's eyes popped open. Round and filled with fear. Settling back, she shifted her weight to give them both more room.

She needed to think. She couldn't grab a gab with Cari. Wasn't able to walk the runway, or pace a show, go to the bathroom, pick up lunch—

Whoa, Jen. Settle down. She swallowed at the lump of wool stuck in her throat. Shutting her eyelids did little but put her other senses on alert. She smelled the peppermint gum from patrol officer C. Bellows, assigned to sit with them. Caught voices murmuring in the hall. The fluorescent bulbs overhead buzzed with the hum of lazy bees. She focused on the faint rose scent emanating from Auggie's curls. The fragrance conjured long-ago memories.

She and Cari had loved acting out fairy tales among Mrs. Ditmar's rose gardens. Their neighbor allowed the two little girls to play there, if they were careful not to crush her new blooms. Jen believed her friend's love of the scent was birthed in the pergola that became their make-believe castle. Cari had often smelled of the nostalgic scene.

Auggie wiggled his fingers, breaking Jen's inward reverie. The police had allowed him to wash up after the photos. Once clean, he had emerged from his thoughts long enough to beg for hand sanitizer. He'd vigorously pumped the spout, squirting a handful. The sharp sting of alcohol was only now wearing off. He dug the rock Officer Henderson gave him from his pocket and rubbed it, smoothing it between his fingers.

Her office chair quietly squeaked in acceptance of the gentle to-and-fro of Eva. How Jen envied the Barbadian and her softhearted demeanor. Eva crooned to the girl in her melodic, Bajan singsong that made her such a joy to listen to.

In a half-wakeful state, Ree's eyelashes fluttered open on occasion, reminding Jen of a flitting butterfly looking for solace among thorns. But the girl's ragged breaths of earlier had evened out.

Eva continued her gentle care, allowing Jen to concentrate on Auggie.

Here he sat, crooked under her arm. Not present, but no longer a shell of himself. His breathing had changed. Morphed into an odd rhythm. A long inhale and a little *chuff*. A labored breath, then chuff, chuff. Repeat. Repeat.

What's that all about? But the professional utterances from across the way kept intruding. Gurney. Chain of Custody. Body Bag.

Stop!

She couldn't hear who they were talking to, only their hushed undertones. Her mind refused to contemplate the words. And the blasted lights. Every pop and flash from the forensic photographer's camera lodged tight between her shoulder blades.

The murmurs started again. Unrecognizable tones mixed with her staff's familiar cadences outside the door. Rose sniffling. Harold's grizzled, ex-smoker rasp—Cari had badgered him until he quit a couple years ago. Richard's oddly tearful resonance. The essence of Lilac Lane was under attack.

"Ma'am?"

"What? I'm sorry. I wasn't listening."

The officer pointed her pen at a retreating uniform. "He said Miss Frazier will be with y'all in a moment." She gave a reassuring smile. "You're in good hands."

The revered Miss Frazier. Queen of the counselors. Gatekeeper to their future.

With her insides quaking, Jen straightened, careful not to disturb Auggie. Squaring her shoulders, she counted and touched. *One*—calm. *Two*—cool. *Three*—collected. *Four*—in control. Emphasis on that last one ... fake it until you make it, right?

Jen listened for the chink, chink, chink of heels beating a path down the hall. After all, strong businesswomen wore three-inch stilettos, Armani power-suits, and rode roughshod over their quarry. Didn't they? She willed herself battle-ready against the wench, for the twins' sake. As their sole safety-keeper now, fear brushed the back of her neck.

Jen closed her eyes, settling her cheek against Auggie's head. His odd sounds of earlier were no longer audible.

He was so still, a rare occurrence for the kinetically active boy. He now leaned heavily on her arm. Was he retreating to Auggie-land? She resumed listening for the clanking of those officious heels.

"Hello? Miss Clark?" The soft words came from near the doorway.

Jen started. She hadn't heard anyone approaching. Schooling her face to show she meant business—Auggie and Ree were hers to protect now—she surveyed the doorway, expecting an immediate confrontation with the gargantuan she'd conjured in her imagination. Her fierce face eased as she lowered her gaze several feet.

The young lady standing there, hand raised to knock again, appeared childlike. Her bright tunic top, fashionably ripped jeans, and hooped earrings did little to dispel the air of youth.

Was this the scout sent to gather them to the front lines?

The officer who'd been sitting with them got up and mumbled something cordial. Nodding, she patted the newcomer's shoulder on her way out.

The woman cleared her throat. "I'm Melissa Frazier. A specialist with the Dallas County Children's Services Center." She stepped into the office, dropping a patchwork backpack from her shoulder once inside the door. "I wish we were meeting under different circumstances. I appreciate you waiting for me."

We didn't have a choice. Jen moved to get up.

"Please, stay. I'll come to you." The waif moved forward, shifting a leather-bound binder in her arm, hand outstretched.

Jen was used to appraising all sizes and nationalities, often on a moment's notice during fashion week, and she did so now without thought. The woman's wide, prominent cheekbones put her in mind of some of the Native American models she'd worked with. An intricately beaded leather hair wrap held a thick ponytail in place with a coordinating neckband adorning her delicate throat. She wouldn't be categorized as a classic beauty in modeling circles, but the genuine empathy pouring from the young woman's mink-colored eyes caught Jen's attention.

I'd love to design for her.

"Is there something wrong, Miss Clark?" The woman cocked her head. "I mean, besides the obvious."

"No. Why?"

"You're staring."

"Sorry, professional hazard." Jen liked her candor. "Truthfully? From how they spoke of you, I expected Attila the Hun, not a little slip of a thing."

The child advocate laughed, the sound kind and soothing. She glanced to where Jen's feet dangled from the oversized chair. "Funny being called 'a little slip' by you. But I'll take it against Attila any day." Her words held no sting. "Please, call me Melissa."

"It don take a big axe to cut down a big tree." Eva's Bajan colloquialism needed little translation. "Our Jen be a little axe, but ..."

"I understand. My own size, or lack thereof, takes nothing away from why I'm here." She pointed to the twins. "Which is for these two."

There was a sharp edge to the tone now, reminding Jen of a momma tiger. *Note to self—don't underestimate this one.*

"Let me be clear, Miss Clark, in as gentle of terms as I can. I will do my best to honor your wishes for these two darlings. But it is my job to make sure they're well taken care of until we determine—at least temporarily—the best course of action for them."

Heat poured through Jen. She swallowed the heart-sick pain of the last hours, mixed with the gall rising in her throat. Time to stand up, in more ways than one.

She moved Auggie from her shoulder and scooted to the front of the settee. Playing for time to ease her rising emotions, she gave him a quick hug and rose. Fear of losing him and his sister pounced on her shoulders. *One*—calm. Nope. Not happening.

Jen forced herself not to waggle her finger in the young woman's face. "And I will do *my* best to cooperate with you," she ground through clenched teeth. "However, these are my best friend's children. My godchildren. Their mother and I grew up together. Same household for six years." Her breath caught, but she forged ahead. "I've had charge of them on and off since they were born. They each have specific needs. I will not allow them to be railroaded. Investigation or not."

Her finger became a weapon of her temper. Remembering the twins sitting there, watching her, she pointed the offending digit toward the chaos in the hallway. "In fact, if those needs are not met, you're all going to have a rough time getting anything from them." Heat hit her cheeks, and her chin wobbled.

Melissa crossed her arms over her binder and held it tight to her chest, saying nothing.

"I want either Eva or myself with the twins at all times," Jen railed. "I can't be in two places if you separate them. So, she stays as well. They're my kids." She swallowed. "For now." Her last words hit home, reason flooding back to her brain, deflating her indignation.

"Good."

Jen's brows wrinkled. "Good? That's all you've got to say?"

Melissa's smile held a world of melancholy. "I wasn't testing you, Miss Clark. Whatever challenge you felt, you've passed with flying colors." Light returned to her eyes. "I intend to work very closely with you. As much as I am able within the confines of the law, for as *long* as I can." She shook her head. "We won't be finished by tonight. The whole ordeal will be ongoing for the next few days, at least. We'll navigate it together."

Jen's stance sagged.

Melissa took a tentative step forward and laid a comforting hand on her arm. "I've been through this a few times, Miss Clark. You haven't."

"Do I get a say in what happens to us?" A small voice sounded.

Melissa wheeled around to Ree, standing next to Eva, still gripping her hand. Auggie stood and leaned against Jen.

The advocate went to Ree and crouched, taking her other hand. "Yes, ma'am. I will listen to both you and your brother." She looked back at Auggie, but his gaze was laser focused on his sister. "I can't make any promises right now, though. I need to ask some questions first." Her glance encompassed all of them but returned to Ree. "Do you feel up to answering?"

"I'll try." She whispered with conviction.

Dislodging Auggie from her side, Jen sat him back in the comfy chair and grabbed a folding seat for Melissa, motioning her toward it. She set another chair next to Eva for Ree. Her goddaughter had always needed to feel in charge when uncomfortable.

So much like you. A voice shifted through the air. Jen's glance darted around the room. The sound reminded her of Cari. Maybe she'd heard someone outside the door.

The panic she'd held at bay since finding her friend whispered along her nerve endings, taking purchase in her left hand. She perched on the arm of the big chair and rubbed her fingers up and down her pant leg, hoping the movement would mask their tremor.

Melissa scribbled in her binder. "I apologize, but I must ask some uncomfortable questions. We don't have to do this all tonight, but I'd like to get a start so I can make some phone calls, if necessary." She flipped to a page in her book. "The deceased's name is Carrie Marshall?"

Ree sat ramrod straight in her chair. "It's Cari. Caribbean Marshall." Her tone resembled that of a young ice queen. "As in Car, like you drive, and a long E. She doesn't like to be called Carrie." Her voice hitched. "She *didn't* like it."

The advocate glanced toward Jen, her eyebrows raised.

"Ree, would you like me to take over?"

"Yes, please." She continued to stare at the stranger barging into her mother's business.

Jen dove in. "Both kids have some very specific requirements when it comes to dealing with people. There's a distinct possibility Auggie is somewhere on the spectrum." Knowing the other woman dealt with kids, Jen didn't feel the need to discuss autism. "I don't believe he's been formally tested. I could be wrong. When he stresses, he retreats." She slid her glance from the advocate to her godson. "Which I'm very concerned about right now."

Shifting back, she fought to explain her goddaughter. "And my girl here is in the gifted range." She winked at Ree, hoping to take any censure from her next words. "When she's distressed, she can get very intense."

Ree's white-blonde curls bobbed up and down.

"She has a near photographic memory. She can usually recall who's in the room, what they're wearing, parts of the conversation, things like that."

Admiration shone in Melissa's eyes. "That's a wonderful gift."

"Only if I hear the conversation." Ree's frosty attitude thawed a degree.

Jen resumed her explanations. "When he withdraws into Auggie-land, it's hard to know how to get him back. He relies on his twin for many of his cues, but Cari was usually the only one who could reach him then. She thought about him seeing a counselor of some sort, but I'm not sure—"

"We see Dr. B." Ree interjected.

"You do? Since when?" Jen turned to the advocate. "This is news to me."

"We've been going to his office for ..." the girl counted on her fingers, "one year. Cari told me I had to go to help Auggie." She rolled her eyes. "But I know she wanted me to see him too. All three of us do." Her glance darted toward the door. "Did."

Eva patted her shoulder in support. "Good on you. Doctors help."

"He's okay. He taught me how to be lion-strong when my stomach gets upset. Maybe he can help Auggie with questions."

So that's where Ree's imaginary lion, Adira, and the monster, Queezy, came from. *That extra bit of information would have been useful, Cari.*

"Excellent." Melissa beamed at Ree. "Dr. B. Do you know what that stands for?"

The girl's brows wrinkled. "I can't remember right now." She appeared stricken.

"That's okay." The advocate assured her. "Maybe you'll think of it tomorrow. We can try to look him up too."

Tears puddled in Ree's eyes. "Tomorrow?"

"Honey," Jen consoled. "I think we're going to be answering questions for a few days."

The girl wilted.

Melissa reached over and touched her arm. "Let's take this in small doses. Would that help? Do you need a break now?"

"Can I get us a drink?" As was her usual, she included her brother. "We're thirsty."

Jen motioned to a door behind Eva. "The fridge is back there, in the workroom. The officer checked it earlier. The only other door is locked, from the inside."

Eva drew Ree's attention. "Do you mind if I come with you? I'm dry as a bone. Sure, the others could use a drink too. I'll help you carry things, love."

Ree fled the room overflowing with responsibilities too great for a nine-year-old.

Eva held out her hand to Auggie. "Coming, sir? You go with us and pick your snack."

He offered no resistance as he got up and shuffled toward her but didn't take her fingers.

Jen mouthed thanks to her friend.

"Seems you two know each other's actions pretty well." Melissa observed.

"We've been working together so long, we're pretty much in sync. There are few who know me better—except for, you know ..." She leveled her gaze toward the dressing room where the murmurs and clanging grew loud again.

Melissa got up and walked to the door. Her pitch low, she spoke to someone beyond Jen's line of vision.

"I'm going to close this. I think it's better if we're not distracted by what's happening in there for a bit." She glanced toward where the other three had disappeared. "They're getting ready to move her soon," she whispered.

A small sob escaped Jen.

Melissa rushed to offer a comforting arm. "I'm so sorry. I wish I didn't have to say these things, but I want you to know the truth. I'll be as gentle as I can."

Jen sniffed back a tear. "It's not that. It's just ... you didn't call her a body. Everyone else has been referring to her like she's not here, as if she's a nothing. To us, she was everything. Thank you for acknowledging her as a person."

The workroom door opened a crack. Eva peered out, and Melissa waved her forward.

"Here we are. Water and chips." Eva plunked the food on the desk. "Miss Ree be thinking our stomachs couldn't handle sandwiches." She nodded her agreement. "On the safe side, I thought it best we all—" She cleared her throat in a delicate manner.

"Did our business." Auggie piped up.

Jen's lips twitched. Bodily functions were still of typical nine-year-old interest to him. A good sign—all things considered.

"Yes. As Master Auggie says, 'we did our business.'" Eva's gaze slid toward the door, eyebrows raised in question.

"Melissa thought we could use some privacy while we eat."

Ree climbed into the big chair with Auggie, whispering to him.

The advocate got down to business again. "Okay, we've established Miss Marshall's name as Cari." She pronounced the nickname properly, smiling at Ree. "And who each of you are. We'll need to contact next of kin."

"Besides these two, myself, and my parents, there's only her older brother, Colin. He's an architect, but I have no idea where he is. Cari hasn't mentioned him in years."

"I'll see if I can establish his whereabouts. But ... you referred to *your* parents as her next of kin. And you mentioned earlier you grew up in the same household?" Her raised brows punctuated the question.

"Originally, she moved in next door to us when we were both seven. But she was always at our house. Her parents were … odd, to say the least. They were killed in an auto accident when Cari was twelve." Jen didn't worry about Ree and Auggie listening. They'd heard the story so many times, there wasn't much to offer beyond facts.

"Her brother is five years older than us. He'd already left for his first year of college. No family that we knew of to take her in, so my parents did." Jen held her cell up. "I put in a quick call to their home office while we waited for you. But I don't expect to hear from them for hours. They're on a science expedition in Manaus."

Melissa added another note to her already extensive list. The questions continued. Their usual showroom routine? There wasn't one. Each day differed depending on the season and event.

Where did the Marshalls live? At the mention of the Beverton-Wise Condominiums, Melissa didn't bother to hide a low whistle.

Where did the twins go to school? A hybrid of showroom tutoring through Cari, Jen, and other worthy staff, as well as in-person classes at a nearby elementary. All to accommodate their various needs and their mother's busy schedule.

Any pets needing care? No. Auggie's lip jutted. The twins had been badgering Cari for a puppy for months.

And finally, anyone else they might stay with? Jen's heart squeezed at the question.

"We get kid-sitted by Mrs. Peter Piper," Auggie said.

Ree agreed. "We stay with Mrs. Peters until Cari or Aunt Jen picks us up. She lives across the hall. By the elevator."

Melissa gave a quizzical look. "They call their mom by her first name?"

Jen grunted. "Long story."

"We can talk later." Then the advocate addressed the twins. "You remembering these things makes my job easier. Anyone else you stay with besides Mrs. Peters?"

Ree's eyes widened. "Engine, who's going to tell her? We were supposed to stay with her tonight until Cari got back."

"Got back from where, honey?"

"She didn't tell me again." Ree's lip quivered. "But she said she wouldn't be late."

Melissa stood, looking sad but determined. "I'll get word to Mrs. Peters. In fact, I'll go find her number right now and let her know you are both okay. I've got a couple of other calls to make. I'll be back as soon as I can." She walked to the door, peeked out, and asked a question of the person stationed beyond it. She glanced back, focusing her gaze on Jen. "Is there something the four of you could do for maybe fifteen or twenty minutes in your workroom? Keep everyone busy?" She eased into the hall.

The earlier officer returned and followed the four of them to the backroom. Jen offered her a stool at the worktable, but she preferred to stand near the door, silent, yet alert.

They didn't do much. Odd jobs here and there. Jen and Ree matched sewing patterns with material. Eva and Auggie picked up pins from the tabletop and floor.

Anything to keep their minds off the return of the child advocate and their futures.

Anything that didn't hold the memory of a tall, beautiful blonde.

Anything to keep them from the long, black bag wheeled down the hall on a silver cart.

CHAPTER 4

Senior Detective Pamela Mason climbed from the department-issued Charger. The clean, well-kept exterior of Lilac Lane Fashion Studio sat smartly among the renovated block, save for the rather dingy building next door. She shielded her eyes from the afternoon sun and a billboard across the street caught her attention. It advertised a recent movie about four female friends and their road trip to the annual Essence Festival. "I still say you look a lot like her."

"Queen Latifah? I'll take that compliment any day." Detective Ozillia Ryan unfolded her tall frame from the passenger side and consulted the dispatch notification. "We're in the right place. We don't usually get called to the Design District."

"Tough break for whoever owns this place." Mason shook her head.

"Tougher break for the kids."

The two entered the showroom and signed the logbook for the young beat cop stationed there. Oz strode ahead while Mason lingered. "Have the uniforms cleared the room?"

"Yes, ma'am. The ME's been here and gone. Most everyone's been questioned and allowed to go home. You've got Henderson and Pratt back there. Miss Frazier just left."

"I spoke with her earlier. We've got an excellent team onboard." She thanked the underling and headed down the hallway in time to witness a minor ruckus in the small room isolated by police tape.

"I don't think the kid did it." The young female officer's voice quavered. "Unless the victim kneeled in front of him."

"Agreed. But *the kid* has a name," Oz ground out. "If you don't know it, find out. They're people too, not just littles who can be pushed around."

"Yes, ma'am." The rookie glanced at her notes. "His name is August Marshall. Age nine."

Mason noticed at the newbie's nameplate and held out her hand. "Good to meet you, C. Bellows."

"The C stands for Charlene, ma'am."

"I'm Pamela Mason, the ogre there is Ozillia Ryan." She chose to consider the grunt she heard behind her as Oz's welcome.

Against her dark uniform, the fledgling officer's flushed cheeks were a beacon of embarrassment, but she shifted her shoulders back.

Mason smiled. Bellows wasn't bolting after a verbal sparring match with Oz like some did. She was still inexperienced, sure, but her composure had only slipped a little. "Why don't you go over what you were explaining to the leads. You don't think young Marshall perpetrated the killing?"

Bellows glanced over her shoulder at Henderson.

"You've done a good job," he spoke up. "But I'll take it from here. The dragon doesn't scare me."

Bellows's lips twitched but she scooted from the room as fast as if chased by the real thing.

"Detectives." Henderson tipped his head. "Glad to have you aboard. And Oz, you can grouse at us veterans all you care to, but you've got to stop making the newbs want to quit before their first month's up."

"If me asking tough questions can scare 'em off that easy, they aren't the caliber we need around here." She nodded toward the doorway Bellows had recently vacated. "That one looked like she was handling things okay until you intervened. She'll do."

"I'll let her know she has your vote of confidence."

"Don't go that far, or I might have to hurt you." She chuckled.

Henderson shook his head at her and sighed. "What am I going to do with you?"

Mason waved a dismissive hand toward her partner. "Don't mind her. She hasn't had lunch yet. Go ahead."

He brought them up to speed on the details. "Fancy, antique dressmaker shears appear to be the weapon. The lead sewer, Roselyn Turnquist, collects the things. States she reported them misplaced last week when other items around the showroom went missing. And yes, there's a police report for those thefts, as well as other incidents spanning several months. Seems they were written up as mischievous actions but never followed through." Henderson frowned.

He pointed to an evidence bag. "My personal and professional opinion ... he likely just picked them up. Clark, his godmother, or aunt, or whatever she is to the kids, swears there's no way he'd do anything to hurt his mother. The kids are home with Clark now."

Mason lifted an eyebrow. "Melissa okayed them staying with the godmother? When we spoke, she said she called an uncle. We haven't gotten a full briefing yet."

"I gather she's still making calls. The uncle lives in Michigan. Needs time to get here. No father in the picture."

Henderson flipped another page of his memo pad and shared the information they'd gathered about the victim, her children, Clark, and the parents. "It's all pretty confusing, if you ask me."

Oz crouched to measure the chalk line. "She was tall."

"The aunt has the kids so often, the mother had a letter of guardianship drawn up. The document names Clark and the uncle as dual custodians. The letter's been in effect for several years. Melissa's got a copy. The boy has some special needs. Nobody said anything specific, but my cousin's kid has autism." He held up a hand to stall Oz's comment. "I'm not saying August has it. All I'm stating is, some of his mannerisms are similar. And if anything is mentioned, I gave him a rock. I always carry a smooth one in my pocket. My cousin's boy likes them."

Mason tipped her head, acknowledging the possible assessment and small gift.

"He and his twin sister, January—"

Oz snorted. "August and January? You gotta be kidding me."

Henderson shrugged. "I guess the mother could be a little eccentric. The kids appear well taken care of. So, they have unusual names. No harm done."

"Fair enough." Oz conceded.

"They're pretty traumatized. With the possible special needs, Melissa felt it better to leave them in surroundings they're familiar with." He licked his thumb, pushing pages forward. "Entry wound is at an approximate height of four feet, four inches. Like Bellows tried explaining, the boy's too short for a straight jab."

He turned his notes so the detectives could read them, two neat columns of names penned down each side of the paper.

"All suspects? Perfect." Mason's deep sigh said otherwise.

"There was only a partial crew today, according to Clark. Still, a lot of people were involved for their upcoming event. Models, technicians, backstage handlers ... the works. Three school-aged boys left before the commotion. Their building had no water. They came in with their dad until mom could pick them up. We'll check if she or the boys remember anything and then piece together a thorough timeline for you."

"Thanks. We'll be in touch." Mason followed Oz away from the crime scene. "This is gonna be one of those tough cases, isn't it?"

"If by that, you mean too many pawns and knights running willy-nilly around a *Life* gameboard with *Monopoly* rules ... no more so than usual."

"What's the good word?" Oz plunked her weary bones onto her office chair across from Mason.

"Looking through some of these preliminary reports."

"Anything promising yet?"

"Not much. We've got Jennifer, with the deceased listed as sibling, but no biologicals. She is godmother and caretaker for—"

"I know all this." Oz sighed. "Melissa verified everything before she could take the kids home."

"Yes, but did we know she had some serious mental health treatment in high school and, again, later in college?"

"Anything we should be concerned with?"

"I thought that might pique your interest. But no. Everyone we've contacted so far ... colleagues, the few old schoolmates we could reach, employees ... all say she's rock solid. The first to give someone a chance, a bit of a temper if they mess up, but the quickest to forgive."

"Sounds like a good friend to have, if you ask me."

Mason nodded, her hair fluffing around her. "So, not much there, other than what we already figured. She'll be good for the kids, if this uncle doesn't make a grab for them."

"Who else did the team ferret out so far?"

"Harold, the maintenance man, basic background. Retiring soon. Brian, the lighting designer was near the ceiling checking a fixture, and Victor, the rigger, whatever that means—"

"That would be your person who suspends the booms, hoists, curtains, and stuff."

"I want to be on your team if we ever play *Trivial Pursuit*, Oz. You know some of the weirdest details." Mason scribbled a memo. "Anyway, he and Harold were helping Brian. So, they're each other's alibis. He seems clean. Maybe a bit of a womanizer. I don't think there's anything there, but I'll check to see if he had a thing for the deceased."

Oz snagged a pen, made a face, and lobbed it over to her partner's desk. "You need to quit chewing on my pens. Ruin your own."

Mason ignored her. "There's nothing yet about the uncle. Not surprising since he's out of state. And this Richard character ... what was it the team said?" She checked her notes. "They called his information, 'elusive.'" She scowled at the paper as if her glare could produce better results.

"What are you expecting? We just got the case today." Oz straightened her desk. "Let's call it a night, go home and get some rest. Patience is definitely not your strong suit."

"Tell me something I don't know."

The radio message earlier had been cryptic. "*Emergên-cia. Filha Jeffer.*" Professor Patrick Clark and his wife,

Elaine, were a day out of Manaus, their home port, when they received the communication. He understood the literal translation of "Emergency. Daughter Jeffer." But exactly what did it mean?

Dallas was only two hours behind Manaus Amazon Time but TéFé, the nearest town with a local airplane transport back to headquarters, was a slow boat ride ahead. The municipality couldn't come into view fast enough. He only hoped they'd be able to get an expedient flight out if necessary.

He contemplated the brown waters of the Rio Negro flowing beneath their *recreo*. Normally, he would watch for *jacaré*, better known to him and his crew as Brazilian alligators—bad business, those creatures. Instead, his mind plunged through scenarios of disasters back home. Everyone had been fine when they'd last talked to the girls prior to leaving for this latest expedition.

He blamed the dense cover from the mangrove trees overhead for their satellite phone's bad reception, resulting in the word *Jeffer*. Jennifer was not foreign to a Brazilian ear. But did it mean Jen had called, or was something wrong with her? If not her, then what could be the matter with Cari, or precious Ree? No mention of *menino* or *filho*. He chose to believe little August was fine. But he probably wasn't so little anymore.

How he missed the grandkids. When had they last hugged Auggie and Ree in person? Three? Four years? Such a long time.

Patrick's gaze turned to his wife, easy enough with only a hammock's breadth separating port to starboard. With little room to maneuver, she'd worn a path of worry around their provisions. Occasionally, she stopped to bow her head, lips moving in silent prayer.

She should be researching, writing, and taking beautiful photographs to share over the internet with their kids, not worrying because they didn't have the full story.

Elaine peered at him from under her floppy brim. Maneuvering around boxes of foodstuffs, science equipment, and specimen bottles only beginning to be filled, she removed her hat. Tilting her head, she wound her arm around his waist. The mercurial hues of her eyes shifted with her moods. Indigo when her emotions were high, as they were now.

"Will we be there soon?" Her words floated on the breeze.

"As soon as this river and our little engine allows."

"The investors group isn't going to be happy we cut this one short, are they?" Anxiety ached through her expression. "I know it's an important trip for you."

"Hang the investors. Our daughters are more important."

"I keep hoping the locker burned, or something else inconsequential."

Ah yes, the infamous keepsake graveyard. After Cari's young life had derailed next door and she'd come to live with them, they'd packed up their girls and moved farther into the Metroplex, away from the memories. But they'd boxed specific relics of that time and put them in storage in case Cari wanted them when she was older.

When the Brazil stationing came along, he and Elaine had culled their own belongings, only taking items durable in the humid Amazon air. The few precious mementos they couldn't part with were packed away with Cari's former life. They could all do without that stuff, as long as the girls were safe.

"What happens if we get there, and it's not as dire an emergency as we're expecting? You know how things get lost in translation," Elaine remarked.

He leaned against the side post of the vessel. Giving her shoulders a light squeeze, he squared his own. "If it's a misunderstanding, I'll likely get slapped on the wrist for making the expedition run late, and afterward, we'll get back on schedule. That's why we started early—wiggle room as you call it—for unforeseen delays. We'll handle the executive board after we get this message from the girls straightened out."

With the renewed mention of their kids, her eyes colored with shades of violet and fear.

Jen startled. Burrowing deeper under her quilt, she took a moment to register her surroundings. No prickles of worry running amok. But what had woken her? There it was again. A muffled, flailing noise.

The nightlight from the hallway silhouetted movement in the living room. Hairs prickled on her arms, whether from the nighttime air or fear, she didn't know. Didn't care. She shot out of bed and rushed past the guest room's closed door, to the edge of the short hallway.

Peering around the corner, her stomach leaped to her throat. Cushions from the couch, chair, and ottoman were thrown in a tumultuous pile. Had someone, somehow, entered the apartment? What were they looking for? But no. There was no intruder. For there, in the middle of the chaos, sat Auggie pounding with furious energy.

She let him thrash. So what if he beat the stuffing from the pillows? He wasn't hurting anyone ... with the possible exception of her heart.

With several low growls, he finally stilled. His breathing slowed to deep, ragged gasps. Should she go to him? As if he sensed her there, he raised his head. She'd expected anger. Maybe tears. But the raw edges of pain swirling in his bright blue eyes took her breath away.

She went to him and helped him up. "Did you need to get the mads out?" Her words landed gently in the stillness.

He heaved a big sigh and regarded the sea of pillows.

"It's okay, we'll get them tomorrow." She guided him to her bedroom and dragged the coverlet from her bed. She settled him beside her in the over-sized reading chaise, covered them both, and rubbed his shivers away.

Even though the chilly air permeated her Dallas Stars hockey jersey, she suspected his trembles were from more than the cold. How to comfort him? She pulled her bathrobe from the back of the chair and wrapped it around his shoulders. He burrowed lower into its softness.

The purple fleece robe, trimmed in satin, had become a favorite of the twins when they were at her apartment and didn't feel well. They had given it to her the previous Christmas. "I tried to tell them you needed something more grown up." Cari had winked. "But they insisted this fuzzy thing was perfect for their Engine. Pfft. What could I say? We had to get it."

"Ree still sleeping?" Jen asked.

"Um-hmm."

"You okay?"

He took so long to answer she thought he hadn't heard. "Cari won't pick us up and take us home anymore." It wasn't a question.

His words were like a gut punch. "No, honey. She won't." A deafening silence stretched before them. The strange rhythmic breathing he'd exhibited earlier started again.

"Auggie?" He seemed halfway down the road to his special place. She'd promised the authorities she wouldn't discuss Cari's murder with the twins. She was thankful they'd allowed them to stay with her. But if she kept him engaged, maybe he wouldn't retreat. She wished she knew how to get to Auggie-land and bring him back.

No one does, except him. The voice, as she'd begun to call it, murmured through her thoughts. *Talk to him.*

She tucked her trembling fingers under the blanket. "I miss Cari."

"You do?" His bright blue eyes appeared glassy, even in the dim light from the hallway. Auggie didn't cry often. A quick temper and quicker contrition were his way. But she'd never known him to shed a tear during a season of meltdown. Thank goodness he was still with her.

This isn't usual for any of you, the voice insisted.

Jen tucked him in tighter. "Did you know Cari and I were besties right away?"

His fingers sought and caressed the satin belt of her bathrobe. The story was an old one, but he seemed to need some type of connection, even a verbal one, to his mother.

"Yup. From the day after she moved in next door with your Uncle Colin and your Grandfather and Grandmother Marshall."

"They weren't nice." His disgruntled tone mimicked his mother's when she'd talked of her biological parents.

"Sometimes they weren't. But Gramma and Grampa Clark made up for it."

He yawned. "They're the bestest."

Her parents couldn't love their extra little family more if they were blood. "Your Uncle Colin had just started his first year of college. He didn't need us so much. But Cari did. She was so young." She thought of her gangly, gorgeous friend who became her foster sister that day so long ago. "She and I were almost the same age, but we didn't look like it. She towered over me."

The grin on his upturned face was obvious in the diffused illumination. Statuesque Cari had loomed over the pint-sized Jen, and they'd often teased each other about it.

"Ho, ho, ho." He imitated their Jolly Green Giant and Little Sprout vegetable joke.

"She was taller than me even then. But I was her protector when other kids taunted her."

"Cari got teased?" This appeared to be new information to him.

"Boy, did she ever."

"Why?" His mouth set in a fierce line. Figuring out how others ticked was a skill Auggie had yet to fully master. Only in the last year had he verbally interacted much with anyone outside of Lilac. He did not take kindly to teasing.

"Because she was different. She was taller, smarter, prettier ..." No need for him to know she had looked like a young woman even at twelve, when the rest of the class still gave every appearance of the kids they were. "After that, they picked on her for being so ambitious."

"Ambi-shush?"

"Ambitious. She wanted more out of life, and she worked hard to get there."

He nodded with the presence of a wise old owl.

"She pushed me to be better and always saw the best in me. We had each other's backs."

"Like Reeree and me?"

"Exactly."

He stuck his foot out from under Fuzz, wiggling his stubby toes.

The motion lessened the tightness in her chest a bit. He always slept with that one foot uncovered. A step in the right direction.

"When I was in fashion school, she offered to model for me and found she had a flair for it. Later, a lot of designers wanted her to work for them. I'm glad she stayed with Lilac." She swallowed a Cari-sized lump from her throat. Auggie's fingers tapped a rhythmic pat on her knee. "She loved you and your sister more than you will ever know."

He held up his thumb and index finger pressed together. "From here to here?"

"Around the universe and back again." Jen quoted Cari's favorite love words to the twins.

He scowled. "Why didn't we call her mom?"

How to answer the gut-wrenching question? No backpedaling would do for this boy. "Well ... we didn't agree about that. I think it's a privilege for a woman to be called mom by her little boy or girl. Modeling can be a hard business, though. If you called her Cari, she could pretend she wasn't getting older." That and her own difficult relationship with the people she'd originally called mom and dad. But that was a discussion for another day, if ever.

Auggie relaxed against her. His fingers slowed their rhythmic burnishing on the bathrobe. "Do you know why she named us what she did, Engine?"

She smiled, tickled that her godchildren still called her by the nickname they'd given her as soon as they were old enough to butcher Auntie Jen into *Engine*. Should she play along? "What do you mean, honey?"

"Our names. August and January. Why she called us that?"

"How about you tell me?"

"Cari said she had a name picked out for one baby, but when she got two, she didn't know who to give it to." He stretched. "So, she named us after the months she got us and when we were born."

Cari's obnoxious streak strikes again. A stab of animosity shot through her jaw.

"That's not okay?"

Now was not the time to disparage his mother. He needed to pour love over her memory. "I know she panicked a little and blurted out names. I think they are as unique and perfect as the two of you. Can you imagine if she'd gotten pregnant with you guys in March and had you in October?"

His quick little mind zipped along the same lines. Cari would have had no compunction to call one "March" and the other "Occie." Her peculiar sense of humor would have run roughshod over decorum. They giggled together.

When Jen scooted further up in the seat, Auggie turned and threw his arm around her middle. She tipped her head to see his face. His eyelids drooped, finally closing. Would he dream of going down to the duck pond with Ree and Cari—one of their favorite places to hang out together? Helping his sister brush their mother's long hair, clipping umpteen barrettes and curlers in it? Or the funny games she played with them—Cari-style?

Jen prayed he remembered all the good things about her. Her infectious laughter and warm hugs. Her penchant for ice cream dinners and Steak 'n Shake breakfasts. And her love of little dogs, old ladies, and playing with her children on sunshiny beaches around the world.

She rubbed her empty chest where her heart should be. "Father God," she whispered. "Please, help me navigate these new waters for the three of us. To be a good caregiver. One Cari can be proud of." She thought of the days ahead. "Help me keep them safe."

CHAPTER 5

Six o'clock Wednesday morning rolled around, and Jen gave up all pretense of sleep. She scowled at her smiley face alarm clock as if the early morning and her sore muscles were its fault. Flinging back the covers, she went to check on the twins, who were still asleep. A quick fluff of her curls and some makeup was in order before she made breakfast.

Reaching her bathroom, she squinted at herself in the mirror. "You're a mess," she informed the haggard reflection. Picking up a tube of concealer, she threw it back in the basket. "No amount of makeup is going to help."

Her homey bathroom, usually so cheerful to wake up to, gave no such comfort this morning. She flicked off the main light, preferring to shower in the peaceful shadows.

Welcoming the stinging heat on her skin, she rotated her aching shoulders and rolled her head from side to side. Tension crackled and popped from her neck. Contemplating the upcoming day, she didn't relish the agenda. The police station at eleven was their top priority.

Auggie had fallen asleep in her arms for several hours. After a restless slumber, he'd gone back to the other room, likely looking for the comfort of having his twin nearby.

But the sandman hadn't been kind to Jen. Her wakeful rest had done little to relieve the tautness around her eyes, nor the pain around her heart.

Paying quick attention to her curls, she finished in record time. The meeting ahead called for business casual of blue chinos, white tailored shirt, and a plum-colored cardigan to complete her ensemble. "At least I feel more human, even if I don't look it."

After retrieving her cell from her nightstand, she padded down the hall in the direction of her requisite morning caffeine. Tea or coffee? Her churning stomach decided. Tea was the wisest choice. A quick detour righted all the pillows from Auggie's grief session.

She had umpteen calls to make before they were expected at the station. Her parents had finally gotten a line through to her shortly after the kids went to bed the night before. Away from their home port, with a sketchy network, she was reluctant to give them the full details. Hearing the news of Cari's murder, her mother grew distraught, and her father finally took over the conversation. Jen relayed what she could.

"Dad, there's nothing you can do right now. Please, get your boat safely back to Manaus. But can you ask for some extended time off? We may need you both for longer than your normal quick visits."

"I'll make it happen." Patrick choked. "You sure you don't need us now?"

"Daddy," she sniffled. The childhood name sounded foreign on her adult tongue, but she needed the man who had championed all her little girl woes. "This is the hardest thing I've ever had to deal with. I wish you *were* here." She swallowed a sob. "But there's little you can actually do right now. The police and their people are filling our calendar for the time being."

"We'll get things shut down here and be there soon, my girl."

She didn't expect them for several days, at least. Next up, calls to her crew. Information was essential. Rescheduling a show was big work. Calling everyone would take time she didn't have if she was going to make it to the station when requested. She toyed with the idea of asking one of her employees to make the calls. But she'd have to explain where the staff phone list was kept, who to call, what to say. It was quicker to do it herself.

She rang Eva first and highlighted her plan. Her friend took the decision from her, offering to split the list since she had many of the numbers stored in her own cell.

"No worries for you. Tell me what you need. I take care everyt'ing." The model's accent was heavier than usual.

Jen cringed, realizing she'd woken her.

"Don' take a six for a nine, Jen." Eva huffed her exasperation.

"I'm not sure I understand." Silence pulsed, but Jen remained quiet. It vexed Eva when she couldn't think of an American equivalent for the Bajan colloquialisms she'd grown up with.

"Ah, got it. It was Nanna's way of saying, 'Don' misunderstand a person's real intentions.' I took it to mean, watch your back. Don' trust no one. Not even me." She giggled.

Jen smiled. "Thank you for everything."

"Jus' call, you need anyt'ing more."

Jen phoned her half of the list in between chatting with several fashion colleagues who rang to offer their condolences as well as their venues, if she could wait a few weeks. Eva must have immediately jumped on her half.

Questions ran the gamut. Did the police have a suspect? Was everyone safe? Would she cancel or postpone Lilac's annual charity event? But there weren't many answers to give yet.

As for the show, she wouldn't completely withdraw. It was the biggest fundraiser for Cari's scholarships at the Wells-Myer Art Academy. But she couldn't drag her staff through the long hours of putting on an event right now, especially without their top model. She'd think about it later.

Her cell rang, and the advocate's number popped up. "Hello, Melissa."

"Hey, Jen. I thought I better update you after I talked to Colin Marshall last night."

His name brought an old flutter to Jen's stomach. "I'm glad you could get hold of him. I'm sorry I didn't know how."

"No worries. I hate giving sad news, but it was necessary. The next steps will be decided once he gets here."

What visitation schedule would he want? Was her apartment too small for them on a permanent basis? Melissa's words interrupted her tumbling thoughts.

"He lives and works in Grand Rapids, Michigan."

"What did he say when he found out about the twins?"

"He wasn't surprised. Apparently, he's known about them all along."

A thought punched Jen in the gut. Colin was blood relation to the twins. She was not.

"I'd like to chat further, but I've got to run. I wanted to give you his contact info right away." Melissa rattled off the information. "He said he'd get a flight out today. But the weather report sounded iffy up there this morning."

"Thank you. I'll see you later."

Hanging up, Melissa's words speared her thoughts. Colin

knew about the twins. Why would Cari keep that to herself? He could legally take the kids from her. Would he want to?

A sudden, sharp stab skewered her chest. Prickles of light danced in front of her eyes. *Stop! Just stop.* She wouldn't make Colin the bad guy before she even knew what his intentions were. Even his awareness of them didn't mean he was ready to be an insta-parent. She willed her galloping pulse to slow as her thumb found its first stop of four.

Melissa had mentioned Grand Rapids—Eastern Standard Time—making him an hour ahead. There was enough time to call him before she woke the twins. Maybe she could get a feel for what he wanted moving forward. If she reassured him, let him know his niece and nephew were well-cared for, that they were comfortable with her, would that play in her favor? She sounded so calculating.

Her stomach attempted a light fluttering again. "Oh, quit that. You aren't ten anymore."

She fumbled with the raw honey lid, dripping the sticky liquid on the counter. Grabbing a paper towel, she nearly knocked over the soap dispenser. *Get a grip, would you?*

Was he as nice as the boy she once knew? The teenager who morphed into a handsome, if aloof, young man before her very eyes all those years ago. He'd always been polite and helpful, but he mostly hung out with her dad in the garage or backyard, if he was at their house at all. In middle school, she'd been much too young to hang out with a senior.

Colin graduated and headed to university to study architecture only months before the Marshall's terrible accident. He had kept in contact with her family for a while, but they'd slowly lost touch somehow. Cari hadn't talked about him in years.

Jen took a sip of tea and grimaced. She slid her cup into the microwave. As the beverage circled and warmed again, she bowed her head.

Father, thank you for your guidance as we navigate this situation.

Over the years, she'd thought of talking to her childhood crush again. But not like this. Never for this reason. Her pulse quieted, but the winged creatures left her stomach and flew along her arm, tiptoeing to the ends of her fingertips, making them tremble with tension. Nerves. That's all.

Get it over with, Jen. The voice breathed.

Quiet, you. It had to be Cari and her familiar snark, pushing her to do a little more. Right? She punched in the numbers.

He answered on the first ring.

"Hi, Colin. This is Jen Clark. I don't know if you remember me. It's been a long time since we've talked." *Lame.*

"Sure." His voice held a note of the grief they'd both been dealt. "Plus, I have your number programmed in my phone."

"Oh, Melissa must have given it to you."

"Cari insisted, a while back, in case of an emergency."

"She did?"

"You sound surprised. I thought she would have said something."

"No. Yes. I mean ..." She paced her kitchen. "I *am* surprised. No, she didn't tell me. Cari hadn't mentioned you in ages. Until a few minutes ago, when I talked to Melissa, I wasn't even aware you knew about the twins."

"Wow." It was his turn to sound confused. "She talked about you all the time. I thought you two were still close."

"We were. At least I thought so. Frankly, I'm unsure of everything right now." Her voice squeaked.

"I can imagine." A quiet moment followed. "No ... I really can't. I can't believe she's gone." His words sounded as if they'd been dragged through gravel.

"Me either." She sniffled. A thought popped into her head. "If you knew about the twins, then you know about the shared guardianship between us, right?"

"Sure." He sounded puzzled. "But Cari being younger than me, I didn't figure I needed to worry about it much." He coughed. "I guess I was wrong."

How far should she push this? She didn't want to put ideas in his head. "I don't know where to begin. Is there anything you need to know? From me."

"I haven't seen the twins in a few years, but I chat with them regularly. We talk almost every week. Mostly Ree."

"Yeah, Auggie hates the phone."

"I don't get to Dallas often, but for some reason they were always busy or away when I was in town."

Jen's stomach lurched. He came to Dallas? "I wish I'd known you were still in her life."

"I'm not sure why she didn't tell you, Jen. But it doesn't surprise me. She always gave me the impression she wanted your family to herself." He huffed. "I wasn't happy about it, but I respected her wishes."

"And here I thought I was calling to fill you in on the twins' lives."

Gee, thanks, Cari. This is awkward. No secrets, huh? Yeah, right.

"I understand you found her." Colin broke into her silent dialogue. "But that's about all I know. Can you tell me anything more?"

She swallowed her irritation. It wasn't Colin's fault. And he sounded genuinely concerned.

"I'm sorry, I can't. They urged me not to talk about it until the detectives question us further. Except, I will tell you this so you understand what you might be walking into when you get here later today. It was the twins who found her."

"Those poor kids." He gulped. "Wait. We got slammed with a snowstorm last night. Everything's shut down. I just got off the phone with the airline." His frustration was palpable through her cell. "I'm on standby. Hopefully, I'll be one of the first out."

"Goodness. Don't worry. I'll make sure the kids are taken care of … until you arrive." Her heart thumped.

"I know you will. You always have." His words barreled ahead. "In the meantime, is there anything I can do for you from this end? Wire you some money for food? Get legal help? Is that even needed? Or—"

"Thanks for the offer, but the kids stay with me a lot. I have a ton of their favorite foods." Would they need anything else? Her mind came up empty. "As for the legal help, I'll have to let you know. I have to take the twins down to the station later this morning. It's my understanding, due to their age, they're going to question them in small sessions over the next couple of days."

"Makes sense."

"Ree's a mess. She was hyperventilating at one point and fell asleep out of pure exhaustion last night. I know she needs to talk things out—that's how she processes—but honestly, I'm not sure what to say to either of them."

"That's got to be hard." A deep sigh emanated from him. "Sorry, Jennifer Bennifer. I'm fresh out of advice."

She gave a small chuckle, remembering a happier time when she used to bug him. The silly nickname and words had always managed to make her feel as if she were in the sphere of his attention—calming her adolescent angst. It did the same now.

"Good. At least I made you smile. But I feel helpless. I wish I were there."

"You will be soon. For now, they're safe and sound." Her cheeks warmed. "I guess I'd better go, since I don't need to tell you about them, like I thought I did."

"I'd still like to hear about them from you. You know Cari. Much as I loved her, her world was a little skewed. Give me an idea of what they're like from your perspective."

She spent the next twenty minutes filling him in on what they all did together, with and without Cari. Feeding the ducks, finding new restaurants with private dining areas for Auggie's comfort, and the four of them lying around reading to each other on Sundays. "Ree's plowing her way through Lewis's *Chronicles*, but they both love to listen to the old classics. Cari voiced the characters so dramatically. You couldn't help but be pulled into the story."

"That does not surprise me one bit. She did have a flair for the dramatic."

"I think that's why she was so good at modeling. She was always herself, but she wasn't. I'm not sure how to explain it, but it was almost like she became who the designer had in mind once she was in the outfit."

"Sounds plausible. I can understand it through my architecture." He paused. "Don't get me wrong, but does Auggie read?"

"He's not big on it, but he can. He likes graphic comics the best. He prefers to draw his own stories and tells us about them when it's his turn."

"And I bet Engine is his rapt audience."

"You know about my nickname?"

"I don't think they've ever called you anything but Engine to me. Yours is better than mine. To Auggie, I'm Collie Dog."

They both chuckled. Reluctant to sever the gossamer link to Cari, she told him about the playroom at the studio and what the kids did there.

"It's big enough they can play games like jump rope and Mother May I. It comes complete with a popcorn machine and a big screen TV for movies. All Cari-approved, of course."

"Naturally."

"Ree and Auggie are older than most of the other kids. They wanted to help out in the showroom this past year. Cari convinced me to find something for them."

"How'd it turn out?"

"Surprisingly well. Ree's a natural. She has a good ear and helps pick out runway music. Plus, she's been trying her hand at designing. She's very talented. In fact, she helped create one of the garments for the next show. Cari and I had a big surprise planned." She realized she was chattering. "If we have the show—" She paused. "No, *when* we have the show, I'm still thinking of having one of the models walk down the runway in that dress accompanied by Ree. If she's in Dallas."

"What do you mean?"

"We can talk about that when you get here."

"Sure." He rushed ahead. "And Auggie? What's his job?"

"He's a whiz at techie stuff. Richard, our sound engineer, has only let him repair small items so far. But when a headset or mic is on the fritz, he can usually pinpoint the problem. He walks around the room, listening. It's like he can hear the difference. He's a big part of the team. They even got him a T-shirt that says 'Junior Sound Engineer' on the back. Well, he's got three now. He refused to take it off, so Cari had to get more." Colin joined in her laughter.

It felt good to joke with him about something so normal. So Auggie.

Minutes later, their conversation wound down. "I'm glad I got to talk with you, Colin."

"Thanks for everything you're doing for them. Everything you did for my sister. I know it meant the world to her. So did you."

"I needed to hear that." Jen sniffled. "Safe travels. I pray our hearts will remember all the good things about Cari."

"Um, yeah. That would be good." Discomfort crowded his words. "See you soon, Jen."

Click. The temporary link they'd shared vanished.

CHAPTER 6

Jen ushered the twins into the Central Patrol District station later that morning.

"Please sign in. Melissa is finishing a meeting. Officer Pratt will escort you upstairs." The desk officer gestured to a door at the end of the counter. "He'll be here momentarily."

Jen picked up the digital pen and marked the screen with a flourish. Clutching the edge of the machine hid the mild tremor dancing along the fingers of her other hand. Upstairs? They weren't being taken to the gallows ... er ... interrogation rooms in some dark, dank basement?

Pfft. You read too many crime novels. The voice chided.

Hush. It wouldn't do for anyone to hear her talking to herself ... or Cari ... whichever one of them was offering the cheeky opinions sprouting in her imagination.

Pratt showed up moments later sporting the latest slick-back and fade, unseen under his cap the day before. He led them to a bank of elevators. The twins stuck to Jen's side like little burrs as the lift lumbered along.

"How's school going?" Pratt inquired of the kids. "What grade y'all in?"

"Fourth." Ree answered but didn't look his way.

Jen counted the flashing numbers as they bumped past each floor. Two. Three.

"Oh. I thought you'd be in about fifth, maybe. Like my nephew."

"Our birthday is late." Ree knew all about kindergarten academic delays, having walked through the paperwork with Cari at the beginning of each school year.

"What's your favorite sports team, champ?"

Auggie stared ahead.

Jen gave the officer an apologetic shrug.

Pratt chewed his thumbnail until the elevator stopped. "Here we go." He held the door for them and pointed to an office across the hall.

Walking into the room, Jen was struck by its homey atmosphere. Floor-to-ceiling gauzy curtains blocked curious onlookers. Multiple shelves housed a jumble of games, puzzles, and books. Various groupings of tables and chairs surrounded a grownup desk piled high with papers. Cheerful, fresh flowers occupied the one clean space on Melissa's worksurface.

The advocate rushed in, a whirlwind of chatter and shoving things into her binder. She placed it gingerly on top of the already precarious mountain on her desk. "Greetings everyone. Sorry I'm late." She blew out a frustrated breath. "That meeting ran longer than I thought. Thank you for bringing them up here, Everett."

He gave her a huge grin, then tipped an imaginary hat toward Jen and the kids, taking his leave.

Auggie heaved a sigh.

"What's the matter, sweetie?" Melissa put her hand on his shoulder. "Did he make you nervous? My colleagues are all nice, but they make me uncomfortable sometimes too. Can you two keep a secret?"

The twins sent concerned glances toward Jen.

"Melissa"—might as well start this off with candor—"Auggie and Ree's mom told them they shouldn't keep secrets from their loved ones." *Too bad she didn't follow her own counsel.* Jen drilled a look at the advocate, willing her to play along.

"That's good advice."

"Now they're older, they know how to keep quiet about some things. If it's good news, like a party, that's a surprise." She waved her hands in the air. "If it's not, like Aunt Mildred's yellow dress makes her look like a school bus—"

Auggie popped his knees back and forth. "We don't have an Aunt Mildred."

"But if you did, we wouldn't want to hurt her feelings, right?"

Everyone shook their heads.

"Those are private thoughts. Maybe we can do the same with you? Then they wouldn't be keeping a secret from me."

"I like that idea." Leaning toward her three conspirators, Melissa brought them into her confidence. "You know those big, scary policemen?" She put her finger to her lips. "They're really teddy bears in disguise."

Ree giggled. "No, they're not. You're being silly." She smiled with sweet acceptance, sending a zing of—what? Jealousy? Concern?—to Jen's stomach. Ree didn't usually take to people at first. Was it because Melissa appeared rather child-like herself? Jen squinted at the pair. What would happen to Ree's heart when they no longer needed the advocate's assistance?

Jen stuck her hand in her pants pocket, in part to keep the worsening tic from notice. Melissa held too many of their cards stacked in her authoritative deck.

Don't borrow trouble where it doesn't exist. The admonition made a fair point. For now, she didn't care who was talking in her head. The words only needed to make sense because her own chaotic thoughts weren't.

Melissa pointed to a table in the corner. "There are games and stuff over there. Do you want to listen to the radio?"

Ree shook her head and went to inspect the artistic offerings, picking up a box of markers.

"Cari didn't let them listen to the radio often because of the content."

"Crap." Auggie spouted. He dropped in a chair across from his sister.

Jen's mouth twitched, remembering her friend's forthright language. "Yup. He's right. She wouldn't let them listen to the radio 'because of all the crap on it.' She played mostly classical."

"She sounds like a very wise mother." Melissa smiled at Auggie.

"You know Cari?" His eyes grew round.

"I didn't, but your aunt told me she was a good mom."

A hopeful look shone in his eyes. He hitched his thumb at Jen. "Her name is Engine."

Melissa chuckled. "I get it. Aunt Jen ... Engine."

His mouth dropped open, dutifully impressed. "She knows your name. She's smart."

"I think Melissa will need to call me Jennifer around her coworkers."

He tipped his head sideways, chewing the inside of his cheek.

My wise old man.

"Okey-dokey." He turned his attention to a puzzle with puppies.

Melissa reached up and flicked a switch above her desk. Orchestral notes danced through the room. "This is one of my favorite CDs. It's by Tchaikovsky."

"Chick who?" Auggie's nose wrinkled.

"He was a music composer." Ree explained. "Cari has some of his music." Her lip quivered.

"Where is he?" Auggie asked.

"Tchaikovsky? He's been dead a long time." Melissa's tone was matter of fact.

"He got killed too?"

"No, he had a sickness called cholera. A very long time ago. But he created a lot of beautiful music before he died."

"Okay." He resumed work on the puzzle.

Melissa's attitude about death was admirable, if hard to pull off at the moment.

The advocate moved to the larger table where Jen sat. "His thought processes are incredible."

"It's hard to keep up with sometimes. Depends on the subject. Ask him about airplanes or dogs if you want a great conversation." Jen grinned.

"Good to know." Melissa made a note. "Because of his special needs, we're getting focused help. With what Ree has going on in here," she tapped her temple, "she's going to need a gentle touch too. I've requested a special team. Detectives Pamela Mason and Ozillia Ryan." Melissa shuffled papers. "They'll handle the actual investigation. But Auggie and Ree are my priority. Along with you as guardian. Once Mr. Marshall gets here, we'll sort out the rest. The Letter of Guardianship names both of you, but legally, things could be swayed toward him."

Jen winced, her chest ached with the thought of what Colin's presence could mean.

"I won't lie to you. Over the next few days, there will be unpleasant discussions. A few may upset you or the twins." She clutched her hands in front of her. "We're all here to help you keep them safe."

Jen blinked. Keep control? Relinquish it? Somewhere in the middle? There were too many questions to ask even one.

"Here's how you can help us. Be as positive as possible." Melissa's eyes crinkled. "I've noticed they defer to you often. Even physically leaning on you. They draw strength from your nearness." She glanced over her shoulder at the twins. "It's okay to let them do that. Murder investigations are tough. It's worse when children are involved. But, like I said yesterday, don't coach them."

"You sound like you've done this a few times."

"More than I'd like." Her smile didn't reach her eyes.

"Do you mind if I ask ... personal or professional?"

"Both." Melissa jotted a note then scribbled through it.

"I'm sorry." Jen wanted to wrap her in a hug.

"Don't be. I'd like to think my experience makes me a better advocate. I understand what they're going through." She fingered the beaded choker at her neck. "You're their rock. But you may hear things about your friend you don't like."

"I doubt it. I don't mean to be flippant about this at all. But Cari and I have been through a lot. And because she was their mom, I already was ... *am* ... their stability."

Melissa's lips formed a tight line.

"Don't get me wrong. Cari loved them to pieces. They were her life." Jen rushed ahead. "She did the best she could after her rough beginning. In my opinion, it gave her some strange notions about rearing kids. I stepped in when necessary. Or when she needed extra support." A squabble brewed between the twins, and Jen turned to them. "Figure it out, you two."

Auggie thrust a blue marker at his sister.

"Thank you." Ree responded, her tone clipped.

"You aren't going to roar at me, are you?" He gave her the side eye.

Jen snagged her lip between her teeth and focused on Melissa again. "I expect *that's* going to get worse in the days ahead. Anyway, Cari had a streak that bordered on callousness sometimes, mostly when tired or overly stressed. But she seemed to be doing better this past year. Especially with them."

"Sometimes we grow up with our kids." Melissa's eyes twinkled.

"You could be right." Jen propped her chin on her fist. "We had a couple major disagreements about how she raised them, but she was fierce about her children. If I didn't like that they didn't go to church or went gallivanting during the school year ... well, that was my problem more than hers. But I became her conscience too. I reminded her of parent-teacher meetings and made sure they ate more than ice cream for dinner six days a week."

Melissa chuckled.

"Cari loved ice cream. Her only vice. Black Cherry Chunk. How she ever got me to love that stuff too, I'll never know." Jen's chin trembled. "I'm not telling you this for a pat on the back. I only want you to understand her better. Sometimes I got angry with her, but we were a good team. The four of us." Rubbing her nose, she sniffled, and Melissa handed her a tissue. "Cari was my—" She dabbed at her eyes. "Like I told Auggie last night, she made me a better person."

Sympathy etched deep creases around Melissa's mouth. "It sounds like she was an excellent momma. She just might not have understood how to be a good *mother* sometimes."

Jen gave her a small smile. "She didn't have a good role model at first."

"Yes, that can happen." Melissa's shoulders pulled taut. "Let's continue."

Had she hit a nerve?

"The detectives will question the twins, probably together. Auggie seems calmer when Ree's nearby." She ran her finger down a sheet and listed specifics to expect.

This young lady orchestrates a whole lot more than I realized.

"Have you been able to talk to your parents?"

"It's an ordeal with the remote locations they travel, but we talked last night." She sighed. "If Colin agrees, we'll wait for the funeral until they're here."

Melissa's quizzical expression lightened. "That's right, they finished raising her."

"They're devastated." Her words scratched at her throat. "Cari had been out of town with the kids the last couple of years when our folks visited. She sent them pictures, and they talked on the phone often, but it seemed like she reduced her physical contact with them. Colin said the same things about his visits." Jen bit her lip. "Anyway, they'll be here in a couple days. Hopefully, we'll be allowed to hold the service once they've arrived."

"That will be up to the detectives and their team. Speaking of them ..."

The atmosphere shifted with a comfortable energy as two women walked through the door. Jen's artistic nature went on full alert watching the mismatched pair. Intrigued, she stood and held out her hand to the first.

Not much taller than Jen's own four eleven, the middle-aged woman wore a dark blue, casual-cut suit, giving the impression of experienced authority. She might have nailed the look, if it hadn't been for the fluff of feathery hair sticking up around her head. Her nameplate read Det. P. Mason. Jen's good manners forbade the grin threatening to sneak out. Growing up, she had loved watching the old courtroom drama with her dad.

"P stands for Pamela, not Perry. I've heard it all before." She winked and patted Jen's hand. "Your fingers are like ice, dear."

Standing behind the warm, encouraging investigator was a statuesque beauty. Jen's usual business etiquette deserted her, but she tried not to stare.

"What's the matter? Never seen a big Black gal before?"

Jen's shoulders tensed, ready for a confrontation, but warmth radiating from the other woman's dark eyes took the sting from her tone.

Detective Mason chuckled and joined Melissa. "Oz can sort that out herself. Let's go visit the munchkins."

"She'll get used to me." The tall one's confident smile lit up her face.

Despite her initial exasperation, Jen's curiosity got the better of her. "I need to know. Call it my professional interest, if you'd like. Exactly how tall are you?"

"Six-three and a quarter. Over six since the tenth grade."

"It must be the hair making you look taller."

The woman turned her head from side to side. Intricately woven braids added a good three inches to her height. "Beautiful, aren't they? My sister does my hair. Takes forever getting it done, but it always looks great afterward."

"That had to have been hard, being so tall in school, Detective Ryan."

"It's Oz." There was no brooking the statement. "What do you mean hard?"

"I bet you were teased."

"Nobody dared to mock me." Oz straightened to her full height. Her grin lessened the bite of her words.

"Hmm ... maybe not."

"You don't seem intimidated."

"Should I be?"

The detective walked over to a table near the door, pulled out a chair, and sat with natural grace. She gestured for Jen to join her. "I tend to unsettle a lot of people."

"Most people didn't have Cari Marshall for a best friend."

"The deceased?"

Jen flinched. "Yes. We've been best friends forever."

"She overwhelmed people?" Oz leaned her elbows on the table.

"Cari?" Jen snorted. "Not by a long shot. I scared people *for* her."

"You? But you're all of five-feet-nothing in your stockings."

"Close. Being so small, I had to learn to hold my own. Cari wouldn't stand up to anyone. I had enough challenge for both of us."

"How come?"

Why did she feel comfortable talking about her friend to this stranger? "Well, for instance, there was this popular football player in school. He liked her, but he was kind of a meathead back then, so he made fun of her. Calling her names like *giraffe* and bumping her in the hall on purpose. You know, annoying." Her jaw tensed. "I'd had enough when he made her cry one day. I tore into him. I didn't think it did any good, but a week later, he asked her to tutor him in math. He's super smart. A McCombs grad. And really nice, now that he's grown."

"McCombs? Who is he?"

"Nathan Banks."

"Git outta here. *You* stood up to Nathan Banks?"

"When we were kids. I haven't seen him in a long time, but I follow his career."

"Yeah. Excellent quarterback. But even I don't know as I would've stood up to him. Not that there's anything to argue about with him. He's a sweetheart."

"You know him?"

"Friend of the family. Roomed with my brother." She paused, seeming to consider her thoughts. "Well, Miss Clark, anyone who isn't intimidated by me and can stand up to the likes of Nathan, I expect we'll get along fine." She stuck out her hand. "Let's start fresh. My name's Ozillia Ryan, but my friends call me Oz."

Jen glanced down at her hand engulfed in the long, tapered fingers. "I won't be able to call you that in front of the twins—especially Auggie. He can get funny ideas about nicknames. How about Detective Oz?"

"Proper upbringing, I see."

"My mom's a stickler."

"Then, you're Miss Jen. For the kids' sake. Speaking of them. How about we head over? The little dude is giving me the once over."

Jen chuckled. "Don't take it personally, Detective, but Auggie has few filters when it comes to his curiosity."

"That happens a lot with ASD. That's his diagnosis, right? Autism Spectrum Disorder, Level One? I'm not an expert, but he seems very high functioning to me."

"Not officially diagnosed, as far as I know. I'm not sure Cari ever had him tested. But I found out about their psychiatrist only yesterday, so who knows?" The corners of her mouth dipped. "If anyone ever got near the subject, Cari shut them down, pronto."

"Momma bear to the rescue. I would have loved to meet her."

Jen's throat thickened. "I think you would have liked each other."

"We'll figure this out, Miss Jen. Together." She unwrapped her frame from the chair. "Maybe I can get a sense of her through her kids."

"Something's caught Auggie's fancy. Fair warning, we can't always predict what he's going to say."

"I'd rather littles ask their questions."

The two moved to the other side of the room.

"Hey there, kids. I see you've met my partner." She pretzeled herself on the floor between them and told them her name. "Officer Oz might be easier to remember though. What are you two working on?"

"Puzzles." Auggie's gaze hyper-focused on her hair. His hand clenched, kneading in a rhythmic back-and-forth.

Ree touched his arm. "You have to ask. Remember?"

"Yes." He snapped, then glanced at Jen. "Sorry, Reeree." He mumbled.

"What do you want to know, papi?" Oz encouraged.

He hung his head.

Ree leaned toward him and whispered. "Ask. It'll be okay."

He peeked from under his lashes. "Can I touch those?"

"My hair?"

"Auggie likes textures." Ree explained. "Especially hair."

Relief washed over his face, followed by a hopeful expectancy.

"Sure, you can." Oz bent her head, giving him free access to her woven locks.

He put a hand on her elaborate updo. He traced the plaits around and over their circuitous route, touching here and poking there. Popping his finger out of the last little burrow of braids, his face burst into a sappy grin.

"Your smile made my day, darlin'." Oz beamed.

The group wrapped up the day with getting to know the detectives, answering cursory questions about the case, and promised to return first thing in the morning.

Melissa reminded the twins she would be with them when they talked to Mason and Oz. "Or anyone else who wants to discuss what happened to your mom."

The mention of Cari brought an instant chill to the room. Auggie's patience, held in check far longer than Jen had expected, was at an end for the day. He swiped at his puzzle, sending pieces to the floor. "Do we hafta come back?" He howled. "It's too ..." Scrunching his shoulders tight under his ears, he wrapped his arms around himself.

Jen and Ree closed ranks, kneeling to pick up the cardboard pieces.

"Leave it there. I'll get it later." Melissa moved to stand behind Auggie and gently pat his shoulder. "I'm sorry, sweetie. You do. But not until tomorrow."

"I don't wanna." He wailed, his face crumpling. "I don't like it here."

"Hey, big guy." Detective Oz caught his attention. "I bet you're feeling like I do in this little room. If it's okay with Melissa and your aunt, how about we meet you first thing in the morning at her apartment with breakfast."

Jen cringed. "Mornings aren't our best."

"Oh, wait, I forgot, I have to go to the dentist first." Oz recovered the moment. "Can we make it brunch? About ten-thirty?"

Jen sighed. "If you want to eat kid cereal and eggs." Her objections sounded petulant, but her composure was as thin as Auggie's wails.

"We'll bring the food, won't we, Mason?" She didn't wait for an answer. "I'm thinking bagels with cream cheese, tomatoes, and cold cuts for the squirts here."

Auggie recovered enough to scowl. "I'm not a squirt. Squirts are little kids."

His sister nixed the tomato slices.

"Okay. No 'maters on Ree's bagel." Oz wrote the orders, looking as if she'd been a waiter in the past. "Got it. How about berry-chicken salad for the adults? Our treat. You in?" Everyone nodded.

"After brunch, you'll come here. We'll be in a bigger room for most of the time." Oz scanned the advocate's office. "But you can come back here with Melissa anytime you want to. Even if it's to get away from us for a few minutes. Deal?"

The siblings nodded in unison.

Oz pushed herself up, almost toppling the little table.

"Oops, careful there. You'll upset the apple cart." Mason held her hand up. "Help an old lady out of these pint-sized chairs."

"Old lady, my eye." But she aided her partner.

Ree watched the two with keen interest.

"Are you riding with us in the morning, Melissa?" Mason asked.

"That would be great, thanks. I'll meet you here."

"Okay, see you all tomorrow." The two detectives started for the door.

Jen hurried to get her purse from under the big table and caught Mason elbowing Oz.

"Dentist? That's not on your calendar."

"Nah. Just back-peddling. I forgot kids don't get up as early as we do."

"No one gets up as early as you do, Oz. You set the alarm for the sun."

CHAPTER 7

Jen's concern grew with each floor as the elevator crawled up to her apartment. Fatigue etched old-woman wrinkles around Ree's eyes. The cares of the entire world seemed to rest upon her slim shoulders.

Auggie chuffed under his breath, matching the mechanical rhythm lifting them. She'd forgotten to ask Ree if she knew why he was making the odd noises. Now was not the time.

The doors whooshed open, and she held the twins at bay, inspecting the hallway before she allowed them to exit.

"Can you open the door, Auggie?" Normally one of his favorite tasks—she handed him the keys—but he stood like a limp noodle. She juggled their takeout dinner and unlocked the latch herself.

She'd expected tears, tantrums, or anger from the kids over their mother's death. Not these quiet little automatons. Was she in for a colossal, delayed reaction with them? She'd have to ask Melissa. Or maybe the psychiatrist.

Inside, the kids chose the kitchen island instead of their preferred seats in the dining room. They didn't even argue over who would sit nearest to her.

Both unwrapped their sandwiches.

"Do I have to eat, Engine? I am so tired. Can I go to bed?" Ree picked up the corner of the bread on her favorite roasted chicken and wrinkled her nose. "I'm not sure it's going to go down."

"Can you try at least a little of the insides? You've got to have some nourishment. Or I can make you some bouillon."

Pulling a piece of meat from her sub, Ree's lips thinned, but she took a bite, chewing in slow motion.

Auggie flipped his bun open, dumped the roast beef on its paper, and shoved the bread aside. Still no words.

Ten minutes later, they were washed up and in bed. In another five, their story was read, and soft breaths puffed from the direction of their pillows. Jen left the door open a crack when she tiptoed out in case they needed her.

She trudged to her bedroom, so spent her bones ached. Seven o'clock, but if she slept now, she'd be awake in the middle of the night. She couldn't face the midnight hour alone today.

Picking up her cell, she swiped the faces next to numbers until she found—

Her hand quaked. The phone landed with a clatter on her nightstand. She'd almost called Cari. The tremor intensified in her fingers.

Phone Sassy. You need each other. The voice filled her room with a gentle kindness.

Glancing at the time, four o'clock Seattle, she punched the icon for her gemologist. She listened for the mechanical tones.

"Hello." Sassy's cheery cadence answered. "You've reached Sassafras Montgomery, Seattle's premier jeweler—at least that's what I tell myself. Right now, I'm working on someone else's baubles. When will I be designing yours? Leave me a message, and we'll talk."

Jen grinned as she did every time she heard the enthusiastic message. Sassy was one of the few people she knew who still had a landline and an answering machine. *Beep*.

"Hey, it's me. Pick up." Maybe she really wasn't there. "Call me when you can. We need to change some of the jewelry for the show. Or—" Her voice cracked.

The line screeched. "Wait," Sassafras shouted into the receiver. "Don't hang up," was followed by plastic hitting tile. "Oh, flipping pancakes. I'm here," she squawked.

Heels click-clacked near the phone. A former clothing design student with Jen, Sassy could create jewelry pieces for the statuesque Cari like no one else.

"Coming, Jen," a muffled shout. More rustling and tapping. Breathless, she managed a labored, "Hiya, honey bunch. You okay?"

"So, you heard." Sassy was one of the few people in Jen's personal life Cari had genuinely liked. They'd appreciated each other's talents and looks. While outsiders thought Sassy lived up to her name—even her hair was the burnt orange color of sweet tea—Cari referred to her as effervescent. The three had meshed well—in business and friendship.

"I heard this afternoon, while I was out getting supplies. I was walking in the door when the phone rang. I've been holed up here for days."

That was nothing new with Sassy. Jen used to have to shoo her from their apartment workroom to get her to eat when they were in college.

"Some old biddy was gossiping about it at a jumble sale. What happened? Was it a car accident? Heart attack? What about the kids? Where—"

Jen went straight to the final answer. "She was murdered."

"Oh, my dear Lord."

Jen pictured Sassy making the sign of the cross at that very moment.

"I just spoke with her yesterday when Ree called about ... I hope you weren't the one who found her?"

"Worse, the twins."

"Those poor babies."

Talking with Sassy, someone who spent plenty of time with the twins ... before ... brought a measure of peace to Jen. She pulled Fuzz over her lap and snuggled under. "I'm supposed to keep my ear out for anything unusual. They're worried one of the kids might have seen something but doesn't remember." She ran her hand through her dark curls. "Auggie's handling it better than expected. But Ree's emotions swing between protective momma and lost little girl."

Sassy tsk'd. "When is it her turn to be a kid? Sorry. That wasn't nice of me."

"But the truth."

"How are you all holding up? I mean, they always went home after a few days. This is going to be permanent, right?"

"As okay as can be. Colin is snowbound in Michigan right now, so we're kind of stalled."

"*The* Colin? Cari's brother? The one you had a massive crush on? I thought no one knew where he was."

"Me either. But it seems Cari's been in touch with him all this time. That's not the only secret she kept, but we can talk about that later. The other reason I called was to discuss changing Cari's pieces for the show. I'm not exactly sure who ... maybe Eva. I can't ..." Jen choked.

"Do you want me to come down? I can be there tomorrow if you need me."

"I know you would. Don't worry. I just have too much information crashing around in my head. It all spills out sometimes. I don't know what I'm going to do without her—or the kids."

"Are you sure you don't want me there?"

Jen sniffed, wiped her eyes, and hiccupped into a semblance of normal. "It's really going to be okay, Sass. I have to get used to the changes, whatever they might be. Colin's their next of kin. I can only hope he'll let me visit." Jen twirled a silver circle of tiny, intertwined lilacs around her finger—a Sassafras Montgomery original. "You're due here in two weeks for the show anyway, if we have it. Besides, knowing you, you've already bought your ticket."

A chuckle confirmed her suspicion.

"That might put you here for the funeral."

"Okay, but if you need me, I'll buy a whole new ticket if I have to."

"I know you would.That will be soon enough. In fact, I may need a big shoulder to cry on by then."

"You got it. I'll bring extra-absorbent shirts with me. Shoulder pads and all."

Jen giggled. She could always count on Sassy to pick up her spirits. Their talk progressed to the jewelry Cari would have worn in the upcoming show.

"So, assuming we still hold the event, if I can make the model changes in the next few days, does that give you enough time to make adjustments?"

"Absolutely. But we didn't discuss the final number. The one with the dripping pearl earrings. They're long. They might overwhelm someone else. It won't take me more than an hour or so to make them whatever length you need."

"I'll keep that in mind. I'm not sure what I'm going to do about that gown yet, if anything. But I didn't realize what time it was. I've got to get some sleep."

"I'll let you go. Oh, wait. I finally broke down and got a cell phone."

"Will wonders never cease."

"Hah, hah. Funny girl. I was going to call from the airport and surprise you, but here's the number ..."

CHAPTER 8

Jen wiped the dining table, listening while the others chatted.

Auggie stood by the picture window and pointed out places of interest along the Dallas horizon for the benefit of Detective Oz. "See those two white arches? And then that one with all the wires holding it up? Those are the Margarets. They're Engine's favorite bridges."

Jen chuckled at his description of the Margaret McDermott Bridge and the Margaret Hunt Hill Bridge. Indeed, two of her favorite Dallas landmarks.

He jumped up and down. "Engine. Come quick." He waved her over to the glass. "Look. Ethan's building is above the trees now."

"Are you sure that's the right one?"

"'Course I am. The boom is right there." He jabbed his finger at the window, indicating the top of a crane. "Ethan tells it what to do. Last week, I couldn't see the top floor, only the crane's hook."

"We've been walking down by that building since it began." Jen explained to the others. "The project manager, Ethan, is friendly and answers all of Auggie's questions about the machinery."

Ree took her last gulp and plunked her glass on the table. "He promised he'd take us inside for a tour when it's done."

"Does Ethan have a last name?" Mason's little notebook was already in her hands.

"I've never asked."

"Can we go see the crane now, Engine?" Auggie bounced like a kangaroo.

"We're not headed to Lilac Lane, honey. Ethan's building is in the opposite direction."

"Where are we going again?"

Oz steered him toward the kitchen. "Mason and I need to go over a few things with you and Ree at the precinct."

Auggie's energy came to a grinding halt. Both kids stared at Jen.

"I'll be with you, " their aunt reassured them.

Ree squared her shoulders, a little warrior girding for battle. "It's okay, Auggie. We'll stick together. I won't leave you."

"You sure?"

Ree crooked her finger. "Pinky promise."

Auggie faced the detectives. "Do I hafta be p'lite there?" He screwed up his face.

Oz's laugh boomed. "Yup. We all do. Even me." She kneeled to eye-level with him. "We'll all be with you, but your Engine will stay quiet, like she has a sore throat."

Auggie's head whipped around to Jen. "You don't feel good? We can't go." He crossed his arms in defiance, a ready caretaker.

A look passed between the detectives. Nuances of speech didn't always translate well to his literal way of thinking.

Oz took back the conversation. "What I mean is, when Engine has a sore throat, does she talk very much?"

"Nnooo." He wasn't giving up his protective armor that easily. "She sounds croaky, like a frog."

"So, like then, we can't let her talk much. We don't want her to remind you about what happened yesterday."

His ire deflated. "She can't." He mumbled into his chest. "She wasn't there. Not me and Ree. Only Cari. And maybe—" The air quivered in silence. He shook his head. "I don't know. Somebody."

A collective ache filled the space.

Jen seized the dishrag and wiped the counter again. Anything to hide her quaking fingers.

You worry too much. The voice caught her attention. *They've got this.*

Bossy much? She tuned back into the real conversation in the room.

"So, we agree? Your Engine stays with you, but quietly." Oz asked the twins. "Deal?"

The kids shook hands with her while Mason watched from her seat at the kitchen island.

Melissa stepped to Jen's side. "You seem unsettled."

"I'm fine." She listened for a moment as the detectives discussed what the twins might bring to the station to pass the time. "This wasn't just a nice little brunch meeting, was it?"

"You're an astute observer. I told you Mason and Oz's team was unique. They've developed a system to help their clients—all children, sometimes adults with special needs—get through the intense emotions and questioning that comes up with their cases. My caseload is frequently the same people, so I ride along on their coattails, so to speak. Their interactions in homes and other places of comfort often give me insight I wouldn't get otherwise."

"Makes sense."

Mason picked up the leftover food, and Ree directed where things belonged. Her brother dawdled near Oz.

"Did you need something, Auggie?"

"You don't hafta call me August?"

"Not unless my boss is here."

"She's not your boss?" He pointed at Mason, who snorted.

Oz ruffled his hair. "Nope. Not yet. She's my partner and friend."

Auggie gave the older detective a toothy grin.

Melissa brought the last dirty plate to the sink. "Okay, everyone. Let's get out in that gorgeous Texas sunshine." Her gaze narrowed on Jen's hand and the wobbling dirty coffee cup she held.

Don't let that one's jolly attitude fool you. The voice cautioned. *Those eyes speak volumes.*

Be quiet, you. I've got enough to deal with. The mild cacophony around her brought her attention back to the room. "I'd prefer the twins rode with me. Otherwise, I need to get their boosters for you. They aren't tall enough on their own."

"Do you have room for me in your car?" Melissa asked quietly.

"Sure. They sit in the back anyway." *Which of us is she safeguarding?*

"We'll follow you back to the station then." Mason buttoned her blazer.

Jen took in the loose cut of the jacket and slight bulge at the officer's hip. Her shoulders relaxed, knowing these women were trained and ready to protect them. She prayed they didn't need it.

The first inquiry of the afternoon flew by. They sat around a conference table chatting. When asked, Jen helped the twins establish who was who at the fashion house. She was not surprised to find they had their own impressions of Lilac's crew.

"What about the *mysterious* guy?" Oz air quoted. "Quiet. Wears all black."

"That's Victor." Ree supplied. She held her hands to her throat, mimicking a turtleneck. "He thinks he's hiding those purple bruises under his shirt. I saw them one day and asked how he hurt himself." She scrunched her face. "He did *not* like that."

Mason sputtered into her coffee.

"He's our rigger." Jen glossed over Ree's observation. "He tends to take the tech crew uniform of all black during shows to the extreme. He started with us as an intern, then was hired as an employee later. Richard might know more about him. They have to work together quite often."

"Richard's my buddy." Auggie blurted. "But not everyone's."

Had her godson picked up on something she should have? If so, it wouldn't be the first time. Nor, she suspected, the last.

He continued. "The little girls screaming in the playroom bother him. But I like when it's his turn with us. More than Rosie." He made a face as if someone mentioned liver.

"Almost our whole crew rotates who's keeping an eye on the kids in the playroom." Jen hurried to add, "Each employee goes through a voluntary background check beforehand." She turned to the twins. "We already took care of that situation. A long time ago."

"Not fast enough." Ree grumbled.

"Rose is my best seamstress." Jen explained. "But she's older than the others. Never had any children. She'd rather be sewing or knitting more than anything else. We decided she's exempt from playroom duty after she tried to teach them all to sew at one time. Little hands and pins—" It was her turn to shiver in mock horror. "Too many poked fingers and tears. She's good with these two, but not the others."

"I like when she takes us to the 'paca farm with her." Auggie bounced in his seat.

"I believe it's time for a break." Melissa stood, brooking no argument.

"Good." He turned to Oz. "Do you gotta bathroom here?"

"We have several."

"You don't have to go in with me, do you?"

She chuckled. "No, sir. One of us can stand outside and wait for you." Oz motioned for the little troupe to follow.

When they returned, a whiteboard occupied the room. They collaborated to draw the plan of the showroom floor. Once done, Mason gestured to chairs at the side of the room. "Miss Jen, care to take a seat over there?"

The placement was strategic. She wasn't in the kids' direct line of sight, but she was a head turn away if they needed her. Soon, the board became like a football strategy session with Oz mapping where the kids had been, what they'd done, and who they'd seen. Jen expected her to break out a whistle and call foul any moment.

Melissa stepped in occasionally to caution her colleagues when their inquiries grew too intense. They immediately backed down.

The twins recreated their movements before, during, and after *the incident*. Ree scowled, and Auggie squirmed every time someone mentioned those words. Or maybe they were typical nine-year-olds. Tired, hungry, and sick of the questions.

Mason erased little points on the whiteboard and drew a blue circle, a red one, and three black dots clustered nearby, presumably to represent the twins and Stan's boys. "So, you were playing a game in the big playroom?"

"Ree told you." Auggie plunked his head on his hand, as if he no longer had energy to hold it up. His other arm draped across his sister's chair.

Mason leaned over the table on her elbows. "I know this is annoying to answer the same questions over and over. But sometimes people think of things if we ask different ways. Understand?"

"I guess so." He took Officer Henderson's rock from his pocket, smoothed his fingers over it, and made his little chuffing noises a couple times. "We were playing Mother May I. That game is okay. But Joey wasn't being nice. He teases me."

"He does that to everyone." Ree sighed. She stared with an odd intensity at the whiteboard. Auggie patted her back. Jen couldn't recall a time she'd ever seen him do that before.

Ree got up and walked to the board, drawing two circles connected by a line from the simulated playroom to her mother's dressing room. She frowned, then slashed jagged marks through them, obliterating any sign of her graphics.

"Are you trying to remember something?" Melissa asked.

Ree jumped and whipped around, her face troubled. "I don't know. Something is ... it's out here somewhere." She pushed at the empty space in front of her. "The more I try, the more it goes away."

"Give it some time. You might recall it later." Melissa commiserated.

"But I don't know if I want to." She flung herself into the chair next to her brother and put her head on his shoulder. "It feels ... scary."

Auggie, his eyes large, held perfectly still for his sister.

The officers sat down across from the twins and beckoned Jen and Melissa over.

Mason's mouth settled into a grim line. "We didn't want to worry you, but you're observant enough to see them, anyway. You'll have a team of officers following you whenever you aren't here. To make extra sure you're safe."

A headache tap-tap-tapped its way across Jen's forehead. She was about to demand a break for the kids—and herself—when Mason's cell buzzed.

She shared the information on the screen with Oz, who headed for the door while Mason lingered.

"We're going to take a breather. I think you could all do with one too."

Something Jen couldn't decipher passed between the detective and advocate.

"Melissa, could you take the kids down to the cafeteria and let Miss Jen have an hour to herself. I expect she needs to regroup."

"Sure, I can." Melissa helped the kids pick up the markers and the sticky notes they'd used. "You guys like pizza?"

Auggie, earlier mood forgotten, rubbed his stomach. "I'm starvin'."

"Aren't you coming with us?" Ree looked at Jen and wrung her hands.

Had Jen interpreted Melissa's pointed stare correctly? "If you two are okay with hanging out for lunch with Melissa for a bit, I'm going to scoot home and see if we have any messages from Gramma and Grampa. I still don't know their flight schedule." She hadn't had a moment to herself in more than forty-eight hours. The break might do her some good. Soothe her nerves.

Mason fished in her pocket and handed Melissa a twenty-dollar bill. "Can y'all bring back a turkey on rye for me and a tuna for Oz?" She turned to leave the room, but Jen waylaid her.

"The text. Has there been some news? Is there anything I can do to help?"

"Nothing yet. We'll let you know." She checked her phone. "It's a little before two. Can you be back around three-ish? We'll finish up with a few more questions. It shouldn't take long. You're familiar with the current officers on your security duty. Henderson and Pratt. Until we know for certain what's going on, they'll follow you." She shook her head. "Don't argue this. Cap's orders."

"Your captain is involved in this? Why?"

Mason grinned. "Small world. She was an enthusiastic fan of Miss Marshall. Her daughter wants to attend that school your model went to. So, no trying to give them the slip, okay?"

Jen went with the twins to the advocate's office and gathered her coat. Auggie went back to his puzzle.

"Before you go," Melissa called to her, "would you and Ree help me understand something?" She turned to the girl. "You seem really troubled not remembering. Can you tell me more about this photographic memory of yours?"

Ree agreed with little enthusiasm. "Dr. B calls it *eidetic* memory. I can see people and places in my head, like a painting. I can almost always draw them. But right now, I can't." The final word ended in a plaintive wail.

"When someone's had a trauma, like you three have, sometimes their normal skills take a vacation. I expect your gift, this eidetic memory of yours, will soon return."

"But I need it now." Ree's hands jerked to her sides.

Jen stepped in. "Sweetheart, why don't you rest for a day or two? After that, we'll draw together, like we always do. You can do a sketch for Gramma. Or Mr. Harper. He's been asking you for one of his new kitten. Maybe that will help."

A tiny gleam returned to Ree's eyes at the mention of the fluffball Jen's octogenarian neighbor had adopted. "I'll try."

"Can you give me a minute with your aunt, then we'll go down for lunch."

Ree went to sit by her brother.

"Listen, what I told Ree ... trauma can do crazy things to us. We rarely know how or why ... or if we'll be the same afterwards. But I expect *her* gift will come back. She's already trying to piece things together." She tidied up the chaos on her desk. "This is the clinical side of me talking, so forgive my text-booking. As her talent reemerges, Ree may exhibit conflicting behavior. While the pictures are murky, that wars with the clarity she's used to. She could become a little manic about her art." She paused. "Or she may never sketch again."

Jen's heart tumbled to her feet.

"Let her guide you. It was a good suggestion for you two to draw together. Something she's familiar with. Go ahead. But keep an eye on her and let me know if you get overly concerned. You have my direct number. Call me any time, day or night."

"I appreciate it. I thought I was going to have to worry about Auggie. He's holding up well, so far." She thought over the questioning. "He's being far stronger than I've ever witnessed. Ree is usually the one in charge. But—I don't know how to put it—it's almost like she's wilting. Instead of going home, I want to stay with them."

"You're not going to be any good to them if you're exhausted." Melissa pointed to Jen's hand. "I've seen the trembles. I'm pretty sure it's stress, but you need a break. Even a short one. We won't be going anywhere except here and the cafeteria." She dug her phone from her pocket. "I have multiple people I can call if we need anything. Including you."

Jen doled out hugs to the twins, and Melissa scooted her toward the door like an errant puppy. Once outside, she waved to the men in the car next to hers. Henderson was in the driver's seat. Both officers acknowledged her with the tip of their hats.

Her Camry purred to life. Pulling into traffic, she headed for home, hoping for news from her parents. In her rearview mirror, the cruiser maneuvered in behind. A shiver tiptoed across her shoulders. She didn't know whether to feel safer or more troubled by the need for extra security.

CHAPTER 9

Jen unlocked her door and dropped the mail on the foyer table. She slumped against the wall and her purse slid down her arm, landing with a thud. Fingers shaking, she took a moment to unbutton her jacket. She was only tired, like Melissa said, right?

Father God, I could use some of that courage you gave to Cari.

Grit had always been the word she'd associated with her best friend. From the bleak days of her childhood, through meshing with the Clark family, and finally, to raising twins on her own. But courage seemed to fit her memory better now.

Pfft. That's life, no biggie. The voice definitely mimicked Cari's self-deprecating tone.

Glancing at the pile of mail, her heart stuttered. A pastel pink envelope with curlicue writing peeped from between the bills and flyers. She recognized Cari's ornate handwriting at once. Seizing the thick envelope, she tore it open. The heady scent of roses drifted to her nose. Pin prickles twinkled before her eyes as she stumbled from the hallway.

Don't you dare. Not now. Inhale. *One*—calm. Touch. *Two*—cool. Touch. Touch. The spots dissipated one by one.

The actual letter was dated at the beginning of November, but the postmark ... yesterday? Was this some cruel joke?

Making her way to the kitchen island, she pulled out the contents of the envelope and smoothed the paper flat.

> Dearest Jen,
> If you are reading this, then I'm gone. Maybe I'm being overly dramatic, but I don't know what else to do. If anything happens—

The ink was smudged where she'd left the pen sitting too long.

> I've asked Mrs. Peters to send you these things, if needed.

Things ... plural? Jen searched the packet. Empty. Scurrying to the foyer, she found nothing else unusual in the stack and raced back to the letter.

> You're the head of my family now, with my brother. There are some things I need to tell you.

Ya think, Cari?

> I'd apologize, but it's too late for that. I hope you'll forgive me and can understand. You have everything I ever wanted. You've been so generous and have always shared your life with me.

Guilt stabbed Jen's conscience. Generosity meant giving with an open heart. Sometimes, she'd shared with Cari because it was expected, but she hadn't always offered or given up things willingly. Especially her "only child" status.

> I am so grateful. But it was your life. Mom, Dad, Lilac Lane. Everything. I got it all because of you. Even modeling. I just wanted the few good pieces of my earlier life to remain mine.

Hurt clashed with understanding in her heart.

To start, I want to clear up something I should have ages ago. The twins' names are not nasty pranks as everyone thought them to be.
Ree is named after you. Or a variation. Jennifer, Jen, Jan, January. Who cared except me? When Auggie started calling her Reeree, no one questioned the rest.

A strangled laugh escaped Jen at the goofy face Cari had drawn.

Then there's my August. He's named after someone very special in my life at that time. I had to turn away from him for the sake of my baby (I didn't know there were two, yet). No, he's not the twins' father.

She couldn't remember another person in Cari's life named August.

When the second baby arrived, I cried out his name. Only the good Lord knows why. I hadn't seen him in months. When January's name was linked with August's as actual times of the year, it suited my purpose to not explain anything further.
I digress. I had a break-in a couple weeks ago. I was going to tell you, but you've had your hands full with the vandalism at Lilac.

Pain jabbed at her temple. Had she been that obtuse to Cari's tension lately?

Nothing was taken, just some things moved around. Things significant to me. Namely, my nail polishes. I know you think I'm a bit psycho about their alphabetical order. Exactly six were pulled out, spelling the twins' initials. A clear message.

Jen's pulse ratcheted. Someone was after the twins?
I came up with a story about a crazed fan so the super would put that second lock on our door. There should

be a police report, but who knows if the officer took me seriously.

Cari had given her another key to her condo a few weeks earlier, saying, "Pfft. You know these frenzied fans." How had anyone gotten past the strict Beverton-Wise security?

Last week, my car doors were jimmied. Again, nothing taken, only the glovebox rifled. Another police report. There was a man talking to the kids outside their school later that day, but he left before I reached them. Auggie said he asked a bunch of "dumb" questions, but the more I grilled Ree, the more I was certain. They'd talked to their father. I don't think they know it.

She gasped. The only thing Cari had ever told her was that she'd made the worst mistake of her life. But she couldn't be sorry because she'd received her two greatest joys.

Jen, don't let him have my babies! He's not a good man. Do whatever you need to keep them away from him. He's not fit to be a father. He's an egotistical, self-centered, misogynistic—

The expletive was underlined.

He won't care about them. Life is all just a game to him. One *he* must win. He'll parade January around like he did me. His trophy until that strong-willed daughter of mine sics her imaginary lion, Adira, on him or he disapproves of something she does. It won't take much.

And he'll have a grand old time making Auggie squirm, purely for fun.

I broke off ties with anyone who knew him or had ever met him. Even his brother ... the hardest thing I've ever had to do.

Confusion swamped Jen's thoughts.

All ties, except two. Mom and Colin. She'd only met him once, so I was hopeful. And I had to take the chance my brother wouldn't meet him through business.

His identity is important for you, but in case he gets hold of this letter somehow, I'll leave the information in the last place you'd expect to find it from me. No secret keys or bank deposit boxes. Sit here in your favorite chair and relax—like normal.

But please! Promise me you won't let him have my kids.

If you need help, call Colin. He's living up north for now. He builds things and takes off for the hills again. You'll find his information in my address book.

Why didn't I tell you or Mom and Dad we'd kept in touch? I guess I wanted to believe you all were my *real* family.

So, Colin was right.

One last thing. I've had Auggie tested. He's considered high functioning, or whatever they call it now. We found a wonderful doctor. Raymond Brasil. He tested Ree too. Majorly smart, my girl.

So much like her mom.

I'll enclose a letter of permission to grant you and Colin access to any of their records. How much weight it carries legally, I don't know. It's the best I can do for now.

Jen glanced at the second sheet of paper. It appeared to be legit.

I trust you completely. I love you even more.
Hug J and A for me one last time.

A dried-up tear fringed the ink, lending voice to Cari's emotions.

Tell them I love them to bits and pieces. From here, around the universe, and back again.

When I get to your beloved heaven, I'll ask if I'm allowed to watch over you three.

All my love,
Caribbean

Jen's breath whooshed from her lungs. The bursting air uncorked sobs held since seeing her friend lying on the floor. Guilt, grief, love, and fear swirled through her like the clouds in a stormy Texas sky. Her stomach lurched, and she rushed to the sink.

"What am I going to do?" She wailed. "Father, I ..." Nothing further made any sense.

A nugget of peace lodged in her heart, bringing with it some clarity. Getting the letter to the detectives was paramount. She fanned her face with the pages. The floral scent fluttered around her awakening a memory, but it hid as quickly as it appeared.

One thought muscled to the forefront. Protect the twins, at all costs. She had to get back to them.

Turning on the tap, she splashed her face and swiped her nose with a paper towel. Dashing to her room, she changed from her tearstained shirt. Back in the kitchen, she put the letter in its envelope, changed her mind, and rushed to her desk to make a copy. She shoved the duplicate in the drawer, locking it away from inquisitive nine-year-old eyes. Leaving the comfort of her home, she turned back to heightened security. Back to the station for more questioning. Back to the twins. Hers to keep from harm.

"Detectives, wait up." Jen ran across the CPD parking lot to catch them.

Oz's long legs had her several paces ahead of the pint-sized Mason, but she paused. "What's up? You look as if you've seen a ghost."

"Sort of. I got a letter from Cari."

Mason leaned back. "Is that unusual?"

"It was mailed yesterday."

They stared at her.

Jen pulled at the flap on her purse and reached in.

Mason stopped her. "Not here. Let's go inside." She gave a quick nod to Jen's security detail, then led the way into the precinct with Oz bringing up the rear.

The elevator stopped one floor below the advocate's office.

Mason paused at the hallway junction. "I'll grab the food from Melissa and look in on the kiddos. We can eat lunch while we talk. Would you like anything, Jennifer?"

She shook her head. "Maybe a bottle of water. I don't think my stomach can handle anything right now. Can I come with you? Check on the twins?" She wrung her hands.

"We have a few questions for you first. Then, I think you've all had enough for the day."

Jen followed Oz across to the opposite passage. They stopped at one of the many glass-enclosed offices.

"This is ours." Oz waved her hand toward the room like a game show host offering a prize.

One side of the room was pristine, void of most personal items. Two frames sat on the desk with an oversized office chair tucked properly underneath. The wall sported a diploma, and two larger photos. Pictures and knick-knacks littered the top of the opposite desk. A smaller seat sat askew.

"Let me guess, that's Detective Mason's side?"

Oz laughed and tapped her temple. "She's got too much going on up in here to think about mundane details like a clean office. I'm okay with it, though. She puts up with me—only partner who's ever been able to do so for this long." Her face sobered. "I'm going to miss her."

"Is she going somewhere? She's too young to retire, isn't she?"

"That woman won't retire until they put the last nail in her coff—" She cleared her throat. "Sorry. I don't mean to be flippant. This mouth of mine. I meant—"

"Don't apologize. My mom says, 'As long as the heart is in the right place.' Yours is."

"I'd like to meet this momma of yours. She sounds like a wise woman."

"The best. She made growing up fun for us. Especially once Cari moved in."

"That's something—your folks adopting her like that."

"They never formally did. They wanted to. But Cari wouldn't give up her last name. She said it was the only thing left from her parents."

"That's understandable."

While Oz grabbed a file, Jen inspected the photos on the wall. One was of a college-aged Oz next to a suited-up Nathan Banks, her head on the up-and-coming football star's shoulder. His arm snaked around the teenager's waist.

"Told you I knew him."

"You never said you were *that* close." Jen winked.

"Well, you know, big brother's friends always hold an extra appeal." Her dark eyes danced. "We were better as friends. Not long after we split, he met his future wife. I adore her. I wouldn't have wanted to fight over him. Big as I am—ooh, the beat down wouldn't have been worth it."

Oz laughed. "Deborah's the best thing that ever happened to him. Settled him, but good." She pointed to the other photo. "That's her there with the rest of us."

A group of young people stood around a beaming Oz on graduation day, with a psychology diploma in her hand. "That's my crew. Family. Friends. We all still hangout. Best barbeque around is found on my brother's back porch with this bunch."

Jen walked around the side of Oz's desk and peered at the other two pictures, expecting a husband or parents. One was of Mason and Oz standing in front of the precinct. The other, a scruffy little pup with a gigantic pink bow pulling its hair back from its eyes.

"One of the best days of my life was when that motley monstrosity adopted me. She found her way to my porch one day ... no chip, no nothing. I took her to the best shelter I could find, but she ended up owning me three days later."

"Animals know a kind heart."

"I don't know about that, but this dog knew a hurting one. I'd recently lost my mom, and another partner had just transferred out." She pointed to the other photo. "That was taken a few months later, the day I was assigned as Mason's partner." Her chest puffed out. "At her request. No one had ever *applied* to be stuck with me. Mason said she needed someone who was situationally aware, 'quick on their feet,' and loves kids." Oz grinned. "I guess that was me."

She motioned for Jen to follow her toward a bank of meeting rooms.

"Mason should be back any moment. You asked earlier if she was retiring. She's favored for the captain's position. She'll get it—if she wants it. Cap's been thinking about taking her daughter abroad for some fancy design lessons."

"I thought the daughter wants to go to the Wells-Myer Art Academy? They're one of the best. Why would she want to leave?"

"You know the Wells-Myer?" Oz asked. "Yeah, I guess you would, being in the industry and all."

"No. Well, yes. I'm familiar with it from there too, but I know more about it because of Cari. She studied there for a while before she went into modeling full-time. And she has two scholarships there. She funds them each year with our *Educate Your Way Up* fashion show. The one we're supposed to have next week."

Further talk of the design school was suspended when Mason showed up. She plunked food in front of the other women.

"You ordered me unsweet tea, right? You ought to try it sometime, Mason."

"Just because you can't have sugar, doesn't mean I can't."

"Simply watching out for you." Oz gave her a cheeky grin.

"Jennifer, whether you like it or not, you have a chicken sandwich. January was convinced you wouldn't eat at home. She wheedled a sandwich out of Melissa." Mason sat next to her partner, across from Jen.

"I am hungry now that I'm seeing food." She reached for the letter, pushing it across the table to them.

Both read in silence as they downed their late lunch.

Mason swallowed. "Mrs. Peters is the neighbor, right? I phoned her yesterday. She never mentioned sending a letter for Miss Marshall."

"That doesn't surprise me. She's been wonderful and a good sitter for a long time. But she's gotten a little hard of hearing lately. Plus, her husband was a private investigator for years—he taught her well. 'No info until you see the whites of their eyes.'" She mimicked.

Mason chuckled.

"But I don't get why she didn't call me to come get it. She has my number."

Oz swallowed a bite. "My grandma was like that. If it's private, you do *not* talk about it over the phone. She probably figured you'd hightail it over there once this reached you."

"The thought had crossed my mind." She gripped the sides of her purse, hoping the detectives wouldn't see the onset of another bout of tremors.

Mason shook her head. "Not yet. There are a couple things we need to check first."

Jen bit the inside of her cheek, her conscience warring with her need to be helpful.

The voice quietly tapped at her armor. *You don't have to do this alone. Let them in.*

You're being entirely too logical. But maybe you're right.

"Full disclosure. I made a copy of the letter." She rushed her words, wanting them to understand. "I wasn't sure I'd get it back. I want to remember everything she said."

Mason folded her hands on the table. "I figured."

"But ... how?"

"New shirt for you. Fresh tear stains. The ones near the middle are smeared. And the letter is unevenly creased. Why, if not for unfolding it again to put on a scanner?"

Jen gawked at her. "I'd planned to go to the apartment this afternoon and do what she said. Try to puzzle out what she meant. I doubt anyone else would get it. Her mind worked in weird and wonderful ways."

Mason smiled indulgently. "That's commendable, Jennifer, but what are you going to do with the twins while you're at Cari's apartment? They can't go there with you."

She sighed. "I know. My mind was in such a jumble after I got this, I'm surprised I remembered to lock the copy in my desk."

"We'll sort this out. You wouldn't be allowed in her apartment right now, anyway. They're not finished."

Her chin hiked.

"Whup. There's that attitude again." Oz chuckled. "Calm down, Miss Jen. It's procedure."

"You're not making a mess of it, are you? I mean ..."

Mason shook her head. "We checked during the break. Everything's in order." She fiddled with her pen. "We should be able to get you in there in the next day or two."

A white-hot core stabbed through Jen's temper. "What if their father's her killer? What if you miss something? What if—"

Oz stood and shut the door.

Mason held up the letter. "This proves it's crucial that you get in that condo. I'll take you there myself. But we must do this by the book, so everything stands up in court later, if need be."

With the promise of being taken to Cari's home legally, Jen's attitude abated.

Mason continued. "A few things came to light this afternoon, and we have some questions for *you*."

Something in her tone made Jen sit tall. She exhaled a prayer. *Father God, please be my rock and my shield.* Her stomach churned, threatening to upset the food she'd recently put there. What had they found?

"Before we get into that, your photographer dropped off a *load* of photos last night from your project. She did a great job. We'll work through them to match everyone we can. I'll call her myself, but please thank her for us when you see her. I know it's not easy to imagine friends through a suspicious eye." Mason commiserated. "There's a random foot here and a bare arm there. The feet are easy to match with people because of shoes. The arms, not so much. We may need your assistance with that."

Jen inclined her head. *Get on with it, will you?* A shred of her earlier temper remained. She added peace and patience to her prayer.

Oz took over. "You mentioned that Cari only drank sparkling water, correct?"

"Yes. Once in a great while she'd have a glass of unsweetened iced tea, but seldom."

"A girl after my own heart." Oz paused and referred to the notepad in front of her. "Did she ever drink tea? The kind with loose leaves?"

"No. That's mine. She blended it specially for me. She has since my last year of college."

"Why was it in her dressing room?"

Jen's forehead tightened. Where was this going? "She kept a tin of it there. I'd stop by the Kingdom for a cup. And just as regularly she came into my office for a bottle of her water."

"Is that the only place you had tea with her?"

"I have some in my workroom and at home in a pretty tin she gave me the first year."

Mason chewed the end of her pen. "How long ago did you receive it?"

"For Christmas, my last year of college ... oh ... you mean this latest batch? My birthday. September."

"We need to check all of that."

"But ... I won't have any of it left." Her voice rose. The thought of losing the last of Cari's best gift *ever* shook her to the core. "It's mine. I can't part—" She clutched her purse strap.

"Jennifer, we need to test it. We'll put in a request that if the tea is okay, you'll get back as much as they can manage."

"What do you mean ... if it's okay?"

"The batch in the dressing room was laced with something." Mason explained. "A tech noticed drops of liquid on the lid as if someone tampered with it."

She didn't need to elaborate for Jen to understand the dire consequences. Her stomach rolled.

"We'll have an officer come and get it when you leave today."

"Do I need to put it in a bag or something?"

"They'll have everything." Mason assured her. "Try not to worry."

"You mentioned a few questions. Are there more?"

Oz launched into the next one. "The white garment ... it was either a ball gown, maybe a wedding dress ... do you remember where it was when you found her?"

"Our final number. The *Wow!* gown." She thought back to the moment she'd skidded over the threshold and shook her head.

"Take your time."

She shut her eyes—a technique she'd used when drawing with Ree in the past—and pictured herself sitting at Cari's dressing table.

"Walk us through what you're seeing, Miss Jen. When you first got there." Oz's deep tones were comforting.

"None of us knew what to do. Richard was behind me. He moved to check on Cari. Eva was near the door. Later—I don't know when—she came in to help Ree." She pointed, trusting the detectives to follow where everyone was. "Harold, our maintenance man ..." They had everyone's names and titles, but if she was going to do this, she needed to do it her way. Her pace. "He has an old smoker's voice, raspy, you know? I asked him to call the police. He's got a bum leg. He couldn't have left the room quick enough if he'd done it."

Scratching noises carried across the table, pen to paper.

"Daphne, our intern, was crying behind me. Rose was standing against the wall. I ... don't remember Stan there. But his kids were in earlier, so he had to be." She blinked and squeezed her eyes shut again, trying to bring the murky details to life. "I'm sorry, I don't think I can offer any more."

"Jennifer." Mason's voice reached through the darkness. "You're doing great. Do you remember anything about the dress?"

"Oh, right. I forgot." Her memories fell into a disjointed pile. She sorted them as if she were starting a new scrapbook with Ree.

She told them how she'd dreaded throwing up in front of her employees. And the feel of the dressing table behind her. She dared not open her eyes for fear of losing the conjured picture. She allowed her gaze to roam the edges of the room. There. The dress. "Yes. I see it now."

"Where was it, Miss Jen?"

"A couple feet from her dressing table. Like someone threw it there. It's crumpled. Right beside the Venetian mask that goes with it." She frowned. "The mask looks worn. A feather is broken. Even if they were only the prototypes, Cari would have put them away properly."

"Prototypes?" Mason's voice sounded puzzled. "Can you explain?"

Jen opened her eyes. "It was a surprise for Ree at the charity show. She codesigned that gown with me. She's only seen the mockup. Cari and I didn't want her to view the final dress until the event. I've been working on it in secret, at home. In my opinion, it's one of the best pieces we've ever produced at Lilac Lane."

Jen reached into her purse, pulling out a drawing. "This is a copy of Ree's original design." She smoothed the paper and turned it toward the detectives. "She was supposed to have walked the runway in a child's version, next to Cari in this gown. We planned photos splashing up on a screen. Transition shots from idea to end-product. And a final one of our little designer. Annie, the photographer from next door, was having so much fun with this project, she kept popping in to take candid shots of everyone."

Mason chewed her lip. Oz marked down through her notes, then leaned over and pointed to something.

Shivers slithered down Jen's arms. "What aren't you saying? Why the looks of doom and gloom?"

"Jennifer, the gown was slashed." Mason's tone was grave.

"What? I know Auggie held the scissors when she was found, but he wouldn't do that. The fashion part isn't his thing, but he would never rip a gown. He helps hang them. He's very careful. He—"

"I said it was slashed. To shreds. Deliberately." Mason's voice held a hard edge. "Probably with those shears."

Jen's thoughts careened from who, to what, and landed on why? "But he knows how much work goes into a design."

"Auggie has been ruled out," Oz informed her. "We think he found her, maybe recognized the scissors, and picked them up."

"Who would want to hurt Cari?" Jen placed her hands on the cool, solid tabletop. Something substantial to bring sense to the craziness.

"We think she might have walked in on whoever was destroying your work. And ... we don't think Miss Marshall was the only target."

"I don't understand."

"We believe *you* may be as well." Mason's sounded troubled.

"Me?" She squeaked. "No way."

"Think this through." Oz's voice drilled through her confusion. "You've told us about the sabotaged machinery. Have you told us all of it?"

She dredged her memory. Only gibberish ran through her thoughts. Inhale. *One*—calm. Where were her fingers? *Two*—

Mason's voice swam through the muck. "Oz, grab her. I'll get a soda."

The room spun like an intoxicated merry-go-round. Warm arms enveloped her.

"Whoa there, Miss Jen. Can't have you passing out. Put your head between your knees. There you go." Oz patted her back. "Don't sit up yet. Mason's almost here."

"Thank the Lord that stupid machine was working today." Mason wheezed out a breath.

Who turned the lights back on? The *sphritz* of a pop-top welcomed her back to full consciousness.

"Nice and slow." Oz's hands were gentle, helping her sit upright.

"How do I get off this crazy carousel?"

CHAPTER 10

Normal. But what did that look like now? Not Cari's way of doing things. Or even time at Lilac Lane. Jen and the twins needed the familiarity of a night spent at Engine's.

She rummaged in the pantry for her pasta pot. Cold water, the pilot light *tic, tic, tic*'ing, and preparations for chicken alfredo with broccoli, or as Auggie called it, Chickens on Trees. All of it was normal ... before.

She smacked the bag of frozen vegetables on the counter to loosen the icebound bundles. Reaching for spaghetti noodles, her thoughts turned to Cari. The rail-thin model hadn't eaten pasta of any kind in her adulthood. She didn't mind if the twins ate it, as long as she wasn't around.

Cari had claimed it was sloppy and didn't suit her figure. Only her family knew the truth. Once she turned thirteen, shortly after her parents' deaths, she'd developed a profound addiction to the starchy stuff. One mouthful and she couldn't quit until her stomach hurt, or worse. Pasta was her kryptonite. Abstinence, her solution.

A long-forgotten discussion with Cari rose to the surface. "Don't you remember? My mom wasn't much of a cook." Her nose wrinkled. "Burned offerings were our norm."

"What about her spaghetti? That was good."

Rosemary Marshall's "company's coming" signature dinner turned out to be spaghetti sauce from a jar—grated veggies and burger added for good measure—served over linguine noodles. Had the recollection of that one delicious semi-homemade meal fueled Cari's cravings?

Jen set the flame to high and turned to find Ree leaning against the kitchen doorjamb. "Hi, honey. You hungry?"

"A little."

"Want to help?"

"Sure." The girl's voice fell flat.

Maybe not so normal. Ree and Auggie usually jumped at the chance to chop, dice, and stir. Although their mother was no domestic goddess, Jen loved to cook, and the twins often pitched in.

"What's up, buttercup?"

"Can I ask you something?"

"Sure. Fire away. But first ... where's Auggie?"

"In the living room, playing his game."

Jen patted the marble countertop next to her. "Hop up here so we can talk while I make dinner."

Ree ambled to the worktop and held her arms up. Part of the ritual for the many girls-only talks they'd had over the years, and she played along. Normal.

Jen hooked her hands beneath the girl's arms. She huffed and puffed, pretending a lack of strength. More familiarity. The outrageous playfulness made Ree giggle, and she counted to three. With Jen's boost, she jumped up and settled in.

Having raised her kids in the sometimes-fickle fashion industry, Cari wanted them to understand healthy bodies and not become self-conscious about their weight, like she had. But she'd left it up to her best friend to discuss nutritious eating habits, share food preparation, and address fit bodies.

Ree grabbed a nearby fork, spinning it.

Jen chopped an onion, giving the girl space to form her thoughts.

"Is it okay to be mad at someone you love? Is that like not forgiving them?"

Definitely not normal. Ree's disposition was mostly sunny, seldom angry. "Would you hand me the ladle behind you?" *Lord Jesus, give me the words she needs to hear.* "Who are you mad at?"

No answer.

"Auggie?"

"Not really. I'm kinda upset with him, but he couldn't help it."

"Help what, honey?"

"Finding Cari."

"You're pretty sure he found her like that?" *I'll be darned if I'm shushing her now.*

"I know he did. He wouldn't ever do that to Cari. He loved her more ... even more than you or me." Ree's voice broke on the last word.

The knife trembled in Jen's fingers.

Relax. Let her talk. The voice encouraged.

She turned to Ree. "Good point. But no matter what happens, don't you ever forget he cherishes you more than maybe even he realizes." She planted a kiss on her goddaughter's forehead. "You're his anchor in a world that changes way too fast for him."

"I know."

Jen dumped the onion in the pan with the chicken. Placing the heat on low, she waited for the proverbial "other shoe" to drop.

Reaching for the paper towels, Ree folded them as napkins. The girl had learned some stellar procrastination tactics. Finally, she looked up, her eyes awash with tears. "I'm mad at Cari." She whispered. "I shouldn't be upset with her. Right?"

Jen didn't even wash the bits of food off her hands before gathering her goddaughter in a hug. "Aww, honey." She patted and soothed. Ree's tears soaked through her shirt as her own waterworks plopped on the curls tucked beneath her chin. Once Ree quieted, Jen released her bear hug and grabbed tissues to mop their puffy faces. "Tell me why you're mad at Cari. And I want to know why you think you *shouldn't* be."

Ree shrugged.

"Could it be because she left you? Or because she died? Or ... I'm out of ideas, kiddo."

"That wasn't her fault."

"Definitely not."

"I guess I'm upset she left you holding the bag ... again."

Blindsided, Jen hoped her expression conveyed her sadness and love for the woman gone. She readied the water for pasta.

"Engine." Ree's voice held irritation. "I might be nine but I'm not stupid. I know Cari had you do stuff she didn't want to."

"Like what?" *A little help here, please,* she implored the voice.

Silence.

"Like ... telling me where babies really came from after Susan told me wrong." She wrinkled her nose. "And going with us to buy my first, um, trainer, for under my dance costume. I'm glad you went but ..."

"You wanted it to be just the two of you?"

Ree's chin trembled. "You had to teach me how to cook, and sew, and babysit."

Jen turned off the gas to the pasta water. It could wait. She inhaled deeply, pressing tears back.

"It's okay." Ree's tone sounded with defeat. "We don't have to talk about it. I know she was your best friend. You probably don't want me to be mad at her."

She took hold of Ree's chin. "You're right, she was my *very* best friend. My sister in every way except by law. But you are so far from the truth. You can be mad at her all you want." Jen gave a curt nod. "I'm so angry at her right now I could spit."

Ree's eyes widened.

"How about we talk this out together, still love her, and only be a little upset with her. Will that work?"

The big blue eyes shone with unshed tears, but she nodded.

"Who first?" Jen stirred the pan of chicken.

"You."

How to start? "I'm mad at her because she left me by myself with you two." She raised her hand to stall the wounded look. "I'm not mad she left me *with* you and Auggie. I'm upset she left me to do this *alone* with you two. Big difference. I might be the bestest aunt in the whole world—"

Ree's soggy giggle tickled the air.

"But I'm no substitute for your mom. She thought the sun rose and set in you guys." Jen leaned against the counter. "And I'm upset because I didn't think we had secrets from each other. I was wrong."

"Like what?"

Her stomach flipped. *Smooth move, Jen. Think.* She couldn't tell the girl about her father. Or her mom's fears these past weeks. "Oh, things like why she named you what she did. Are you aware she named you after me, in Cari's own goofy way?"

"I was?" Ree's smile lit up her face. "How do you know?"

She heaved an inward sigh of relief. "She left me a note. I can read it to you after the detectives give it back."

"Why did they need it?" Ree sat up straight. "Does it tell who killed my mom?"

"It doesn't. I promise. They wondered if there were any clues about where she was a couple days before she passed. They thought it might help."

"I'm old enough to hear the word killed." Ree rolled her eyes. "Even if it is my mom we're talking about."

Copping a bit of an attitude. Good. "Fair enough. So, there you have it. Now, what about you? What are you mad at her for? Besides leaving me holding the bag with two adorable twins inside?"

Ree snickered, followed by a bone-deep, wise-beyond-her-years sigh. "I don't know how to explain it. Lately, my mom needed more than us." She threw her hand in the air in exasperation.

In that instant, Jen realized Ree referred to Cari by her given name when speaking of her with fondness, but by "my mom" when needing emotional distance. Interesting. Useful information to tuck away for Melissa and the psychiatrist.

"You're doing fine. But tell me more, so we're on the same page," Jen fibbed. She had no idea how to respond.

"She always seemed to be searching for something she couldn't find. Like we do in hide-and-seek. I don't know if it was for someone to love ... you know, a guy." The girl's cheeks pinked. "Or whether she wanted more adventure. She took us everywhere, before. But we stayed here a lot more lately. Why weren't we enough for her? Me and Auggie." A tear leaked down her cheek.

"I have a feeling her disappearing more than normal lately was all about you two." Navigating through the conversation with age-appropriate information was like treading through pudding. "Or she could have made a new friend. She wouldn't have introduced anyone to you until she was sure they were nice."

"Maybe."

"Well, whatever it was, I'm sure she thought it was important."

"Okay. But I'm still upset with her right now." Ree pouted.

"Here's my take. I believe it's okay if we're mad, especially at first. I think it's how our hearts protect themselves after someone we love dies. It gets a little upset, so it doesn't break into tiny bits. Only a couple big ones we can stitch back together with good memories and some time." She retrieved plate settings and handed the silverware to Ree.

"But if I'm still mad at her … does that mean I don't forgive her? I don't love her?"

Jen shook her head. "You get mad at Auggie. And you forgive him, don't you? You still love him?"

"Sure."

"There's your proof. You can be a little upset at Cari and still forgive and love her." Jen smiled. "If someone told you otherwise, I bet you'd make Adira eat them."

"You know about her?"

"Cari told me last week, after you lost your cool with me." *Although, she conveniently forgot to mention it was a coping technique you learned from your psychiatrist.*

"Yeah … sorry." The girl cringed. "Adira had to learn to be a respectful lion. She only roars when I need her to now." A small giggle escaped her. "She doesn't eat anyone, yet."

"Maybe you could have your lion pop them in the nose."

"I'd *pop* them for you, Reeree." Auggie bounced into the room, holding up his fist.

"No one really needs hitting, honey. We were talking about being upset with someone."

"Are you mad at me?" He asked his sister, his lip jutting with hurt.

"I'm not mad at anyone, anymore," she reassured him.

"Good, 'cuz I'm starving. When are we eatin' trees?"

"Oh geez, the chicken." Jen checked the meal, relieved to find it still edible. "Auggie's stomach to the rescue. You two wash up and set the table while I get the pasta going again."

Ree and Auggie picked at their meal but ate enough to satisfy her. Their eyelids drooped, but it was only seven o'clock. She got up and took the leftovers to the counter. Normally, they'd have jumped up to help. Those were the rules at Engine's apartment.

Her phone vibrated. Voicemail could get it. Moments later, her message notification dinged. She'd get back to them. The kids needed her first.

"Auggie, you get in the shower. Call me when you've rinsed your shampoo."

"Do I hafta?"

"Shower? Or call me when you rinse your hair? Yes, to both."

"Oookkay." He trudged toward the bathroom. When younger and starting to shower by himself, she'd been reluctant to check on his hair rinsing. After a sticky mess of Blue Goo shampoo on her pillowcase one morning, Cari came to her rescue with the solution. It required a sopping wet towel around his middle, allowing aunt and godson some modesty while he stuck his head out past the shower curtain for a shampoo inspection. Part and parcel of life with Auggie.

"Can I get my craft stuff?" Ree asked. "Or do I need to clear the table first?"

"I'm giving you both the night off from chores." Hope leaped in her heart at the mention of art supplies.

Her phone buzzed again. She glanced at the screen and nabbed the cell immediately. Propping it between her shoulder and ear, she scraped plates. "Melissa, I'm so sorry. I forgot you were calling. We were finishing up dinner."

"I figured. Checking in with me takes some getting used to. Especially the nighttime call." Her normally chipper voice grew crisp. "I'll ask for a wellness report if I get worried."

Having police nearby, Jen didn't need to be told who would make that check. Melissa's message rang loud and clear. The advocate's first priority was the care of the children she was tasked with. "It won't happen again."

Melissa cleared her throat. "I don't mean to sound cold."

"You have a job to do. I hope to make it easier."

"Thank you for understanding. Like we discussed, since more caution is warranted at this time, I'll call each morning and evening. You have security at your apartment, so we don't need an officer right with you. But don't open to anyone you aren't expecting."

The spoon shook in her hand. She plopped it in the dishwater and turned her back to the sink. Ree walked into the kitchen with paper and scissors. Jen's heart twinged at the lack of colored pencils.

All in good time. The voice consoled. *At least she's creating again.*

Agreed. She tuned back into Melissa's words.

"Do I need to let the officers know when Colin finally gets here, or my parents?"

"They've been cleared, but maybe notify your detail when they first arrive, so there's no undue commotion trying to figure out who's who." Mirth laced Melissa's voice.

"Yeah, we don't need any more drama than we've had."

"Now for the routine call. Everyone okay?"

The instructions she'd received that afternoon were a jumbled mess in her memory. "I need to get some ginger ale." She gulped. "No, wait. That means we need help." She closed her eyes, hoping to trigger the right words.

Ree set her scissors down. "Tell her everything is shipshape."

Melissa chuckled on the other end. "January is correct."

Heat moved over Jen's cheeks. "I'll remember better next time."

"Do *not* worry about it, Jennifer. You have plenty on your mind. I think your little wonderkid overheard our conversation. It's probably a good thing she knows it so well already. It might help her feel more in control too."

"It's all good. With Ree on my side, we'll be fine." She sat down at the island across from her goddaughter. "She'll help me remember. By the way, thank you for picking a soda I can't stand as the emergency code."

"That's the idea. It has to be something you're familiar with so it comes out easily, but not a word you would generally use."

"So, why the check-ins? I don't mind. I'm just curious."

"To make it routine. Having a code word has saved a couple tense situations in the past. Things can happen and escalate, especially with estranged spouses." There was a pause on the other end of the line. "I know this gives tones of histrionics, most advocates don't even require it. But since a good majority of my cases aren't normal, it's imperative I follow my usual protocol with my clients. I'm sorry to put you in that same category but, you kind of are."

"That makes perfect sense." A cry floated to her ears. "Is there anything else you need? Auggie's yelling for me."

"We're good. I'll talk to you in the morning."

"Ennngggiiinnneee." The boy's tone rose in panic. "It stings. Help. I can't get it out."

"You're next, kiddo." Jen called to Ree on her way to rescue her godson from the Blue Goo shampoo.

Eating Chicken on Trees, normal. Shampoo in the eyes, mostly normal. Crafts, a movie, and their bedtime routine. All normal. Life went on as normal. Or not.

Jen's cell buzzed, breaking the quiet she'd relished since the twins went to bed. She bolted up from the couch like she'd been caught napping on the job. Colin's name flashed across her screen. "Hey, there. Did you finally get a plane?"

"So many flights were canceled, they're still backed up. The airline's trying to get one out tomorrow. It'll be last minute, though."

"Wow, it's that stormy?" Dad had taken the family along on a couple business trips to Michigan. She pictured towering trees and the beautiful capital in Lansing. They'd even stayed in Grand Rapids, where Colin currently lived, a time or two. But never during a winter squall. "Do you want me to book a room for you? I'd offer to have Ree bunk with me and let you stay here, but I'm supposed to keep things as normal as possible for the kids."

"Thanks, but Corporate's letting me use the suite there."

"That's great. A suite?" She swallowed a wad of worry. "Do you want the twins to stay with you?"

"I don't think that'd be a good idea, do you? At least not at night. Definitely not right away. They only know me as the fun uncle on the phone." He chuckled. "We should get used to each other first."

She didn't detect pity in his voice, only a down-to-earth common sense. Same as the Colin she knew in her girl-crush years. Good thing blushing wasn't audible.

"Maybe you guys can come swimming some afternoon. You'll know if they'd be comfortable there. And with me. I understand they haven't been around a lot of men."

"They'd like that." She paused, thinking. "We have guys at work. My dad when they were young and ... wow. I guess you're right."

"Cari didn't bring dates home? She wouldn't talk about it."

"Because she didn't. Date that is."

"Seriously? She didn't have clandestine assignations? No intimate trysts? Not even a secret social calendar?"

She giggled. "Not even a temporary tête-à-tête."

Colin gave a low whistle. "I mean, she was my sister, but even I knew she was beautiful."

"Not because men didn't try. Cari never accepted." Jen walked to the kitchen, poured herself a glass of milk, and pulled a dark chocolate truffle ball from her hidden stash. "She told me once she'd given her heart to the wrong guy, and it was too late to hand it to the right one. To this day, I don't know who either one is."

She wouldn't tell him about the letter ... yet. How could she say, "Oh hey, your sister feared for her life the last few weeks, and I was too busy to notice. And by the way, her killer might be the twins' father." Not something one mentioned over the phone. "She didn't want to expose them to anyone she didn't plan to keep in her life." Jen hoisted herself up on a stool.

"My sister could be pretty wackadoodle sometimes, but it sounds like she made good choices for the kids."

"You know, she really did. Occasionally she drove me nuts with some of her decisions, but most of the time everything revolved around them." She whispered the chocolate from its crinkly wrapper. She wasn't ready to share her biggest vice with anyone.

"Speaking of the kids, we haven't talked in a few weeks. Do they have time?"

"I'm sorry, they're already asleep. It was such a long day, talking with the detectives and counseling with Melissa ... they were exhausted."

"But they're okay?"

"Yes—" Her hand flew to her mouth, narrowly missing her glass. "Oh my gosh, I should have told you first thing. They cleared Auggie. They still have questions, but he's officially a non-suspect." She popped the creamy chocolate into her mouth in celebration.

"You made my day. How did they *finally* come to that conclusion?" Did she detect a hint of irritation?

"They were convinced he hadn't done anything except pick up the weapon. But they still had to go through the motions. The timing was off. He'd been in the playroom earlier with Ree and Stan's kids, playing 'Mother May I.' Once Stan's wife picked up their bunch, Auggie went looking for Cari."

"'Mother May I?' I thought he didn't like playing group games."

"He doesn't. That's one of the few he tolerates. They played it at home. He understands the rules and what's expected of him. Cari always had them rolling on the floor laughing by the end of the game. Some of her antics were so far-fetched."

"Like what?"

"Let me see." She took a swig of milk. "You know how the player asks, 'Mother May I,' and then something like 'take two steps forward?' Cari would come back with a doozy like, 'No, you may not. You may take a giant leap in the air, stand on your head, and bunny hop thrice.'" Colin's answering chuckle warmed her insides.

"I'm surprised she didn't add a belch or two."

Jen covered her mouth to keep from spitting another gulp. "Sometimes she did, and Auggie usually tried it."

"What boy can resist a good burp, especially if his mother tells him to? Those would have been my favorites at that age."

"I didn't know you back then. Was it hard relocating? I'm not sure I ever asked."

"You were only six or seven when we moved in. All I can remember is you were thrilled to finally have a playmate next door in that stuffy neighborhood."

"It was great. It must have been awful for you, though. I can't imagine being a twelve-year-old boy there."

She thought back to her old house with the retirees walking their dogs and working the abundant flowerbeds nearby. Scowling about local boys throwing footballs in the street and racing their RC cars down the sidewalks.

"It wasn't too bad. I had Jose Baker in my class and Tommy Norton down the street—"

Jen snorted. "That little toad? He was not nice. He always punched me or jammed gum in my locker latch."

"You're kidding, right? You know he had a huge crush on you. After you hit middle school, every boy within a five-mile radius did."

"No way. And not everyone." *Not the most important one.*

"I don't know what *you* remember, but yeah, the whole neighborhood's male population under eighteen was smitten with your don't-give-me-any-guff attitude."

For a moment, he sounded like the cheeky but kind fifteen-year-old she'd swooned over ages ago. "Anyway, it was wonderful news to have Auggie cleared. Now they need to figure out who did it."

"Well, I couldn't be happier. I will get on that plane tomorrow a lighter man."

Dishes clanked on the other end of the phone. Was he just now eating? She shook herself. She had enough people to worry about.

"Tell me some more about the twins."

"Didn't you get enough the other day?"

"Never. I only knew them through Cari. I think she was a bit prejudiced."

"Hah. And you don't think you'll get favoritism from me? I may not be their mom, but ..."

"I understand. She told me more than once you were their—what did she call it?—their normal. For all three of them."

Her eyes stung. "I thought she got annoyed with me for getting on her about the kids."

"Sometimes. But she also knew she needed it. Like I said ... sister ... whackadoodle. Sweetness herself in some ways, but not always the most stable."

Jen strolled into the living room, plumping already puffy pillows. "When you say things like that, it doesn't make me feel so guilty for being upset at the way she treated people sometimes."

"This is Cari we're talking about. From the family of dysfunction extraordinaire. Do you blame us after every-

thing we went through? Especially those last few years."
His voice cracked.

Jen's heart reached across the miles to give him a hug.
Maybe one day she would be brave enough to hug him in
real life.

CHAPTER 11

Friday morning, Jen paced her living room and left a message for Detective Mason. "If you could please call me back, I have a bit of a dilemma. No emergency." *Click.* Moments later, her phone rang. "That was fast."

"I was out in the hall conversing with a colleague. What's up?"

"I've been battling with myself for the last hour. I got a phone call from a vendor. They need to see me at Lilac briefly. I planned to call Melissa and ask who of my crew could come stay with them, but the kids overheard, and they want to go into Lilac. Give me a moment, please." She covered the mouthpiece. "Guys, I'm on the phone. Cut the apple in half if there's not enough for both of you."

Mason chuckled on the other end.

"Sorry about that. They're going a little stir crazy. They can't get their things from the condo like they're used to, and there's only so much here to keep them occupied."

"I don't envy you. Let me check …" Her voice was muffled. "Your regular detail isn't available, but someone can be at your apartment within an hour to follow you over. The room is still secured?"

"I believe so. To be honest, Detective, I've got work to do too. I'd like to go in for a while, if it won't hurt your investigation or the kids to go there."

"I can understand that. Get in touch with Melissa. She'll likely want someone from CPS there for the kids."

The idea of more officials around didn't sit well. "Maybe this isn't such a great idea."

"It might do you all some good. Get back on the horse, so to speak."

"I don't know how Cari did it all. Until Colin or my folks get here, there's not enough of me to go around."

"She had a Jennifer. You don't. Oz and I will pop in later. See you then."

Hanging up, she decided coffee was next on the agenda. Ten minutes later, with a steaming mug of liquid determination in hand, she strolled into the dining room. The twins' earlier squabble had turned into an art project involving halved apples, potatoes, and lots of craft paint. She shook her head at their rainbow-colored fingers.

"I like those bug impressions. Finish soon. We're going to Lilac. As long as you're sure you both want to go."

"Yay! I get to see Richard." Auggie hopped up and down. "He's still there, isn't he?"

"Of course. Why wouldn't he be?"

No answer. *Was this another of Auggie's intuitive moments?* She couldn't keep up.

Melissa said much the same as Detective Mason had when she called. The advocate had another family in crisis, but she would send a friendly young man to attend to the kids while Jen worked.

Family in crisis. She hoped to never fall into that category for the advocate. Choking on a mouthful of coffee, it occurred to her ... they were.

When they arrived at Lilac Lane later that morning, Richard offered to work with Auggie on the soundboard, but he declined. A rarity for the boy who adored anything tech related, and spending time with his buddy, even more so.

"I need something from the office, first." He captured his sister's hand and pulled her along.

From behind, Jen scrutinized the twins' walk and the way they clung to each other. "Don't get too far ahead of me." Had she made the wrong decision to bring them with her? Should she have called Colin to ask his opinion? Too late now.

Skirting the runway to enter the workroom from there instead of near the dressing rooms seemed to help. Their shoulders appeared relaxed.

"Can I have some paper to draw, Engine?" An unusual request from Auggie. He grabbed a pencil, and his sister gave him one of her drawing pads before she resumed her own search. Standing in the doorway, he bounced up and down in one spot.

"You okay, honey?" Jen rubbed her arms, cool in the confined workroom. She should have worn a jacket. A memory niggled at the back of her thoughts, then raced away again.

"Yup. I'm waitin' for Ree."

Cari had often claimed people underestimated him. Jen took comfort in his gesture of care. Her happiness multiplied when Ree pulled her art satchel and colored pencils from her cubby.

She took the twins up front near the sound booth. "Remember to stay by Richard, at least until Melissa's coworker comes."

Both gave solemn nods.

"I'll check on them in a bit, Richard."

"We're good." He turned to the kids. "Hang around where I can see you. Promise?" He held up his little finger.

Auggie thrust his pinky in the air, and the two curled them together.

Ree rolled her eyes but smiled.

Having arrived back in the office, Jen welcomed Eva's company and input. "This is a lot easier with your help."

Together, they studied the runway roster for the Educate Your Way Up event. Eva, Jen's first choice to take over the lead model spot, would need to consult with her on business details if she accepted it, including the rosters. The Barbadian beauty rose to the occasion and helped where needed, as usual.

An odd sense of déjà vu passed over Jen, as if Cari would walk through the door at any moment. When she was in business mode, Cari had been a force to be reckoned with and a whiz at directing backstage outfit changes. Exactly enough time to prevent most wardrobe malfunctions, while maintaining the energy that translated well to the thumping bass on the catwalk.

Now, Eva chewed her lip. "You really think Stella be built to pull off my golden outfit?"

"I don't know. I'm second guessing everything. The last gown, though. I can't let just anyone wear it, so I'd probably have to switch you into it."

"The one wrapped in secrecy? I thought it be ruined."

"I'm ..." She skirted the truth. "Hoping I can resurrect at least the idea of it." A knot formed in her stomach. She didn't like fibbing to her friend.

"Mmm. But—" Eva leaned on the arm of the overstuffed chair, the roster dangling from her long fingers.

"If you have an opinion, say so."

"I was to be wearin' the golden gown." Eva's Bajan accent thickened, hinting at her discomfort. "I know it's in your spring lineup, but ..."

"That's partly why I can't decide. There wouldn't be time for you to change in between the two dresses." Jen scrutinized her copy. "You have the correct proportions for the last design, but I'm hard pressed to find someone who looks as stunning as you in the golden one."

Eva's cheeks flushed, making her brown skin even more striking. "Thank you. I love that dress. I would like to wear it when ... well, some day."

Why so guarded? "It's settled." Jen made a notation on the paper next to Eva's name. "Golden Goddess."

Eva glanced toward the office door, opened her mouth, and shut it again. The corners of her generous lips tipped down.

Jen ignored the odd look. They were all stressed. "Now I have to figure out what to do about the last number ... if I can fix it." Her stomach flipped.

"It's important to you?"

"Very much so. It's the one I designed from Ree's drawing."

An inscrutable expression passed through the other woman's dark eyes.

There didn't seem to be malice there, but what? Rivalry? Reflection? Her emotional compass spun out of control. "It's got to be someone Ree's comfortable with."

"Why?"

"She planned it with her mother in mind." She wasn't ready to share the surprise. It was still hers and Cari's.

"Makes sense." Eva's head bobbed with a slow rhythmic gesture, as if listening to soft island music only she could hear.

"You seem preoccupied today."

Eva pressed her lips together.

"Out with it." Her tone was harsh. She glanced at the Big Boss sign on her desk. Time to grow up and act like it. "I'm sorry, I didn't mean to be so abrupt. Please, say what's on your mind." Jen leaned forward.

"What about the new model at TBM Agency? Lily." Eva hedged. "She tall, and willowy, like Cari was."

Jen snapped her fingers. "I forgot about her."

"I noticed she wasn't on here."

"She's so new. If she's free, I'll need your gift of mentoring her. Are you up for that?"

Eva's eyes shone. "She be a quick study for your surprise. Ree will be comfortable with her."

"You know, don't you?"

"I figured. You've been working from home more lately. And that sweet little pattern you designed. She'll look adorable."

So much for keeping it a secret.

Eva glanced at the roster and took a bold breath. "I don't want to overstep, but ... I can call the agency. Ask if Lily is available for the show?" She held up the sheaf of papers. "Maybe rearrange a few outfits. Make it more worth her time. She be similar in proportion to Stella and me."

"That's an excellent idea. Show me the end lineup and we're good."

"Of course. You are Big Boss, after all." Eva winked.

"You sound like Daphne. She's always calling me boss lady."

"She mean it as a sign of respect."

"Maybe. Speaking of her, I wonder where she is. She's almost an hour la—"

The office door banged open, making them both jump. Daphne charged in. "Sorry I'm tardy. The hospital wouldn't release ..."

Eva gulped, dropping the show lineup papers on the floor.

"Hospital?" Jen shrieked. "Is everything okay?"

Daphne waved her hands. "I'm fine." She beamed at them. "I was visiting my sister. They might let her come home soon. The logistics of it ... the meeting ran later than I thought it would. I should have called."

"It's okay. But anything to do with hospitals and ..." Jen let out a slow breath. "It's a touchy subject right now."

"You have a sister?" Eva asked. "She is very ill?"

Daphne stared at the model.

"I didn't mean to pry." Eva bent to pick up her papers.

"It was a long meeting. I'm tired." Daphne rolled her shoulders. "She's not sick. She was hurt a while back." Her voice seemed to come from a flat, dark place. "She's getting better."

"Good to hear." Eva stood. "I'll check on the twins. Give you two some privacy."

"Thank you. I'll talk to you later about the lineup."

Watching the model retreat, Daphne shivered. She turned to Jen and hung her head. "Again, I'm sorry. I know I was supposed to be here to help you with Ree when you brought her in. And Auggie. Although he's usually hanging out with Richard."

Jen gestured toward the now vacant seat.

"Am I in trouble?"

"I want to hear more about your sister. Like Eva, I didn't know you had one."

"She's doing good." Daphne grinned. "They're very pleased with her progress."

"That must be a relief. Is there anything we can get her?"

Daphne tilted her head to the side, considering. "What does January like? But Tabby doesn't draw."

"Tabby? Your sister?"

"Tabitha Elizabeth Carmichael. She's the best sister I could ask for."

"And she's Ree's age?" Jen scooted her chair around the desk, inviting more information.

"A little older."

"Well, let's see. Ree still likes dolls—the ones she can dress like fashion models—go figure." She tapped her finger to her lips. "She loves reading. Right now, it's the *Narnia* books. Would Tabitha like a basket of any of those things?"

"Maybe." The girl picked at her nail polish.

"Do you want to check with your mom first?"

Daphne's chin hitched upward. "I'm responsible for my sister."

"By yourself? Oh, my goodness, I had no idea. That must be hard." And expensive. So that's why she wanted more hours lately. Interns at Lilac didn't make much. She got up and leaned her hip against her desk. "We'd like to help."

A shadow crossed Daphne's face, then she brightened. "I'll keep it in mind." She stood to leave. Glancing down at Jen's desk, strewn with event papers, her expression darkened. "When can I be in a show?"

Jen swallowed a sigh. "We've been over this before. Design house interns generally don't model, or construct sewing patterns, or any higher tier activities. They begin by learning the business. Which you've been doing. Get some more classes under your belt first."

"Oh yeah. I forgot." She bent to pull at her shoe strap. "Is there anything else you need me for now?"

"Not just yet. But please, let me know if you're going to be late again. I don't want to worry something's happened to you."

"Will do, boss lady."

"What hospital is—"

"I'll go check on the twins. I haven't seen them since …" She flapped her hand. "Then, I'll finish cataloging that material you asked me to the other day."

"Thank you. Oh, there's a CPS caseworker with the kids. He should be here for another hour or so."

Interest flashed across Daphne's face.

Oops, she'd mentioned a member of the male species. "If you have time, will you catch the lunch truck and ask for the menu for next week? I'm hoping we'll all be back in swing by then."

The young woman's face became animated. The lunch truck owner was a favorite among the unattached in the neighborhood.

"Before you go, can I ask you a personal question?" Jen didn't wait for an answer. "Does Eva bother you?"

"Why would she?"

"I noticed your expression when she left the room."

Daphne glanced toward the door. "I don't want to speak ill of anyone."

"You know you can discuss whatever you need to with me, right?"

"She's your friend."

"I consider all my employees my friends."

The girl's lips pursed. "I don't know how to get her to warm up to me. She's so secretive."

Jen's brows drew together. "It may be her culture. Or more a privacy thing. She's gone through a lot to get here."

"Culture. Right." Daphne paused. "I'll give her some space. Let her have her secrets … for now."

Jen stood and stretched the creaks and crackles from her back. She shoved her office chair away, the wheels rasping against the concrete floor grated her nerves.

She missed the twins gallivanting down the hall, racing to see who reached the office or the Kingdom first. A dull ache thumped between her eyes. Would they ever get used to walking past there without remembering? Should she start looking for another showroom site?

She'd have to do something about the Kingdom, sooner or later. Jen peered into her workroom and pondered how to fit more of the twins' things in there. An uneasiness mingled with her thoughts. She might not have to worry about it after all.

Jen and Richard had fallen into a routine of popping into the playroom to check on the twins. It was her turn. It didn't appear to faze the CPS caretaker Melissa sent. He seemed like a nice guy. She found him admiring Auggie's take-apart box while Ree rummaged through a bin of fabric. Swatches flew in every direction.

The girl's cheeks were flushed. "What's going on, honey?" Jen reached to feel her forehead, but Ree pulled back.

"I'm looking for a color."

"Do you want some help?" She picked up a strip of purple near her.

"You can't."

Jen winced. Putting the fabric back, her fingers quaked.

"I mean, you can if you want. But I don't know what color it is. It's in my head. Can I do this myself? I'll know it when I see it."

She'd heard that same phrase from her own mouth many times. It would be humorous hearing it parroted back from Ree, if not for the girl's frantic actions.

Don't rush. The voice pressed forward. *She needs to process in her own way.*

If you're going to keep talking to me, would you please be more consistent and help when I ask you to?

She patted Ree's knee. "I'll leave you to your hunt. Let me know if you want an extra pair of hands."

The CPS social worker walked over. "Auggie offered to help. So did I. But I think we were in her way. We'll help her pick things up when she's done. Right, sport?"

Auggie bobbed his head, too busy screwing a wire onto a piece of metal to spare energy on words.

The guy pulled Jen aside. "I texted Melissa to update her. She said you're the best one to know if Ree's okay."

"She's got more confidence in me than I do." She adjusted her headband. "I'll let Richard know I checked on you all."

Up front, the sound tech was talking with Detective Oz. Jen hung around in case she was needed. Oz asked what sounded like inconsequential details, but the detective seemed satisfied with the answers.

Mason stood up front and gestured for Jen's attention. "How have things been around here this morning?"

"Way too quiet. Even the neighborhood seems muted." It was almost as if the area was in mourning. Cari had been a big part of the artsy block. They both had friends in many of the businesses nearby.

Detective Mason's eyes radiated sympathy. "How was it coming in today?"

Jen shrugged. "I've got to keep this place running. My employees rely on their paychecks." She scanned the length of the showroom. "I'm busy revamping the charity event as sort of a memorial. Do you think we'll be able to hold it here, or will I have to rent someplace?"

"Too early to say for certain. Have a backup in mind, in case. It may not even be a good idea if you're having any more mishaps, though."

"Would it help if I gave you the list of names we invite and who usually attends?"

"That would give us a huge advantage."

"I'll print one off for you. It's public knowledge who's asked to come so there shouldn't be an issue."

Mason chewed her pen top. "Our team did a cursory check of everyone who lives in both your buildings."

"Oh great, they're going to love me for that."

"Folks generally understand. Is there anyone there who has an overzealous attraction to you or Cari?"

"Not that I can think of. The only guy who seems strange would be classified as having the exact opposite of interest. He avoids me like the plague."

"Interesting. Weird vibes from someone are always worth checking out. What's his name?"

"Ned Bass. But he's harmless."

"We'll be the judge of that."

Oz cruised up to join them. "Hey, Miss Jen."

"What a pretty blouse."

The detective posed. "My niece, Deidre, made it." She turned to her partner. "You good, Mason?"

"Almost. I was asking whether there had been any more misadventures."

Jen shook her head. "Everyone's at odds with each other. But that's it."

"How so?" Oz's voice resonated in the small reception area.

"Harold is grumpier with everyone but the kids. Conversation with Richard is more technical than usual—which is a lot. He's preoccupied with something ..." Some of his jargon had sailed right over her head that morning. "And Daphne was later than usual. I guess her sister is getting out of the hospital soon. Poor girl. She's the caretaker.

None of us knew. But that's one of the disadvantages when working with short-term interns."

"Tough break," Oz commiserated. She swished a couple pages through her notepad. "What about the one with the accent? What's she been like this morning?"

"Eva? Now that you mention it ... strange. Really off for her. She always gets along with everyone." Jen walked over to the silver mannequins and straightened a bouquet. "But this morning, she acted like she needed to say something, then clammed up. She's almost skittish, which is not like her."

"We haven't found much about her, yet. Her citizenship status, but little else." Oz shifted her weight. "Do you know, was she documented when she began working here?"

Jen smiled. "That question I can answer with one-hundred percent certainty. She started shortly before her citizenship ceremony. I was honored she asked me to attend."

"Any relatives staying with her?"

"I think she only has a couple left—no one here. She hasn't mentioned anyone visiting."

Oz's brows drew together.

Mason continued down a list. "Do you know what hospital Miss Carmichael's sister is in?"

"We didn't get that far. She seemed tired and wanted to finish a project I'd given her. I'm sure she's exhausted with everything we've had going on around here. I know I am."

Mason snapped her notebook shut. "I think that's all we need for now. We'll go check on the young'uns."

Daphne careened around the corner, nearly knocking Oz over. The detective stumbled into one of the silver mannequins but made a grab for it before the fiberglass form hit the ground. She righted the faceless body and smoothed the wedding dress around it.

Daphne closed her eyes, grimacing. "Sorry, Detective. I'll be more careful next time." She had a stack of folders clutched in a death grip. She turned toward Jen. "The lunch truck is here. The menu is on your desk. I got the kids each a corndog from him." And off she went again.

"Thank you," Jen called to the retreating figure. "The detectives want to know—"

The intern waved her hand as she disappeared around the next corner.

"She always that high-strung?" Oz brushed at nonexistent lint on her suit.

Jen leaned closer to the detectives and kept her voice low. "Unfortunately, yes."

Two o'clock and Lilac Lane was done for the day. Its normal energy had fizzled out like the bubbles in Jen's soda. Eva had left an hour earlier, feigning a headache, and the CPS dude had left moments before.

Richard texted to say he was wrapping things up and would bring the twins back to her. Something about his words troubled her.

She replied, saying she'd shut things down and be right there. Rolling her neck to stretch out the kinks as she walked down the hallway, it was her turn to collide with Daphne. "Oof, sorry hon."

"No problem. I'm looking for Harold. The storage room is cold again." The intern rubbed her bare arms, shooting past her for the nether regions of backstage.

"He's already gone." Jen yelled. "It can probably wait until tomorrow." *Wear a sweater, girl. Even Texas has its frigid days.*

Once she reached the showroom, Richard motioned her to the catwalk, away from the twins.

"Everything okay?"

"Yes ... no. I'm not sure." He sat on the corner of the structure, bringing his height more level with her. "I'm worried about them." He bobbed his head toward the kids. "I knew about the—what did Cari call them? trances?—that Auggie gets into when he's troubled." He pulled at his chin. "But I've never seen Ree get upset, especially with drawing."

Jen glanced at the girl, sitting next to her brother, furiously scribbling, sketches strewn around her on the floor.

His phone chirped. Looking at the screen, he massaged the back of his neck. "There's somewhere I have to be this afternoon. But I can call and cancel if I need to."

She patted his sleeve. "Thank you for your concern, Richard. Unfortunately, I think I kept them here too long today. We're leaving shortly."

"You're sure?" He hesitated.

"Positive. You do whatever you need to. Big date night planned?"

He hemmed and hawed.

"I shouldn't have pried. Take care." She gave him a quick wave, regretting her inquisition, and scooted over to the twins. "You guys hungry?"

Ree shrugged, intent on her frenetic drawing. Jen walked around to the front of their chairs and crouched, looking between them. So much alike, yet so different.

Auggie didn't seem to be retreating. His stare appeared more dreamy than vacant. Not for the first time, she struggled to understand how he saw the world.

The kids had seemed so eager to be at Lilac earlier. Had they paid for her own need to immerse herself in work? The charity event was important to her. Doubly so now. She and Cari had hosted the first one for the Wells-Myer Art

Academy four years earlier. Annually since that time. But it wasn't worth the twins' mental health. She could have done some of the work from home. "Do you want to go back to the apartment?"

Ree continued her scribbling. "Maybe after you're done pulling the show?"

Her goddaughter's referral to gathering the clothes and accessories for an event proved how much she knew about the industry, even at this young age.

"We won't do that until next week, honey. Would you like to help? You're so good at it."

No reaction. Strange, she usually loved assisting. Jen's earlier happiness over seeing her goddaughter draw again now mixed with concern over the feverish actions.

In the past when creating, Ree's fingers resembled a vibrant porcupine of multi-colored art pencils poking between each finger. Cari had often teased her about having the waxy pigment running through her veins. Today, there were only three shades clutched tight in her fist. A sea of dark green scratched across the paper, red splats slapped down, and purple blobs—centers askew.

"Not your normal lively rainbow. What are you drawing?"

Ree shoved her hair away from her face and continued the erratic pace. She scraped through her drawing so hard the paper ripped. Tearing the offending sheet out of its binder, she threw it on the floor with others. "I don't know what it is," she wailed. "It's in my head, and I can't get it out."

Jen hugged her tightly. Auggie unfolded himself from his chair and came to stand by theirs, leaning against Jen. Big as he was, she pulled him onto her lap and turned back to Ree. "It'll come to you. Let's work through this. How about you tell me why you picked those colors?"

"I tried all the tricks you've taught me during our lessons. Drawing it in different colors or another pattern.

Like when I designed the princess gown. I drew swirls at first, remember? When I changed it to the dots, my drawing finally went right."

That design would be etched in Jen's memory forever. She'd created the secreted gown from it. Ree's first professional runway piece—credit where credit was due.

"Daphne said to draw all kinds of other stuff, like she does at school. To mix things up. Nothing worked." She threw her hands in the air, her precious box of pencils upending like a game of pick-up sticks. Sliding to the floor, she swallowed gulps of air between whimpers.

Auggie retreated from Jen's lap to sit next to his sister and pat her back. Ree heaved a sigh and wadded the nearest drawings.

"Don't throw those away. Put them in your carryall for now." Jen picked up the satchel and held it open. "We'll look at them later. I'm hungry. I know you had pizza yesterday, but are you game for more?"

At the mention of food, Auggie came to life. "Yay, pizza. I'm starvin'."

His outburst broke the tension. Ree gave him a crooked smile and smoothed the crumpled pictures.

"Mark that one." Jen pointed to a single paper Ree kept looking at. It seemed familiar somehow. But not. The girl drew a star on the back and shoved it in her case with the rest.

"Let's go to Antonelli's. I can get a salad, and you two can get that pizza you like."

"I can't wait that long." Auggie grumbled, rubbing his stomach.

The three headed toward her office down the back hall, the twins holding hands once again. They were a team and let everyone know it in their own quiet way.

Ree flung her binder on the work island and pitched in to help pack up the design table. Technology was Auggie's thing. He requested time to work on his latest project with her computer. He'd eat, sleep, and breathe computers and tools if allowed.

The twins were seven when Cari finally broke down and allowed them a computer game. She'd chosen a "build it" amusement, thinking they'd tire of it soon. To her chagrin, Auggie turned out to be her Mr. Fix-it.

Jen could still hear her friend's laughter when she shared a story soon after the purchase.

"I was late yesterday because my clock annoyed me, so I threw it across the room. Auggie put it back together, complete with a quieter ringer. He said it was angry because it was too tight, 'like Ree's pig tails.'" Cari had preened. "I didn't know he even understood what the business end of a screwdriver did." The take-apart box was created after that to keep him in devices to dismantle so he didn't "fix" his mother's small appliances, whether they needed it or not.

"Ten minutes for your project. Set your timer."

"'Kay," he chirped.

Later, standing outside the studio with Auggie and Ree at the bottom of the loading ramp, she locked the back door. Turning, she froze. There, near the dumpsters in the back corner sat a guy on a cycle. She glanced around the parking lot. No other vehicle. Only her old, trusty Camry ... directly across from motorcycle man.

CHAPTER 12

Jen blanched. Their ever-vigilant police escort was nowhere to be seen. She'd been so preoccupied with a financial spreadsheet earlier that she'd forgotten until now that they had called to say they were checking a lead and would return shortly.

She couldn't see the man through the dark shield of his helmet. Was this masked rider the twins' father? Would he be so bold?

Prickles ran up her spine. Whoever it was, she wouldn't let him get near the kids. "Come on, guys. I forgot something." She waved them closer.

The rider hoisted his leg over the bike.

"Let's go." A note of hysteria edged her words. She spun for the door, dropping her phone. The cell skidded partway down the ramp, landing in pieces at Auggie's feet. Ree helped him scoop them up. Working to keep her voice even, Jen jiggled the keys in the lock. "Can you hold that, Auggie? Maybe put it back together later?"

She glanced back. Motorcycle Man had his hands on his helmet. She couldn't let them see his face. If Cari was right, and they remembered him from his visit to their school, they'd start asking questions.

Lord, help me. Her fingers fumbled with the lock. The sticky latch finally gave way. She ushered them inside, bolted the door, and headed toward the front. "We can walk to Antonelli's and get some fresh air on the way."

"But I'm starving." Auggie moaned.

"We'll hurry."

Ree gave her a questioning glance. "What did you forget?"

"Pardon?" Her fib already forgotten.

"You said you left something."

Breathe. *One—* No time to count. "I uh ... forgot my, um, clicker thingy." The laser pointer she used during presentations was a lame excuse for coming back inside, but it would have to suffice. "I need your brother to take a look at it, it's being fussy again."

"I fixed it good." His tone was indignant.

"You did. I'm probably not doing it like you showed me. We can practice at home."

"Engine?" Ree squinted at her. Her goddaughter stood under the dim hallway light, hands on hips.

"I'm okay, honey. Hunger makes me fuzzy headed sometimes." She shooed them toward the front entrance.

"Ookkaay." Skepticism tinged the girl's words. "I saw the remote by the sound booth."

"Let me get a light."

"I can see." Ree went galloping in the shadowy beam of the exit signs. "Here it is," she yelled from the catwalk. "Will you get my art case, Engine? I left it in your office."

"Good idea." She grabbed the satchel. "Now, let's go." Escorting them out the front, she listened for footsteps and loud motors as she locked the heavy doors.

Finger touches and counting ensued.

She ushered the twins across the street and around the corner. For now, they moved. Toward Antonelli's. And away from the unknown, masked by a motorcycle helmet.

Blocks later Jen's nerves still sang. Such a stupid idea. She should have locked them in and called the police from Lilac. Too late now.

Ree trotted to keep up. "Who was that guy, Engine? Are you scared?"

"I don't know. Can you two remind me to call our detective friends when we get to the restaurant?"

"Your phone's broke."

A muscle stitch stabbed her side. Switching Ree's art case to her other hand, she slowed, counting out her pattern with each step.

"I can fix it, Engine." Auggie jumped over each crack in the sidewalk as they scurried to Antonelli's.

"I'm sure you will, honey. Mrs. A will probably let us borrow their phone until you get it back together. I don't want anyone to worry about us."

"Mrs. A is nice." He bounced next to her. "She gives me extra 'shrooms on my pizza. And she doesn't put those yucky little fishes on my half."

Despite her apprehension, the memory of Auggie arguing with his mother about anchovies on their pizza brought a smile to her face.

Why hadn't Cari said how hard it was being a mom? *I was so tough on her sometimes.*

A dark crew-cab truck rolled by on the one-way street, slowing to a crawl. Keep walking. Maybe they'll go away. It came to a stop and backed up.

"Jen, is that you?"

"Isn't that Ethan from the skyscraper?" Ree pulled on her sleeve.

Relief swept through her. They walked over to the truck. She stopped the twins a pace away on the curb.

"Hey, Ethan. What brings you here?"

"I'm looking for a business but can't find it. Do y'all need a ride?"

"Thanks. We're fine. The fresh air is good for us." She reached up and shoved an errant curl behind her ear. "Who are you looking for? I know most of the businesses in this area."

"I ... uh. Well, I'd rather—"

The growl of a motorcycle roared in Jen's ears. Her stomach leaped to her throat. "On second thought, we'll take you up on the offer." She heard the click of the locks and grabbed the back handle, yanking the door open. Ree's satchel went tumbling inside. She took hold of Auggie's hand. "Get in." She hoisted him up by his belt.

Ree stepped in front of her, eyes full of questions.

Auggie turned to get out. "He doesn't have boosters. We can't ride in here."

"I'm making an exception this once. We're only a few blocks away."

Ethan leaned over the seat, his face a mask of concern, and clasped Ree's hand, helping pull her inside. Jen scrambled in front and slammed the heavy door. A prayer for protection swam through her mind, both from the unknown they'd left behind and the little-known in the driver's seat next to her.

What have I done?

She gave their rescuer a weak smile. "We're going to Antonelli's. Do you have time to join us?" Her words sounded cheerfully brittle. "If not, could you drop us off there?"

She wasn't letting him know where they lived. No one knew where they were. Was it a coincidence running into

Ethan? Or by his own design? She turned to the twins, "Everyone buckled?"

Auggie bounced on the backseat. Ree's hand, all Jen could see of the girl sitting behind her, landed on her brother's leg, steadying him.

"This will be fun, guys." An adventure? Seriously? Her insides churned.

Mrs. Antonelli waved at them when they walked into the family-style restaurant.

Ethan insisted on paying for everyone's lunch. "It's not every day I get to have pizza with friends. Especially ones who admire my work." Once the kids were fed and playing a game of Pacman in the corner, he leaned in. "Mind telling me what's going on? It's great seeing you three, but you seem very jumpy."

Jen surveyed the open dining area. Too early for the dinner crowd, there were few people to overhear. She hunched her shoulders over the picnic-style table and told him about their week. Everything. The sabotaged equipment. Cari's death. And her suspicions of the guy on the motorcycle. "I think I overreacted, though."

Ethen shook his head. "Go with your gut, Jen. You got a bad vibe, and you paid attention. Good for you."

Tension leaked from her shoulders.

"Always listen to that still, small voice. Or the hairs rising on your arms."

"Or my *skitters*?"

"Pardon?" His eyes filled with mirth.

"Cari said she could always tell whenever something was hinky because I rub my temple like crazy. When something unnerves me, those little nerve endings feel like a bug skittering through there."

"Then listen to your skitters." His laughter was rich and hearty, but his kind face turned serious. "I'm surprised the police are—"

"Oh, my gosh. I need to call the detectives right away. I dropped my phone." She fished it out of her purse, pushing buttons. "Auggie shoved it back together, but he didn't have time to really look at it, yet. Crud. It's still dead. Can you excuse me? I need to ask Mrs. A to use their phone." She pushed away from the table. "I hope I remember the number."

"Here. Use mine." He swiped at his screen and handed it to her with the nearby precinct's number already pulled up. "I've had to call them a few times for mischief at the job site."

She didn't relish the dressing down she knew she was due.

Minutes later, she wound up her conversation. "Yes, we're fine. And in a public place." She glanced around her. "Which is getting busier all of the sudden."

She could hear the irritation in Mason's controlled response.

"Please don't be upset with them. I take full responsibility. Can they pick us up here at Antonelli's? No, we won't budge. I promise." She handed the phone back to him. "As you probably heard, Detective Mason is *not* happy, but she's glad I called. Our detail has been looking for us since they got back. Her exact words, 'No lights. No kids. No Jennifer. Only a locked business and an empty car.'" She laid her chin on her cupped hands, fingers scorched by her flaming cheeks.

"From what I could hear of the conversation, all is well."

"You say that a lot."

"It's usually the truth."

Jen glanced at the twins in the corner. They squabbled over who was making the little ball eat the most dots. She grinned. "They're having fun for a change."

While they waited for the none-too-happy police escort, Jen asked why he had been in the right place at the right time.

He finally admitted he'd been looking for a lawyer near her building.

"That would be Mr. Santos. He retired a few months ago."

Ethan's face fell. "I'm not sure I'd have had the nerve to go in anyway."

She hated being nosy, but he seemed so miserable. "If you want to talk about it, it might help."

"It certainly can't hurt. I've never said this about a job before, but I've had enough. As a construction manager, it's my responsibility to oversee a project. But this guy is micromanaging everything." He leaned in close. "And, I think he's cutting corners where he shouldn't. But I can't prove it. I've been fortunate to work for some of the best builders in Dallas. Real integrity. You know? I'm not sure who to talk to."

"That's got to be tough." Jen listened with one ear toward the twins until she recognized a name. "What did you say?"

He shook his head. "I shouldn't have mentioned anything. I'm just so frustrated."

She leaned forward. "Please, repeat it."

Ethan hesitated, his lips forming a grim line. "The company is Midas Industries, but the checks are signed by Bart Golden. I've never met him in person, only on the phone. I usually deal with his assistant."

"He's the guy who owns the building next to mine."

Ethan turned pasty.

"Don't worry. I won't say a word to that shyster. Besides, I've never actually seen him either. He bought the building about a year ago. The whole block is old. It needs constant maintenance. He refuses to do anything to help his tenants."

"If it's the same guy, sounds about right." He spoke in hushed undertones. "I wish I'd never taken this job, but I was between contracts. The guy offered decent wages, and I needed the money." A goofy grin passed over his face, then he turned serious. "I'm proposing to my girlfriend at Christmas. But no ring is worth people getting hurt."

"Congratulations!" Jen's thoughts jumped tracks. "You could mention it to the police. They're probably going to talk to you anyway, after the trouble I caused today. They're being very careful about everyone I know."

"Send them my way."

Having a techie whiz for a nephew was a godsend when phones needed fixing. Grateful that hers had only required being snapped together more securely and restarted, Jen picked it up on the second ring.

"Hey, sorry, this is hurried." Colin panted. "I just got to the airport. They're trying to get a plane out between storms. I had to rush to get here." Another gulp for air. "Boarding starts soon. I'm finally on my way."

She pictured him as the athletic teen she used to know. He would have sprinted back then with little problem. But he was older now.

"They're routing us to Chicago with a puddle jumper." He audibly shuddered.

"Are you a nervous flyer?"

"Not usually. But I'm not crazy about little planes. Thank goodness I left my bag packed in the car. I hope I remembered everything." His words were stronger. "I'm glad Gggrrr isn't as big as DFW. I'd have never made it on time."

"Did you just snarl at someone?"

He laughed. "The call letters for this airport are GRR. Most refer to it with a little growl."

She appreciated the trivia that still flowed easily between them, even after all the years. "If you're missing something, we can get it here." Thankfully, the butterflies traipsing through her stomach didn't affect her voice. "Do you need a ride when you get in?"

"No, I'm picking up a rental."

"Quick, before you go, what's your flight number?"

"For Auggie? Hold on a sec. Ah, here it is." He rattled off the information. "It's gonna be kind of late when I get in, but ... would you mind me stopping by? You know, see the kids. If that's okay." He hesitated. "And you. I'd like to see you too. It's been a long time." His words tumbled over themselves.

"Of course." She mentioned the detour near her building so he could plan a reroute. "When do you get in?" Pacing between the living room and dining area, she closed the curtains on a dusk that had yet to settle for the night, and straightened this, while picking up that.

"We're scheduled in by eight Central. So, I'm guessing somewhere around nine."

"They might still be awake. I'll pop in a movie and let them stay up. They'll be excited to see you, I'm sure." She hesitated. "Colin, I need to tell you what happened—"

"They're calling final boarding. I'll talk to you soon." And *click*, he was gone.

She placed her phone on the counter. Staring at it as if it would bite, she turned it over on its face. Her hand fluttered to her hair.

Get a grip. She'd known Colin for years. He couldn't be that different, could he? She morphed back into an infatuated tweenaged girl in two seconds. But there was no sense wasting time pondering the differences between the young, hunky boy and this grown-up, manly-sounding Colin. She'd find out soon enough.

Searching for the twins, she found them on their bedroom floor, finishing an airport-themed puzzle.

"I just got off the phone with Uncle Colin." She grinned. "By now he's in the air. He'll be here later tonight."

"Woohoo." They peppered her with questions.

Auggie finally shouted above the noise. "What's his flight number?"

"Ree, do you want to help me with dinner while Auggie does the flight tracking?"

Under the pretense of a school project, Cari had involved him with aircraft tracking a year or so earlier. Before that, he'd been a mess as soon as his mother or aunt left for the airport. They researched headwinds, turbulence, and other fascinating flight details. Once he learned to use the *Flight Aware* app himself, he had their arrivals pegged within minutes of landing. He'd bounce into the room and announce their call moments ahead of the first ring.

Now, Auggie rushed to the kitchen and handed Jen her cell to swipe in her password and the child safety code. He hopped up and down while he entered his uncle's flight information. His running commentary of the altitude and location of Colin's plane bubbled over. It remained to be seen whether he would have the same uncanny connection with his uncle as he'd had with his mother.

Jen alerted her doorman, Leo, and their security watch of Colin's impending arrival. Their protection team informed her they would meet him in the Sheffield's lobby. Afterward, Leo escorted him up to Jen's flat.

"Sorry to meet you under these circumstances, Mr. Marshall." Leo shook Colin's hand outside her door. "Everyone here at the Sheffield loved your sister. Almost as if she was one of our own tenants." He turned to Jen. "Speaking of our residents, please tell little Ree that Mr. Harper asked when she could visit the new kitten. Spoiled old thing. The cat *and* Mr. Harper." He laughed at his own joke and doffed his doorman's cap. "Take care."

The moment the door shut behind Colin, Jen's nerves kindly took a leave of absence. Remnants of the boy she'd crushed on were visible under the calm, confident man that stood before her.

The twins rushed from their bedroom and the next hour was consumed with giggles, jokes, and shy smiles.

I don't know what your reasoning was, Cari. But you and these kids missed out on a lot of extra love by keeping them away from your brother. She didn't know who to feel sorrier for, the twins, Colin, or her best friend. Admittedly, maybe even a little herself.

Two exhausted kids finally shlepped to bed but coaxed a story from their uncle. While he read to them, Jen warmed some leftover dinner, hoping his adult stomach still liked the same food he had as a teen.

He walked into the kitchen with a melancholy grin. "I can't believe how big those two have gotten." His eyes lit up at the plate of tacos waiting on the island for him. They sat down across from each other and chatted as he ate.

"While I was reading, I did some quick calculations. Do you know this is the first time they've seen me in person in over four years." A mixture of emotions played across his face. "Ree said she didn't remember that I had white hair above my ears." He chuckled.

"Then let's make sure you get to know them good and proper now." She quite liked the silver at his temples.

The two caught up on the decade since they'd last seen each other shortly after Cari and Jen graduated high school. Neither brought up Cari's death. There would be time for that later.

CHAPTER 13

Saturday morning, the showroom teamed with people. The whole crew had decided to get ready for the upcoming charity show as best they could, until they knew different. Jen leaned in to hear better.

"Busy day." Colin winced at a toddler's piercing screech.

"Noisy, you mean. That's Olive, Annie's granddaughter. She's three."

He nodded as if the age did indeed explain everything.

Jen took his arm and pulled him away from the chaos. "I'm glad you could come today, but are you sure you're up for this?"

"I don't want to miss a moment with them for anything." He glanced away. "Or reconnecting with you."

Despite the slight chill in the air, Jen's cheeks warmed.

As they walked toward the sound booth, she searched for its main occupant. "I'd introduce you to Richard, but he seems to be MIA. It's quieter here behind the audio desk." She shepherded him to chairs nestled beside the mahogany bay.

He sat and leaned his elbows on his knees, angling toward her. "Tell me more about Lilac Lane. You didn't say much last night."

"I didn't want to scare you off when I invited you along."
She forced a laugh. *Relax. Pretend he's the curious boy next
door.* She pointed toward the back room. "That commotion
is the playroom I told you about. Cari and I built it with my
dad's help."

"That would have been fun to be part of." His tone was
wistful.

"It's like this on Saturdays for a couple weeks before
a show ... holidays, school breaks, and most days off. The
kids have the freedom to run around there. It gets loud
if the door's not shut. I'm thankful they're quiet during
shows." She leaned over and stage whispered. "Plus, they
don't know the room is semi-soundproofed."

Colin snapped his fingers. "I'll bet that's why Cari
quizzed me about padded rooms a couple years ago."

"During shows, we hire college students to keep the
kids occupied with movies, popcorn, soda—the whole bit.
Ree and Auggie often opt for their jobs, but not always. One
moment." She stood and caught Daphne's attention. "Will
you tell the kids to pipe down?"

The intern touched her forehead in a mock salute and
disappeared.

Moments later, childish moans and groans filtered
through the doorway, but the decibel lowered to a dull roar.

"They must be playing some rousing game today." She
glanced at her watch. "No wonder they're getting restless.
It's past lunch time. He's not usually late."

Richard's head appeared between the stage curtains.
"Bucket's here," he bellowed.

"Bucket?"

"The Lunch Bucket food truck." Jen explained. "The
owner's a great guy."

Colin flicked fuzz off his shirt sleeve, not meeting her
gaze.

"He's a young chef who figured out the fashion district eats well, if you feed us mostly healthy food."

"You like helping up-and-comers, don't you?" Colin smiled.

"Just paying it forward. He's been catering for us about four months. It's simple, good food. Plus, his prices are reasonable." She shrugged. "And it's another way I can repay my staff for our weird hours. When he knows the kids will be here, he tries to have stuff they like."

"Was he on the list?"

"Of what?"

"People who were here that day."

Jen stared at him, eyes wide. "I never even thought of him. I honestly don't know. But that brings up a couple other vendors we see on the regular." She pulled her cell from her back pocket and sent a text to the detectives. She motioned for Colin to follow her. "We'd better herd the kids into the lunchroom before the crew, so they get some food."

Daphne appeared at Colin's elbow. "Hello, there."

He jumped.

Jen masked her annoyance at the intrusion. "Hey, Daphne, where did you come from?"

The comment was ignored, as was Colin's personal space. "Who are you?" Blatant eye batting ensued.

He took a step back.

"Colin, this is Daphne, this semester's intern. Daphne, this is Colin Marshall. Cari's brother."

The girl turned wounded-doe eyes on him. "I'm so sorry, Mr. Marshall. I didn't know your sister well, but I'm sure you were close. You're the twins' uncle then, aren't you?" She peered into his face. "Yes. I can see the family resemblance."

"Daphne." Jen's patience ran thin with the girl's prattle. "Will you corral the kids for lunch? They need food before they declare mutiny."

"Sure." Her tone held a crisp edge. "Anything else you need done? Do you want the stage curtains opened?"

"Yes. Thank you."

Moments later, the kids spilled from the playroom. Auggie came bounding onto the stage. Spotting them, he charged forward, clutching a metal creation in his hand.

"Cool mask." Colin kneeled and took the piece, running his fingers over the screwed-on-washer eyes and wired mouth. "But weren't you working on a microphone a little while ago?"

Auggie's shoulders pumped up and down. "I fixed it. Richard checked."

"This is awesome, bud." Colin's eyes shone with admiration. "Tell me more about the mask." He handed the craftwork back.

"Lots of people have them."

"Like clowns and actors, right?" Colin stood.

"Not real ones like this." Auggie scowled. "Inside masks." He pointed to his chest and paused.

Jen let him puzzle through his thoughts. Colin remained quiet.

"Like when Ree and I pretend. We wear 'nvisible masks. I like to be Albert Einstein. Cari said he was really smart. Like me. Cari said so."

"She was right." Jen's heart burst, hearing him talk of his mother with pride.

"Ree likes to wear a painter's mask. Money ... Mooney ... ooh." He stamped his foot. "He paints floaty flowers. And ladies carrying umbrellas when it isn't raining."

"You mean Monet?" Colin quizzed.

"Yeah, him." He swiped the air as if holding a paintbrush and twirled the ends of an imaginary mustache. His smile lit up when Colin laughed. Auggie held the metal mask over his face but immediately brought it down, frowning. "This is no good. I forgot eye holes."

Jen was used to his quicksilver changes. "It's a handsome mask, Auggie. If you don't want it, can I put it up in the office?"

He shook his head. "You can have it. But not here."

Jen started. He usually loved to have his creations on display. "How about over my desk at home?"

His caterpillar brows scrunched together. "Okay. No one wears a mask at your 'partment."

An idea formed in her thoughts. "Does someone here wear a mask? Are you afraid of someone?"

"I'm not afraid of no one." He puffed out his chest but glanced over his shoulder.

Colin watched their exchange with intensity.

Auggie's face scrunched, then he perked up. "Daphne wears a mask." He mimicked a goofy face. "Mr. What's-his-name wears one. Nobody else can see it. But I know. And Richard has one too." He made a face like he was crying, swiping at a tear.

"Richard has Comedy and Tragedy hanging in his cubicle." She explained to Colin.

"No. That's his real masks. I mean his pretend one."

"Let me get this straight ... Richard, our always smiling sound man, and one of your best friends, is really sad on the inside?"

"Yes. He cries in there. Especially after Cari died." Suddenly, he grinned. "But he still likes me."

Jen wasn't sure this was getting them anywhere, but it seemed important to her godson. She'd continue as long as he went with it. "And Daphne? What about her mask?"

"She wears different ones. Sometimes she's a grizzly bear." He held up his hand like a claw. "Then that guy with the flute. Those kids followed him."

"The Pied Piper?" Had his fanciful imagination teetered toward pretend?

He nodded and mimicked the literary musician. "When we watch movies with her. But sometimes, she gets sad-mad like Cari."

"Cari was sad-mad?" Colin's eyes reflected his question.

"She was my mom. She said people made her mad sometimes."

He seemed to be getting used to the idea of Cari not being around. A small fissure in Jen's heart healed.

"But not Ree and me. Even when we made her sad, like breaking her favorite vase." He grimaced with the weight of his guilt. "But she couldn't be mad because she loved us. See? Sad-mad."

"That makes perfect sens," Colin praised.

Auggie's face was wreathed with happiness.

While Jen enjoyed their interaction, she hoped Colin was up to the possible fallout the first time he had to discipline his nephew. Auggie responded well to defined rules. But like any nine-year-old, special needs or not, he pushed boundaries.

"You said there were three people wearing masks." She prodded. "Who was the other one?"

He thought for a moment. "Oh yeah, Mr. Golden."

"The guy who owns the building next door? You've met him?"

"His face looked like this." He smiled with artifice, heavy on the fake.

Jen fought a giggle. Was her boy puzzled, acting sly, or had gas rumbling in his stomach?

Abruptly, his face changed as if made of molten plastic. Without warning, it hardened. His eyes narrowed. Lips sneered.

She gasped. She'd never seen Auggie look mean. Ever.

His features relaxed, but he appeared worried. "When he did that, he was scary." Auggie leaned toward his uncle and confided. "I was kinda afraid of him then."

"I would be too, bud." Colin regarded him with concern.

She needed to get to the bottom of Auggie's worry over that stink-face Golden. "When did you see him make *that* expression?"

"The day he yelled at Cari."

"Mr. Golden shouted at her? Why?"

He pretended to cover his ears. "He was loud."

"Where? Here at the studio? Can you remember?"

"'Course I can. On the sidewalk. Where we live." He folded his arms across his chest.

Cari used to be so good at channeling his conversations. Why hadn't she paid better attention? She turned to Colin. "What reason would Bart Golden have to be at Cari's?"

Not knowing the players of this all-too-real drama, he shrugged.

Auggie chimed in. "Cari didn't call him that."

Her pulse leaped. "Well, of course she didn't. She probably called him ... Fred." Turning the inquisition into a silly guessing game peaked Auggie's attention. "Rupert? Beauregard?"

The last one elicited a full belly laugh.

"I give up." She threw her hands in the air for dramatic effect.

"I can't tell you the first name she said." He drew Colin into his confidence again. "It was a bad word."

"Good thinking." Colin's puzzled expression was nothing new around Auggie. The boy's swift emotional changes took some getting used to. "We wouldn't want Engine getting upset at us if I let you say a bad word."

"Engine's not mad." He peered at her through his lashes. "Are you?"

"We're good. You can't tell me the first word ..." No use having Auggie fixate on swearing. "But did she call him something else?"

"Bill Gee or Gill Bee ... I think."

She fished through men's names. "Could it have been Gilby or Gilly?"

"Maybe." He considered the new information, then shook his head.

Jen's mind swept back through the years. She couldn't get a firm grip on the rather unusual name, but something sounded familiar about it.

"Do you know who he's talking about?" Colin asked.

"I'm not sure."

Auggie's voice broke her reverie. "Engine, I'm starving." Colin agreed.

"Do you like roast beef?"

Auggie rubbed his stomach. "Roast Beast sammiches from the Bucket? Yummy."

"Sounds good to me too." Colin licked his lip with exaggeration. "Look, here's our girl. Right on time."

Ree was quiet when she joined them. "I'm not hungry."

"You love their blueberry muffins. How about that and a cool drink?" Jen smoothed Ree's curls back, brushing her hand along the small forehead at the same time. *Cool as a cucumber. Overtired?*

"I'll try."

Jen touched Colin's arm. "Come on. We'll introduce you to the gang."

"Meet my buddy, Collie Dog." Auggie hopped up and down.

"Remember to use real names." Jen reminded him.

The hops stopped. "I *know* that." He pulled a face.

"Okay, smarty pants." Jen poked his shoulder. "What is it?"

"Uncle Colin?" His eyes twinkled with mischief.

"Take Ree with you and introduce him by saying, 'This is our Uncle Colin.'"

"Okey dokey." He beckoned. "Come on, Collie Dog." Auggie gave his mask to her, grabbed his twin's hand, and led the way to the lunchroom—chattering good-naturedly.

Ree glanced at her, mouthing "help me," then turned back to her brother and giggled.

"I'll be right with you." She wheeled by her office to put the mask away.

She nestled the creation inside her desk drawer. The fractious guise sulked. "Grumpy old thing." She slammed the drawer and locked it away.

CHAPTER 14

Sunday, Jen shut her binder. "I'm sorry, honey. Was I ignoring you?"

Auggie flopped on the living room ottoman at her feet. "You were going to."

"Okay, I'm all ears."

"No, you're not. You have hair and teeth and eyes and feet." He held his sides with his belly laugh.

A recent Bible study in Romans came to mind, "We have different gifts, according to the grace given to each of us." *He uses his gifts well, doesn't he, Father?* Her godson's quirky sense of humor never failed to make her heart smile. Jen reached over and ruffled his curls. "All right, funny guy. What did you need?"

"Is Collie Dog coming today?"

"He said eleven o'clock." She checked the time. "That's thirty more minutes. Let's say forty in case he gets caught in traffic."

"What are we doing?"

"He wants to take you both someplace for a while. Are you good with that?"

"But what if Detective Oz needs me?"

She smiled. Oz was his buddy, Mason was Ree's. Interesting how he split the loyalties. "Uncle Colin said you wouldn't be far. I'll let you know if she calls. Deal?"

"What if I get starving?" Heading up the hill toward puberty, he was always hungry.

"Ask him if you can bring snacks."

"Lots of them?" He wheedled, wiggling his eyebrows.

She laughed. "Will you tell Ree to get ready? I haven't seen her since breakfast."

"She's readin' ... again." He bunny hopped out of the room.

Thirty-five minutes later, Leo buzzed her, announcing Colin.

"Collie Dog." Auggie whooped at the top of his lungs and bounded for the door.

"August, wait." Momentary panic sent Jen running from her bedroom. "Don't go to the door without me. It might not be him." Catching up, she placed her finger over her lips. "And indoor voice, please."

"Oh, right." He skated around the slippery floor in his socks.

Jen glanced through the peephole and opened the door. There stood Colin with a plastic bag—taller than it was wide—and a satisfied grin. "Come in. You have one rambunctious nephew waiting."

Auggie danced around him.

"I hope I don't disappoint."

"Whatcha got, Collie Dog?" Auggie reached for the bag.

"Hang on, champ. Can you get your sister?"

Ree slogged into the room. Her cheeks were flushed again.

"Uh-oh." Colin kneeled by the girl and felt her forehead.

A stab of jealousy hit Jen's stomach while he performed what she'd considered her job. But his obvious concern for his niece won over her own discontent.

"She's a little warm, but I don't think she's feverish." He turned to Jen.

Her fingers twitched with the need to check, but she tucked her hands in her jeans pocket.

Let him take charge. The voice demanded.

You sure are pushy. She shot back.

"Don't you feel well, sweetheart?" Colin asked Ree.

"I'm so tired." She plunked down on the couch.

Auggie's bouncing ceased. "Now we can't go."

Ree's face clouded.

Jen turned to Colin before the kids started bickering. "What did you have planned? Maybe we can come up with a fix?"

"Sounds good." His excitement seemed forced. Standing, he grappled with the bag and pulled out two bats. One had Auggie's name written in black marker. The other was pink—Ree's favorite color—with her name. Turning the bag over, out tumbled two balls, junior-sized mitts, and a well-worn adult one.

"I thought we'd go to the batting cage. Maybe throw some balls back and forth and get ice cream afterward, so Engine has some time to plan her show. But since Auggie doesn't like to go places without Ree, we can go another time."

Go ahead. Try it. The voice advised.

She sat on the ottoman and grasped Auggie's hand. She didn't want him wandering away while she talked to his sister. "Sweetie, what would you think about heading back to bed for a nap? When you get up, we'll make cookies for the crew."

Ree was crestfallen.

Jen glanced at Colin. "Do you have anything going on tomorrow morning?"

"Nothing I can't change."

"Good. I need to get some bookwork done. Would you mind doing something with them for a while then? Ree can rest up today."

"Great idea. There's a special place I haven't been to in ages. It'll be fun to go there with you two."

Ree's smile was wan but accepting. "You don't mind if I don't go today?"

"Of course not. I want you to get better."

Auggie squirmed, tugging Jen's hand. This was unfamiliar territory for all of them. She pulled the boy close. "You know that big, green building we pass when we walk to Ethan's high-rise? That's where the batting cage is. What if the two of you go throw some balls for a bit?"

"But ..." His forehead creased like the Shar Pei puppies he loved.

"If you get anxious, I'm sure Uncle Colin will bring you back here."

"I have to go by myself?" Popping his knees back and forth, Auggie reminded her of a Jack-in-the-Box toy stuck on go. Apprehension filled his eyes. "Not Reeree? Not you?"

Everything was changing so fast for him. *Where do we go from here, Father?*

Colin sat on the floor next to her and focused his attention on Auggie.

The wiggles eased and he turned to his uncle. "No sisters? No Engines allowed?"

"Just us guys. You good with that?" Colin didn't wait for an answer. "Here's our code word. Stop. That's it. If you want to stop, you say so and we can leave."

"Pinky promise?" Auggie squinted at him. "You won't be mad?"

Jen's heart warmed as she watched their fingers inter-twine.

"This is supposed to be a fun day." Colin said. "If we stay here, we can enjoy playing games or building with your blocks. I'm fine with that too."

"But I have to take care of my sister." He said to no one in particular.

"Oh, for Petey's sake," Ree snapped. "I'm not sick." Her tone softened. "And I'm not upset you're going without me."

"You sure?"

Her eyes flashed a quick sparkle. "Will you take my bat and hit some balls for me?"

Colin winked at her.

"Sure." Auggie turned to their uncle. "Thirty minutes?" Often the extent of his patience.

"Yes. Scout's honor."

"You were a scout?" The boy's mouth hung open.

"I was." A shadow crossed Colin's face. "For a while." Was that something else his parents ruined? "I can tell you more while we're throwing the ball around."

"What if I get starving?"

"Let's eat here. We can bring a bottle of water and snack bar with us."

Auggie's curls bounced up and down with enthusiasm.

"Sandwiches coming up." Jen stood. "How about you, Ree? Do you want some soup?"

"Not right now. I'm going back to bed." She walked over to Colin and clung to his back, hugging around his neck.

He reached up and patted her cheek, leaning his head next to hers. "Feel better, sweetheart."

Ree meandered from the room.

"Do you have sweats here at Engine's, champ? You'll be more comfortable."

"Okey dokey." With his spirits and energy returned, Auggie ran from the room. A moment later, he raced to the bathroom.

Colin leaned back. "You think Ree is okay?"

"When she's overwhelmed, she shuts down sometimes. A nap should help."

"I hope so. I'm not so good with sick kids—or children in general. I don't exactly know what to do with them." He rubbed the back of his neck. "I figured playing catch was something I wouldn't have to think much about. I can concentrate on them. We never had little kids at our house, except you." The past seemed to swallow him for a moment.

What could she say? *A quiet mouth is a listening heart.* A conversation with Ingrid Reynolds, her Bible study leader, flooded her memory. She'd said much the same following Cari's death.

"How are you such a good listener, Ingrid?"

"My ears are my best ally. When my mouth wants its way, I try to remember Proverbs eighteen two, 'Fools find no pleasure in understanding but delight in airing their own opinions.' I don't have any solutions for you, but I'll be here to listen whenever you need me."

Jen followed her advice in this precious moment and kept quiet.

Colin shook his head. "I think about it sometimes. I don't know if it's because we never really had the opportunity to be around kids, or if I stayed away from them on purpose. I don't want to be like my parents and mess things up."

Her insides warmed to know he trusted her with these memories. She laid a hand on his arm, hoping her touch radiated comfort. "You're doing fabulously with them. They trust you, or Auggie wouldn't even entertain the idea of going by himself."

Gratitude shone from his eyes. He stood and offered his hand to help her up. His mouth was inches from hers when the whirling dervish named Auggie returned to the room.

"What kind of sammich do you want, Collie Dog? I make a good jelly sammich."

A grin snuck onto Colin's lips.

Jen spun toward the kitchen, hoping to hide her flaming cheeks. "I'm hungry for chicken sandwiches."

Prancing beside her, Auggie made a face. "Jelly ones are better."

"But they aren't as good for you. Remember? You can have half a jelly sandwich after you eat a chicken one."

Colin caught him around the waist and carried him like a sack of potatoes to a chair at the island.

"Ketchup on mine, Engine."

"I know. Ketchup on Auggie's everything."

"No sticking out your tongue, Collie Dog. That's not nice. Is it, Engine? Do you like ketchup? Or yucky mustard? Oops. I'm not supposed to stick out my tongue, am I? Can I get some—"

The adventure awaited.

Colin and Auggie had Reno's Batting Cage to themselves for almost an hour. Although cool, they'd built up a sweat in the indoor sports center. Colin flapped his shirt and smiled when his nephew mimicked him. "Your timer is buzzing again, bud."

"Do we hafta leave?"

They'd thrown a Frisbie disc for a short time and got the bats out. Auggie remembered to hit a few balls with Ree's bat, but he'd been more curious about pitching.

"Engine's expecting us, and I want to check on Ree."

"Oh yeah." Auggie dug in his pocket and retrieved Officer Henderson's rock. He smoothed the stone under his thumb. His forehead grew deep furrows. "I need to take care of her."

"I don't think she's ill. Engine said this happens with Ree sometimes." He wished Jen was here to help him navigate this burgeoning relationship with the boy. "What does your stone do?"

"It helps me be brave, like David. Engine told us all about him. He took care of that guy, Goliath. He was a filly ..." He paused.

Colin dug through the few memories he had of attending church with the Clarks. "Philistine?"

"Yeah, that. He was mean." Auggie tucked the rock back in its hiding place. "David was nervous, but brave. Like Dr. B said I can do." Auggie looked thoughtful. "And he gave Ree aminals so her tummy doesn't throw up."

Colin wondered what wildlife had to do with his niece's stomach. He'd ask Jen. "How many more minutes do you want to play catch?"

The boy stretched his arms wide. "A hundred zillion."

"We need some sleep before then. How about thirty minutes." Colin fluffed his shirt again. He hadn't played this hard in ... he couldn't remember how long. "Afterward, we'll stop by that store you told me about. I need to get a few things."

"Some fortune cookies?"

"We'll see. Set your timer." Colin picked up the ball, threw it in the air, and whacked it with a bat. It careened into a net at the other end of the room.

Auggie's gaze snapped to attention, consternation written across his face. "I want to throw a ball between the eyes."

"You mean hit the bull's eye?"

"Yeah. Hit the ball between the eyes."

Colin smiled at the misconstrued words. "To do that, you have to keep practicing." He laid his bat down and stood behind Auggie. "Decide how you want to throw the ball ... overhand or underhand." He demonstrated what he meant.

"Over."

He positioned Auggie's shoulders and feet in the correct stance. "Concentrate—that means stare at your mark." He pointed toward the pitching target. "Now throw it at that spot."

Auggie scowled. "But how will I know when it's okay to throw the ball?"

"What do you mean?"

Auggie's shoulders hunched, but he didn't say anything.

Colin searched for what he'd said or done to confuse the boy. He dug back through Jen's remarks and remembered a helpful nugget. "You have to think ahead, even if you don't know where ahead is. But when he understands, he really gets it. That makes everything worthwhile."

"When you said, 'How will I know when it's okay,' do you need someone to tell you when you're allowed to throw the ball?"

Auggie moved out of stance and faced him with a huge grin. "I want to hit things. A lot. But I'm not s'posed to. I might hurt somebody for real. Cari let me know when I could hit."

"How did she do that?"

"We have rules at our house. She said I could pound my pillow any time I was mad. I miss my pillow. It takes a good punching. Once she gave me a roll of toilet paper to toss, but I made a mess all over my room. I wasn't allowed to throw toilet paper anymore." His nose wrinkled. "Engine made my happy hitter. I get to hit my bed until I'm happy. No one gets hurt."

Colin took mental notes. "Do you sometimes want to break stuff when you're mad?"

"Yup." Auggie threw the ball up in the air and caught it with a thwack to his palm.

"And you're not sure if you're allowed?"

The boy's head wiggled so hard, the rest of his body followed.

"You know we should never hit people, right?"

Auggie's eyes narrowed. "Even if they deserve it?" He cocked his fist on his hips and grunted.

This was definitely a redirection moment. "So, what if we had a signal? Like catchers, pitchers, and umpires do."

"What are those?"

"I'll have to explain what each of them does later, but for now, the catcher needs to know what kind of ball the pitcher will throw."

He squeezed the sphere in his hand. "It's a hard one."

Colin chuckled. This was going to take some time. "There's a fast ball and curve balls and there's even a sl—"

"No spit balls?" Auggie wrinkled his nose. "I don't like those. Joey throws them at me. They're yucky."

"Definitely no spitballs."

"Good. What signal will we have?" He threw the ball to Colin.

"What about …" Colin stalled. He enjoyed the give and take with his nephew. "If you want to throw the ball at something you shouldn't, you tell me. But here's the rule—"

Auggie sighed. "Another one?"

"This rule isn't hard. You can only throw *this* ball when I'm around." He held it up, feeling the worn spots, from years of use. "I'll let you know if it's okay. Deal?"

"Pinky promise?"

"About what?"

"You won't get me in trouble with Engine?"

"I promise." After hooking fingers with his nephew, he lofted the ball into the air.

Auggie leaned forward and caught it. "What if I want to throw the ball at something I shouldn't?"

"Then I'll either shake my head or tell you no. You're a smart guy. You'll know what it means. If I can think of something else for you to throw it at, I'll point to it."

Auggie's eyes sparkled. "Point now."

They stood and Colin signaled to his gym bag on the floor about twenty feet away. Auggie wound back and let the ball fly. It missed the duffle by mere inches. "Excellent job."

"I didn't hit it." Auggie stubbed the toe of his sneaker against the floor, scowling.

"Striking the target will take practice. You'll get there. But you understood what I was pointing at. And your speed was great."

Auggie flashed him a grin. "Can we practice more?"

Some forty minutes later, Auggie's timer sounded.

"You want to come here again?"

"Do we hafta bring Reeree? I can't practice when she's bossing."

"Yes, we do. Maybe she can point at targets for you."

The boy scowled.

"I still need to be in the room when you throw the ball."

He brightened. "I want to be good as you."

"I've been playing more years than you. But I think you can be even better than me."

"Better'n you? I can't ... can I?"

"If you keep training."

Auggie blinked, as if pondering a deep thought. "Can I throw some more?"

"One. Then we go to the store."

"Okey dokey."

Hearing Auggie's favored acceptance, Colin understood the day was a hit. A stab of anger at his sister caught him in the gut.

Irritation washed into heartache. Would Jen let him see the kids after she gained custody? He was confident they'd work out a fair visitation schedule. He was not going to miss out on the kids' lives any longer.

"You mad at me, Collie Dog?"

"No, why do you think that?"

"You looked mad. Then you looked sad."

"I was thinking about something."

"Do you want to throw the ball? It helps with the mads."

Colin smiled at the boy who wasn't supposed to understand the subtleties of life. He knew more about the important stuff than most people. Like throwing a ball at something to make the mads go away.

"I'm good. But I promised you one more pitch. What do you want to throw it at?"

"Can I pretend the target is something else?" His eyes danced with mischief and a hint of trouble.

"I guess so. But what's the rule?"

"I don't throw the ball at anything—or anyone—'less you say okay."

"Anyone?"

Auggie stared hard at the target, and let the ball fly, narrowly missing the center.

Jen's worry over Ree stirred. Two hours later, and the girl was still asleep.

Snick. The guest bedroom door opened and Ree padded out to the living room. She snuggled in next to Jen on the couch.

"Hey, sleepyhead. Feel better?"

Ree covered her mouth for a yawn. "My brain won't shut off. I keep seeing those scary blobs in my dreams." She swirled her hands together to mimic the shapes, like she had at the police station. "They float and grow sharp teeth. They look like they're going to bite." She smacked her hands together. "Kind of like those drawings I did." She laid her head in Jen's lap, her soft hair tickling against Jen's arm. "I think I left my satchel in Ethan's truck. He won't throw it away, will he?"

She stroked Ree's downy-soft curls. "I'm sure he wouldn't do that. He probably hasn't even noticed it's back there. We can go by his work tomorrow or Tuesday, okay?"

"I guess." She murmured. "Can you call and ask him?"

"I would, but I don't have his number. And it's Sunday."

Ree bolted upright, almost colliding with Jen's chin. "Hey, where's Auggie and Uncle Colin?"

Sometimes her change in mood could be as mercurial as her brother's. How had Cari ever kept up with them day in and day out?

"Uncle Colin texted an hour ago and said they were doing fine. Hopefully, Auggie's having fun, instead of dealing with a meltdown."

"He hasn't had a bad one in a long time. Not since we started seeing Doctor B. He said Auggie got frustrated because he couldn't express himself. Now he does some exercises when he's uncomfortable. Like that funny noise he makes."

Ah, the huff-chuffing. One question answered.

"I noticed he's been more outgoing at Lilac. I thought it was because he's older. And thank you for reminding me. I have to call Dr. Brasil tomorrow. Uncle Colin and I need to know some of these things about you guys." She tweaked the girl's nose.

"I don't see him for myself much anymore. I mostly go in with Auggie when he wants me to. But that isn't very often. He likes Dr. B."

"I ..." Jen rolled the edge of the blanket between her fingers.

"You're beating around the bush, Engine."

"You're pretty astute at this grownup stuff, aren't you?"

"I had to be sometimes ... when Cari wasn't doing good."

"Yes, you did. I'm sorry, sweetie. I should have stepped in more often."

"You took care of us when you needed to. Some people don't." Ree grabbed a couch pillow and crushed it to her chest.

"How so?" Where was this going?

"Like my friend, Gretchen. Her dad left them." She sighed. "Her mom stays in bed all day. Crying. Now, Gretchen gets herself and her little brother ready for school. Even their breakfast. She makes their lunches and dinner and puts them both to bed." She whispered the last words.

No wonder she's overwhelmed. Concern for her best friend, on top of everything her own heart was going through, couldn't be good for her.

Jen's fingers vibrated. She tucked them beneath her lap blanket.

Let her talk it out. The words puffed past her thoughts.

Worry edged Ree's mouth. "But I'm not supposed to tell. You won't report it, will you? Gretchen will be really mad at me."

Flexing her fingers beneath the cover, the jitters took full purchase. "Tell me more."

"She's afraid her and Toby will get taken away from her mom. Like what happened to that boy in our class last year." She rushed on. "I haven't talked to her since last week. I'll bet her mom's all better now."

"Do you think Gretchen or Mrs. Millbrook knows about Cari?"

Ree shook her head. "I haven't been in school since she died."

"Her mother is Georgia, right?"

Ree squinted. "Yes, why?"

Scrambling for words, Jen threw out an idea. "Here's my take. When I dropped you off one time, Mrs. Millbrook mentioned she's only worked for her husband before. She's probably worried how she's going to keep a roof over their head and food on the table. Raising kids isn't cheap."

Ree strangled the pillow. "At least she *gets* to raise hers," she murmured.

Jen's stomach twisted, but she focused on the immediate problem. If Gretchen and her little brother weren't being taken care of, she needed to do something. But what? "Georgia is a good mom, and a strong lady. Here's what I'm proposing we do. First, when I get back from Bible study tonight, I'll call her."

Ree's rigid jawline marked her protest.

"Hear me out. I won't mention our conversation, unless Georgia brings it up." She made a cross over her heart. "I'll let Georgia know what happened. And tell her you miss Gretchen. We'll see if we can get you two together soon." Would she be able to discern if the Millbrook kids were being cared for? "*If* I think there's a problem, we'll plan from there."

Ree gave her a watery smile.

"You good with that?"

"You promise you won't tell anyone first? Or call Melissa?"

"I won't until after I talk to Georgia. I *can't* keep that promise if the kids are being neglected." Jen smiled, hoping to offer Ree some reassurance. "But, from what you said, she's probably coping better already."

Ree sniffed. "I do miss Gretchen."

"It's settled. We'll ask Uncle Colin what day we can get you two girls together. Maybe sometime next week."

"Uncle Colin?"

Jen swallowed hard, but noticed the thought didn't sting as much. "He's your next of kin. And along with me, for now, your legal guardian. Now that he's here, we're going to have to figure out this whole situation."

Wide eyes stared back at her.

"Let's get this Gretchen thing figured out first. Okay?"

Ree's head bobbed, and she blinked away tears. "You were going to ask a question earlier. What was it?"

"I ... It's not important."

"Ennngginne—"

Jen could almost hear Cari scolding her. "You sounded like your mom just then."

Ree smiled angelically. "Good. Now I will sound like my aunt." She sat up prim and proper and wiggled her fingers toward herself. "Out with it."

A bubble of laughter escaped Jen. "Yup. That's me." *Here goes.* "Cari told you and Auggie not to mention Dr. Brasil to me. Do you know why?"

Stillness permeated the room. She wished she could take back the ask.

Ree sat in thoughtful silence for a moment. "She said you'd say, 'I told you so.' But I think she was embarrassed."

"Why? She knew I've went to a shri ... er, psychiatrist for years. I don't understand."

"Cari thought you had all the answers."

Jen snorted. "Far from it."

"She thought so. She didn't want to disappoint you."

"I never meant to make her feel bad." Jen's shoulders sagged. "I shouldn't have gotten mad at her so much."

"Pul-ease." A snarky teenager blossomed in Ree's tone. "She needed that sometimes."

"How did you get to be so wise?"

"By watching you two."

She smiled and patted Ree's leg. "Well, my dear. I'm not sure where those boys are, but for now, let's make cookies. We'll keep some for us too. Auggie is sure to be ..."

"Starvin'."

CHAPTER 15

Jen pointed to a clump of flour. "Don't forget that bit."

Ree squished the blob into the mix with buttery fingers. Chocolate chips peeked from folds and flaps of dough.

When a knock sounded at the door, Jen peered through the peephole.

"Who's there?" she asked the swath of bright blue blinking back at her.

Giggles erupted from outside. "Engine, it's me." Auggie's muffled answer drifted back.

"I don't know anyone named me."

He huffed. "She doesn't know it's us, Collie Dog."

Whipping the door open, she caught him still squinting with one eye. "Auggie, how did you get so tall? You've never been able to see in the peephole before."

He snickered. Colin lowered him to the ground and gathered the bags at their feet.

Auggie sauntered through the doorway. "You were gonna make cookies, Engine. I don't smell no cookies."

She ignored the bad grammar. He'd obviously had a good time with his uncle. She was leaving it at that.

"Auggie, you're forgetting something out here," Colin called from the hallway.

He dashed back, picked up a bag, and rushed into the living room. "Wait 'til you see, Engine. Where's Reeree? We got some cool stuff."

His sister poked her head around the corner.

"Feeling better?" Colin walked over, leaned down, and kissed the top of her curls.

She graced him with a bright smile.

He glanced over his shoulder at Jen. "Even though I had plenty of time to pack, I still forgot a few things. Auggie assured me Central Market is the best store."

Ree laughed. "He would. They sell his favorite fortune cookies."

"So I've heard. Several times."

"Our cookies are ready to go in, Engine." Ree turned and headed to the kitchen, a girl on a mission.

Colin set his bags on the side of the island not filled with baking bowls, spoons, pans, and flour. Lots and lots of flour. Jen was a messy baker. Ree had learned well.

"The Meijer by me is bigger, but Central Market is impressive."

"I haven't seen a Meijer in ages. Not since we went up north with my dad as kids." Nostalgia colored Jen's words. "It was huge."

Colin pulled a red box of fortune cookies from his bag. "Do you have a safe spot for these?" His cheeks matched the hue of the treat's container.

"Don't worry. We've all been suckered into buying those. They're good, especially with a cup of hot tea."

"So, you're telling me you need to hide them away from *all* of us?" His eyes crinkled beneath an errant shock of hair.

Jen's stomach flip-flopped with his look. She tossed the cookies in the basket on top of her refrigerator.

Colin continued as she circled back. "I moved away before Central Market became established. That was the first time I've been there. They had everything I needed." He chuckled. "And some stuff I didn't."

"Cool stuff." Auggie bellowed.

Jen put a finger to her lips.

He lowered his voice, but not his enthusiasm. "He got a comb and some stinky stuff."

Colin held up a bottle for inspection. "Aftershave balm."

"Yeah, that. And guess what? They have pit juice. Collie Dog got me my own stick." He pulled a container of teens deodorant from the bag clutched in his hand. "I have to try this first. But when I get older, I get big juice."

Jen clapped her hands. "I haven't heard anyone call it that since ... your dad."

"Pit juice?" Ree tilted her head.

"Deodorant. Your Grandfather Marshall always called it that." A sharp edge cut through his words.

"So, if he gets big juice later, what is little juice?" Jen inquired.

"All-natural and unscented. I wasn't sure if he was allergic to anything."

A wisp of thought played for Jen's attention, but she couldn't grasp it.

"Collie Dog said it's a nestity...nesit."

"Necessity." His uncle supplied the word.

"It's important for growing boys to have pit juice." He mimicked Colin.

Jen made a mental note to check on growing girl requirements.

Colin rummaged around at the bottom of a bag. He put one hand behind his back and held the other in front of him. On his palm lay a bottle of the brightest, grapiest purple nail color, and another of bubblegum pink. "Auggie helped pick these out. Pink is Ree's favorite color. Right? And purple for Engine." He bowed and presented the gifts as if they were Cinderella's glass slippers.

Ree put her hand over her mouth and giggled.

Jen wasn't quite so ladylike, laughter burst from her. Even her heart smiled at Colin's antics. This was the boy she remembered.

"I figured you might like these as well." He winked as he presented two more bottles—a soft, cotton candy pink and a breezy, light lilac.

"Thank you, both. They're lovely." Jen planted a kiss on Auggie's forehead. He seldom tolerated smooches, except on the rare occasions he initiated it, but he accepted her appreciative affection.

Ree hugged her uncle and grabbed her brother round the neck. She waggled her eyebrows at Jen. "Aren't you going to thank Uncle Colin too?"

"I already did. But I'll say it again." She turned to her old friend. "*Merci*, kind sir. I'll enjoy wearing these."

"I mean, like Auggie, with a thank you smooch." A cheeky grin spread over her face.

"Yeah, Engine." Colin pointed to a spot on his strong jawline. "You know ... to thank me for the lovely nail polishes." His eyes twinkled.

Heat rose high on Jen's cheeks. She'd longed to show her feelings to him all those years ago, but now?

Don't be a prude. The voice chided. *They're only teasing you.*

Hush up in there.

She leaned forward and planted a light peck on Colin's scratchy cheek. His spicey aftershave lingered near her nose, setting her heart to dance a little jig.

"Oh, yuck." Auggie covered his eyes with both hands.

Ree beamed at them.

"All right, you two." Jen pointed toward the bathroom. "Wash up. Lunch and then milk and cookies while the guys tell us about their day."

The twins hightailed it out of the room, good-naturedly pushing and shoving.

Jen turned to Colin. "Are you still planning to spend the afternoon with them?"

"Sure am. You're okay with us staying here?"

"Absolutely." She reached into her junk drawer and pulled out two keys. "I had these made for you. This is to the apartment, and this one is Lilac Lane's back door. It sticks sometimes." She stumbled over her words. "Now you and the kids don't have to work around my schedule while you're here."

"Thanks. That will help." He clipped them onto his car rental ring.

"And I'll make sure Leo and the others know you're welcome here, even if I'm not home."

He appeared relieved. "Wouldn't want any of them giving me the third degree."

She sought a more comfortable subject. "When we visit your hotel, would you mind if Ree's best friend, Gretchen, comes with us?" She wouldn't break the girl's confidence until she knew more about the happenings at the Millbrook household. "Ree misses her."

"Sure." He helped wipe up the flour. "As long as you're there, I don't mind another kid along. What about Auggie?"

"He's a little short on friendships right now. Gretchen's brother can tag along, maybe. He's a little younger, but I think they've played together before." They could give Georgia a break.

193

Colin seemed intent on rubbing a spot on her counter. Emotions over the boy he was getting to know? Or remembering a childhood short on friendships due to his volatile home life?

She cleared her throat and trudged on. "They both have some games and treasures here. Don't let them railroad you into getting everything out at once." She snapped her fingers. "That reminds me. I have to pick up some things when Detective Mason takes me to their condo."

Squabbling noises sounded from the bathroom. She listened, then waved her hand in dismissal. "They'll get over it." She pulled her phone, leaned over the island, and dashed out a list.

"Can you add his happy hitter? He mentioned it today."

"Absolutely. I'd forgotten about that. That's one of his nestties." Auggie's new word tickled her funny bone. Her phone pinged, and she shoved it back into her jeans pocket. "I don't want to forget what they need, especially if we find a ..."

"A clue?" He finished for her.

The twins raced back into the kitchen, skidding across the floor in their stocking feet.

Colin gave them both a light scowl. "Whoa, you two. There's no reason to go galloping through Engine's apartment."

"Neigh-gh-gh." Auggie whinnied, prancing around the small kitchen.

Ree shook her head. "Uh-oh, now you've done it, Uncle Colin."

"Auggie. I didn't mean a real horse. Calm down." Colin frowned.

He hung his head.

"I'm not mad, bud. But you need to chill." He pointed to the cupboards. "Where are the glasses?"

Auggie bounced, pointing to the cabinet by the sink. "They're too high for me. Engine has to drink yucky milk, but we get the good stuff."

Colin pulled down the cups and turned to Jen, his eyebrows raised in question.

"Lactose free."

"Mmm-hmm." He made a face. "I'll have the good stuff too."

Jen served up lunch and listened to their chatter.

"It was fun, Engine. I can throw a Frisbee disc far."

"He's got a strong arm. We worked on accuracy with the baseball too."

"I'm not so good with that. But I can practice. Collie Dog said so. My new glove isn't like his old one."

"He means his leather isn't broken in yet."

"My baseball has little bumps from the stitches. I can hit the target sometimes. I catch better than I can throw." He stood tall. "But I'm not really good with—"

You'd be proud of your brother, Cari. He treats these two like they were his own.

A shard of hurt pierced her middle. She shoved it aside, intent on enjoying the afternoon with the Marshall trio. She'd worry about the rest later.

Jen entered Ingrid Reynold's home following the faint "come in." She followed the kitchen sounds through an arched doorway into a large eat-in.

There, bent in front of her oven, was the host for Jen's weekly Bible study. With her dark hair pulled back and big glasses encircling kind, brown eyes, she appeared as comfortable as her home.

"Please, tell me you didn't make those sinfully delicious chocolate cherry oatmeal cookies." Jen groaned.

Ingrid's smile disappeared. "I thought you liked them."

"I do, *way* too much. I think I gained three pounds from your last batch."

The smile was back. "I only made enough for two each this time."

"I can stick to that." She visually devoured the pan of cookies. "Unless someone doesn't show, then I get dibs."

"I don't know if Mary Francis is coming. I haven't heard from her in a couple days. She and Fred are traveling again." Rancher Fred McDonald's penchant for traveling had blossomed in the past six months when their son took over the couple's massive farmstead. *Old McDonald*—Mary Francis's endearment for her husband—was enjoying semi-retirement and keeping her busy crisscrossing Texas and the surrounding states. "But the others will be here. You doin' okay, darlin'?"

"With all that's happened, I feel like I can't keep my head on straight."

"Jesus understands, I assure you." Ingrid patted her shoulder. "You wanna talk?"

Ingrid was the only one of the group Cari had meshed with. According to the model, Ingrid "was solid," which may have been why she'd asked her to join the scholarship committee.

"There's not much I can say yet. Everything's still under investigation. All I know at this point is Auggie has been officially cleared."

"What a relief. I couldn't believe they honestly thought that sweet baby could hurt anybody, let alone his own momma."

"I guess it was purely protocol. They're thorough, so no stones left unturned is my guess." Jen shrugged. "I'll let you know more when I can."

"You know where to find me." Ingrid handed the cookie plate to Jen. "I'll get the coffee and tea if you'll take these to the dining room. No snitching."

"As if." Jen placed the forbidden cookie back on the edge of the plate. She'd have to remember which one she'd touched.

The front door opened after a quick rat-a-tat. "Yoo-hoo." Mary Francis walked in. As usual, her outfit was adorable and fashion forward. Chocolate brown leggings tucked into knee-high suede boots and a woolly sweater peeked artfully from under a puffy fall vest. Her flaming orange pixie haircut topped the ensemble and made her look like a gamine elf ready to wreak fun on the party. Mary Francis, a retired schoolteacher and older than all of them, appeared ageless.

"Hello, hello." She called. "Sorry I didn't let you know I was coming. I made Fred rush back so I could be here. You know how slow that man drives. Actually, you probably don't. But let me tell you, if he has a mind to, he could make Grandma Grunt look like a race car driver. Wonderful traveling companion but ..." Her chatter continued while she kicked off her boots. She turned to Jen. "Whatever's the matter, dear?"

"Nothing. Why?"

"You're staring."

"I didn't mean to."

"I thought I was wearing half my lunch or something." She craned her neck to search her backside. "I'm not, am I?"

"You look perfectly lovely, as always. It's just ... is that a new sweater? The design is so unusual." And unsettling.

The pullover was a beautiful chocolate brown confection topped by a swirl of pumpkin orange and sage green dots. "It's from a new boutique in Waco. Fred said if it was yellow and white it would look like over-easy eggs. Aren't the colors gorgeous? I didn't end up buying it, but I guess I wouldn't shut up about it because he went back and got it for me."

Mary Francis was well-known for her lively prattle whenever she walked into a room. She was celebrated even more for being the first to lend a hand when needed.

"My dear, I was so sad to hear about Cari. Bless her heart." Mary Francis hugged her. "Ingrid filled me in. I didn't feel it appropriate to ask you about it over the phone. Are you okay? How are the twins? And where are they?"

As the explanations started, the others arrived. All was stalled for greetings and warm hugs, followed by a tear or two, memories of the late, great Cari, and commiseration over the whole ordeal. A bit of Bible study was even thrown into the mix.

Jen left Ingrid's more relaxed than she'd been in days. The women's friendship, along with their journey together through the Good Book, had always revived her spirits. Tonight was no exception.

Returning home, she fixed a light dinner for her little troupe. The jovial atmosphere of the afternoon had somehow turned somber. The twins picked at their salads and poked their baked potatoes.

Tiredness pulled at the corners of Colin's eyes, and he begged off dessert. "I'm sorry. I know you've been going all day. I don't know how you and Cari kept up with these monkeys. I'm beat. If you don't mind, I'm going to go and turn in early."

She smiled. "I'm sure you're exhausted. They're not used to having your undivided attention."

After he hugged the twins, she walked him to the door, stepping over car tracks and books. "Looks like everyone had a good time, though."

"It was fun. There were a couple moments of tears when Cari's name came up. But we got through them. Are you sure you don't want my help cleaning up?"

"Positive. Thanks for everything. I needed my Bible study friends to recharge my soul." She was too tired to even try interpreting the odd look he gave her. "Tomorrow morning? You're sure you don't have to work?"

"Go into the showroom for a while. The small amount I'm doing this week is keeping me in good standing at the office. They weren't expecting anything."

She gave him a quick hug. "Sleep well." What more could she say to this man who was a welcome piece of her past, a partner of hope in the present, but embodied more than one question mark for her future? She shut her door on all the uncertainty.

With the twins watching a movie, it was time to call Georgia Millbrook. Jen moved to her bedroom for privacy.

After three rings, a young, female voice answered. "Hello. Millbrook residence."

A child answering the phone, hmmm. "Is this Gretchen?"

"May I ask who this is?"

Good girl. Let the caller identify themselves first. "This is Jennifer Clark, January Marshall's aunt."

There was a pause. "Oh, you mean Ree. Is she okay? She wasn't in school all week." Her concern pulsed through the line.

It was clear she hadn't heard about Cari. "She's all right, sweetie. Is your mom there?"

"Hold on, please. I'll get her."

Moments later, the line was active again. "Hello, Miss Clark. This is Georgia. What can I do for you?" Her words dripped, thick and sweet as Texas honey.

"Please, it's Jennifer, or Jen. I'm calling because ... well, I need to let you know about Ree's mom."

"Is she ill? If you're calling, it must be serious. Is she in the hospital? Do y'all need help getting the kids back and forth to school?"

Offering her assistance. Good. "I'm not quite sure how to tell you this, but ... Cari was killed earlier this week."

Georgia gasped. "Was it a car accident?"

How far do I go here, Lord? Peace washed through the truth. "She was murdered."

Georgia inhaled sharply. "Are the kids okay? Do they need someplace to stay for a while? I might could find room here for a bit. How are y'all holding up?"

Jen explained what little she could about Colin and why Ree wasn't in school.

"Can't say I blame you. I wouldn't let mine out of my sight if something like that happened. It's been hard enough this past month."

Lord Jesus, guide my words. Don't let me betray Ree's confidence. "Oh? Now I guess it's my turn to ask if everything is okay there."

"Better now. My husband left a few weeks ago. At first, he was threatening to take Gretchen and Toby away, but we got that little issue squared away right quick." Her sarcasm was palpable.

"I'm sad to hear about your parting. But it's good you're able to work together."

"Together?" Georgia grunted. "I wouldn't go that far. I was a mess for a couple of weeks, but I'm getting through it. Bennett and I had a come-to-Jesus moment, so to speak. No one will be taking my kids from me."

Georgia's tone wove a cable of determination through the phone lines, lodging with certainty in Jen's ear. The

Millbrook family would be fine, at least the part she was concerned with.

"But enough about that nonsense. How's Ree? And Auggie? Poor babies. Gretchen was worried, but with everything going on here, I didn't even think of calling Caribbean."

"We're taking it one day at a time." Jen appreciated the woman's concern. "For now, you can call my cell if Gretchen wants to talk to Ree. I gave you my card last time I dropped her off, didn't I?"

"I think so. But I'll have to look for it. To be frank, I hid it. Defense mechanism, I guess. I'm fixin' to go find it when we hang up."

"I can give you my number again. But I don't understand."

Georgia cleared her throat. "Honestly? You're living my dream." A fragile laugh escaped her. "I was attending university for fashion merchandising when I met my husband. According to Bennett, his endodontist career was far more important than me playin' dress-up dolls." She made a rude noise. "Lord knows, his everything was more important."

Jen almost snorted at the derision reaching her ears. Georgia seemed to be slicing through the stages of grief at a decent clip.

Fashion Merchandising. A thought bubbled at the back of her brain.

"I apologize, Jen. I went on a tangent there again. Please continue."

"I was hoping we could get the girls together. And Toby, too, if he'd like to come along?"

"Um ... I—"

"It's okay. Maybe just the girls."

"No, I'm not being clear. Toby has no problems playing with Auggie. They've chummed together with the girls a few times. But to be honest, I'd rather ... how do I put this delicately? I'd rather my kids not be around there until you know who did this to Caribbean. Ree and Auggie are welcome here if you want. A few weeks back, maybe not." Georgia grunted. "I couldn't put one foot in front of the other and take care of my own kids, let alone someone else's. But we're good now. I can come get them next week."

A momentary panic fluttered in Jen's chest. "I'm not able to do that yet. Surveillance and all." The fib didn't sit well, but she really couldn't be without the kids—police orders or not.

"Sure. How about this ... when things get back to normal ... well, you know what I mean ... in a couple of weeks, why don't we all get together? Maybe pizza, or a movie out. Something easy. A moment, please."

There was a rustle from the other end of the phone. Georgia's muffled voice floated through the earpiece.

"Toby, what have I told you, young man? Gentlemen do not blow spit balls at their sister's boots. Yes, I know they fly through the straw really awesome. You're fixin' to get your butt dusted if you don't knock it off." Georgia came back on the line. "Sorry, Jen. We're going through some attitude adjustments here. Anyway, their uncle can come too, if y'all want. I'm sure he's eager to spend as much time with them as he can before he goes back home."

It was sweet of Georgia to assume the twins would remain with her. "Sounds like a plan."

"We'll wait on your call. I'll be easiest to reach in the evenings. I'm ... I've started job skill training while the kids are in school." Her voice cracked. "Being a dedicated wife and mother might give you great nurturing skills, but it doesn't translate well to a résumé. And running Bennett's *oweffice* finances from home—" her accent kicked in heavier. "Yeah, his halfhearted recommendation isn't being taken serious by any employers yet."

"What are you looking for? Are you going through an agency?"

"Thankfully, the church I attend works with the Dallas Christian Women's Job Corp." A thread of hopefulness permeated the woman's voice. "I'm after something that will work around my kids' schedules."

DCWJC? Good to know. She'd check Georgia's credentials. But the earlier bubble of thought became a full soda. The woman could be an answer to prayer.

A young girl's angry cry trampled her eardrum.

"I apologize Jen, I need to go. My young'uns need feeding and put to bed. Too much of each other's company today. We'll be in touch soon."

Thankfully, she could relieve a bit of worry from Ree's shoulders. The Millbrook household would be fine. But would their own?

That remained to be seen.

The evening routine of showers and snacks was over. Jen snuggled in the oversized chair in her room, curls still damp where they lay against her cheek. Her worn leather Bible waited patiently in her lap. She listened to the hushed tones from the room next to hers. The twins' usual pattern of chatting and drifting off to sleep after story time commenced.

Planning to catch up with her Bible study work, she opened the cover, but the gentle influence of the book of Psalms beckoned. Leafing through the pages, she stopped on chapter 34. A phrase near the beginning caught her attention anew. "I sought the Lord, and he answered me; he delivered me from all my fears."

Father God, please guide us as we go forward without Cari. Allow the kids to always remember the fierce love she had for them. Settle my fears ... whatever happens.

The lack of noise from next door signified blessed sleep. They needed it. Now, if she could only shut down her own brain. Her mind wandered further afield, to time spent with Cari and the twins over the years. Bowling with big kid bumpers, impromptu dinners on the weekends, and traipsing through the many museums of the Metroplex. Time stood still for those few moments. So engrossed in the memories, she startled at a light tapping on her door.

"Engine?" Ree peeked in.

Jen waved her forward. "I thought you'd be asleep by now."

The girl shuffled over, attached by a handhold to her twin.

"What can I do for you?"

"Would you pray with us?"

Auggie pointed to the book lying in Jen's lap. "And read something?"

"Of course. Is there anything specific you want to pray about?"

Auggie elbowed his sister.

Ree nodded then looked at Jen. "Is it okay to ask him for something?"

"You mean ask God for things? I think it is. But remember, like we've talked before, he may not answer our prayers the way we want. Especially when we ask him for stuff." She glanced from one sweet face to the other.

"I'm scared," Auggie confessed. "I don't want to be afraid."

Understanding dawned. "Come on over here." She scooted to the middle of the oversized chair. The twins climbed up, one on each side, in a tight but welcomed squeeze. Bowing her head, she reached for their hands.

"Father, we thank you for this time of seeking you and the comfort and safety of your presence. We come to you in prayer because we're floundering. Frankly, Lord, the three of us are scared silly." She peeped through her lashes to see if she was on the right track. Both nodded, eyes squeezed shut. "We need your guidance and protection and ask for peace for our hearts and minds."

Ree pressed her hand.

"Father, cover Auggie with your strength. And allow them both to discern the truth. In the name of your Son, Jesus Christ, we pray."

Their young voices chimed in, "Amen." They relaxed, but neither moved.

"What does dis ... dis—?" Ree frowned.

"Discern? It means to discover, or to ... notice. Like Sherlock Holmes. He detected things and discerned the truth."

"With his magnifying glass?" Auggie made the motions of looking through a lens.

"Something like that."

Ree pointed to the Bible. "What were you reading?"

"The book of Psalms. I often study it when I'm troubled. It's very comforting to me." She opened her Bible to the same spot and continued through the verses, this time out loud. "'Taste and see that the Lord is good; blessed is the one who takes refuge in him.'"

Refuge. The three of them—no, four—she would include Colin in the count whether he wanted it or not, needed God's refuge. She snuggled the twins close. All arms and legs, bony elbows, and jutting knees, she gained comfort from their nearness.

Tomorrow could take care of itself.

CHAPTER 16

Monday brought a reset to the long, stressful weekend. Time for Jen to enjoy a cuppa and a few minutes of quiet before she and the twins started their day.

Her thoughts turned to Colin and the planned outing at the zoo. A morning with the animals sounded way more fun than her scheduled bookwork.

She scribbled notes on her bedside pad of paper. Figure out how to get Ree's satchel from Ethan and let Richard know Auggie requested his help. Not one to put his creations to paper, the boy had an idea for a mic box stuck in his head. "So we don't have any more vlanalism."

Wishing her nine-year-olds didn't know what vandalism was wouldn't make it go away. Her heart swelled that he'd chosen to fix the problem, instead of wallowing in worry over it, like she'd been doing.

Harold had conducted a full inventory, as requested, and called with a list of other damaged equipment, including one of Lilac's best industrial overlock sewing machines. How they would keep production flowing without it was a mystery, but she wasn't going to rush a new purchase. Insurance would cover much of the cost, but it had to feel right.

Thankfully, her personal machines were still in their cabinet here at home. She opened her closet doors and wheeled the console out into her bedroom. The serger it housed was only a few years old, but the other apparatus, a hefty metal Singer, had served her well through university, including those first designs for Cari. It was still going strong.

She opened her doors wider and pulled two garment bags forward. The secret projects, hidden from a certain nine-year-old designer. Pulling out the dresses, she examined each with a critical eye.

The showstopper was a slinky, bright white silk charmeuse ending in a trumpet-style skirt with a tulle underlay. The bodice of the gown, liberally sprinkled with embroidered polka-dots and clear sequins, shimmered in the light. The wide, minimally capped, sleeveless straps dipped in a graceful arc to create an elegant sweetheart neckline. Ree's artistic design, though inexperienced, required only minor adjustments.

The other dress was a perfect puffery of dotted Swiss cotton. Ladylike and adorable, the outfit would beautifully fit the young designer, dreaming away in the next room.

Cari had been so excited to bring Ree on stage with her. The surprise didn't seem appropriate without her. Another topic on her list to consult with Colin and her parents about. Jen shoved the garments to the back of the closet and closed the doors on any immediate decision.

But she couldn't shut out plans for the charity show as easily. Being the main fundraiser for Cari's scholarships, a determination was needed soon. Maybe the others would have some ideas. She'd have to dig out her old mic, find a new venue, send updated invitations ... *Whoa, Jen. Slow down*. One step at a time.

She headed for her kitchen and the coffeemaker. One. Two. Three. Four. And an extra half scoop for the perfect pot. Her nerves didn't need a full carafe, but the rest would go in the freezer for iced lattes later.

Cari's wrinkled nose passed through her thoughts. "I don't know how you stand drinking that stuff. It's so bitter." Patting the top of Jen's head, she'd add, "And it's probably what stunted your growth."

She chuckled at the memory. While the coffee maker gurgled and burped, she'd run down to retrieve her mail. Her Dallas Stars jersey and matching lounge pants were presentable enough.

A quick scan in her hall mirror confirmed no latent makeup, in case she ran into anyone besides Leo or one of the other Sheffield Apartment's attendants. She could resemble a racoon, and they would still treat her like a queen.

She checked on the kids and wrote a quick note in case they woke up, making sure to print her letters. Although Auggie's reading had improved, he still took issue with cursive. She snickered, remembering his recent assessment of her writing. "Sorry, Engine. I like Cari's words better. Yours make my brain itch." She had to admit her own flowery, artistic penmanship could be a bit over the top.

Snatching her keys and phone, she locked the apartment door and hit the elevator's down button for the mailroom, next to the main entrance.

Eight. Seven. The elevator slid past the various floors. Four. The wood paneled car slowed, coming to a halt on level three. Crud. Who would she be embarrassed in front of? Maybe Mr. Harper. He thought she was cute even when she was all sweaty after a good run. Her lips twitched into a grin at the thought of the dapper octogenarian and his flirty winks as the doors whooshed open. Her smile slipped. Definitely not Mr. Harper.

"Hello, Jennifer." Ned Bass gave her a quick wave.

"Hey. How's it going?"

"Good. Good. Enjoying a day off." He ducked his head and entered the car. "Running errands?"

"Getting my mail. It's probably chock full. I haven't picked it up for a couple days." Did he turn sheet white? With his light complexion, it was hard to tell.

"Um. Yeah. I'm sorry to hear about ... your friend."

"Thanks. I suppose the news is all over the building. Cari knew almost everyone."

He refused to make eye contact. "We all liked her. She was great to wo—um—get to know." His cheeks turned scarlet.

Odd. Cari had never mentioned him much, except to call him Nedward in her best snark. The elevator resumed its descent. "Did you know her from somewhere besides here?"

He shook his head so hard he had to right his retro specs. Another unsuccessful attempt at fashion.

The guy had moved in months earlier. Over the following weeks, her good manners warred with her fashion sense each time he'd braved her opinion about style. She admired his pocket watch, even though it didn't seem to work. She tried to be nice about his black and white wingtip shoes, too-short suits, and crazy socks. The last time she saw him—a blustery day around Halloween—she caught a glimpse of his hazel eyes, usually shrouded by dark-rimmed glasses, when the wind blew his brown-sugared locks off his forehead. She remarked how nice his hair looked, smoothed away from his face. He immediately brushed his bangs down flat against his forehead and shoved the glasses back on. He whipped away from her faster than she could say "you look like—"

She tuned back into his words.

"I might have heard of her death someplace else." He stood tight against the elevator wall. "I'm not around here much. I work a lot of hours."

"Where are you employed, Ned?"

"Um. I, uh, well ... I travel a lot. With a design firm." Ned swiped his hand down his highwater pants. The elevator dinged at ground level and the doors whooshed open. "Gotta go, bye."

"What—" She hurried after him, but he rushed out of the building.

Leo stood out front, hailing a taxi for a resident. He frowned when Ned pushed past him and nearly tangled with the Sheffield's dog walker and her four-legged charges. Entering the complex's foyer, he glanced outside. "That young man sure is an odd one."

"What's your take on him?" Jen fiddled with her mailbox key. "He's not very talkative."

Leo resettled his doorman's cap at a jaunty angle and shrugged. "It's more his mannerisms, like he's uncomfortable in his own skin. He skulks around here, waiting on something, then barrels out. Odd hours too, sometimes gone for weeks at a time."

"He did say he travels a lot for work."

"Well, to each his own. And he doesn't seem to bother anyone—" He peered at her meaningfully over his spectacles.

"No. He actually avoids me at all costs these days."

"Well, if he, or anyone else, troubles you, holler for us. We'll take care of it, or we can get the police here in a jiffy." It didn't take a rocket scientist to know why police were on his mind.

"So, they've been to see you already. About Cari? Or me?"

"Yes. And yes."

His slouch was so uncharacteristic of the proper gentleman, Jen's heart ached for him. She couldn't think of anyone at her complex who hadn't appreciated Cari's vibrant personality.

"I'm sorry all this questioning has upset everyone."

"Can't be helped. We want you and them young'uns safe."

"Thanks for thinking of us. I'll tell them you said hello. And speaking of them, I'd better get back upstairs."

He rolled a newspaper with his special tuck and handed it to her with a brisk nod.

Stepping into the mail alcove, she shoved her key into her box. The latch caught on the catalogs, fliers, and other mail jammed inside. With an armload, she waved goodbye to Leo and turned back toward the elevators.

When she returned to her own floor, the doors whisked open, giving her a full view of the apartment entrances, with hers halfway down the hall. Her heart leaped into her throat.

A bright red paper lay on the carpet in front of her door, shoved halfway underneath. Had someone tried to entice the kids out?

She pulled her phone from her pocket to call the police and dashed forward. Glancing down the hall for the intruder, she bent to pick up...

Good grief. A housewarming invitation for a new tenant.

Instead of their security detail, she phoned the doorman's kiosk. "Hi, Leo." Her tone sounded breathy and laborious.

"Did you forget something my dear?"

"I don't want to be nitpicky here, but could you mention to our new residents in ..." She consulted the flyer. "6G, that all correspondence is to go through the building's email or our mailboxes, *not* shoved under doors." *Calm down.*

"I certainly will." His tone was gruff. He paused. "Seems they've not cleared an event with our schedule, either. Looks like they'll be getting a little reminder session from the office. Are you okay?"

"Yes, it just gave me a momentary start." She rang off after a final goodbye.

Letting herself into the apartment, Jen threw the pile of mail on the kitchen island, sending envelopes and magazines flying.

The twins' door was still shut, the room behind it silent. She set her phone alarm as a reminder to wake them in an hour. Muffins and fruit would be breakfast, but first, coffee for her. Pouring a cup, she generously laced the hot liquid with hazelnut creamer and turned to the island. Spying the latest issue of *Silhouette*, she pulled the pile closer to reach it and made a mental note to opt out of so much junk mail.

She'd almost missed a bill last week, scuttled between papers advertising fresh steaks, cheap milk, and winter snow tires—in Texas. She shoved the stack of bothersome papers aside and opened the magazine. A longtime subscriber, she loved the smell of the fresh ink and the first crinkle of the fine, glossy pages.

The March issue did not disappoint. The sleek photos and tasteful ads were as classy as ever. She never inspected the cover, or article highlights until she'd thumbed through the magazine at least once. Seeing photos of her own designs or those of colleagues, as well as models she knew, was enjoyable. But most often, the layouts were a complete surprise. Eye candy for a creator.

She flipped through the articles, admiring the new line of a rival stylist, and planned a visit to an art gallery recommended by the editor.

Her alarm beeped. Time to wake the twins.

Five more minutes, her inner fashionista cajoled. Obliging the whim, she flipped to the middle, flattening the center spread. And choked on her coffee.

There, splayed across the middle of the magazine was a two-page layout of Cari. She was draped luxuriously over an antique fainting couch and adorned in a flowing, sea green gown Jen had recently made for her. She vaguely remembered the conversation.

"I've got a modeling gig, a photo shoot, and a party afterward. Can you design something stunning for me? This is a big deal."

Jen had thought little of the statement. Many of Cari's jobs outside of Lilac were notable and tended to bring in more business for their showroom. But a main spread in Silhouette—their favorite magazine—why hadn't she said anything?

The cutline answered her question. "Gown designed by Jennifer Clark, founder of Lilac Lane Fashion Studio and business partner of Caribbean Marshall." The copy near the photo was a pull quote from the article. "This is a surprise for her. We're celebrating our ten-year anniversary as partners soon."

Jen sucked in a breath. Ten years? She ran through the numbers in her head. She'd been making clothes for both of them for ages, but Cari was right. Twelve years ago, when they were seventeen, she'd asked her tall, beautiful foster sister to model her designs for a semi-professional show. Twenty-four months later, although Lilac was still a couple years in the making, Jen graduated and the two teamed up to rule the runway, even after Cari had become pregnant with the twins.

Jen raked through the magazine spread, careful of the papery preciousness, and found Cari on four more pages throughout the monthly.

There was a beautiful photo of her sunning herself on a boulder near a large body of water. Her happy place. The accompanying story discussed Cari's longevity in the industry, the scholarships she'd started at Wells-Myer, being a mother and how proud she was of her kids—although she didn't divulge much information—and how she'd gotten her start. She praised her bestie for shepherding her into modeling and choosing her as the lead for Lilac Lane Fashion.

Shepherding you, Cari? I shoved you into it. If she'd let her friend be the teacher she wanted to become when they were growing up—guiding kids, instead of her photo adorning adolescent teens walls—would she still be alive?

She hugged the magazine to her chest, knocking several other pieces of mail to the floor. She didn't dare take the time to read more of the article or she'd be a blubbering mess. She needed to hide it away from young, inquisitive eyes for the time being.

Silhouette was one of Ree's go-to mags for inspiration and industry news even a nine-year-old could enjoy. This would not be the best time to stumble on photos of her mother without warning.

One last look. She pulled the thick magazine away from her and spread it on the counter, flipping to the last pages of the article. The montage was of Cari and other female models, along with one lone male figure. Only his profile showed, but she could tell he was quite handsome. One photo caught her eye. In it, Cari peeked over his shoulder with her hands splayed possessively across his back muscles. Rachel was right. Cari did indeed know Edward Baas. Currently, the highest-ranking male model in the industry. He reminded her so much of—

Crunch. The telltale snap of plastic cracking sounded beneath her foot. Bending, she picked up a mangled envelope lodged between two fliers.

She pulled the damaged packet from the rest. Black smudges skidded across the back. One corner was ripped, but the rest appeared intact. The envelope bore the signs of a fight with a mechanical postal sorter. Turning it over, her heart lodged in her throat. Return address: Caribbean Marshall.

Stamped across the top in red letters was the message, *Damaged in Transit.* The cancellation date verified its mailing on the same day as the letter. Not only damaged but delayed. Here was the other item Cari had mentioned.

Yanking on the silverware drawer, Jen grabbed a table knife, pried up the defective corner, and pulled out a plastic CD case. Cracked. Inside, a photo with a sticky note that read, "Received this in the mail yesterday. Sending for safe keeping."

She recognized the photograph as one taken when she and Cari had attended an elite black-tie gala some two months back. The two of them were laughing at something off-camera. Cari had her hand on Jen's shoulder ... or would have if the other half—the one where Jen stood—wasn't missing. The deliberate tear severed the two friends.

On the back was scrawled, "It's my turn."

She couldn't get enough air. Her lungs spasmed. *Not now. I can't—*

Her insides jellied, shaking worse than her hands. The gray-and-black marble counter turned monstrously dark and pulsated.

Breathe. The voice counseled.

Are you real? Am I losing my ever-loving mind?

A ragged breath wheezed from her lungs. Pain radiated through her chest. She turned her back to the island and slid to the floor. Experience had taught her it was better to sit than wake in a heap. Pin-prickles of light sailed before her.

A door opening sounded from somewhere far, far away.

Her pulse galloped. *Please don't let them find me here. Not like this.*

She gulped mouthfuls of air. *One*—calm. Finger touch. Black dots exploded in her vision. Old images of chaos and anxiety taunted the edges of her consciousness. Threads of remedies floated and popped through her memory.

The toilet flushed in the hallway bathroom. Water running. Then muffled grumbling reached her ears.

"I don't wanna get dressed, Ree. I'm hungry. I'm gonna find Engine." He stomped from the bedroom.

Relax. The voice coached. *You know what to do.*

She inched the lower drawer of the island open. Trembling, her fingers dug for a paper sack. Curling the edges of the bag, she managed to take a shallow gulp of air.

"Auggie, you get back here right now." Ree's mom-voice squawked. "Stop. I don't want to pillow fight. You have to make your bed before breakfast. You know the rules."

The pain in her chest finally lapsed enough to allow a nugget of air in her lungs. With Herculean effort, she pushed it back into the sack.

Is that how she sounded to them? All rules and regulations? So be it for now. Stick to those decrees a few more minutes, please.

She took even, slow breaths. *One. Two.* She didn't bother with her finger touches. Instead, a Bible verse came to mind. 1 Peter 5:7 from her beloved NIV, but the particulars bobbed from her grasp. Mom had suggested the comforting words after Jen's first major episode. Why hadn't she kept it at hand? *I need your help, Jesus.*

Peeking through squinted lids, the room stayed blessedly still. She twisted toward the island and pushed herself up. Needing a moment, she leaned over the cool marble and laid her head on top of her arms. At least if the twins found her, she could feign a headache. *Whew! Too close for comfort.*

"There." Auggie groused. "I'm done. I'm gonna make Engine fix me some eggs."

"August Isaiah. You have to ask. You can't make her."

"I know, Jan-you-air-REE."

A chaotic laugh escaped Jen's lips. Taking a deep breath, she stood. Shaky, but good enough. She retrieved the threatening photo by the corners—realizing she probably shouldn't have touched it at all. She shoved it along with the cracked case, envelope, and the Silhouette magazine into a bag. She couldn't have the kids finding these. She tossed them in the basket on top of her fridge, right beside Auggie's fortune cookies.

She moved gingerly around the kitchen, setting out the kids' favorite cereal, along with milk, bread, apples, and oranges. Digging the toaster from the appliance garage, she glanced at her reflection. Her pupils were enormous.

Auggie bounded into the kitchen. "What's for breakfast?"

She busied herself at the stove. Buy some time. Cook something. "Good morning to you too. One or two eggs?"

"Two, please. I'm starvin'."

"Where's Ree?"

"Brushin' her teeth."

"Did you do yours?"

"'Course I did."

"Auuugggie?"

"Oookkkay. I'll go."

Ree padded into the kitchen. "That's a lot of food, Engine."

Jen eyed the spread she'd doled out in her haste.

"You might be right. We'll do the best we can."

That's all you expect any of us to do, isn't it, Lord?

CHAPTER 17

Pacing the length of her living room, Jen ticked down through her list of to-dos. Call Melissa for morning report—check. Anxiety attack from earlier under control—ditto. Security escorts in place—check. Their captain must have really admired Cari. Was the extra policing detail available for others? Doubtful, but she honestly had no idea.

She continued her mental inventory. Phone call to her parents—she'd left a message. Dishwasher started. Hair done. Makeup on. Check, check, and check.

After admitting to Colin about Ethan rescuing them from Motorcycle Man, and Ree's frenetic drawing on Friday, the two had agreed the twins needed some fun and a break from the stress of the showroom. Lions, tigers, monkeys, and bears at the Dallas Zoo won their vote. Getting them ready required a flurry of details, including the detective's approval.

"Do you have any disposable cameras, Engine?" Ree was the only one Jen had ever seen who could coax artistically unique photos from one of those throwaway things. She dug one from a box of show extras and Ree stashed it in her pink drawstring backpack.

After asking for permission, Auggie jingled coins from her change jar. He squared his shoulders. "I want to feed the lambs in the petting zoo." The slobbery mouths usually made him squeamish. Bravery was easier with a tall uncle by your side. "We haven't seen the aminals since we went there with Cari." He stopped short, seeming to remember the past few days. Tears sprang to Ree's eyes, and Colin gathered them both in his arms.

"I've gotta get something from my bedroom." Jen spun toward her sanctuary. She didn't have a clue what she needed but chose to give that time to the Marshall trio.

Once Colin and the kids were gone, Jen grabbed her favorite loafers. She couldn't spare the time for the two-mile trek to work, no matter how much she craved the fresh air. Not to mention a certain security detail trying to follow her in Dallas traffic. She headed out the door, not looking forward to the dreaded bookwork.

To take her mind off the future, she drove by Ethan's job site. She liked how the clean lines blended with the skyline, but she had to agree with her friend, the high rise did seem a bit boring. Colin would have designed better. She made a mental note to connect the two guys. The power of community networking could never be discounted.

Traffic prohibited little more than a glance at the project. She didn't recognize any of the workers milling around. She'd have to figure out how to get Ree's satchel another way.

Nearing Lilac's back parking lot, Jen turned on her blinker. Friday's fiasco raced through her thoughts again. Had that only been three days ago? Nerves skittered up her arms. She made a quick circle around the block, parking in front of the worn, but cheery building.

She glanced at the grimy facade next door and wrinkled her nose. If Ethan's suspicions about his current boss were true, and the guy was indeed the owner next door, what did that mean for Annie and the rest of them? No time for that now.

An hour later than her normal arrival, she hurried from her car. Richard's cryptic text saying he needed to talk to her—it was important—was concerning. She hadn't noticed his car in the parking lot when she'd circled, only Daphne's jalopy. Strange.

The front doors of Lilac were already unbolted. She yanked them open and was met with a blast of chilly air. "What in the world? It must be fifty degrees in here." She reached over to flick on the overheads. Nothing. *Not again.*

Digging her phone from her purse, she touched the flashlight app, illuminating a small swath of floor in front of her. Voices reached her from backstage. She took a step farther into the showroom but thought better of it. "Hello? Who's here?"

A flashlight beam waved in her eyes.

She blinked against the glare. "Can you get that out of my face?"

"Sorry." The shaft of light was lowered. "I didn't expect you to come this way." Daphne rushed to hug her.

Jen stiffened but forced her shoulders to relax from the unexpected affection.

"I'm so glad you're here. It's terrible. There's no air." Daphne took a quick, shallow breath, as if to prove her point. "Well, there's air. But it's cold. There's no lights. Plus, the backroom reeks."

"Like what? It's not gas, is it?" She thought of the older water heater.

"It smells like the stuff my dad used to spray so the deer didn't catch his scent. Pheromones or something."

"Wonderful." She pinched the bridge of her nose, hoping to stave off the headache scratching behind her eyes. "Did anyone call Eagle Electric?"

"I got here right after Richard. I think he called. He's getting more flashlights from Harold's closet. We heard you call out. I came to see if you needed help." Daphne reached into a deep pocket of her sweater and pulled out a penlight.

Heavy footsteps thudded down the hallway leading from backstage.

"Who else is in? Besides you and Richard?" The sound tech most often wore loafers or sneakers.

"No one. Why?" Daphne gave her a quizzical look.

Another beam of light bounced around, ahead of the clonking boots, but it didn't blind her as it came down the hall ahead of ...

"Ouch." Thud. "Oh, crud."

A motorcycle helmet rolled around the corner.

She stiffened.

"What is it? You're frightened." Daphne's voice rose. She pointed her light in Jen's face again. "Do you want me to call that nice young man, Colin? Or the police?" Her free hand fluttered around her throat.

"Relax, Daphne." A distinct voice reached them. "Jen's not used to seeing me in my motorcycle gear." The unfamiliar figure appeared and picked up his helmet, scanning it under the glow from his light. "Good. This thing was expensive. Glad my new GoPro wasn't on it yet."

Jen's breath whooshed out of her. Richard? Motorcycle? She recognized his jacket as the same from Friday night. Where was the next hole she could crawl into?

Richard focused on the intern. "Daphne, the electric and H-Vac guys are here. Can you see if they need anything? Hold the flashlight or something?"

"Um. Yeah. Sure. I guess." She sulked toward the backroom.

Jen fisted her hip. "You? You were on the bike last week?" Her voice grated.

"I forgot you didn't know I have a motorcycle. I was out enjoying the great weather."

"Why didn't you take the helmet off while you were sitting there?"

"Helmet? No wonder why you seemed so rattled." He unzipped his jacket. "While I waited for you to come out, I was messing with my traffic cam. It's on the fritz."

"Waiting? You could have come back in the showroom."

He made a face. "We need to talk. I don't want the rest of the crew to know about it yet. Not until you do."

That didn't sound promising.

"I debated back and forth whether to talk to you Friday or not. I figured it could wait. I was getting ready to leave when the three of you came out."

The lights flickered once. Twice. Then remained steady.

She blew into her cupped hands. "Let's get this temperature up, then I'll meet you in my office." He had some explaining to do.

Walking side-by-side down the hallway, she reached up and poked him in the shoulder. "You scared the crud out of me."

His grimace spoke volumes.

Thirty minutes later, Harold and their heating expert found the culprit of the icy air. A mix up with the thermostat and blocked air intakes. A discussion of storage and safety protocols was in order with her crew.

Harold walked from her office grumbling about locks, new keys, and everyone needing to leave the boss alone. Pulling her jacket tighter around her, she agreed. She smiled at the old curmudgeon's back. He was nearing retirement, by his choice, and she was going to miss him. He was a gruff but loveable grandpa to all of them.

Richard stuck his head around the door. "Everything okay in here?"

"Yes. Why wouldn't it be?"

"Well ... you know. I ... um, I thought you might still be mad at me."

"I'm embarrassed more than anything. It sounds like an honest mistake on your part and a huge overreaction on mine." She waved him in.

Richard closed the door and took the chair across from her desk. "You've got every right to be spooked."

"Can we not discuss that right now? I'm kind of on a tight timeline. What did you need to see me about?"

"It can wait." He leaned forward, making ready his escape.

"I'd rather we get this out in the open. Colin won't be here with the kids for at least another hour."

"That's right." He shifted positions. "The uncle came in Friday night. How are the kids adjusting to him? Is he good with Auggie?"

"You're not getting out of it that easy. Spill."

A bead of moisture trickled down his hairline, and he rubbed his hands on his jeans.

She sat back in her chair and waited, letting the space stretch between them. He wasn't going to quit, was he?

"I ... I knew Cari."

"Of course, you did."

"No, I mean, I knew of her before I started working here. My best friend—" His Adam's apple bobbed. "Let me start over. First of all, I took this job under false pretenses. I don't need to work at Lilac."

Not what she expected. He was always there. "Go on."

"I'm surprised those detectives haven't already told you. I own Keane Intelliware."

"Get serious. Even I know that company." She narrowed her eyes to slits. "Then why would you accept this job? There's no way I could pay high enough wages."

"I didn't take it for the money. I took it to watch over Ree and Auggie."

She shot from her chair and loomed over her desk, her voice a low growl. "You what?"

Richard put his hands up as if to stave off danger. "Please, hear me out."

"Make it quick. Before I call the police." She clenched her cell, sitting at the edge of her chair.

"My best friend is August Guildane."

The one Cari referred to as her "other" August?

"He asked me to keep an eye on the kids for a few months. He was worried about them. I'm not sure why. He's been pretty closed mouth about it all."

"You're talking in the past tense. Did something happen to him?"

Richard shook his head. "August has been in a wheelchair for over ten years after a bad accident. He went overseas in February to try some experimental treatments. Mr. and Mrs. Guildane think he's traveling. They aren't aware of the twins. *I* didn't even know about them until he told me before he left. For some reason, Cari swore him to secrecy a long time ago." Richard shifted in his chair. "Anyway, it was up to me to watch over them while he's gone. Besides, the company pretty much runs itself with the team I have in place. I was bored."

"So, the kids are your rich-boy distraction?" She scowled.

"Nothing like that. I'd do anything for August. My promise was so important to him. I kind of ... they could be—"

"They're not his, if that's what you're thinking. At least according to a letter I recently received from Cari."

"Whew. I was afraid he wasn't taking responsibility, which would be totally out of character."

"I'm still learning a lot about Cari and her relationship with your friend. But reading between the lines ... how did she put it?" Jen bit her lip. "He was her one. She said she didn't realize it until it was too late. Whatever that meant. Speaking of Cari, did she know about you?"

"I told her right after I started working here." Richard's shoulders hunched. "Don't be mad at her, Jen. I begged her to keep it to herself. Frankly, I didn't want the publicity my company or Lilac would get if anyone knew." His hand dove through his hair. "Anyway, the 'too late' part Cari referred to could be around the time of August's accident. He shut everyone out for a while."

His thoughts didn't jive with Cari's note, but she wouldn't divulge that information yet.

"His brother walked away with little more than a scratch—lucky jerk that he is." Richard sneered. "August ... well, I've already told you about the wheelchair."

"All right. We can talk about this more later." She wasn't happy about the secret, but she might as well hear the rest. "You said you had things—plural—to discuss?"

Richard's cheeks matched the redness of his ears. "I ... um ... I know you don't—"

Jen willed his words toward her with a wave of her hand. "Out with it."

Jen stewed on Richard's news until Colin and the twins arrived.

Waiting for her to finish her computer work, Colin occupied himself with his phone while the kids settled at the workroom table. Auggie had looked for Richard then asked his sister to help design the new mic box.

Coward that she was, Jen didn't have the heart to tell her godson she'd sent his buddy home for the day. She wasn't sure what to do about the Richard situation yet. His revelations had unnerved her. She'd seek the counsel of her parents and Colin. And pray about it. Lots and lots of prayers. Then deal with him after that.

Richard's tale was a bizarre one. This August person … apparently monitoring Cari and the kids' well-being … Richard surprising himself by becoming so attached to the Marshalls … and what seemed his biggest bombshell, at least according to him, was he'd fallen in love with Eva.

It explained why he was so awkward around the lovely model at first and had avoided her at work in recent weeks. Lilac Lane had a 'No Fraternizing' policy.

She'd never minded her crew bringing family and friends to the showroom, but she didn't like the fallout from broken work relationships. Her trust in Richard, and admittedly, even a little with Eva, was teetering in a precarious spot. Was the longstanding policy more important than dear friendships? Another thing to think through.

Finished with the work neglected from the hectic morning, she switched off her desktop with a final flourish and turned to Colin, sitting across from her. "Thanks for waiting."

"No problem. I caught up on a few emails." He held up his smartphone as proof.

She thought to ask his advice about Richard's confession, but he beat her into conversation.

"You said Auggie couldn't play with the other kids here most of the time, didn't you?"

"I said wouldn't, not couldn't. There's a difference."

"Oh right, sorry." His gaze dropped to his tennis shoes. Classic Chuck Taylors.

"That came out wrong. It's been a long day. I apologize." She stood and went to sit near him. "From what I hear, regular kids are hard enough to parent. A child with special needs, plus one who's probably at the other end of the spectrum ... it's downright tough. Especially on us aunts and uncles." She smiled to take any lingering sting from her words.

"I know. I'm just trying to do my best by them." He picked at lint on his pants. "And you. I don't always get the words correct. But I'm trying."

"I appreciate it. It will make the inevitable easier to accept. When they go with you."

The collection of emotions rushing across Colin's face would have been comical if they weren't so raw and real. She touched his sleeve. "We'll worry about that later. You wanted to talk about something?"

He took a deep breath and smiled, which she accepted as his thanks. "Auggie's been really getting into this pitching stuff. He's trying hard. But ..." He grimaced. "The bottle of Blue Goo all over the bathroom floor is proof he still needs work."

How could he manage to look embarrassed and pleased all at once? She giggled with him.

"He's working on his accuracy. I was thinking if he had a place he could practice unless he's with one of us ... it might save some furniture and both of our sanity."

"That sounds promising. Did you have any place in mind?"

"I was hoping I could commandeer that room next to the kids' retreat."

"The storeroom? What would I do with all the stuff in there?"

"I'd build storage shelves and new racks to one side where you can hang the clothing and material. We'd put up heavy netting to separate the pitching area from your show items."

"It's really sweet of you to offer. And doing this for Auggie. But one, I can't afford it. And two, as much as it would boost his confidence, Auggie and Ree already get preferential treatment around here. There can't be more, purely for him."

"I'm countering your arguments. You don't have to afford this. If you'll allow me, I want to foot the bill. I have access to building materials at cost through my company. And an Auggie-only place? Not happening. Any of them can use it to blow off steam, but they'll have to sign up for a time. Even him. I'll show him how to do it, and we'll talk about responsibility and sharing and all that guy stuff."

He gave her what she'd come to refer to as *the grin*. An endearing mixture of the excited boy she imagined him to be before his parents got so messed up, the slightly cocky teenager she knew years ago, and this shy, confident man he'd grown into, all rolled into a lopsided smile. And it seemed he didn't even realize how devastatingly handsome it was.

Her cheeks grew warm. "Let me think about it. Can I get back to you?"

"Totally. And I meant it when I said you would not have to pay for the materials. I can request whatever permits might be needed, and we should be done in a couple days."

"The problem is, the twins might only be here another few weeks, maybe even days. It wouldn't be fair to the other kids to put it up, only to take it down when you go back to Grand Rapids. It would have to be a gift to them all, whether the twins are here or not. A very generous one at that."

The grin was gone, replaced by a sheepish snort. "It's not completely altruistic. Pitching is how I unwind. Ever since college. I still clear my head with it. I was hoping you'd let me come over, when you're here, of course, and use it myself. That sports center near your apartment is nice, but ..."

"But it means you can't be near the kids if you're there and paying for an hour or two."

"Exactly."

A quiet comfort grew between them.

Jen placed her hand on top of Colin's. "Tell you what. You can build it if you keep it simple. I can't have the upkeep on something all fancy later. You already have a key. But watch your back. I still don't know who I can completely trust around here anymore."

"You got it." He leaned toward her. "Between you and me, do you have a favorite suspect?"

"I wish. But I can't imagine anyone here. We're family."

His smile returned. "I've always liked that about you. Your people are *yours*."

Good grief, that grin could do a number on a girl's heart if she let it.

He rubbed his hands together. "I haven't even asked how your day went around here."

Jen sniffed. "It was eventful, to say the least. But I can tell you about it tonight. For now, go ahead and start designing your batting thingamajig."

Colin bounced up and called the twins.

"Only adults moving my inventory, please."

"At your service, ma'am." He laughed and shooed the kids out the door.

She giggled. *What have I gotten Lilac into?*

CHAPTER 18

"You wore them out." Jen marveled.

The twins and Harold had helped Colin clear the area for the new pitching space. The physical labor acted as a splendid sedative for Ree and Auggie. They were already firmly ensconced in slumberland.

Taking her laptop from its carrier, Jen set it on the island and turned it on. "Can I get you something to drink? I have soda, tea, decaf and regular coffee, and … sparkling mineral water."

"Cari's favorite. I'd like that, in honor of her. But it's gotta be over ice."

"Sounds perfect." She fetched the commemorative drinks in two antique Imperial amethyst water goblets.

Colin held the glass to catch the light. "I like this pattern."

"Cari thrifted them. She discovered the antique chalices she brought back from a modeling trip were leaded glass and could be dangerous to drink from." Jen gestured to the shelves where those gifts were displayed. "These were her answer."

"Smart. And I see they're purple." He grinned. "To Cari. My intelligent, ambitious, whackadoodle, wonderful little sister." The raw emotions roaming beneath the surface of his words tugged hard at Jen's heart.

"To Cari." Clinking her glass to his, the mineral water splashed over the edge. She concentrated on wiping the droplets from the counter. Prickles of familiarity danced across her shoulders.

"That's it? No hearts and flowers or tears and temper for your best friend?"

"I don't want you to think ..." Emotions engulfed her, crushing her ribcage in a stranglehold of longing for what was.

He reached across the island and squeezed her fingers.

Warmth spread from his touch to the middle of her hurt. "How do you get to know someone you thought you completely understood once they're no longer here?" She took his silence as license to continue. "The woman who wrote that letter ... I don't know how to explain it, other than she seemed so ... with it." She shrugged.

"Consider this. We've been given a rare privilege. A glimpse into more than who she allowed others to see. Not many people receive that honor." He leaned on the island. "Not to sound too philosophical, but it's intimate and it's intimidating all at once because we know we'll only learn so much before it's gone."

A comforting warmth blanketed her. "I think your sister would approve of your theory."

They sipped at their bubbles, lost in their own thoughts and memories. Colin took a swig of his drink and belched. "Good grief. Excuse me."

"Cari loved sparkling water, except the burping. This brand has less fizz, that's why it was her favorite. And it isn't expensive."

She turned on her stool to face him, their knees touching. "Did you know, even as much as your sister made, she was extremely thrifty most of the time."

"Like what?"

She lifted her glass. "For example, she could afford Dom Perignon but chose sparkling water. She didn't throw money around at all. She saved for the kids' education. Whatever they needed."

"Makes sense. Single parent and all."

"And she taught Mom and me not to use a whole dryer sheet. Even though I teased her about it, I do it myself now." She scissored her fingers. "Cut them in half, put one in a lingerie bag, and throw it in the dryer. Add a new sheet now and then. Why are you laughing? It's a good money-saving tip."

"Sorry, I'm not making fun of you. But she picked that up from *our* mom. Rosemary used to do it all the time. Cari hated when it was her turn to cut them."

"I didn't remember that."

"Mostly when we were younger. Before ... well, you know." Wonderful laugh lines reappeared around his eyes. "Of all the weird things she could have maintained from home, I'm glad it was that."

"Someday I'd like to hear your side of growing up Marshall. Before and after. I think Cari colored a lot of it."

"I doubt it. More like downplayed everything." A flash of anger washed across his face.

She'd touched that sore spot again. "Well, as much as I'd like to continue reminiscing, we should get this obituary written."

"Do you mind if I get a glass of milk? I don't think my ego can take another belch."

"You know where everything is. Mind getting me some while you're at it?"

He peered at her over non-existent dad glasses.

"What? You're no longer a stranger in this household." She snickered. "You gotta start pulling your own weight."

"Bossy, aren't we?"

"Haven't I always been?"

"Anything else while I'm at it, Your Majesty?"

"I'm kind of snacky. Toast and jam?" She started to rise, but he held his hand up.

"After being around the jelly monster, I know where you stash both."

"Thanks. See, I told you. No longer a stranger."

"Maybe not, but I still ask before taking. Your mom taught me some manners too, you know." He went to the refrigerator. "So, how do we begin?"

"Should we say anything about how she died? She wasn't given the chance to accomplish so many of her dreams and goals yet. How do we let people know about those." She swallowed the loneliness stuck in her throat.

"Maybe we can't in public. But privately, I think we need to get back to remembering who she was to each of us and move forward."

"I'm not sure I can. I'll have to take this one to my knees."

His brows drew together.

"I mean pray about it. Something this heavy ... I need to surrender this to Jesus."

Colin silently busied himself around the kitchen.

"Sometimes we chat. Occasionally, I send him a bucket of tears. And every so often, like when my cat Louie died, I hold a shouting match."

"You yell at God?" His brows disappeared into his hairline.

"He can take it. Besides, the noise is in my head." She clicked the mouse to wake up the screen. "I haven't ever had anything this crushing to share with him though." She produced a tissue from her pocket and blew her nose. "And if I cry much more, I'm going to have to buy stock in these."

"Does it help?"

"Prayer? It helps me. You don't think so?"

"I've never really known what to believe. I mean, your mom and dad readily accepted me along on Sundays, but to be honest, Stone ruined a lot of good things for me. Going to church with your family and learning more about your God didn't get far once he found out."

"That makes me sad. I always wondered why you quit coming with us."

He brushed a lock of hair from his forehead. "Maybe that's why you're only now finding out these things about Cari. We learned to hide things from people on the outside, so they didn't know how damaged Stone and Rosemary had become. And then from our parents, so they wouldn't wreck more stuff for us. It was easier."

"Makes more sense than anything I've come up with."

Colin grabbed paper towels and returned to the island with the toast and glasses of milk. "Your yucky milk, madam." He squinted at her screen. "You haven't written a word."

"Somebody keeps interrupting me." She took a bite of the bread. "Mmm. Always better when someone else makes it."

"Wait until you see what I can do with a steak." Reaching over, he wiped jelly from her cheek with his thumb.

Her face warmed. "Well, this thing's not going to write itself."

Swapping information back and forth, twenty minutes later, she was satisfied. "Listen to what we've cobbled together so far."

Caribbean "Cari" (KAR-ee) Anita Marshall, 29, Dallas, TX, was taken unexpectedly on Tuesday, November 14, 2017. Her children were the center of her world, around which revolved a tight-knit group of family and friends.

Marshall was the lead model and a contributing creative of Lilac Lane Fashion.

She was sought after in the modeling world as much for her dedication and artistic expertise as she was for her beauty. She earned many awards and accolades, but her most treasured was Mentor of the Year 2015 from the Wells-Myer Art Academy. She was a generous supporter of the organization, as well as the founder of the AIM Higher and JEM Young Designers scholarships.

Marshall is survived by her children, January and August, brother Colin, foster parents Patrick and Elaine Clark, and best friend, Jennifer Clark. She is predeceased by her biological parents.

"You're certain you don't want Stone's and Rosemary's names in there?"

"I'm sure. Your folks were better to her than they were." He seemed determined. Jen left it at that and kept reading.

Caribbean is best remembered for the unconventional style with which she lived her life, including ice cream dinners, quirky thrift store treasures, and spontaneous trips traveling around the world with her children.
Cremation will take place with a private family service. A celebration of life with extended family, friends, and colleagues is planned for the spring.

Jen rubbed the kinks from her neck. "I'm glad you told me Cari wanted to be cremated. Of all the things we discussed over the years, that wasn't one of them."

"We hadn't talked about it since our parents died, but a couple weeks ago, she brought it up again." A shadow crossed his features.

"Whatever the reason, her decision takes the burden off us. So, what do you think?"

"I still can't wrap my head around the fact my sister was a mentor to teenagers. She never said anything."

"I wish you could have seen them with her. They hung on her every word." She turned the stool so she could lean over the back of it toward him. As much a prop for her tired bones as a shield for her feelings. "Her schedule was erratic, but whenever she could drop by, the profs opened their rooms. It didn't matter what was going on, they allowed the kids time with her. She was cherished there."

"Sounds like an amazing program. I'll have to check it out."

"Please do. The kids would love meeting you." She bent her head forward and circled her shoulders.

Colin walked behind her and kneaded the knots from her neck.

She tensed at first but allowed herself to relax. The warmth from his hands ministered to something deep within her. No counting needed.

He finished and sat back across from her. "You look troubled. What's wrong?"

"I don't know how we're going to accommodate everyone. Where are we going to fit them all? Even though we're waiting for spring to hold the memorial around the duck pond—"

"You really think there will be that many?"

She started ticking numbers on her fingers. "There's Lilac's crew, fashion colleagues, and most of the Wells-Myer's faculty and students. All the JEM and AIM scholarship recipients, past and present, plus the two new ones for this year. They're going to want to visit with Ree and Auggie. If they're able to attend."

"Why the twins?"

"Cari always brought the scholarship namesakes with her to the awards night."

"I don't understand." He rubbed his chin.

"The scholarships are named after the kids. January Elaine Marshall—JEM. August Isaiah Marshall—AIM. Cari used their initials for more privacy. The recipients knew it, but not many others."

He snapped his fingers. "That must be what she was hinting about when school started. She asked if I'd ever thought about donating to an artistic foundation for kids. I thought she was talking about the twins. Auggie tolerated all those people?"

"Not his favorite night, I assure you." She smirked. "But he went to please Cari. They stayed a short time, then she took them to their favorite Italian place for dinner. The owner always reserved a special room for them that night."

"Tell me more about these scholarships."

"This year's award ceremony is going to be difficult. We already know who the recipients are, but *they* don't find out until the spring. The two who won were favorites of Cari's. I have never seen her as affected by anyone as this year's winners."

"What makes them so special?"

Jen propped her chin on her hand, thinking. "I just realized, they may have reminded her of you two. They've both had rough lives, that's verified. And they're very talented. The young man will receive the JEM. He's a gifted clothing designer already—he only needs some guidance. Plus, his looks are really striking. He asked Cari to mentor him through modeling. I'll check if Eva would be willing. And then there's the young woman. She's handy with theatre sets and things, but where she excels is architecture."

"Why do you verify if they have tough backgrounds?"

"These are financial needs-based scholarships, in addition to their artistry. I'm on the committee that chooses who they're awarded to. The stories can be heartbreaking—if they're true."

"Some of them aren't?"

"Let's just say one or two have embellished, hoping it gave them an edge. It didn't."

"Who else is on the committee?"

"There's six of us, but only five have a vote. There was Cari, of course. And me. Professor Thompson, he's the non-voter. He brings the scholarship requests to us and is the one who verifies their need. He's the only person who knows the identity of the applicants until they're chosen. Although ... someone leaked the names of applicants this year." She frowned. "We still haven't figured out who did that. One of the many police complaints we've made over the last few months. We'll have to figure out tighter security if we continue with the program." She shook her head as if to clear it. "Number four is Eva. That girl can ferret out a fib in a student like no other. And my Bible study mentor, Ingrid Reynolds. She has a heart of gold with a steel rod of sweetness down her center."

"Never heard that one before."

"Wait until you meet her. You'll understand. She's so nice and caring to everyone, no one dares question her decisions."

"That's five ..."

"The final one is Sassafras Montgomery. Did you ever meet her? She was my college roommate."

"She's a terrific jewelry designer. I don't know her, but my sister gave me not-so-subtle hints one year."

"I wondered how she got so many of Sassy's designs."

"My office admin, Deborah, who I couldn't get along without, loves it when I give her a piece occasionally."

Jen's stomach flip-flopped, but he was entitled to give presents to anyone he wanted to.

He leaned toward her and whispered, spy-like. "Her husband was so jealous of the first one—I think it was a pin, or do ladies still call them brooches?—he started getting more creative with his gifts after that." He winked. "From an artistic standpoint, they're unique."

Her nerves settled into a soft samba. "That's our Sassy. If she can, she flies in when we make the choices. If she can't—like this year—we narrow the field to six, score and number them privately, and ship the applications to her to do the same. The ones with the highest tallies at the end are the recipients. That's when we find out their identities. You can meet Sassy at the charity event if we still have it. She always flies in for it."

"I look forward to that. I might even get one of her pieces and have her sign the authentication card. I think Deborah's husband needs another shakeup." Waggling his eyebrows, he grinned wickedly.

"Goodness, I can't believe it's so late. You must be exhausted."

"I uh, I was wondering if you had time for a cup of tea or something. The hotel is a little too quiet, and there's nowhere to get a snack after hours. Could we sit and visit for a bit?" He ran his finger through the condensation on his glass. "I mean, if you're not too tired."

"I'd like that. But I only have one type of tea right now." She got up and put the kettle on. "The detectives confiscated my favorite. The one Cari always blended for my birthday and Christmas."

Colin choked. "This I have to hear. I'm curious which story will be better. My sister mixing tea or why it was seized."

Colin slipped in and out of the funeral all night, his little sister clutching his hand. Tall for her age, she still only reached his shoulder. Her tears drenched his shirt. His own were pebbles, resting rock solid where his heart should be.

How was he going to raise a twelve-year-old? He had only recently turned eighteen himself. *I don't know the first thing about parenting kids. Let alone an almost teenage girl, sister or not.*

Quit school. That's what he'd do. Mr. and Mrs. Clark weren't going to like that. He was grateful they'd helped him plan the service, lending their assistance like they had over the summer. Grownup stuff Stone & Rosemary should have been doing.

He wanted to hate the two people lying in the simple wooden boxes, but he could still remember when they were good parents. In the end, they'd cared less for the children they'd born into the world than the drugs that took them out of it.

He longed to touch his mother's cheek one last time. So soft and papery thin. Could he make her understand the grief choking him? Heartache wracked his body. Reaching out he touched—

Cari? Where was she? No longer at his side. Heart racing, he searched for her. Only Tragedy stood there, clawing at him, pointing to the casket. Not a haggard, drug-addicted mother. Instead, the beautiful golden one. His confidant in life. No longer twelve to his eighteen, but twenty-nine.

No!

He held up his hand. His fingers, wet from her youthful tears, gripped a metal monstrosity made by a creative boy. The mask sneered at him.

Where did she go? She was just—

"Uncle Colin?" A soft, sweet voice whispered to him through the haze. "Wake up."

He startled. "Ree?"

"You were dreaming. You sounded ... scared." Her eyes appeared troubled.

He sat up. *Where ...?*

"Why are you sleeping on Engine's couch?"

Pieces clicked into place. The late night had taken its toll. "We were talking. I couldn't keep my eyes open. She didn't want me driving so late."

Ree gave him a mushy grin.

His watch lit up for a moment, illuminating the three o'clock mark. "I'm sorry if I woke you, sweetheart."

"You didn't. I wanted a drink of water."

Standing, he was glad he'd had a change of clothes in his car. Sweatpants were always more comfortable to sleep in than jeans. "Sounds like an excellent idea."

He got their water while Ree climbed on a stool. She sipped her drink and remained quiet, squinting at him.

How could he find out what went on in that brilliant mind of hers? "Do you want to draw in the morning? The view from the window in the hallway would be a good perspective." He'd have to check their pencil supply.

"Sure."

"When are you headed back to school?"

"I don't know. Engine said we probably shouldn't go back for now."

"It's not a regular school, is it?"

Her eyes twinkled. "That's what I like about it. It's for different kids. Like Auggie and me. The teachers call us Creatives. We do some of our schoolwork at Lilac Lane anyway, so it won't be hard to catch up. Engine's getting our books after the funeral."

He shuddered at the word.

"Are you okay, Uncle Colin?"

"I am now. I haven't had a dream like that in a long time."

"You called for Cari." Her chin wobbled.

His own eyes stung. Leaning over, he hugged the girl who reminded him so much of his sister at her age. He gave one of her curls a light tug. "Finished? You'd better get back to bed before we wake up Engine."

Ree slid off the stool. "Are you going to be here when we get up?"

He nodded.

"Promise?"

He kissed the top of her head and crossed his heart. "Yes, ma'am."

She sent him a loving smile and padded out of the kitchen.

His insides quaked. Chest heaving, he laid his head on his arms. Having his niece and nephew nearby was a blessing. What was he going to do without them when he went back home? He'd rack up a lot of flight points from now on, assuming he was offered generous visitation.

A warm hand touched his shoulder. Jen sat next to him with her own glass of water.

He looked up with a sigh, silence stretching between them. He hoped her thoughts were more peaceful than his.

She took hold of his cold, wet fingers and gave them a squeeze, throwing him a lifeline back from the hurt strangling his heart.

CHAPTER 19

Jen's soapy, agitated fingers fumbled the pan Tuesday evening. The dish landed in the sink with a plop. How could one week go by so fast and drag so excruciatingly slow at the same time?

You should be in there playing games with them. Not here contemplating things you can't change. The voice whined through her thoughts.

Shush. You're not helping.

Worry fizzed like the bubbles that splashed on her shirt. Auggie's nail biting and cross words had gotten the best of all of them today, especially Ree. Even Colin's calm demeanor hadn't helped with the boy's handwringing.

"He's jumpy, almost as bad as when you or Cari traveled." Ree grumbled. "Remember, Engine?"

How could she forget? She'd often kept the twins extra busy on those evenings, waiting for the phone to ring. Once he knew his beloved mother made it to her destination or was on her way to pick them up—only then did he settle.

Since she herself was here in person, and there was zero chance he was neurotic over Cari flying any longer, she was at a loss for this uncharacteristic behavior. Grasping for the proverbial straw, she'd even contacted Detective Mason to ask if any significant changes in the case might be causing his mood. There weren't.

Hoping to ease the boy's fidgets and fears, Colin offered to be the Blue Goo shampoo inspector and sat in the bathroom talking while Auggie showered. Their voices drifted through the door while they discussed airplanes and drowning in bathwater. Thankfully, Colin nipped that conversation with some well-placed subject changing, trivia about puppies, and statistics about their treasured baseball.

For the most part, Ree drifted through the day in a haze. After dinner, she curled up on her bed.

"Do you want some company?" Jen had asked.

"Maybe later." Ree stared at the artwork above her bed but seemed a million miles away.

Opting for busyness in the kitchen, Jen finished the dishes. She rinsed the last pot and pulled the sink plug. Dread circled the drain with the dirty water. She prayed Auggie's anxiety wasn't a signal of an impending meltdown, but with everything the twins had been through the last few days, it wouldn't surprise her. Would she and Colin be able to handle a complete disintegration and bring Auggie back? Only time would tell.

In short, her little family wasn't having a good day. Her heart hiccupped to think of them as hers, only to remember it was nothing but make-believe.

She recalled her phone call to Dr. Brasil, the twins' psychiatrist, earlier in the day. The conversation had taken less time than she had expected. His clipped attitude mystified her, as if he held a personal grudge against her. He'd agreed to be on call for the kids as needed. A consultation with Auggie and Ree would happen in the company of Colin or herself, in-person or by video, whichever the police allowed. Done and over.

Whatever, buddy. Don't think you're the only shrink in this town who's good with kids. She picked up her phone and scrolled through the directory. Yup, the old, not-used-in-years number was still there. Jen tucked that bit of information away and went in search of the others.

Walking into the twins' bedroom, the shower and downtime seemed to have worked by the looks of them draped over their uncle's lap while he read a story about a fantastical make-believe world hidden beneath a staircase.

"Secrets of Droon. Excellent choice. Which one are you reading?"

"'Journey to the Volcano Palace,' *again.*" Ree rolled her eyes. The book was Auggie's favorite of the fantasy series by Tony Abbott. Ree usually preferred to read to herself, but uncle time was a treat to enjoy.

"Are you feeling better, Auggie?" Jen sat across from them.

"Yes. They're safe now."

"Who is honey?"

He shrugged.

Before she could question him further, her intercom buzzed.

"I wonder why Leo's calling this time of night."

Bbzzz. The mechanical box screeched a second time.

"What's up, Leo? Did I leave my mailbox key down there again?"

"No, ma'am." The tinny voice sounded through the intercom. "But I think you forgot some parents down here." He laughed. "Sending your folks up."

"What?"

"Miss Elaine is looking as beautiful as ever."

She could hear the elevator door swoosh shut on her mother's lilting laughter.

"Thanks, Leo."

"Sure thing. If I'd known they were coming, I would have made sure to be watching out for them." Was that the slightest reproach in his tone? "Sure is cold to be standing outside waiting."

"Rest assured, Leo, if I'd known, I would have been down there to get them myself."

"Haw! She pulled another one on you, did she?"

"That she did. Thanks again for taking care of them. I hear the elevator. I'd better go let them in. Have a good night, friend."

"I expect those little 'uns need to see the grandparents for a bit. But give me a call if you're needin' a cab later. Happy Thanksgiving if I don't see you before."

"Always a step ahead of me, Leo. Thanks. You too." She disconnected and went to intercept her parents.

She greeted them outside her door with her finger to her lips. "I wasn't expecting you today. Why didn't you call? We would have gotten you from the airport."

Mom enveloped her in an overdue hug, followed by a woodsy-scented embrace from her father. "Phone lines were all messed up from the storms before we left. Once we landed, well, you know your mom. She wanted to get here as fast as she could to see how everyone was doing." Dad shook his head. "Can't say I blame her."

"It's been so long since we've seen the twins." Mom chimed in. "I'm sure they've changed more than I'm prepared for. But since you met us in the hallway, I'd say we've come at a bad time." Her expression was crestfallen. "We can come back tomorrow."

"Not at all. I'm so glad you arrived safe. In fact, that's why I met you out here. Auggie's had a rough day, but I think I know why now. You two traveling."

Dad stared at her. The logic didn't seem to compute with his scientific mind. "None of you even knew we were coming."

"I don't know what to tell you, Dad, but whatever it is inside him that connects him to his people seems to have transferred to you two." She relayed the little scene from earlier. "And right then, Leo buzzed that you were here."

"Poor boy. I'm so sorry I caused all these problems." Elaine's shoulders slumped under her fluffy coat.

"You couldn't have known. We'll have to get him used to your extended traveling schedules." She caught an odd look between her parents. "In the meantime, you'll be welcomed by two sets of gangling arms, legs, hugs, and kisses. As well as an adult Colin. He got in a couple hours after I talked to you last."

She gathered their coats. "Just so you know what's going on, there's a huge elephant in the room. I didn't say anything before because I didn't want to worry you further. Colin may wind up with custody of the twins since he's their blood relation." She tried to smile. "Their advocate is handling everything."

Mom's hand flew to her chest. She and Dad cherished the twins and at this point, Colin was a familiar but unknown factor.

"Until this whole thing with Cari is over ... we're taking it one day at a time." Thumb to finger, she stopped and flexed her hand. *Don't go there.* "He's trying to get to know them in person. They love him. Surprisingly, they were in regular contact by phone. Seems Cari kept a few secrets from all of us."

Dad's jaw stiffened.

"Anyway, you will now be bombarded by the twin typhoons." She opened the door to her apartment. "Ree. Auggie. Can you come here? You too, Colin."

The twins bounced from the room, followed by a quieter, taller, darker-haired version of them. Happy chaos ensued.

Auggie's "Gramma! Grampa!" mixed with Ree's little-girl squeals grew deafening. The kids flung themselves forward. Mom kneeled to receive their loving ministrations.

"Well, what am I? Chopped liver?" Dad growled and bent to gather in his share. But before they released their grandmother, both twins held her at arm's length, staring deep into her eyes, as if saving every detail of her for the future.

She gasped. "Oh, my word. It can't be." Recovering, she shooed the twins toward their grandfather. She stood, appearing shell-shocked, and embraced Colin with a mamma-bear hug.

"Mrs. Clark, you haven't changed a day since I last saw you." His grin was wide.

"It's Elaine, dear. You're an adult now. You don't have to call me Mrs."

"Yes, ma'am. I mean, sure. I think I can."

His discomfort was palpable, but Jen figured he'd get used to it. Her mother would see to that. Few were a match for her Midwestern charm.

With the twins dancing around them, her dad pumped Colin's hand.

"Sir."

"Good to see you, son. It's been way too long. I'm sorry it's under such sorrowful circumstances."

"Thank you, sir."

"Please. It's Patrick. No need to stand on ceremony with us any longer."

Colin ducked his head toward the older gentleman he'd looked up to as a teenager.

The twins turned their attention to hanging on Colin's legs.

"Jen? Can we get the monkeys settled with a game or something? I think your mother needs a glass of water. I'd like to get it for her." He gave Jen a meaning-filled look.

"I'll get Gramma water." Auggie bellowed. "I'm good at water."

"I'll float away if I drink all of that," she teased. "Have you two eaten yet?"

The kids' curls bounced up and down.

"Grampa and I haven't. Let's say we raid Engine's cookie box, we visit for a little bit, and then you can scoot off to bed."

"But Gramma, you just got here. We haven't seen you in *forever*." Ree drew out the word in a tired whine. "Why do we have to go to bed now?"

"You'll see us again in the morning, precious girl," Mom said. "For now, we'll sit and have milk and cookies. If Engine's okay with it?"

"Absolutely." She'd learned long ago not to get in the way of her mother's plans, especially when they involved children. She was convinced her mother possessed unique gifts bestowed on only the kindest, most giving hearts. She could talk any child around to her way of thinking with a few gentle words, a twinkling smile, and a hug.

"And while we're eating, and slurping just a little ..."

Auggie snickered.

"... we'll have a chat. We're going to be here for a while. Right, Grampa?" She wiggled her eyebrows at Patrick, conveying some secret message.

"Right, dear. I'd like my milk warmed up."

"Warm milk? Gross." The twins broke into giggles.

"Why, yes." He picked up each child and sat them on the counter. "Warm milk is the best on chilly nights." Sounding like an old radio narrator, he recited. "It gets you all cozy and comfy. From your toeses all the way to your cold little noses." He tweaked said appendages.

Jen leaned toward her mother. "I take it this is your way to get them to bed sooner so we can talk?"

"My dear girl, would I do such an underhanded thing?"

"Says the woman who bribed two teenage girls to clean our rooms and think it was our own idea." She marveled at her parents' ability to corral the situation at hand.

Minutes later, Jen stood at the stove, stirring milk. She called over her shoulder, "Why don't you guys tell Gramma and Grampa what you've been doing with Uncle Colin."

Nine-year-old chatter never sounded so good as it did while they ate homemade cookies and sipped warm milk. They spoke of shopping with Colin, drawing, batting cages, and introducing him to their Lilac Lane family. It didn't take long for the bedtime treats and the late hour to do their magic.

"Goodness. You need to quit that before I start yawn—" Mom covered her mouth as she melted into a tired sigh.

"Do we hafta go to bed?" Ree fussed.

"You guys finish up those last bites. I think we can entice Gramma, Grampa, and Uncle Colin back here for breakfast. Remember, they stay at the hotel down the road when they're here."

"The mon mi tha...?" Auggie questioned around a mouthful of cookies.

"Eww. Shut your mouth." His sister squawked.

He swallowed. "The one with the swimming pool? Can we go in it again?"

"The same, sport." Grampa scooted them to the sink to wash their hands. "It's been a long time since we've seen you two swim. I bet you're little fish by now."

Ree erupted in a torrent of tears.

He patted her shoulder. "You don't have to go swimming if you don't want."

She sobbed harder.

Colin's eyes were saucers of panic.

"We can ..." Dad searched for help from his wife and daughter.

Auggie stared in confusion at his sister, while Mom distracted him as best she could with the handwashing chore.

Jen kneeled and handed Ree a towel. "Honey? What's wrong? We'll sort it out."

Ree looked stricken. "We—" She hiccupped. "We can't."

"Take a deep breath. There you go. Here, Uncle Colin brought you a cool rag. Now wipe your face." She waited. "Better?"

Ree hiccupped again, drawing a giggle from Auggie. She scowled at him, but his interruption seemed to help her.

"We can't go swimming then." She choked out her words. "We have to bury Cari in a few days."

All the air in the room sucked into four pairs of adult-sized lungs. Inhale. *One.* Jen ordered herself to remain composed for Ree.

Mom shuffled a still baffled Auggie to his sister's side for moral support. "Sweetie. Grampa didn't mean we'd go swimming that day. We won't. I promise."

"But I want to," she wailed. "I want to go shopping for a new bathing suit. And water toys. And towels." She snuffled. "I want to go to the hotel. And swim. And play. I don't want to bury my mom. I don't want to bury Cari. Forever."

A memory tapped Jen's shoulder. It had been such a normal family time it barely registered, but it made perfect sense of Ree's current state. "Like the last time we all went swimming at Gramma and Grampa's hotel. Right?"

Ree bowed her head.

A glance at the other adults confirmed they were following along now.

"We got swim noodles and catch rings." Auggie caught up to what he understood.

Jen pulled him close. "A pink noodle for Ree. An orange one for you. And a bright purple one for me, if I remember correctly."

"I wanted a blue one, but they didn't have any left." He pouted.

Ree's lip trembled again. "Cari picked a yellow one. But we didn't bring any for Gramma and Grampa. I don't remember why."

"Gramma had her hair done for an awards banquet they attended that night. Your mom knew they couldn't have used them anyway."

Ree was too quiet.

"Sweetheart?" Jen caught her attention. "What if, the day before Cari's funeral—"

"Can I call her my mom?" Ree murmured, as if afraid of the answer.

"Absolutely. She will always be your mom."

"Mine too." Auggie piped up, not to be left out.

"Yours too. So how about the day before the funeral you, and Auggie if he wants to—"

He readily agreed, once again in sync with his twin.

"We'll take Gramma and go shopping for new bathing suits."

"And a pool toy?" Auggie yawned.

"Sure. Then we'll go swimming the day afterward. When we have less to do."

Ree considered. "Can we invite the detectives to go swimming with us? And Melissa. I don't think they get to have much fun."

The swift return of Ree's generous heart made Jen's own feel lopsided with love. "They may not be able to get off duty, but we'll ask. I'll even let them use my purple pool noodle if they want."

The phrase snagged Auggie's attention. He started jigging around. "Purple pool noodle. Purple pool noodle."

"Okay, goofball, give Grampa and Gramma a hug, then march Uncle Colin into the bathroom with you and brush your teeth. Ree and I will be there in a moment."

Auggie did as told, then high-stepped it out of the kitchen with Colin following as if trailing the Pied Piper, both sing-songing the new phrase caught in the boy's fancy.

Jen pulled Ree close. "We'll get through this all together. You, Auggie, Uncle Colin, me ... and now we have Gramma and Grampa to help us too."

"That you do, dear girl." Dad leaned down to give her a hug.

"We're always and forever here for you, sweetheart." Mom kissed her forehead.

"Not forever." Ree whispered.

Tears sprang to Mom's eyes.

Ree hurried on. "But I'm glad you're here now. Cari ... my mom ... talked about you a lot. Especially after you called."

"We can share our memories with each other. We loved her to pieces."

A sad, sweet smile finally reached the girl's eyes. "I'd like that." She yawned and blew her grandparents a kiss, then drifted out of the room.

Jen looked at her parents. "Make yourselves something to eat. Colin and I will be back in a few minutes to find out what spooked you, Mom."

Later, sitting at the dining table, the farthest point from the twins' bedroom, Jen sipped a cup of decaf coffee, the aroma buoying her spirits. Dad joined her, while Colin rubbed the condensation on his glass of ice water. They studied Elaine as she sipped her tea and told them of two very striking eye colors.

"A few years before we left for Manaus, I went to lunch with Kimberly Noble and some of our book club ladies. Do you remember her, Colin? She's been my best friend for ages. We went to Eggzactly, that cute little café downtown. When we walked in, I saw Cari across the restaurant with two men. A tall, suave one and a younger one. I was going to say hi after I ordered, but the restaurant was busy, so it took a few minutes." She seemed lost in thought. No one dared break her reverie.

"I could only see her profile, but she seemed agitated. Her body language suggested she was arguing with the older one. When he pounded on the table, she picked up her glass of water and doused him."

Jen snorted. That sounded like Cari.

"I thought he was going to hit her, but the younger man reached up and grabbed his hand." Mom blew through tightened lips. "I got up, but Kimberly held me back and asked me to wait. She was right. By this time, the whole restaurant was looking at their table. Cari would have been mortified if I'd made it worse." She winced. "The nasty one played it off like they'd had a lovers' spat."

"Sounds like a jerk to me." Colin groused.

"I couldn't tell if it was an act, or if the other young man really had put his temper in check. Anyway ..." She waved her hand in dismissal. "They all got up to leave. Cari hadn't realized I was there. When I spoke to her, she was startled but introduced them. They were brothers."

"Did they live around here?" Jen asked.

"She'd met the younger one here, evidently. The older one was in from New York for business. We had a pleasant enough conversation." She shrugged. "The mean one—did I mention he was exceptionally good looking?—was making friendly with the other ladies. They ate it up." She *tsk'd.* "Kimberly and I thought he was a piece of work. The younger man seemed nice. Embarrassed. He was concerned for Cari, for sure. What struck me the most were their eyes. The nasty one had brilliant green ones. Obviously, contacts." Her face held a pinched expression. "But the younger man had beautiful, ocean-blue eyes. With his darker hair and grownup face, I never connected him with the twins until today. He's related to them somehow. I was so angry that day, I've forgotten their names."

Jen figured she already knew one of them but held her tongue until she had the rest of the information. "It's okay. We'll figure out something."

"Wait." Mom set her cup down with a rattle. "Maybe Kimberly remembers."

Twenty minutes later, she walked back into the room. "Sorry, that took so long. We made a time to get our nails done next week."

"It's okay, dear." Dad's eyes twinkled. "I've been catching up with our young man, here. I'm proud of him."

Colin's cheeks flamed, but he appeared pleased.

Elaine plopped in the chair she'd vacated earlier. "I can't believe I never knew this. The whole incident made such an impression on Kimberley because she'd never seen me so angry. I didn't know. We might have been able to see the twins more if I'd said something to Cari."

"Dear, you're not making sense."

"She remembered their names. The older one," she pursed her lips. "Such an affectation ... he referred to himself as Gill-B."

Jen turned to Colin. "I'll bet that's what Auggie was trying to tell us when he showed us his mask. The guy who yelled at Cari. He said it sounded like Gilby, but not exactly."

Mom continued. "The younger one is ..." Her eyes were wide. "August. Kimberly never put it together with our Auggie, but we rarely refer to him by his full name. Their last name was Guildane."

Colin leaned forward. "Did she remember anything else?"

Elaine shrugged. "Not really."

Jen's stomach flipped. "Mom, was August in a wheel-chair?"

"Yes. How did you know?"

"He's their uncle. Gill-B is their father." She went into the kitchen and dragged a stool toward the refrigerator.

Dad followed her. "What are you doing, dear?"

"I need to get some things down from the basket on top there."

"Here, let me. Cookies?"

"No. There should be a magazine and a padded envelope up there. Plus, I have to get a letter from my desk. With all the chaos going on, I forgot. You all need to see this stuff."

CHAPTER 20

Wednesday morning Colin arrived with doughnuts and hopeful plans to take the kids to the Perot Science Museum. Jen had mentioned Auggie handled the lighter weekday crowds better. One look at her bloodshot eyes had him suggesting he take the twins for the full day. What he was going to do with them, he hadn't a clue.

His sugary breakfast treat wasn't the wisest choice. He chuckled at his own folly. *Dad material, you're not.*

Jen added eggs and bacon to his sweet offering. She would be such a good caretaker for the twins. Maybe they could visit him in the spring. He would enjoy showing them around Traverse City or Mackinac Island.

"Auggie loves Legoland, but I suggest you get in and out quick." She lowered her voice, pulling him along as a co-conspirator. "He can get overstimulated by the choices."

He cherished how her eyes twinkled when she gave him hints to know the twins better. "You okay if we go to Lilac Lane and work on the pitching alley if there's time?"

She clunked her forehead. "I forgot to tell you. Richard called. Harold is still trying to work out the kinks with the building permit, so we can't start that part yet."

Would a call from his firm smooth that blip in their plans faster? He'd ring Deborah and ask her to check into it. He longed to ease Jen's worry any way he could.

Detective Mason's call the day before had set her on edge. She'd been making lists of what the twins needed from their condo ever since. He felt better knowing the seasoned officer would be with her and help her puzzle through his sister's cryptic message. He wished he could take that burden from her, but they'd agreed he wouldn't know what was out of place. Neither would her parents.

Patrick and Elaine. His mind wrestled with what to call them. Former neighbors didn't begin to do justice to the roles they'd played in his college years. The word mentors, especially Mr. Clark, was a closer fit, but still didn't feel right. Friends would have to do for now. They'd popped over to Jen's for a quick morning visit—as promised to the kids—and were now on their way to some big meeting with Patrick's colleagues.

Colin was glad they were back in his life. Why had he allowed his sister's wishes to overrun his desire for a continued relationship with the Clarks? "We'll come back here to eat dinner with your folks as planned."

"I'd better get going, myself. Would you mind getting the photo and things down for me? Take a few of those fortune cookies for you three. You might need the bribe later." Her hand jerked when his fingers brushed hers, as if she'd received an electric shock. Her wide eyes reminded him of a bunny, ready to bolt from the big bad wolf.

Rubbing his fingers where they'd touched, he watched her retreat from the kitchen and turn toward her bedroom, clutching the fashion magazine to her chest. She held the envelope by a corner as if it crawled with bugs.

He struggled to recall the little girl they'd moved next door to so many years ago. All pigtails and skinned knees, folding origami cootie catchers with his sister, the paper game better known as a fortune teller to his older crowd. The only picture he could conjure was the smart, funny, beautiful woman intent on guiding everyone through this trauma.

He broke a fortune cookie in half, pulled the fortune, and popped the treat in his mouth. Flipping the tiny slip of paper over, he nearly choked on the sweet confection.

YOUR FUTURE IS AROUND THE CORNER.

"I'm so sorry I held onto the photo." Jen's stomach plummeted, as it always did in this elevator, racing to the floors upward. "After the anxiety attack and everything about Richard came out, I completely forgot."

"Oz already told you—no harm done." Detective Mason scanned the posh courtyard from the clear enclosure as it ascended. "We were going to ask you about it, anyway."

"You didn't seem very surprised when I gave it to you. What's going on?"

"We found the other half in the garbage behind your shop. No fingerprints or words. Nothing."

"So that's why Oz snapped up the part Cari sent me so quick. I wondered why she didn't come with us."

"I can handle a condo tour with you. She's better suited to getting results at the lab faster." Mason snickered.

The elevator doors whispered open, and the two women walked to the condo at the end of the hall. Jen dug Cari's keys from her purse. The crystal bauble at the end of the chain clanked against the door. She grasped the trinket and shushed it as she had so many times before. "I always meant to change this noisy thing. I guess it's a moot point now."

Once inside, the living room appeared both serene—with its quiet colors and tasteful art—while lived-in and loved. A board game lay open on the dining table in the alcove, and boy's tennis shoes lounged beneath. "She really was distracted the last few days."

"How so?" Mason took her notebook from her jacket pocket.

Jen pointed to the shoes. "That is a no-no in Cari's house."

"But the board game didn't bother her?"

"It meant they were learning. Personal things out of place meant being lazy." Remembering other quirks of her friend, she smiled. "Cari was a study in opposites sometimes."

She strolled into the living room, running her fingers over the back of the buttery leather sofa. "She said I'd find it in the place I least expected it. With her, that could be anywhere."

"I've got a copy here. Let's see exactly what she had to say." Mason flipped open a folder and her eyes tracked the words. She repeated the phrasing. "Let's work through this systematically. Did you come here often?"

"Not as much as we did at my apartment, but yes, I was here a lot. The view of Dallas is even more stunning than at my place, especially at night."

"When you were here ... where did you usually sit?"

She pointed to a lounge chair cornered to the couch.

"Sit where you usually did your—" she consulted the transcript. "—relaxing."

"Ah, follow her *exact* words." Jen sank onto the cushy chair. Wiggling around, she worked to dispel the jitters coursing through her.

"You look uncomfortable, not relaxed."

She swung her feet onto the matching stool. "I'm so short, I always have my feet up."

"Look around the chair. Is anything out of place?" Mason stood near the windows and directed the search.

Jen ran her hands between the cushion and arms. No pieces of paper, books, anything, not even dirt. "Nothing here." Her fingers pressed under the nesting tables beside her. "This feels so cloak-and-dagger. That wasn't Cari."

Mason walked around to the front of the chair. "Good to know. Now, do what she said. Relax. She's underlined that word."

"I unwound with the kids here quite a bit. But relaxing? Not unless Cari was here. Then she was in charge, and I could loosen my worry strings. We used to love putting the kids to bed and hashing out the day or talking about music, other designers, new models. You name it."

"So, if she was here, where would she be sitting?"

Jen pointed to the closer end of the couch.

Mason sat where indicated. "Here? Like this?"

"Yes." She snorted. "Except you're about a foot too short."

Mason kicked off her shoes and kneeled on the sofa. "Better?"

Jen's shoulders tensed, but Cari no longer cared whose feet were on her couch. "Yes, that's about right."

"See anything unusual?"

"Mason, you're a genius." Jen jumped up and raced to the bookshelf behind the sofa. "She's always had her books sorted by color, ever since I've known her. She wouldn't have put this blue leather one here in between these purple—" Memories engulfed her.

"What is it?"

"I thought she'd gotten rid of this years ago." Jen pulled the brightly colored book from the shelf. "My parents gave this to her when she moved in with us. Her first Bible." She held the leather-covered volume close. "I haven't seen this in years. Never out here. I've read quite a few of these books. I would have noticed."

Mason steered her to the couch. "Let's sit you down. This is exactly why you were needed. So many people have Bibles sitting around, our team didn't recognize this as out of place."

Jen opened the book with care, peeking under the front cover. When nothing jumped out to startle a soul, her shoulders relaxed. She moved to flip the book over, but Mason stopped her.

"If there's something in here for you to find, we don't want to lose where she hid it. She seems to have appreciated symbolism."

Fanning the pages, the first clue to Cari's frame of mind jumped out in color, or the lack thereof, in the family history record at the front. She'd filled out Stone and Rosemary Marshall's births and marriage in jet-black ink. Their death date was penciled in.

In contrast, she'd penned Patrick and Elaine Clark's information with a subtler blue. Jen's, Colin's, and Cari's births were there as well.

Jen touched the blank line next to Cari's name. "I suppose I'll have to fill this in later, for the twins." She hiccupped. "Can I take this home with me?"

"We'll have to see what it produces first."

Cari's beautiful script testified to the births of her children in a vibrant pink ink. Underneath, she'd penciled the word *conception*, then wrote *New Year's Eve* next to it. Important info for the twins' health records. Jen fingered the corner of the page to turn it, but a faint pencil line drew her attention. She walked to the floor-to-ceiling windows to catch the light. "This might be what we're looking for." Faint strokes of lead appeared when she held the book at an angle.

Mason squared her glasses and squinted at the page. "I can't read it, even with my specs. Good thing you saw it."

"It's written in a slim line down the side of the *Births* page. She wrote biological donor." Jen grunted. "Gilbartson Bartholomew Guildane III. What a mouthful." She flipped the paper to what looked like a mostly blank copyright page and pointed to the light pencil lines. "Here's a list of names she titled *Aliases*, including Gill-B Guildane and Gilbert Goldman." She read the long list of similar names, then inhaled sharply.

"What's up? I thought you already guessed who their father was." Mason leaned closer.

"What I didn't know is this one." She pointed. "Bart Golden. That's my friend's boss and the guy who bought the building next to ours last year." Jen gave a short account of Ethan's suspicions. "This is too much of a coincidence. Somehow, this guy knows about the twins."

"You might be right. I'll get our people involved in that. But for now, let's finish here. We'll figure out what to do with the other information later. But this could end up being an ace up your sleeve if needed down the road." She didn't elaborate.

Jen continued to leaf through the pages. The second clue was a small sticky tag underlining *Acts* 16:34. A name was written on the slip of paper. *Pastor Hicks.* She read the passage out loud. "'The jailer brought them into his house and set a meal before them; he was filled with joy because he had come to believe in God—he and his whole household.'" Tears prickled behind her eyes.

Detective Mason paused in her notations. "Do you have any idea why she marked this?"

Jen rummaged for tissues and blew her nose. "I think she's trying to tell us ... me ... she did have a relationship with God after all. I wish I'd known."

She fluttered the pages again but only found one more tag. It held the initials GBG3 and pointed to *Exodus* 23:2. "Do not follow the crowd in doing wrong. When you give testimony in a lawsuit, do not pervert justice by siding with the crowd."

Mason paced. "Strange way of going about it, but if she found something incriminating about the guy, we have a possible motive."

CHAPTER 21

Jen plopped on her bed and kicked off her shoes. "Mom, is there any way you could maybe come over earlier?"

"What's wrong, honey?"

"Nothing major." She collapsed back on the duvet. "Everything just piled up today."

"Hang on." Muffled rumblings sounded through the phone. "I'll be there in half an hour. Are the kids back yet?"

"They're still with Colin. He called and said his secretary was able to plow through the building permit issue. They're probably at Lilac by now. I bet he'd appreciate an extra hand if Dad wants to go over there."

"Let me check with him … oh, he heard you. He's nodding his head. I guess I have this thing turned up too loud again. I'll drop him off there."

Some forty minutes later, Mom apologized for running late. "Colin said they would pick up pizza for dinner. I watched the twins for a few minutes. They're getting good." Grandmotherly pride laced her voice. "He looked relieved when we got there. I gather Auggie was getting a little intense about pitching, and Ree wanted to bat more. Dad can use the exercise."

She raided her candy stash and gave Mom a chocolate truffle ball. "I was getting some coffee. Do you want tea?"

Mom nodded. "Your dad is so used to being busy. I'm not sure what he's going to do when ..." She unwrapped the treat and popped it in her mouth, closing her eyes. "Mmm. I can't buy these down there easily." She finished chewing. "So, what's all this about you and Cari?"

"Was I mean to her, Mom? I remember being less than thrilled about giving up my "only child" status at first, but once I got used to that ..."

"You were two bugs in a rug growing up. Two vastly diverse species, but compatible and living on the same carpet most of the time."

She smiled at Mom's analogy.

"But mean? No. At least she never said anything. Did you find a diary or something?"

Jen shook her head. "After going to the condo today and talking with the twins' doctor and Pastor Hicks—" She sighed. "I don't recognize who Cari was any longer." She slid a hot cinnamon disk from its wrapper, needing something stronger than chocolate to settle her mood. "Did you know she was a believer? But she didn't tell me."

Mom put her hand over her heart, eyes tearing. "You could not have delivered better news." She was quiet for a moment. "As for the rest ... honey, do you think maybe that's your grief talking? This is so hard for all of us to wrap our heads around. But it's got to be doubly so for you, with how intertwined your life was with hers. And now you have the worry over the kids' futures." She rubbed Jen's shoulder.

"Maybe. I sure hope they can give me the rest of my favorite tea back soon. Coffee is getting old."

"I don't understand."

"Something else I forgot to mention. The police confiscated the last batch Cari made for me. The stuff at the showroom had something mixed in with it."

Mom flinched.

Why hadn't she kept that to herself? In for a penny, in for a pound. "They wanted to make sure what I had here wasn't tampered with."

"Was it?"

"No. And Mason said the drops in the showroom tea were Syrup of Ipecac. It would have only made me nauseous." She grimaced. "But she was honest that there might not be much left to give back. I'm going to miss having a cup when it's gone."

"Gone?"

"I don't know the tea-to-fruit ratio, or what spices she used."

Mom chuckled. "She didn't mix anything to make that tea."

"What do you mean?"

"I thought she'd have told you by now. You know Cari could barely boil water. You think she came up with that blend on her own?" Mom's mouth twisted to the side. "I think it's time I give away another of her secrets. Your last year of college, you were rushing to get your finals project done before Christmas break. You couldn't get home until the night before she left for that modeling job in France."

"I remember. That was her first big professional gig." Jen grinned. Cari had been so excited.

"Sweetheart, she was strapped for cash. She had to pay a hefty last-minute flight fee until she got to Paris, where they reimbursed her. Dad wanted to give her the money, but she wouldn't hear of it. She was determined to make her own way." Mom smiled at the memory. "You were due home, and she hadn't found your gift yet. She wanted something special to help you get through your last semester. Cari was so proud of you."

"She gave me that beautiful basket filled with the relaxation CD she burned, a cute little tea infuser, my mug, and her tea mixture in that gorgeous tin."

"You were holding the tin when she said she made it. She meant putting the basket together. You thought she meant the tea."

"But I've never been able to find anything close to her brew. I've tried. Come on, Mom, we both know I'm kind of a coffee and tea snob."

"Kind of?"

"Guilty. But I've pretty much tried them all. Hers is so refreshing, citrusy, and smooth. She had to have made that."

"Sorry to burst another bubble, Jen, but if you were to get three boxes of Bigelow brand Constant Comment tea bags, cut open each sachet, dump them in a special tin, and throw in a handful of love, you'd have Cari's special brew."

"Tea bags? Seriously? I mean, even my corner pharmacy carries that brand."

"I know." Soft crinkles around Mom's eyes made the tattling a little more palatable. "I used to pick it up for her once in a while."

"Constant Comment, huh?" Jen propped her chin on her fist.

"Don't be hurt."

"I'm not."

"I can see it in your eyes. I'm as much to blame as her. When you raved about how the tea helped you breeze through your last semester, I begged her not to tell you until after you graduated. Then you asked her for more halfway through the semester because you'd already run out. And you requested another batch as your graduation gift. She didn't have the heart to tell you by then. Neither did I."

Jen pinched the bridge of her nose. "So once again, I turn out to be the brat and end up making more work for Cari."

Elaine took her daughter's chin in hand. "No pity party allowed. Your pleasure with her gift was priceless. You wanted to experience that feeling every time you had a cup. Do you still have the mug?"

"Of course. It's locked away in my desk at work."

"Why not sitting out on top of it?"

"I don't want someone else to use it. It's too special."

"My point exactly. You know she didn't make that, but you cherish it."

A moment of quiet ensued. "She opened each single pouch from three boxes. Really?"

"Every batch."

Jen calculated. That many boxes, four to five times a year, twenty sachets per box ... for the last seven years. "That's a lot of tea bags." She giggled.

"That's better. Now, call your dad. Tell them the coast is clear, and they can come home." She winked. "Tomorrow is Thanksgiving. Have you given it any more thought?"

"Low key. Beyond that, I don't have a clue."

"Mind if I handle it? One of our neighbors taught me how to make the most wonderful *Pamonha de Forno Goiana*." She kissed her fingertips. "It's a type of Brazilian corn casserole. You'll love it."

"Sounds perfect."

Mom grabbed the notepad off the refrigerator and started a list. "Shopping the day before Thanksgiving in the States." She shuddered. "Not ideal, but we'll hurry. What else do we need?"

"Nothing I can think of." She eyed her cold coffee. "On second thought, let's pick up three boxes of Constant Comment. I can't throw in Cari's special brand of love, but maybe the kids can help."

"That's my girl."

Settling into the passenger side, Mason buckled. She hated it when Oz drove. Without the driver's side mechanisms to raise her seat, she felt the full weight of Dallas traffic pressing down around her.

Oz checked her mirror and pulled out into the gnarled Thanksgiving traffic. She honked at a wayward car. "Working holidays when the creeps are out in force isn't fun."

Mason agreed. "It makes getting work done harder too. No one is around when you need them."

"Melissa said Miss Jen was doing her check-ins like clockwork until Tuesday night. Said her folks flew in early, surprising her. Guess it's a regular thing with the mom."

"She mentioned it yesterday. Can't be easy for Miss In-Control." Mason grunted.

Oz grinned. "Melissa made an impromptu visit on her way home last night. Mainly to get an impression of the parents. She said they're a lovely couple." She glanced over the rim of her sunglasses at her partner. "Especially the mom."

Mason hooted. "That's something coming from Melissa."

"You got any plans when you get home?"

"A shower, sandwich, and bed."

"That's no way to celebrate. I'm officially inviting you to my brother's cookout for dinner." Oz chuckled. "After being around my whole crew, you'll be thankful you can go home."

Jen walked Colin to the door after he'd said the rest of his goodbyes.

Dad clanked dishes in the kitchen as he cleaned up after dessert and Mom occupied the twins in their bedroom teaching them a new game she'd learned in Brazil.

"I appreciate you including me for Thanksgiving dinner," Colin said.

"You're family. You're always welcome." She squeezed his elbow and stepped back. "It was good for all of us to have a quiet day—well, except the squabbling."

"Whew." Exhaustion pulled at his chiseled features. "They were a handful, weren't they? You're sure it's okay if only Auggie and I go to the batting cage for a while tomorrow? I'll be glad when we're finally finished with the new one."

"I think the twins need a break from each other. You guided them through the worst of it today, though. They respond well to you."

His crooked smile rewarded her compliment.

"You're beat. I can see it in your eyes. I've got help here. Go get some rest."

After seeing Colin out, Jen went back to the kitchen and hoisted herself onto a stool next to her father.

He looked up from the extra helping of dessert he'd secreted away. "I sure enjoy that young man's company. He always was one of my favorites from the old neighborhood." He bit into his key lime pie and eyed her. "You're blushing. You don't have a crush on him again, do you?"

"Again?"

"Sweetheart, I may not be the most observant father, but I don't live under a rock. Even I knew you were sweet on him." He cocked his head sideways. "Since when?"

"Forever?"

He gazed straight to her heart. "Does he know?"

"I don't think so. It has to stay that way, Dad. He doesn't need to worry about his kid sister's buddy crushin' on him with everything else happening."

Dad lifted his mug and took a long swig from it, his go to for *I'm not saying a word.*

"Will you tell me about the Marshalls after they got mixed up in drugs? When they first moved next door, they seemed so nice." She fiddled with the salt and pepper shakers. "Mom won't say much. Colin even less."

"Your mom blames herself."

"Why?"

He pushed his glasses up his nose. "Stone and Rosemary Marshall were your average young parents, but they didn't fit in with the PTA crowd." He rose and took his dessert plate to the sink. "Remember the house on the corner?"

"The creepy old place?"

He chuckled. "It was nice when Mrs. Pritchard owned it. When she moved, another young couple bought it. They were a bit odd, but they kept to themselves, so no harm. Your mom said they were nice enough."

"Mom thinks everyone's nice."

"One of her charms." His eyes twinkled before growing serious again. "They said they didn't have any family or friends, so Mom introduced them to everyone in the neighborhood, including the Marshalls." His jaw clenched. "I can't remember their names. They looked like such a wholesome, clean-cut couple. No one knew they were dealing."

"Drugs? Right on our block? And the Marshalls got involved with them?"

"The worst though ..." He appeared lost in thought. "... were the last few weeks before Stone and Rosemary died. They'd started—"

Crash. Shushes, whispers, and giggles interrupted their conversation.

Dad leaned over and planted a kiss on her forehead. "We can pick this up another time, but right now it sounds like I better rescue Ree and Auggie from Gramma. Better yet, your apartment from the whole troupe."

Watching him trudge from the room, her heart grieved for the kids who had lived next door. The one she later called sister, and the other who'd recently reentered their lives. Would Colin ever let her into that part of his world?

CHAPTER 22

Oz strolled into her office Friday morning with a renewed sense of determination. "I got the forensics report. Nothing we hadn't already figured." She set a sandwich, chips, and bottle of water near Mason. Her partner spun the scroll wheel on her mouse. "You're going over the files again? For what, the third time?" She wheeled her chair around to view Mason's computer. "Anything new jump out at you?"

Mason pointed to her screen. "I've got Daphne Carmichael's report. Why can't we find out much about that girl? It's like she's been redacted from society." She pulled the plastic tab on the sandwich container and sniffed. "Ten o'clock is too early for lunch."

"Have you eaten anything since the barbeque last night?" Oz squirted vinaigrette on her salad.

Mason wrinkled her nose.

"Yeah, that's what I thought."

"Your family fed me so much I don't need to eat for a week."

"And if I didn't make sure you had food in front of you, you wouldn't either. Happens every time we get a case with little ones who touch your heart. It's January this time, isn't it?"

"And you're saying it's not getting to you?" Mason held up her little finger. "August has you wrapped tight."

"At least I admit it and still take care of myself."

"Can we get down to business?"

"No need to bust my chops."

"Let's see ... we've got Jennifer. Parents, Patrick & Elaine Clark, normally out of the country."

"Did you talk to them?"

"Briefly. Melissa was right, they're a nice couple. Level-headed." She fluffed pages of her notes forward. "They even chimed in about the uncle, since they knew him when he was younger."

"So, what's up with him?"

"He's an architect for Kent & Langston Design, based here in Dallas. Travels all over the United States. Sometimes overseas. Usual stints are nine months to a year. He has the authority to make changes on the fly when necessary. Word is, he's a bit of a whiz kid with structures." She scrunched her nose.

Oz bit back a smile. The brother hadn't proven himself enough to Mason, yet. She hoped he was a good guy, or he'd find himself in a world of hurt with her partner.

"He's been in Michigan for over a year, working on two different projects. His company expects him to be there at least another six months." She sniffed with disdain. "Too cold up there for growing bones. Besides, what's a bachelor going to do with those two, away from everything they know?"

So that was the problem. "It wouldn't give me heartburn if the kids were around here, either. To keep an eye on them, mind you."

Mason waved her hand in dismissal. "Enough about that. Here's where things get interesting. The bit players. We've got this Richard Kerne."

"Were you finally able to get what he told us verified? He's seriously Ricky Keane, the famous recluse of Keane Intelliware? Is he down on his luck or something?"

"Far from it. He's left the helm of his *very* lucrative tech company in the hands of some trusted underlings to take the job at Lilac. That hermit schtick I've read about him, though, it might not be a fake. No one outside of his company seems to know much about him. According to the little his employees divulged, he makes twice daily check-ins, and they say he comes running if needed—which is seldom." Mason jotted a note. "But something's not adding up."

"If he has a crush on Miss Jen ... or had one on the deceased ... those brainy types do some goofy things sometimes. Which could put him as a possible suspect if she turned him down."

"Good point, but from what I gather, he's well-liked by everyone, especially the women. There were more than a few pouts when I asked if he had any specific lady friends. Especially from Eva and Daphne."

"Kind of boy crazy, isn't she?"

"Ya think? She moons over every Tom, Dick, and even Harold in that shop." Mason laughed at her own pun.

"So, more digging on this Kerne or Keane guy. You got anything on the model?"

"She seems legit, if aloof. Brought up by her grand-mother in Barbados. She's a naturalized citizen. Nothing too out of the ordinary ... except—" She leaned forward and shuffled through papers on her desk, pulling one from the bottom. "Seems she takes side trips when she's in New York every chance she gets lately." She pulled the sheet closer to her face, before unearthing her reading glasses from her desk and putting them on. "Well, looky here."

Mason turned the map toward Oz and pounced her finger on a pink star south of New York City. She underscored a neighborhood in Richard Kerne's file.

"So ... this Eva chick is spying on the guy?"

"I think it's time we get down there and have a chat with both of them." She crumpled her sandwich wrapper, lobbing it into the trash. "And Oz ... thanks for caring."

"Gotta keep you healthy so you stick around." She pushed print on a file and grabbed the papers from the printer. "You're driving. I'll read Daphne's info to you on the way."

Oz recited from the sheaf of papers.

Stuck in Dallas traffic, Mason glanced at her partner. "Poor girl. No wonder she looks for attention."

Their team hadn't found much on Daphne Carmichael but the small amount in the girl's file squeezed Oz's heart. "Tough break to have your sister in a home from such a young age. Especially if you're the only two kids. I don't know what I'd do without my whole crew bugging me. As you said earlier, though, not much else. Grades are spotty. She's an English major and theater minor at UT Arlington."

"You sure drama isn't her calling? She's got enough of it swirling around her."

"Mason, you're being downright snippy today. What's gotten into you? I'm usually the grumpy one."

The diminutive detective shrugged. "Too many loose ends."

"Give it some time, Mase. When you quit worrying so much, that's when things start happening."

"Well, they're not happening fast enough."

Jen paused and listened to the tune coming down the hall in a Barbadian singsong until Eva rounded the corner of the office. "Great, now I'll have *Going to the Chapel* stuck in my head all day."

"Sure and I'm sorry." Eva held out a black leather art case. "You had a visitor. A Mr. Ethan. This is Ree's, yes? He said he's running late for work, but he'll catch you next week. Is there something you not be telling us?" Her dark eyes danced.

"Ethan is very much taken. He's merely a friend. The one who rescued the twins and me last Friday when I mistook Richard for the boogie man."

Eva cringed.

"Ree left her drawings in his truck." She stood and arched her back, the pops and crackles more pronounced than usual. "If you aren't too busy, would you mind taking the carryall to her? She's been waiting not-so-patiently for it." Glancing back at her desk, she scowled again, in real consternation this time.

Eva stood rooted to the spot. "You good? You be looking troubled."

Jen held a pile of papers. "Bank statement. You haven't used Lilac's debit card recently, have you?"

"I don't think so. Not since I stopped at Stoff for that dotted Swiss for a special young lady's dress." Eva moved her lips back and forth, deep in thought. "About a month ago?"

Jen shrugged. "I thought so, but I can't reconcile these withdrawals to any purchases. Nothing huge. But it adds up to a good chunk these last few weeks." She shook her head to clear it. "Either that, or I'm losing it and can't subtract straight."

"That not be." Eva disagreed. "You're one of the most careful businesswomen I know."

"Thank you. I think I'm just too tired to deal with it right now." She wrinkled her nose. "This was usually Cari's job. Not my favorite."

"The night classes I take might help. Should we look at it together this afternoon?"

"Careful, I might take you up on that offer." Jen sighed. "If I don't find it soon, I'll let you know."

Eva shifted from one foot to the other, glancing at the floor. "Do you mind if I, um, go for an early lunch? Richard too." Hope shone on her face.

"Where are you going?"

"Sadie's Salads. You want we should bring something back for you and Ree?"

"That would be great. Their grilled chicken and berry salad sounds yummy. Ask Ree what she wants when you give her that, will you?" She dug in her purse and handed Eva cash. "That should cover it. Thank you."

"No lunch for Colin and Master Auggie?"

"They're having a guy's day. I'm guessing they'll get something while they're out."

"Good on them." Eva dawdled. "Would you mind if we took a little more than an hour?" She blushed. "We haven't had time to sit and talk much. We might take longer than my darlin' Richard thinks this be needing."

"Uh-oh. Is he in trouble?"

"Not yet." Eva's tone held mischief.

"Sure, go ahead." Jen laughed. "You've been putting in some massive hours for this show. I can't pay overtime until we get all the damaged equipment replaced, but extra time ... that I can afford." She glanced at the clock. "It's eleven now. How about ... one thirty-ish? I'll bring Ree a snack in a bit to tide her over. And don't be too rough on poor Richard."

At noon the detectives pushed back out the doors of Lilac Lane. Mason's smile was cherubic.

"Ha!" Oz slapped her thigh. "Well, if that don't beat all. The guy's practically giving away a multi-million-dollar company because he's gaga over a girl."

"True love. I told you it exists."

"Yeah, right." Oz shuddered, but grinned. "At least it answers all the secrecy with those two." She bent to move the sedan's seat back as far as it would go and pushed the lever to ratchet it toward the floor. "Could you be any smaller, Mason?"

"Shorter every day. That's what happens when you're old, like me."

Oz hooted. "Care to make a quick stop by that convalescent home while we're waiting? We can check on Daphne Carmichael's sister. Miss Jen mentioned something the other day about her getting out soon. I'd like to find out more details."

"Sure. We have time. Jennifer said Eva and her beau aren't scheduled back from lunch until early afternoon. That'll teach me to call first to make sure everyone is available before popping in."

"You're just anxious, Mase." Oz put the car in drive and pulled onto the road. "Miss Jen sent Daphne to Stoff Fabrics to pick up an order. Ever been to that place?" Oz purred. "I could drop a month's salary there, easy."

"But you don't sew."

"I might not. However, Deidre, my niece, does. She works at Stoff to save up for fashion school." She glided her hand down the length of her torso, shooting her partner a saucy grin. "You don't think I could afford these fine duds on a detective's salary, do you?"

"I've wondered about all the silk shirts you wear. They are pretty."

"She wants to design for full-figured women. You're looking at her number one guinea pig."

Mason whistled, low and slow. "Some digs. This is a convalescent home?" She surveyed the address again. "This is the right place."

The narrow pathway led to an expansive, tiled veranda dotted with rocking chairs. It connected to a Mediterranean-style home, complete with manicured lawns.

Walking up the wide steps, Oz shivered. "Place gives me the creeps." She rubbed her arms through her jacket. "Like ... this big, beautiful porch and no one's sitting here enjoying the day."

Mason glanced at a small brass plaque. "Tarrington Manor. Please ring bell." The faint tones of an aged chime announced their arrival.

"You get the feeling we're being watched?" Oz whispered.

"Get your badge ready, you old scaredy-cat."

A disembodied voice sounded from overhead. "May I help you? Visiting hours don't start until four o'clock. Our residents are resting at the moment."

Mason held her badge up to a camera discreetly tucked in a niche above the door. "We're from the Dallas Police Department. We need to see your director."

"Someone will be with you shortly."

"If an old, grizzled butler answers, I'm outta here." Oz muttered.

The heavy walnut doors sighed open, revealing a nurse in full uniform. "This way, please. The doctor is waiting for you in her office."

They were ushered into a large, sunny room off the foyer. Pickled oak paneling and overstuffed leather gave the room an air of genteel refinement. Behind a cherry Roosevelt desk stood Dr. Granger, announced by a gilt-edged nameplate.

The doctor's professional demeanor was accentuated by her pure-white chignon crowning a graceful, if angular, face. She extended her slim hand. "How may I help you, detectives?"

"Thank you for seeing us. I'm Pamela Mason. This is my partner, Ozillia Ryan."

Oz inclined her head, her gaze darting around the room, sizing up the executive and her surroundings. She'd give a full report when they returned to the car—missing little.

"Dr. Granger." Mason seized the woman's attention. "We're here to learn what we can about one of your patients. Tabitha Carmichael."

The doctor breathed in sharply.

"Is there a problem?"

"Yes ... I mean, no." The clinician waved her hand toward visitor seating. "I will be as forthcoming as I can, within HIPAA Privacy, unless, of course, you have a warrant. But please be aware, the Carmichaels are heavy supporters of Tarrington Manor. With that patronage, they expect—*and receive*—as much confidentiality as we can manage."

Oz jumped into the conversation. "Wait a minute. The parents are alive? We were under the impression Miss Carmichael and her sister were alone."

The doctor inclined her head. "You've been speaking with Daphne." Sadness etched her face. "The dear girl is ...

how do I put this delicately? Quite delusional. I wanted to intake her after the accident. Unfortunately, we don't offer the type of psychiatric treatment she requires."

Mason folded her hands, the picture of cooperation. "Would it be possible for us to talk to Tabitha?"

"I'm afraid you can't."

Oz straightened, adding weight to her words. "Then we need to speak to the parents."

"Detectives, you don't understand." Her smile gone, the doctor's countenance was a grim earnestness. "You can't speak to her because Tabitha can't talk. She's been in a vegetative state for years. Ever since she was ten, when Daphne almost drowned her."

Mason grasped the armrest with clenched fingers. "What? Tell us all you can. *Fast*."

Deidre Ryan wished she was home working on the new blouse she'd designed for her Auntie Oz instead of staffing the front counter at Stoff Fine Fabrics. She was already late for her lunch break. "Hi there. May I help you?"

"I'm here to pick up an order. And I need another sewing pattern for my little sister. She's going to look so cute, dressed up like me. Not all that fussy stuff her mom used to put her in."

Oh no, here we go again. Maybe I can head off her spiel. "You're the intern from Lilac Lane, right?"

"Yes." She didn't supply her name. "But I won't be there for long. I'm moving on up to the big times." She fingered a gift-boxed pair of scissors.

She got a better job than a first-year intern at Lilac? How? The girl had proven over the last weeks with her many purchases that she knew very little about fashion, particularly couture style.

"Glamor wear is my thing," she'd mentioned during one of her many monologues for which she'd snagged Deidre's ear. Her questions and ideas suggested otherwise.

I'd gladly take her place as apprentice under Miss Clark and her team.

"While I'm here, I need better needles than the ones you sold me last time. Every one of them broke."

Diedre gave her a sidelong glance. "That whole pack of Schmetz needles? Those are some of our best. You had an entire box go bad? Bring them back. We can return them for you."

The other girl waved a dismissive hand. "I threw them away. Can you hurry up? I need to go pick up my little sister. Oh yeah, and that order for Lilac Lane too. Dopey silk or something."

"Dupioni silk? Sure, wait here, I'll be right back." Diedre marched to the storage room. It took a few moments to find the misfiled special-order bolt in the backroom. Carrying it to the front, she admired the color variations and shadow play when the light washed over the peacock and lime green iridescent fabric. She hoped Miss Clark would show them the jacket once it was finished. Her designs were always killer.

Deidre plopped the material onto the cutting mat and grabbed her scissors. "Remind me how much Miss Clark needed ... Where did she go?" She turned to her coworker, Pinky, who was hunched over the counter, drawing. "Did you see the girl I was talking to a few minutes ago? I have to cut her material before I go on lunch."

"That chick from Lilac?" Pinky pointed to a hodgepodge of items stacked on the counter nearby. Sewing patterns lay jumbled on top of a stiff, tweed suiting material. Pinky made a face. "She came over here, looked at my drawing, dumped that stuff on the floor, and left." She went back to sketching. "I'll take care of it in a minute."

"What are you working on?" Diedre leaned over and peeked at her friend's sketch. "That's pretty." The fitted bodice and trumpet skirt would look great on Pinky. It was reminiscent of one of Miss Clark's drawings. *I've got Lilac Lane on the brain too much.*

Pinky grinned. "It's for my Arwen gown. I have an idea for a matching mask. Would you mind helping me with it? Yours are always so pretty."

"Sure." Diedre blew an errant zigzagged lock of hair out of her eye and scooped up the pattern envelopes. "Come over this weekend, and we can work on it together."

She hiked the sewing patterns to the storage drawers, then went back for the thick, somber suiting material. It looked like it belonged in an old English novel complete with M'lords and M'ladies. *Sometimes that girl dresses older than my Gigi's car. She could be a real looker in the plus-sized model world.* She picked up Lilac's bolt of dupioni silk to reshelve it, but Pinky waylaid her.

"Do you think Ms. Clark would give me some tips for the corset part? She's been so helpful with your costumes."

"She might. You should see the finale gown her lead model is wearing in that charity event they sponsor every year. You know, that tall, pretty blonde that comes in here with her once in a while." She gave her fingers a chef's kiss.

Pinky's eyes grew enormous. "You mean the one who was murdered a few days ago?"

"No way." Deidre's hand flew to her mouth.

"Where've you been? It's all over the news. Hey, where're you going?"

CHAPTER 23

"Where is that thing?" Jen rummaged around on her desk for the model roster. Paperwork seemed to have exploded over every inch of its surface like the newsprint feathers on the turkeys the kids crafted yesterday.

Her fingers twitched with nervous energy. *Not this again.* Pushing the concern away, she concentrated on finding the show timetable. Would Eva be as adept as Cari had been at managing events for Lilac? Those were tall heels to fill.

Pfft. Let her be herself. The voice instructed. *She'll find her own way.*

Jen agreed. *Unbelievable. I'm taking the advice of ... what?* Should she talk to someone about this unseen counsel? *Later.* For now, she had enough concerns to go around for days.

She went into list mode, indexing the ones uppermost in her thoughts. Could they hold the show where Cari had spent most of her modeling career—right here at Lilac Lane? Would the event take place at all? Should she replace the last two designs on the model roll? If not, would Ree be up for wearing the one and seeing someone else in the other?

Pulling open the top desk tray, her keys rattled against pens and paper clips. "Oh, right, I locked it away." Her brows scrunched together. She couldn't remember why. She removed the list from its hiding spot. Underneath sat Auggie's metal mask. She lifted the creation and admired his clever use of nuts, bolts, and wire. She mimicked its grimace. The mask glared back.

"I can see why Auggie doesn't like you." She turned it around and raised the façade to her face. The cold metal touched her temple and a skitter ran through her hairline. She dropped the mask as if it were scorching hot. "He's right. Something about you is ... almost menacing." From the looks of things, Auggie had used his hand-cranked drill to bore holes where he wanted fasteners. She could imagine his tongue sticking out for better concentration.

Maybe the metal monstrosity would look friendlier with a good dusting and polish. Grimy fingerprints covered the bits and pieces of brass, copper, and ... red? She pulled the thread.

The strand was caught around the screw he'd used for a nose. She plucked at the bright wool fiber and threw the yarn in the trash.

Visions of squashed pumpkins, sunny side up eggs, and flattened Christmas trees ricocheted through her thoughts. Dark alleys, discarded evidence, and stogy smoking bad guys came to mind. She dug the thread from the garbage and wound it around her shirt button for safe keeping, laughing at her fanciful imagination. "Time to get some food in you. You're getting slap happy."

With that, she went into the workroom to get the promised snack for Ree. Passing her desk on the way out she gave the mask a pat. "You stay here. Out of trouble."

MURDER MAY I

Ree sat crossed-legged on the stage Uncle Colin and the others had built in the new pitching alley room. Her drawings and art pencils arced around her. She'd missed them.

She flipped the ends of the beautiful, crocheted scarf over her shoulder to keep it away from her waxy pencils. Engine and Rosie had helped her and Auggie buy the gift for Cari at last year's Educate auction. Engine said it was hers now. She closed her eyes and inhaled. Tiny wisps of her mother's favored scent met her nose. If she pretended hard enough, it was like Cari sat right next to her.

Clip, clop. Clip, clop. Daphne's heavy Mary Jane platform heels announced her before she arrived in the room.

"There you are." The intern chirped. "I've been looking all over for you. Come here. I want to show you something."

Hackles rode the back of Ree's neck. She couldn't wait for the new intern at Lilac. Maybe this one would help Engine more. Ree extended her legs and plopped her drawing pad on her lap. The new little stage was perfect for sketching. "Give me a few minutes, okay?"

Daphne glared at the drawings. "I told you to throw those away." Her tone grew icy. "Why didn't you listen?"

Ree swallowed a growl. Cari said Adira, her imaginary lion, was only allowed to roar when Ree needed extra courage, not just because she didn't like something.

Daphne rolled her eyes. "If you want to become a famous fashion designer, you need to take criticism from those of us who know better."

She glanced up at the older girl, towering over her. Sweat drenched the intern's red face. "Can you please back up, Daphne?" Ree's insides wobbled. She put her hand over her stomach. The monster hadn't wanted to escape since the day Cari was killed.

Her eidetic memory—her gift, as Cari had called it—damaged though it was the last few days—stumbled forward and a memory surfaced. Dr. Brasil's office with Cari and Auggie. "But this ... monster in my tummy wakes up when people get mad. It makes me want to—" She gagged.

Dr. B had her pay attention to the rumblings before they got too big for her stomach. "You don't have to be quiet when you're upset," he encouraged. "You can be a fearless lion." She'd named the brave creature, Adira.

He said it meant *strong* in Hebrew, and he roared with her. Cari and Auggie joined in. Later, she practiced inside her head. Dr. B called it attitude. He gave Adira permission to ask questions and speak up for Ree when she didn't feel strong enough herself.

The picture vanished. She'd nearly forgotten about the visits after Cari died. Until her stomach squirmed again. Squaring her shoulders, she roared, "It's my artwork. You're not the boss of me."

"Get up." Daphne ground through tight lips.

Maybe too much attitude?

"You won't need these where you're going." Daphne spat the words and kneeled, shoveling the drawings into the leather case.

"Stop that." Ree wrestled for the satchel, catching her hand on the zipper.

Daphne yanked it away.

"Those are mine." Not as confident as she'd wanted, but her hand hurt. The metal teeth had gouged her palm. Scarlet droplets forced their way through the scratch.

Daphne's gaze riveted to the blood. She squinted, her eyes narrow and tight. She reminded Ree of a cat—all teeth and claws—ready to pounce and bite. Nothing like her confident Adira.

"I said let's go." Daphne flung the art sheath at the back wall. Drawings fluttered through the air. "Come along." Her voice turned syrupy. "There's someone I want you to meet." She gripped the girl's arm and yanked her to a standing position. "You sure are getting heavy." Her voice sharpened. "Just like Tabitha."

Wrestling with Daphne's hold, Ree's heart pounded. "Where are you taking me?"

"It's a secret."

"Does Aunt Jen know?"

Neither the grip nor the pull was gentle now. "I said—" Daphne gritted her teeth. "It's a secret. No one else can know. Tabitha is precious. Mummy and Daddy said so. Only special people get to see her."

Ree wrenched her arm away. "I'm not going anywhere with you." Her knees quivered, but she stood straight. "I can't go anywhere unless I tell Aunt Jen first." Ree clutched Cari's scarf.

"She won't let you go." Daphne sniffed the air and wrinkled her nose. Her lips smiled. Her eyes did not.

An icy finger of fear ran down Ree's spine.

"Come on. It'll be fun. I'm sure you'll like her. She's a nice little girl." Her lips twisted. "Do you know how to swim?"

"Yes. Why?"

"I wanted to teach you, like I did Tabby." The older girl pouted. "It doesn't matter. Let's go." She held out her hand.

Ree tucked her fingers away from the girl. "Not until you tell me who Tabitha is."

"My little sister, silly." Daphne's face took on a pained expression. "She never wants to talk to me anymore. I'm too old for her now."

She seized Ree's wrist, twisting it until she could see the abrasion. The trickle of blood had smeared. Daphne pulled a tissue from her pocket and wiped at the gouge, her eyes glazing.

"Ouch. You're hurting me."

"You remind me so much of Tabitha. Smart. Pretty. Artistic." Daphne pouted and dropped the tissue on the floor. "Daddy's little girl." She cackled. "You don't even have a daddy."

Ree whimpered but searched for an escape.

Daphne's chin quivered. "I had a daddy. I loved him. But Tabitha is his favorite. It's not fair. I always have to take care of her." She stomped her foot, her platform heel crashing against the newly laid wood. "I have to play the games she wants and always let her win." Her voice softened to a little girl's cadence. "January will play dolls with me."

The monster returned to Ree's stomach with a vengeance, blocking Adira from her grasp. If she threw up, Daphne would be really angry with her. What would Engine do? Maybe pray. *God* ... the rest deserted her, but an idea popped into her head. "Daphne?"

"Hmm?" The intern's look sharpened. "What? I told you, it's time to go." She made a grab for Ree's shoulder, nearly catching her.

"Go find Aunt Jen. I think she's up front. Tell her ... you're taking me to lunch. I'll get my jacket."

Daphne tilted her head to the side. "Then you'll go with me?" The older girl spun and skipped across the room. At the doorway, she glanced back over her shoulder. "Well? What are you waiting for? Hurry up. I'll be right back." She disappeared through the backstage door.

Ree dashed toward the office and rammed straight into—

"Whoa. What's the matter?" Jen hugged her goddaughter to her. The girl's pulse pounded against her chest.

"She's going to take me away, Engine!"

"No one's taking you anywhere, honey. Not today."

"Daphne wants me to meet her little sister. She tried to ruin my pictures."

Jen held her at arm's length. "Where is she?"

"She's looking for you. I told her you were up front."

"Hurry, show me your sketches."

They rushed to the papers strewn across the floor.

Jen scrutinized the drawing. "There's something familiar about this design."

Clip, clop. Clip, clop.

"She's coming," Ree screeched.

"Quick, out the other door."

"Not so fast." The words boomed. "Get back here."

Jen rushed Ree ahead of her. "Not on your life."

"Maybe not mine. But it will be yours."

Jen turned back, looking straight into the barrel of a gun.

Mason and Oz raced to their car. While Mason punched numbers into her phone, Oz activated the emergency system and gunned the Charger toward Lilac Lane.

"The showroom phone's going straight to voicemail." Mason grabbed the panic handle overhead. "You tried Jennifer's cell?"

Oz gripped the steering wheel. "Twice. Colin's and Melissa's too. Messages on all of them." Honking at a slow driver, she yelled. "Get out of the way. What do you think this siren means?" She swerved around the lagger.

Mason planted her feet for stability in the careening vehicle and called the precinct's number. Finishing the call, she updated her partner. "Dispatch can't get them either."

"Try her detail again." Oz took the corner, fast and tight.

Mason called Lilac's security detail. "Where are you?" Her voice roared through the car. "No, I didn't send word for you to check another lead. Get back to that showroom. Pronto. See if you can get in. No one's answering." She gripped her cell. "Daphne Carmichael is to be brought in for questioning. We're on our way there now."

Oz stole a glance at her partner. "Mason. Breathe."

"I am."

"You look like you're about to hyperventilate. That's not going to help."

"I've got a bad feeling about this."

Oz's cell buzzed. She passed it to Mason. "Maybe that's her."

"It says Deidre."

"My niece. Hang up. She'll understand."

Mason went to hand it back when it rang a second time. "It's her again. I'll tell her you can't talk." She put the phone to her ear. "Detective Mason speaking." She paused. "No, she's driving. She'll have to call—" She listened then tapped the phone screen. "Deidre, I have you on speaker. Say that again."

"The intern from Lilac Lane was here. She saw my friend's sketch and for some reason, she panicked. She ditched everything and hauled it outta here—"

They drove under an overpass and the reception garbled.

Oz leaned toward the phone Mason held. "We lost you for a moment. Repeat that."

"Auntie! She told Pinky she's making matching outfits for her and her sister." Deidre drew a quick breath. "Auntie Oz, I think she was talking about Miss Marshall's daughter. She's been here with Miss Clark before. She'd *never* wear that stuff. That little girl has some serious fashion game going on."

"I know, lovey. You two did great remembering everything. I'll call you when I can."

Mason disconnected Oz's phone and braced as the car fishtailed through a curve.

CHAPTER 24

Colin parked his rental in the back of Lilac Lane near Jen's Camry. No other vehicles were around. Where was her security detail? Maybe they were at lunch. The police following him and Auggie all morning had left moments before, running their emergency lights as they whipped around his car. Probably an accident on the nearby expressway.

"Got your ball, champ?"

Auggie held up the leather treasure. "Wait until Engine sees how good I can throw. She's gonna be surprised. Can we go back tomorrow with Ree?" Auggie bounced his way up the ramp, all the while smoothing the ball with his fingers.

"We should have the new net up here tomorrow. You can practice then." Colin yanked at the back door. Locked. *Good. My girls are safe.* The protective thought caught him by surprise. He fished his keys out of his pocket and searched for the showroom spare. Opening the door, he ushered Auggie inside.

"I'm gonna find Engine and Reeree."

"Wait a minute, tiger. This door's sticking. I want to lock—"

The boy was already out of earshot.

Jen choked back a cry when Auggie skidded into the room, all squeaking tennis shoes and excitement.

"Engine. Guess what? I—"

"Stop!" She yelled. "Go back."

"No." Daphne barked. "I want him over there with you. I need to keep an eye on y'all."

Auggie's tightened jaw announced he was spoiling for some sass.

Jen reached over and pulled him to her, nearly dislodging the baseball he gripped with both hands. She tried shoving him behind her with Ree. He refused. She clamped her hand around his wrist to keep him nearby.

Daphne held the gun as if it were a plaything. Was it a prop she'd kept from her theater days? Jen couldn't take the chance. "Let the kids go. It's me you want."

Daphne's lips curled. "No, actually, they will be coming with me."

"How are you going to take care of them? You know they need special attention."

"They'll be fine. You baby them too much." Daphne huffed. "They should play with normal kids. Go to a regular school." Her eyes shrunk to slits. "Not the horrible one you sent me to."

Jen's thoughts raced to keep up with Daphne's volatile mood shifts.

"I don't wanna go to your school." Auggie shouted. "I wanna go to mine."

Ree held a tentative hand toward her twin.

He shook his head. "She's a meanie-face. I need to tell Engine someth—"

"Auggie, sshhh." Ree hissed. "She's going to hurt Engine if we don't be quiet."

He stood ice-crystal still. One blessed moment.

If Daphne hurts the twins, there'll be nothing left of me. They could sweep her up with the dust. *Lord Jesus, please keep them safe.* Her prayer looped as she searched for a way out. "I'm not sure what I've done to upset you so much, Daphne."

"Done?" Daphne squawked. "You've *done* nothing. Really. Nu-thing." She spat each syllable. "Not for me. You always took Cari's side. Or huddled with them." The gun jerked between the twins.

Ree's fingers clutched the back of Jen's soft chenille sweater, tugging her backward. Her goddaughter gasped.

"But, Engine—" Auggie interrupted, his tone insistent.

"Auggie. Please. Not now."

He stomped his foot and pulled away from Jen.

"Stop moving!" Daphne snarled.

He scooted sideways. "Let me see."

Jen could barely make out Colin in the shadowy light from the hallway behind Daphne. What was he doing? Signaling? This wasn't a game.

"What are you looking at?" The intern pivoted toward the hall.

"Daphne, what do you need?" Jen fought to draw the girl's attention to herself. Back from Auggie. Away from Colin.

Daphne whirled on her, voice dripping with syrup. "You want to help now? You all think you're better than me. Everyone does."

"I don't." Ree's voice wavered.

"Then why wouldn't you *listen* to me?" Daphne shrieked and jabbed the pistol toward the sketches littering the floor.

Ree flinched.

"You're scaring her."

"And you." All sweetness was gone, replaced with pure venom. "Big Boss Jennifer. Large and in charge. Except you're not now. Are you?" She poked the gun at her ample chest. "No. Because I am."

Jen inched her way toward Auggie, pulling Ree with her.

"I'm giving the orders now. Ordinary ol' Daphne." Her whine returned. "Nobody notices me unless they need something." She waved the gun as if tracking a bouncing balloon. "I'm a glorified gopher. Babysitter. Lunch lady. The one no one takes seriously."

Only a couple more feet. Inch by inch.

"Well, you will all pay attention now." Daphne paced a tight line in front of them.

Jen couldn't see Colin. He wouldn't rush Daphne, would he? The kids needed one of them alive. Inhale. *One*—calm. She touched her thumb and index finger together. *Two*—

"Counting's not going to help this time." Daphne sneered. "I know you do that one-two-three thing when you're frustrated. And it's usually with me." She reached for Ree. Her cheeks stretched in a macabre grin. "Come here, Sissy." Her tone carried the lilt of a little girl. "We'll go swimming after we visit Tabby."

Daphne spiraling concerned Jen more than the gun. Her thoughts swooped through her brain, searching and discarding answers, exits, and solutions.

"Did you even hear me?" A howl scraped through the plea.

"I heard you, Daphne. I didn't know you felt that way. I'm paying attention now."

"A dollar late and a day short." The intern paused and rubbed her brow with the barrel. "Or is it a day late?" She shook herself and stomped closer, holding the fisted gun above her head. Her eyes blazed with hatred.

Jen raised her arms to ward off the blow that never happened.

"You're afraid of me?" Daphne cackled.

Patchouli, manufactured coconut, and orange assaulted Jen's nose. "You're wearing that perfume again. It's—" She coughed. The dense, earthy fragrance made her stomach heave. Ree hugged her middle.

Cari's delicate roses wafted around her, coming from Ree's scarf. Roses and patchouli warred for dominance. The truth speared through her. All nausea vanished. She stood straight, girding for battle. "It was *you*. You killed Cari."

Ree loosened her grip and peered around Jen with caution.

Daphne's lips puckered. "I ... no ... she ... she caught me with the dress. I was ... redesigning ... fixing it. We struggled over the scissors." She paused and her face morphed into a sneer. "Cari got what was coming to her."

"I went to find out why my mom was yelling."

"So, we're calling her mom now, are we?" Daphne's shoulders deflated, but not her gun hand. "She was *always* screaming ... at me."

Ree peered at the older girl. "You brushed past me in the hall. Your sleeve touched my face. Then, you rushed into the playroom. I remember now."

"You and that photographic memory of yours. The perfect little girl." Daphne pouted.

"After they accused Auggie ..." Ree shuddered and focused on Jen. "When I touched your sweater just now ... it's fluffy. Like hers was that day."

"I know, honey." Jen eyed Daphne but hugged her girl. "Cari's perfume from your scarf mixed with Daphne's cologne. The smell was similar in the dressing room." She wrinkled her nose. "I *don't* have an eidetic memory, but I do have a photographer who took a photo of you later rubbing your bare arms. No sweater in sight." She tugged on the thread wound around her button. "A *red* and green jumper. I bet it came from the same boutique as my friend's squashed pumpkin sweater."

"My ... my scary blobs." Relief flooded Ree's voice.

"It was dirty. I hid it until later. Why did you have to remember that?" Daphne cried. She whirled on Auggie. "What are you doing?"

He stood, rigid in his stance, and rotated the ball in his hands. He squinted at the darkened hallway behind her.

"Quit fidgeting." Daphne stomped toward the boy. "Give me that."

"No. It's mine. Uncle Colin—"

"I don't care." She snatched it from him, throwing the ball across the room.

A muffled pop and the sharp chink of shattering glass sounded from the showroom. Daphne seemed to take no notice.

Auggie reached into his pocket. He stared at the intern with intensity. Retribution was written across his face.

Jen moved toward him, wishing he could mask his emotions as he charged others of doing.

"Stay where you are." Daphne screamed at her.

Jen strained to hear his whispers.

"Mother May I ...?" He moved his feet a fraction to the right.

Daphne wheeled toward Jen. "Tell him to shut up, or else."

Glaring, Auggie continued to murmur. "Mother May I ...?" He angled his body and took a deep breath, shifted his weight, raised his knee and let loose his weapon, straight to its target. "Bean her between the eyeballs!"

Daphne landed with a thud at Jen's feet.

Moments later, Jen sensed the stampede of people, more than heard them. Mason and Oz pounded into the room, followed by others. Uniformed officers added to the chaos.

Ree's eyes were huge, swimming with concern.

Where was Colin? There he was, running toward them. The room began a slow carousel around her. Counting was useless. Instead, she focused on Auggie.

He picked up Officer Henderson's rock, threw it in the air, and caught it with confidence. Holding his fingers an inch apart, he glared at the small welt already raising on Daphne's forehead. "Off by that much."

"I think ... I'm going to be—" Darkness engulfed her.

Mason's voice floated somewhere nearby. "Get back. Give her some air." So loud for such a little woman. Jen's thoughts scattered.

"Secure the weapon." Oz bellowed.

The rock? Or the gun? Reality pulled her back to the commotion in the room.

Colin hugged her to his chest. "I thought I'd lost you." He choked. "All of you."

Mason scurried around, shouting orders. Oz made sure they were followed. Under their care, the mayhem was stabilized in minutes.

Auggie patted the top of Jen's head. Ree sat next to her, holding her hand. Colin helped her sit up and stayed glued to her side.

Listening to the others, Jen pieced together her missing moments. Mason and Oz had finally breached the front door—that was going to be an expensive fix—and ran for the back room. The detectives seemed caught between their frustration with the whole lot of them and proud as peacocks over Auggie's accomplishment.

Oz helped raise Daphne to her feet while another officer recited the Miranda rights. Handcuffs were secured around the young woman's wrists. She regarded the silver shackles as if they were so much pretty jewelry. The only sign she gave of recognizing their dire significance was the black mascara that ran in harsh rivulets, vandalizing her pretty face.

Another officer picked up the revolver with gloved hands.

"It's empty." Daphne sputtered. "I promise. It's from my daddy's desk. Why won't you believe me? No one ever believes me."

The deputy hit the release and a single round landed in his palm.

"He always said it was empty." Daphne crumpled before their eyes.

CHAPTER 25

Late the next morning, Jen contemplated the city from her dining room windows. Even her beloved bridges offered little comfort. *No more, please?* She glanced skyward, beseeching in silent prayer. Yesterday's chaos churned through Jen's mind like the creamer in her coffee until her cell rang again.

"Good morning, Detective Mason." Jen exhaled audibly, too tired to care if her emotions spilled over the airwaves. "Do you need Colin here too? He should be back shortly."

Earlier, Colin had sat at her dining table, ostensibly working on his laptop. After she didn't hear his keys click for long stretches, he'd offered to go get takeout lunch for the four of them.

"You can fill him in. This shouldn't take too long." Mason paused.

Jen imagined the detective putting her pen to paper, complete with a chewed cap, and checking the boxes as she went down a list. What she wouldn't give sometimes to be more methodical like that and turn off her creative brain.

"Daphne will not be bothering any of you for a good long time. And I quote, 'Of that you can be sure.'"

"Exactly what does that mean?"

Mason cleared her throat. "Mr. and Mrs. Carmichael asked me to convey their sympathy and express how sorry they are. Their daughter has *finally* been committed to a psychiatric hospital."

Mason's clipped tones mirrored Jen's thoughts. Too little, too late.

Why couldn't more parents be like hers? Mom and Dad had called this morning to check on everyone. They weren't happy but seemed to understand Jen's need for a temporary buffer zone around her little family. They assured her they were but a phone call away.

She gave herself a shake. She could dwell on a past of what ifs or be grateful for the here and now. For the two children sprawled on her living room floor, waiting for their uncle to return. *Father, thank you for keeping us safe. Help me forgive Daphne. For my own sake, if not for hers.* Was that a true pardon? She didn't know, but it was a start.

Mason broke into her contemplation. "Hang on a second. I have to get this." The phone went to canned music.

With their discussion paused, Jen's thoughts hopscotched over the previous afternoon.

Melissa had arrived soon after Mason, Oz, and the others. "I'll take the kids to the playroom. Come get us when you're done." She requested an officer to accompany them.

"You're sure you're okay, Engine?" Ree appeared torn between mothering and the offered sanctuary.

"I'm good." Jen gave her a hug. "Go with Melissa. I'll fill you in later with what you need to know." *Which won't be much.*

She squeezed Auggie's empty hand. His other one clutched Henderson's rock. *Should we memorialize that thing or bury it?* He probably wouldn't let it out of his sight for a while.

Once the twins fled the room, clinging to the advocate's hands, Daphne's convoluted, confusing tale unfolded.

Her personal delusions of grandeur encompassed more than the damaged equipment she'd caused at the showroom, but she started there. The broken serger? "No one would teach me how to work it. So, I taught myself." The mangled new mic? "I was practicing my announcements for the charity show. Stupid thing wouldn't turn on." The list continued.

Still on hold, Jen pulled her thoughts from the intern's brokenness. Her next reflection brought a needed smile to her face.

Colin and Grampa had pulled Auggie aside after a light dinner the night before. They explained beaning people with a ball ... or a rock ... wasn't to be a regular occurrence.

"But I can if they wanna hurt Ree, or Engine, or Gramma, right?" The boy's logic left them with little to say in the moment. He was ready to slay Goliath for his family.

Mason came back on the line. "You still there? I just got word that the extra detail for the memorial service is granted."

"You're sure having it here in the community room tomorrow will be okay?" She pulled a glass from the cupboard, intent on assuaging her thirst.

"I'd rather you have it there then at some big church. We can keep an eye on things better."

"Did you find out anything more from Daphne ... that you can share?"

"Not much, but she did cough up a few details that could help you make some sense of things."

"Like what?"

"For starters, she'd rummaged around in your backroom at Lilac and found that photo of Cari and you at some exclusive shindig. She took it and pinned it to her bedroom door, pretending it was her private dressing room."

The snapshot she ripped in half?

"She kept moaning, 'They never take me with them.'"

"That was an invitation-only event," Jen cried. "I had no control over that."

"I know." Compassion lodged heavy in Mason's words. "Do you want me to continue?"

"Please."

"Seems she thought if you drank the contaminated tea, you'd be sick and put her in charge of the show."

Jen grunted. "Where did she get that stuff? We had some in our medicine closet when I was a kid, but I thought they discontinued it years ago."

"We haven't figured that out yet. But she finally revealed where she got the gun and why she killed Caribbean."

Jen's heart skipped a beat.

"During a visit to her parents' home—a rarity from what I understand—Daphne searched for her mother's scissors. She planned to alter an old suit of her grandmother's, like she'd seen some YouTube influencer do. While she didn't find the shears, she did come across her father's gun tucked away in his desk. Then she returned to Lilac and filched Rose's dressmaking shears." Mason whistled. "Expensive buggers. Anyway, she planned to add 'her own special touches' to your design. She actually got mad when Oz told her she'd only ruined a copy." Mason huffed. "Caribbean walked in while she was slashing at it and things escalated quickly."

A sob lodged in Jen's chest. "I don't need to hear more. At least for now."

"I understand." Mason's words became monotone. "Before I go, sorry to be the bearer of more bad news, but Melissa's tied up with another delicate case today. She received a call last night. For some reason, your custody hearing was moved to Monday morning. *Tsk*." The click of her tongue held volumes of irritation. "She will meet you and Colin at the courthouse."

Hanging up, Jen bypassed the refrigerator and dragged herself to the living room, near the kids. No amount of water would quench her parched spirit.

After lunch, Jen sat at the dining table, staring at nothing. A few of the takeout tacos Colin brought back remained. He insisted on cleaning up and shooed her from the kitchen. The twins took a rare afternoon nap, having protested little.

I should do the same. Sleep had eluded her most of the night.

Colin finally walked into the dining room and sat next to her. His shoulders slumped. After a few minutes he spoke. "I felt so helpless yesterday. I couldn't see a way to get in the room without making Daphne's drama worse." He picked up Jen's hand from the table, playing with her fingers. "Auggie was so excited to tell you about his latest target practice and ran ahead." He winced. "With that gun waving around ... my whole family in there ... I tried to get him to throw the ball. Toward me. At the target practice. Anywhere. Just cause a distraction, so I could stop her." A muscle along his jawline tightened. "I'm sorry if I put any of you in danger."

His touch overloaded her raw emotions. "You did no such thing." Giving his hand a soft squeeze, she gently pulled away. "None of us knew what to do. We all did the best we could." That small comfort was all she had to offer for now.

Daphne's drama. Colin's description was perfect.

She filled him in on Mason's call. "The only problem is, Daphne doesn't seem to be the one who stalked Cari. They've gone over all the timelines and testimonials." Daphne was not Cari's boogey man. "They'll keep digging."

Sunday morning, Jen opened the blinds in the dining room allowing light to spill into the apartment. Her frayed nerves had settled to a dull ache since Daphne's capture two days ago. As much as she wanted to be with her church family today, Cari's memorial took precedence.

She joined her parents at the kitchen island. "Thanks for texting, Mom. I don't think I could've sat here one more minute by myself."

Perched on a stool, Mom cradled a cup of tea in her hands. "I figured you were awake, but I didn't want to call in case you were able to sleep in a little."

"I wish." She poured the last dregs of coffee in her dad's cup. "I'll make a fresh one for us. There's not enough coffee in the world to keep me from dreading today." Rinsing the now-empty carafe, Jen pushed a new filter into the drip basket and measured the grounds while contemplating what was ahead of them. "I'm glad it's supposed to be warm and sunny later. Cari deserves a beautiful day."

"Jen?" Dad's voice sounded puzzled. "Don't you think that's enough?"

She looked down at the coffeemaker. The filter nearly overflowed. Her giggle strangled her breath, but she welcomed the comic relief. Pouring the grounds in a bowl, she started over. "One. Two. Three. Four. And a half." She propped her fist on her hip. "Geez, Dad. You don't want your weekly allowance of caffeine all in one cup?"

"I'll pass, thank you."

Mom dabbed the corner of her eye with a tissue. "Remind me of the time schedule."

"We'll get the kids up about eight-thirty. Colin will be along about ten. I'm thankful the service is here, where we're relatively comfortable. She was cremated so we can hold it where and when we want." Jen leaned on the island, opposite her parents. "No casket. No urn. Only photos and flowers. Mason will have police there as *guests* for the kids' safety. They don't think the stalker is anyone from Lilac. Thank goodness. Plus, we all need some closure."

Lethargy had consumed Ree and Auggie since yesterday morning. Even the promised shopping trip for pool toys and swimsuits had produced little excitement. Life unsettled had never been a good thing for the Marshall twins. Even more so now that their helm was missing. Cari's routine may have seemed chaotic to the outside world, but she had been their constant.

Mom chewed her lip. "Do *you* think it's a good idea to have the twins there?"

Jen shrugged. "Colin and I plan to stick to them like glue." She rubbed an imaginary spot on the counter. "I have a favor to ask. Mason wants our family to mingle. Keep our listening ears open if anyone says anything unusual. The regulars from her past know you. New ones don't. Would the two of you be the minglers?"

Dad huffed. "Much as I don't like this cloak and dagger stuff, we'll do what we can."

Watching her parents interact, her heart warmed. She longed to be that well-matched, both physically and mentally, with someone, someday. And she had to admit, they looked dashing today.

The rainforests of South America hadn't given them much need for elegant attire, but events for their girls, Elaine's publishing life, and the ever-present need for "schmoozing" donors—her father's words—meant they both still kept a few dressier clothes on hand.

For this solemn occasion, Dad had chosen a tie gifted by Cari. Jen could still recall the playful banter between the two.

Cari had plucked the handsome present from its gift wrap. "Dad, that brown striped tie makes you look like you have a noose around your neck. Try this one."

He'd finally agreed to wear whatever she chose on two conditions. "Number one, your clothing tastes run bigger than my needs. It cannot cost a week's salary."

"Daadd." She'd used her teenage whine on him, the one good enough to wheedle a few extra bucks from him back then. "I can't find any to fit your good looks for that pittance."

"And two, with you both dragging me to these shows, it must contain purple. I will show my allegiance to Lilac Lane and my favorite girls, wherever I go."

The French blue of his shirt accentuated the soft lilac and blue paisley print of today's tie. His navy sports coat gave him an air of suave authority. Not for the first time, Jen wished she could talk him into modeling. He'd be a favorite.

Mom's dress was lovely. One Jen had designed for her back when the twins were babes. The garment's tailored tucks, from bustline to hips, complimented her mother's trim waist. A smoky-gray satin lining under crocheted, midnight-blue lace still looked stunning on her. She chose little adornment. Only small hoop earrings, as well as a silver cross at her throat.

"That's a pretty necklace. Is it new?"

Mom reached up and touched the filigreed cruciform. "Cari sent it to me for my birthday, with some matching silver studs."

A lump fought its way up Jen's throat. She'd only seen the earrings. "It's beautiful."

"When did you say Colin is supposed to be here?" Dad opened the fridge, perused inside, and shut it.

"Ten o'clock. I'm guessing he'll come early, though. He's having a hard time keeping himself busy at the hotel."

Mom shook her head. "Poor boy. He sure has had a lot to deal with being a member of the Marshall family."

Dad walked over to look out the dining room windows. With his hands in his pockets, he jingled his keys. He stalked back to the island, leaning into the granite, as if it could support his sadness. Dad was a fixer. He couldn't fix this.

Jen eyed the door of the Sheffield Apartment's spacious community room as people came and went. She and Colin bookended the twins while her parents mingled, as requested. They knew much of the crowd. Colin did not.

The twins sat in folding chairs or retreated to a corner, tabled off for their privacy.

She was grateful her apartment management agreed to the last-minute get-together, even offering punch and cookies—gladly accepted by the family. She'd contacted Cari's condominium director to alert those who had known the model. The Wise-Beverton's association sent their condolences along with a beautiful spray of flowers. She placed it on a credenza surrounded by many of the photos they'd collected of Cari.

Colin had somehow procured pictures from the Silhouette magazine spread, nestled in silver frames. "They're just pulls from the magazine." He confided with a wink.

Those were sprinkled among several Elaine had taken of Cari as a teenager and young woman, along with Annie's photography from Lilac. Only two photos were missing. Jen couldn't bear to look at them yet.

With her permission, the complex had alerted their tenants to the gathering. Mr. Harper, minus his new kitten—much to Ree's consternation—shambled in, swiping his ancient eyes. "Such a waste of a nice young lady." He patted the twins on their head and shuffled away, grief weighing heavy on his cane.

Leo and the other Sheffield staff members took turns at the door so each could pay their respects. Many reminded Auggie and Ree to stop by and chat when they had a chance.

Even Georgia and the kids had dropped in for a short visit. Gretchen and Toby gave the twins a respite from the many adults crowding in on them to offer condolences.

Jen glanced at her phone. Only ten more minutes. Almost two hours and nothing untoward had happened. A flurry of giggles near the door caught her attention. Colin motioned for Dad, asking him to stay by the twins.

Jen guided Colin through the remaining throng of sympathy bearers. Mason and Oz beat them to the entrance but hung back.

All eyes were on the man who had arrived. No wonder he'd caused such a stir. Cari's partner in the Silhouette spread. The one whose shoulder she peeked over in the photos now standing next to the memorial flowers. Edward Baas graced them with his presence.

Now that Jen could see him in the flesh—tall, his spun-sugar hair combed back, strong jawline, suit immaculately cut—she could see why he'd become a fashion favorite when he'd arrived in the States the previous year. The only thing marring his handsome features were his red-rimmed eyes. Bad contacts or teary? He was a looker all right. And familiar somehow.

Scanning the room, his gaze darted past Jen and settled on Rachel. The model, fully made up as she was today, commanded the room. Of course, he'd gravitate to her.

Jen didn't give him another thought when Richard and Eva appeared in the doorway. She caught Colin's eye and nodded toward her friends. "I'll get them and bring them over by you and the twins." She whispered in his ear. "We can visit for a bit."

Evidently, Auggie had been keeping an eye out for his favorite Lilac team member. "Richard," he bellowed and ran toward him, bumping into Edward just as the model rubbed his eye.

"Sorry." The boy hurtled himself into Richard's arms.

Without missing a step, the Adonis look-alike brushed the jostling off with good grace and a shy smile. *Well, what do you know, the great Edward Baas is bashful.* A thought flickered through her memory then retreated. Ignoring the minor commotion near the male model, she turned to Eva until she heard a groan behind her.

"Oh, no." Edward addressed Rachel. "I must have rubbed my contact out. Can you see it anywhere?"

She searched his jacket. "I can't, sugar. Are you okay?"

"I'm as blind as a bat without them." He bent to look at the floor, seemed to realize the futility, and stood, shoving his hand through his hair. A shock of it dislodged and hung down his forehead. Red crept up his neck and onto his cheeks. "I knew this was a bad idea." He reached into his pocket and pulled out brow line spectacles, placing them on the bridge of his nose.

Jen gasped. "Ned? How did I not know a supermodel was living in my building?"

"Hello, Jennifer." Several women gaped at him. "Can we talk? Somewhere private?"

Oz placed manicured fingers on his shoulder. "Not until *we* have a conversation first ... Mr. Ned Bass." Her tone was quiet, but firm. "You've been hard to locate, sir."

He flinched. "My publicist is not going to like this."

CHAPTER 26

Monday morning, once bright and filled with hope, seemed a million miles away now. Jen's throat grew raw from shoving aside sobs.

Colin's knuckles shone white on the steering wheel. "I can't do this, Jen. Not on my own."

She laid her hand on his cheek. "You can."

I, on the other hand, must go upstairs and tell my heart and soul goodbye.

Earlier that day, she and Colin sat in the small courtroom, flanking Melissa, their counsel for custody, and suffered the old wooden chairs. They hoped guardianship would be theirs to share, working out the twins' lives together.

Instead, the judge brought down her decree with a cold finality and nasty glare. "Good day, sir." She bobbed her head toward Colin. Then the pinched, angular features sneered at Melissa and Jen. "Ladies."

As the twins' only living blood relative—the judge's flimsy excuse for the life-altering edict—Colin had just been awarded full custody. Whether he wanted it or not. Staring straight ahead, his normally tanned skin held a greenish pallor.

Jen sat in stunned silence, hearing little else. *Father God, I—* Her brain stumbled to a halt. A low snarl rumbled in her chest.

There was nothing tender about Melissa's grip on her leg, keeping her planted in her seat. A quiet hiss slithered between the advocate's parted lips—a warning to remain still. Melissa kept her eyes downcast.

Jen's breath skidded between her ribs. Everything Jen ever wanted ... needed ... was now gone. Her heart shattered into a million miniscule, twin-sized shards. One large, man-sized chunk cracked off and tumbled after them into the abyss.

Melissa kept her gaze hooded, saying little as they left the judge's chambers.

"Wait here." She stalked to a reception desk and asked the lady a question. Whatever the answer, Melissa's expression turned thunderous. She beckoned them forward. "Follow me."

"But—" Jen protested.

"Please."

The ragtag trio trudged down the block to a coffee shop. The warmth of the café was useless to Jen's frozen heart.

"What can I get you?" The advocate's expression was now a blank mask.

Colin still hadn't said a word.

Jen glanced at him. "I don't think either of us is—"

"Trust me, you want something hot. Sweet. Calories. We have *work* to do." Melissa's tone was bitter.

Colin finally emerged from his fog and glanced at Jen with a questioning grimace.

She shrugged. "Herbal tea?" It didn't matter what kind. All would taste sour right now, anyway. "Maybe split a muffin?"

"I guess." His voice fell as flat as the concrete counter they stood next to.

Melissa gave their order to the barista.

Jen followed Colin to a corner booth in the nearly empty cafe. He removed his coat and held out his hand for hers.

"No, thanks. I can't get warm."

He sat and moved close to the wall, gesturing to the seat next to him. They left the other side for Melissa, who plunked their tray on the chipped, laminate table. She threw her leather bag on the bench seat and trudged to the condiments bar. Grabbing a handful of sugar, creamer, and a wad of napkins, she returned and dumped them beside the mugs, sliding into the booth.

Her cheeks blazed identical spots of red as she dug in her satchel. Slapping her binder down and flipping it open to a blank page, she finally looked up. Dark storm clouds grazed the horizons behind her eyes. Lightning flashed and sparked. "Are you two okay?"

Colin glanced around them as if unsure who the question was directed to. "I think so."

"I'm ... I mean, I knew Colin might be awarded custody." Jen croaked. "I was still hoping for at least shared. But to not be able to see them, visit, even talk to them for three months. That will be after Christmas." She wiped her nose. "That's ... I can't ... I don't know."

Colin's nod quickened. "When she asked if I had someone who could help me with them in Michigan, I thought she meant for visits. I really did. I love my niece and nephew. But what am I going to do with them?" His words tumbled over themselves. "All of Auggie's needs. And Ree is a little girl." Panic rose in his gaze.

"But you said you have this Tiffany person." Jen's heart still stung a bit from his answer.

"She's my next-door neighbor. I travel a lot. She feeds my fish and gets my mail. I water her plants when she's gone. She's capable, but she's not going to want a long-term gig. She's got a serious boyfriend." He peered at Jen. "Who isn't me. I thought the judge was going to ask us what we wanted."

"She's supposed to," Melissa muttered.

He breathed a heavy sigh. "I don't know ... I mean three months." He turned to their ally. "Can she do that?"

Melissa's pen bounced against her paper. "She can. But she shouldn't have. At least in my opinion. Most judges understand, if everyone doesn't buy into the arrangements, it usually doesn't work." She scribbled some notes. "Now that I know where you both stand—" She smacked her hand on the table. "We are not going down without a fight. I need to think." She paused, then glanced up, her eyes watery. "Judge Arbuckle took Judge Crandall's place, but she should have recused herself." She stared into her mug as if it held all the world's answers. "If only I could have warned you."

"Warn us about what?" Jen asked.

"That y'all couldn't get a fair shake from her. No matter how hard we tried." A strangled whimper escaped her lips.

"Recuse herself?" Colin asked. "Do you two have history?"

"I'm not real familiar with her. But yeah, you could say we share a past." Pain poured from Melissa's gaze. "She's my mother."

"Your *what*?" Had she heard correctly? Questions exploded in Jen's mind.

Colin beat her in voicing them. "I thought you couldn't—"

Melissa held up her hand. "You deserve answers. For now, the abridged version. Judge Arbuckle walked away from us, my dad, brother, and me, and went back to her family name when Raymond and I were small. Our dad raised us with the help of his aunt, Lora. A hired hand ... the son of family friends ... caused this." She pulled her ever-present choker down to expose a ragged, angry scar.

Jen winced. "You don't have to tell us. Not if you don't want to."

"Y'all need the truth. This is where it begins. I was sixteen. My dad died because of him." A sob escaped her. Reaching for a napkin, she mopped her eyes. "A month later, my *mother* reappeared, staking a claim on guardianship of us kids and the generous life insurance policy that went along with that to finish raising us. She forgot she wasn't the only one gifted at law in the family. Aunt Lora put her dusty law degree to good use." Pride shone on her face. "We got to stay with her. My mother was *not* happy. And it seems she can be quite vindictive."

Some of the fire had come back in her eyes. "I've had exactly one run-in with her since returning to Dallas." Her nostrils flared. "Since that incident, I've been able to stay out of her way and off her docket. Until today. I don't know how she orchestrated it, but I aim to find out. All I know is there was a last-minute switch with the original magistrate. And I do mean last minute. I found out about the replacement at the same time as you, when she walked in."

"I wondered why you looked like you were going to throw up when we first sat down." Colin pulled a face.

Melissa chomped her sticky bun. Swallowing, she wiped her fingers and attacked the paper in front of her. "We need to cross all the *Ts* and dot every *I* from here on out. I don't want any loopholes available for her to squirm through. Let me outline my plan and see if you two are up for it."

They listened with rapt attention.

"You're going to have to follow her orders for now. We'll have Doctor Brasil weigh in. We need to prove Jen is more familiar with their care." She pointed at Colin. "And he's going to need your help ... in the best interest of the kids."

Colin frowned. "I thought we were going to try for shared custody, and they stay with Jen."

"First things first." Melissa tapped her pen on the pad of paper. "We have to convince another judge you want the kids with you. However, you need help from Jennifer specifically." She scribbled something on her notepad. "We don't want the kids taken away from both of you."

And here they were, two hours later, sitting in Colin's rental car, in the garage beneath her apartment. Neither seemed capable of moving.

Colin shuddered again. "Melissa was right. I can't do this. Not without you."

Jen caught Dad's eye when they entered the apartment. He sat on the couch reading the paper with the twins sprawled at his feet, thumbing through books. He took one look at her and Colin and folded the newsprint with a whoosh of crinkles. "Auggie, Ree, what say we get our coats and go over to the park? I need to stretch my legs. We'll bring ice cream back for everyone."

Auggie whooped, jumped up, and ran for the coat closet, nearly colliding with his grandmother, coming from the kitchen.

Ree stood. Her gaze darted between them, and her color drained.

Could she go to her sweet Ree and hug her without breaking what was left of her own heart?

"Hey, champ," Dad called to Auggie. "Go to the bathroom before we leave, will you?"

Stalling? Whatever ... it worked. Auggie headed down the hall with no argument.

Mom went to Ree, enveloped her in a loving embrace, and whispered in her ear. The girl nodded, silent. She trudged to the closet and dragged her coat on. The only sign that the lively, creative girl Jen was used to was in the rigid little automaton was a brief touch of Jen's fingers as the child stumbled out the door.

Jen's strength deserted her. She leaned against the entry wall, still clutching her purse. Her keys clanked to the floor.

Auggie returned to the living room and started for the door. He stopped in front of his godmother and picked up her key ring. "Here, Engine."

The warmth of his fingers placing the cold metal in her hand, somehow shifted her brain into some semblance of order.

Auggie smiled. "Don't worry. It's okay. I asked God. He's going to make it all better." He whirled and bounced out the door after his twin.

Her dad gave Colin's shoulder a manly squeeze and inclined his head toward his daughter. "Allow Elaine to assist you with this, son. It looks like you could use some cheering yourself. Everything has been too much for the both of you." He took Jen's chin in his hand and gave her forehead a kiss. "Let Mom help."

Auggie's words resounded in Jen's ears. *All better*. So simple. Like kissing a boo-boo. She wished life was that easy. He'd asked God and God was going to make things right. His optimism blanketed her, covering her own inadequacies. *Help me be more like him, Jesus.*

She closed her eyes and shut out the world for eternity. Or the length of time it took one lone tear to slip down her cheek.

Dad's kind voice interrupted the nothingness. "Do you want me to say anything to the kids, Colin?"

"I guess ... tell them—" He cleared his throat. "Tell them we'll discuss this as a family when you get back. Over ice cream."

If only Colin's words were true. But she was on her own now. Even her parents wouldn't be here until their next furlough. What was she to become without Cari? Was there anything left of her without Ree and Auggie?

Life could not be fixed. Her best friend torn from her. For what? Because a psychotic young woman imagined she could change the mistakes of her own past if only she used different players.

The little ones she'd helped usher through the last nine years exiled from her. To assuage a mother's desire for vengeance on anyone whose story mirrored the broken reflection she held of her daughter.

And the man she'd loved since before she knew what the word meant ... would he ever know? She couldn't tell him. Not now.

Her fingers tingled. She shoved them behind her.

You're not angry with him, are you? The voice pressed. *He's only doing right by his family.*

Be quiet.

She needed help through this, not some intangible voice in her head telling her what to do, when and if it felt like it.

Yes, he would do right by his family. *His* family. But Colin Marshall's life was not entwined with hers like his sister's had been. His day-to-day would now include the twins, without the presence of either woman. He was an innocent pawn in this macabre game.

What game? You're being melodramatic.

One—calm. *Two*—No. You are not in control. You never were!

Mom moved toward her with arms raised to hug.

She stiffened. "I'm okay. I'm … I need a minute."

Mom gazed deep into her eyes, distress constricting her features. "I'll be in the kitchen getting dinner ready. Something simple." She touched Colin's shoulder and left.

Jen stared at him. "I don't mean to flake out on you. I'm sure Mom could use the company if you want to join her."

He put his hand on her arm and gave a light squeeze. His mouth opened and shut. He tried again. "Jen. We need—"

She fled from the foyer.

Planning to sit on her bed and gather her thoughts, instead she fell to her knees beside it. Grabbing a tissue, she bowed her head. An unbearable anguish seeped from her soul. She expected the room to start spinning. Tears to gush—

One thought pushed to the forefront. Pray. Not with words, but more like her pastor's message months back. Pray. Repent. Ask. Yield.

"Where do I begin?" She croaked into the stillness. "What do I say to you?"

Her pulse quickened. He'd understand, even without sound.

Lord, I haven't been doing much of this lately. I'm not sure what to say. But I have so much to be thankful for. Can I start there?

Comfort flooded her heart, easing the pinch.

I'm grateful the twins are safe. And Colin is reconnecting with them. With us. Most of all, praise Jesus, learning Cari knows you.

A soothing warmth glimmered in her chest. Peace followed each tiny twinkle of hope. She took a deep, cleansing breath. *Please forgive me. Help me to know I can still be calm, cool, and collected. But the control ... it's not mine.*

The vise of hurt around her heart dropped away as if a lock had been unfastened.

Tap, tap, tap. "Jen?" Colin's deep voice startled her. "Can I come in?"

She wiped her eyes and blew her nose. She probably looked like a raccoon. No matter. It was time he knew the truth. She moved to the edge of her bed. "Sure."

Colin stuck his head around the door, his expression wary.

She waved him in and patted the space beside her. "I won't bite. I promise."

The corner of the mattress dipped when he sat. "I wanted to make sure you're okay."

Busy noises from the kitchen meant her mom was processing things in her own way. "I'm sorry. I didn't mean to act like that earlier."

"No need to apologize. I wish I could make this go away for you. For all of us—" He shrugged. "You're fine."

"No. Actually, I'm not. I'm a mess. I've tried to hide this. But it's time you understood how badly I can react when things go haywire. In case ... you let the kids come see me later."

"Jen. I'm not—"

She put up her hand. "Please, let me finish. If I don't get this out now, my bravery might desert me later." She ran her hand over the soft, purple nubs of her duvet cover. "I've battled depression and anxiety since I was in high school."

"I know."

She pulled at a string. "I'd been doing okay until Cari was killed. But I've had a couple bad episodes this week. I can't promise the kids would never see a doozy. So, there you have it." Her head snapped up. "Wait. What did you say?"

"I've known for a long time. Cari called me after you had the first one in high school."

"She did what?" Her stomach churned.

He lifted his finger to her lips, shushing her. "Now it's my turn. She'd call after you had a bout and say things like, 'she went off the deep end again,' or 'Jen had to go away to rest for a couple days.'"

Her chest tightened, heartbeat racing past her ears. "I feel like a dissected frog—after the fact. I can't believe she gave away my secret."

Shaking his head, he explained. "She called because she was scared. The one she depended on was in an emotional tailspin. Her rock had cracks."

She snorted. "*Was* cracked, you mean. Still ..."

"The call wasn't about you, Jen. It was about how she should handle things. What she could do for you, especially at first. Besides, Cari wasn't sure what would happen to the other daughter if their real one needed the parents more. She figured they'd say adios."

"They wouldn't have."

"You know that, but remember where we came from."

"Fair point."

"She was afraid for you. And worried you wouldn't make it." He placed his hand on her shoulder. "She couldn't have handled that. The only person she trusted about you, besides your folks, was me."

The bass of her pulse quieted to a background tempo. "I guess I can understand that."

He laced his fingers in front of him. "Forgive me?"

"That obvious, huh?"

His eyes crinkled. "You wear your emotions. I knew you were mad, maybe not *at* me, but—" He sighed. "I don't want to be the bad guy."

"God and I were just having a talk about it. None of us can make this disappear, but we can move forward. And I can be thankful for what I had."

He pulled at the crease in his khakis and shifted toward her. He reached up, tucking an errant curl behind her ear. "I'm not sure how to request this, but would you mind being my rock too? Like you were for Cari. At least for a while."

"Even one with cracks?"

He smiled, crevices of sadness sitting heavy around his mouth. "We'll comply. Somehow. But I need your help. Is that too much to ask?" He stared into her eyes. "Jennifer Bennifer, I'm fresh out of advice. Got any for me?"

When had the past and present mingled? The boy whose heart she'd longed to catch all those years ago was reaching out to her as a man. Unsure. Unprepared. She wanted so badly to touch him. Hold him. This was not the time. "I'd be honored."

His breath whooshed from him, hinting of cinnamon, mixed with his spicey aftershave.

"We'll get through this." She bumped shoulders with him, as she'd done all those years ago, sitting next to him on the curb between their houses. "Together."

He leaned his head on top of hers.

"We should probably check on my mom."

"She's okay. I looked in on her first. She told me if you were hiccupping with a squeak to come get her—fast." Colin lifted his head and grinned, the one that made her heart flipflop. "I don't hear any hiccups. Or squeaks." He leaned over and planted a soft kiss on her forehead. "I think we're good."

Jen wanted nothing more than to hug Dad when he returned with the kids. Finding the perfect plant specimen and ushering it through the medical world was his comfort zone, not accompanying traumatized youngsters to the park. But he seemed to have survived. He even sported a warm smile for Auggie and Ree before bidding them to wash the duck goo off their hands. "How was it, Dad?"

Mom brought him a bottle of water while Colin hung up his coat for him.

"Quiet. Not many ducks at the pond this afternoon. A couple of cranky geese. Auggie explored the edge for tadpoles, but it's not the time of year for them."

They all waited for him to get his bearings.

"Ree and I mostly sat and talked. We plan to ask the Parks Council to add two benches around the pond. One in Cari's name. And one in Daphne's."

Surprise registered all around.

"It was her idea. She decided no one was nice enough to ... that girl ... when she was little." His lips pressed in a thin line. "I wish it were so simple. But I'm not going to be the one to dissuade her tender heart." His stern look encompassed all three. "And neither are any of you."

"We wouldn't dream of it, dear. We'll figure out a way to put two beautiful, durable seats out there. Thank you. I know that was rough on you. But they needed a quiet, sturdy ship in their current storm."

"I could use some lessons, sir." Colin placed his hand on the older man's shoulder. "Would it be okay if I called to talk this fathering type stuff over with you?"

Another of those odd looks passed between her parents. Dear Lord, there was nothing wrong with either of them, was there?

"You're welcome to call whenever you want, son."

"Can we come in now?" Ree peeked around the corner.

Jen waved them forward.

They both appeared and circled the counter. They did not reach out to her, as she'd expected. Or to Colin. Without a word, both went to their grandmother, encircling her waist and each other.

Jen hadn't witnessed a gramma sandwich since the last time they were all together. Had that really been only three or four years ago? It seemed like a lifetime. She embraced the trio, and Dad followed.

Colin observed his little crunch of people. Familiar to him in so many ways. Strangers in others. The group was missing something. Someone. From here on out, they would always be minus Cari. He plowed his hand through his hair. *Man up. Uncomfortable or not, you've been welcomed into this family again.* He ambled toward them.

Miss Elaine seemed so sad. He didn't know how, but he vowed to fix that. For now, he could only think of one thing to do. Being taller than the rest, with a wingspan to match, he folded his arms around all of them. Family.

Muffled from the middle of the pack, Auggie hollered, "Group hug."

Later, Jen stood with her back to the sink, sipping a cup of decaf. Her heart skipped a beat when her mother clasped her dad's hand.

"Patrick, honey. Can you come help me find my glasses?" She rubbed her eye. "I need to get these contacts out."

"Aren't they in your purse, Mom?"

"I couldn't find them, earlier. Your dad will be able to." She stared hard at her daughter. "Can you all clean up the dinner dishes? We'll have ice cream and talk more."

Message received loud and clear. Her parents needed a moment.

The remnants of their pork chop and sweet potato dinner—Elaine's idea of something simple—sat in the sink. The twins pitched in with their usual chores, albeit at a snail's pace. Colin helped where he could. Once the grandparents returned, ice cream melted in dishes while conversation stuttered along.

A few tears mixed in with the judicial orders, court expectations, and plans. What was to be expected of them in the next weeks and months? They tried to explain it in nine-year-old terms.

"This will all turn out okay." Colin assured the kids.

By unstated consent, all three Clarks let him handle as much as he chose, only jumping in when asked or needed. He was the head of the Marshall family now.

"Engine and I talked things over." His baritone leant a strong assurance to his words. "We have to do what this judge says, or we could get in trouble."

Auggie scowled. "I didn't do anything bad."

"None of us did, champ."

"Then why are we being punished?" Ree wailed. "It's not that I don't want to live with you, but—"

"I know." He took a mouthful of the now soupy dessert, made a face, and swallowed. "All your stuff and friends are here. I get it. Do I know why the judge says we need to move you? No. But we have to."

"I don't like that judge. She's a meanie face." Auggie laid his chin on his arms.

"Let's not worry about her anymore." Colin's gaze shifted between the kids. "I'm not going to be perfect. I'll need your help. Not only yours, princess." He eyed Auggie. "Yours too, sir."

"What am I gonna do? I don't know nothin'." His brows pulled together into one fuzzy, grumpy little caterpillar.

Elaine bent over the table to look at him. "You know plenty. Plus, Grampa and Uncle Colin are going to chat, at least once a week. You think I'm going to let them have all the fun? I'll want to talk to both of you too."

Two pink circles dotted Ree's cheeks. "I don't want to leave Engine." Her voice was harsh. "She needs us. She's going to be all alone."

A significant look passed between Mom and Dad. "She won't be sweetie. At least not for long." Mom held Jen's gaze. "We didn't say anything before because we weren't sure when it was going to happen. Your dad is retiring. We found out tonight the board accepted his replacement."

Jen's heart quickened. She wouldn't be by herself after all.

"We'll go back for a few weeks." Dad said. "I have to transfer the program over, and Mom needs to pack up the house. But we'll return soon."

Mom pulled the kids' attention back to her. "Tomorrow, let's go get three calendars and mark them up with all the dates we need to remember as a family. One will go with you guys to Uncle Colin's, we'll pack one in our suitcase, and the last stays here with Engine. You watch, time will fly by. Are you game?"

The twins shrugged.

"I think that's a great idea, Mom." Too bad turning a calendar page couldn't really make time move faster.

CHAPTER 27

Jen's last-minute decision to hold the Educate Your Way Up show late Wednesday afternoon instead of the upcoming weekend had surprised nearly everyone except her, the family, and their law enforcement team. Having the twins here to close out the show with her had become an ache since Monday morning. Jen still couldn't think about it without the breath whooshing from her lungs. So, she didn't.

The whole crew pitched in all day Tuesday and that morning with phone calls and last-minute details. Aided by her parents, Colin, and the twins, the charity-turned-memorial event became a reality. Whether it would be the last one, she didn't yet know.

Many of the original invitees attended the rescheduled time. And all her regular models—save the most important one—were available. A minor miracle.

As a final precaution against Cari's as yet unknown stalker, and to share a piece of what and whom Lilac Lane was all about, Jen invited Melissa, Mason, Oz, and Oz's niece, Deidre, as guests.

The only change to the original program was a small slip of paper dedicating the fund-raiser to Caribbean Marshall and introducing Miss Lily.

I am so glad Eva was able to book her. The new model was a natural, needing little coaching. And wonder of wonders, she fit Cari's proportions with no need for last-minute alterations.

Now, the event wound its way toward the end. Jen took the moment to reflect while waiting for Rachel to finish her runway stroll.

The after-show reception would be smaller and less grand than normal, but she didn't think anyone minded. So be it if they did. Take-out dinner, popcorn, and a movie awaited her family at home.

She had entertained canceling the show. But her creative soul longed for the closure. And Cari deserved it. Devoting the program to her, with the extra splash of photos, would create a backdrop of reminiscing for fans and crew alike. She hoped her dad had purchased enough tissues.

Rachel was almost back up the runway with her last set. Jen glanced at her notes but didn't need them. "Eva Corbin, in the Golden Goddess gown," she announced.

The music changed tempo. Eva stepped from behind the curtain and a buzz rose from the audience. The model's sable skin enhanced the gown to perfection.

Yesterday, she'd asked Jen's opinion of sheering her natural locks short and wearing only a beaded headband nestled among the tight curls. The hairpiece was meant for another show, another dress, but it completed the gilded vision to perfection. No need for further adornment except a pair of Sassafras Montgomery yellow citrine earrings dangling to the model's shoulders. The audience was mesmerized. More than her majestic stature or the glitz of the gown, the person and garment were one.

Eva wanted to buy it. Hefty discounts were a perk Lilac models enjoyed. Instead, Jen had already decided to gift it to her friend. No one else could look as gorgeous in it. Tweaking the pattern before it went public would produce a similarly pretty, but different dress. This one-of-a-kind design would remain precisely that.

Larger-than-life photos of Eva and Cari splashed across the backdrops as Lilac Lane's newest lead model took the runway where the former had dominated. The two of them relaxing in Jen's office. Cari zipping Eva into an outfit. And laughing with other crew members.

The event was almost perfect. The only things missing were Cari and Sassy. But Cari would never attend again, and Sassafras had shocked her the night before when she texted to say she couldn't make it after all and had shipped the jewelry order Next Day Express with no further explanation.

Jen shook herself back to the present. Eva worked the runway giving her time to search out her parents, front and center, sitting next to Colin. Dad whispered something to Mom, and she wiped her eyes. There would be no mascara left on those lashes tonight. This was their daughters' last show together. A tribute to one. A declaration from the other.

Scanning past the crowd, the shrouded light of the sound booth allowed her to see the outlines of her sound techs. Richard, in his dark shirt and tie, pointed. Auggie stood by his side, intent on following instructions. Her boy. She wanted to reach back there and hug him. But he'd not tolerate mushiness during a show. He was a 'fressional.

Eva stopped at the staging end with a flourishing twirl. She posed, showing off the crisscrossing gilded straps at the back of the gown. With a regal strut, she returned upstage, halted short of the curtain, and blew Jen a kiss.

Many of their regulars were in the audience, dabbing their eyes. If they thought this was something, they were in for a jolt.

If a wedding dress or *robe de mariée* wasn't closing out the lineup, a show-stopping spectacle like Eva wore was usually the end of any Lilac Lane Fashion event. The audience expected it.

This time, though, the curtains closed while photographs continued to flash onscreen for several moments. The audience seemed to enjoy the novelty. Pictures rotated of Cari with Harold, Richard, and other Lilac Lane colleagues. Moving on to snaps of the beauty with her family, Patrick and Elaine, Jen, Ree and Auggie. They'd even included a couple with Colin when the two were younger and one precious photo Colin had of the siblings when their schedules had coincided in Europe a couple years back.

The lights dimmed further, and the imagery stopped. A deep, gray haze cloaked the podium where she stood. Delicate notes drifted from the speaker system. The stage draperies parted.

There, bathed in subtle light, stood Miss Lily in the secret gown—Ree's and Jen's collaboration—the one Cari was to have worn. It draped and dripped in an ethereal shimmer around the stunning model. Lily held a silver-plated stick at a jaunty angle to showcase the luxurious Venetian-styled mask attached to its end. She peered over the top, mannequin perfection. Posed. Poised. Waiting.

A young girl walked onstage. She wore a knee-length dress, similar in style, but one fit for an up-and-coming young designer. A smaller, more delicate eye mask—tied with a huge satin bow over white-blonde curls—hid her identity. But those in the crowd who followed Jennifer Clark and Lilac Lane, those who had been a fan of Caribbean, knew who hid behind it. January Elaine Marshall. Protégé of one, daughter of the other.

Lily and Ree walked forward, and the curtains closed again. Another photo splashed on the side panels behind them. Cari at her finest. As a mother. Photographer Annie's best work, in Jen's opinion.

The portrait featured the model with her daughter, heads bent together, poring over the girl's initial sketch. Ree, clearly animated, explaining the cut and design—eyes twinkling. And Cari, made up only as herself, in the rare jeans and T-shirt, hair pulled back in a sleek ponytail. Her face shining with pride over her daughter's burgeoning talent.

The small auditorium grew eerie in the near silence. The only sound—soft, tinkling music. Lily gestured for Ree. The girl walked over and tucked her fingers into the model's gloved hand.

Jen counted the beats. *One*. Pause. *Two*. Pause. *Three*. Wait for it—

Boom. The music blasted, one heart-pounding crescendo, and settled into a staccato beat for the final number.

The two paraded the catwalk together, Lilac's newly signed model keeping a gentle pace to match the smaller footfalls beside her. The two stopped at the end of the runway. Ree dislodged her hand and Lily stepped back.

The young designer curtsied to the audience, then turned to her new friend. They finished the show walking back, hand-in-hand toward Jen. She stepped from behind the podium, and Ree ran the last few paces to hug her waist.

Two final portraits, side-by-side, splashed upon the screen. Knowing which ones played to the spectators' heartstrings, Jen did not—could not—look at them. If she did, she'd lose the tenuous grasp on her composure. The audience erupted.

CHAPTER 28

Jen clicked off the call to Melissa Thursday morning. She looked forward to the day she would be able to talk to the advocate about nothing in particular. Friendly things.

Technically, the check-in calls weren't required since Cari's killer was no longer a threat. The two had continued the visits more for companionship it seemed, and to keep abreast of the legal situation. Cari's stalker still needed apprehending as well.

She hadn't seen Ned ... er ... Edward since he'd accompanied Oz and Mason to the police station after the funeral. But they would have told her if he was the culprit. Right?

Her cell rang.

Mason's greeting was brief. "I'd like to stop by in about an hour. Will you be home?"

"Sure. I'll have coffee ready."

"Oz and Melissa will be with me."

"Ookkaay." The advocate hadn't said a word. "Do you need the twins here?"

"I'd rather they not be. Can your folks get them? But we'd like Colin there if possible."

Jen's heart stuttered. "I'll see what I can do." This didn't sound good. The call ended as abruptly as it began.

Colin answered with the first ring, and she relayed the information. "They'd like you here. Can you make it, or do you want to join us by video call?"

"They?"

"Correct." Worry laced the word. "Mason, Oz, *and* Melissa. Mason was in a big hurry."

"Give me five to call the office. I'll be there."

After Colin, Oz was the first to arrive and accepted a coffee. "Sorry if Mason worried you guys." She took a sip from her mug. "She'll be here in a few minutes. She had to meet someone and make a zillion phone calls along the way."

If Oz was at ease, why was Mason on edge?

Bzzz. Bzzz. "Sending up Detective Mason and Melissa Frazier."

"Thank you, Leo."

"Mind if I ask? Should we be watching for anyone else, Miss Jen?"

She gave Oz a questioning glance.

"No one they need to look for." The detective's grin reminded her of the Cheshire cat.

A tentative knock sounded.

"That was quick—" She swung the door open. A stab of irritation shot through her. "Ned. I mean Edward."

"Hello, Jennifer." Edward Baas stood on her threshold. "I was asked to come here when I got back. May I come in?"

The elevator dinged and Mason rushed out, followed by Melissa. "I didn't expect him to beat us here." The senior detective huffed and puffed.

Jen waved them all inside. She didn't trust herself to say anything kind.

The little entourage trekked to the dining room. Colin's eyes narrowed when the male model entered. Oz snorted.

Jen jerked at her sweater sleeve. "You're having entirely too much fun with this, Oz."

"My apologies. You need to hear the whole story. I knew once I started spilling the beans, I wouldn't be able to stop. Better to zip these lips." She ran her thumb and index finger across her mouth.

Mason smirked at her partner. "Were you able to get hold of our other source?"

"Yes. He couldn't make it. Too short of notice. But he did confirm."

Mason pulled out her notebook.

"Anyone want coffee or tea before you start telling us exactly what's going on?" Jen's lips felt like cracked dirt. She licked them, to no avail.

"Sorry for all the mystery." Mason acknowledged. "We've had a lot happen the last couple days. Everything came to a head this morning. I'll take you up on that coffee."

Jen brought cookies to the table while Melissa retrieved another mug, appearing comfortable there. They were all welcome in her home, anytime. Well, maybe not Edward. That would depend on this meeting.

Mason stirred sugar into her coffee. "First things first. I think Mr. Baas has a couple things to say, then we'll let him be on his way."

Edward's cheeks reddened. "I'd like to apologize."

"What for?" Jen's tone was sharper than she'd intended.

"For asking Caribbean to deceive you. For not telling you the truth about my real identity. For not trusting you like she said I could. For—"

Colin raised his hand like a crossing guard. "Back up. You've lost me. For not trusting Jen? What does she have to do with any of this?"

Her insides tingled at Colin's irate tone. It was kind of cute. She let him take the lead. Edward's explanation better be good.

"When I first moved to the US, wherever I went, people kept mobbing me. It didn't matter what time of day or night. I wanted to be left alone, maybe make a few close friends. Breaking leases was getting old." He stared at his cup. "I'd met Caribbean before the photo shoot in Silhouette. We connected—for a lot of reasons." His eyes misted. "I phoned her one night after a particularly zealous fan incident. She said I should move to Dallas, near her. Get a place with greeters so they could keep gawkers away. But there wasn't anything available at her condominium at that time."

"Let me guess." Sarcasm laced Jen's words. "There was an opening here. I remember when you moved in."

Edward had the grace to look sheepish. "She was going to tell you about me. I begged her not to. I didn't want to draw attention to myself again." He reached up to finger a silver chain. "I'm good at modeling. But it's not who I am."

She hadn't noticed the jewelry before. Ned always had his shirts buttoned up tight. Edward didn't. The necklace ended in a handsome, blue-inlaid cross. She was sure she recognized the designer. It was not cheap. More importantly, it marked Edward as a believer.

He cleared his throat. "I'll get to the point and let you have your privacy. I'm not good at being sociable." His tone fell flat. "I was working on that with Caribbean."

Colin clunked his coffee cup down. "Just how close were you with my sister?"

Edward looked him in the eye. "Not as much as I would have liked. But I respected her wishes. Her kids and family came first. She wouldn't even let me come to the showroom because of the fuss it would cause for everyone."

He deserved a break, but Jen couldn't resist one last jab. "I bet you had a big laugh when I kept giving you fashion advice."

"I thought it was nice. You were trying to help. But I figured you'd recognize me immediately if I did what you said." He cringed. "So, I did the opposite. That and stayed out of your way as much as I could."

The pit of anger Jen had been holding onto dissolved. "I guess I can see how this all happened. Rotten timing though ... what do we call you?"

"Edward, please. You couldn't be more right about the timing. Caribbean and I were—" He palmed the table and made to stand up. "A story for another day."

Colin stalled him. "Just a minute." His annoyance seemed to have lessened, but his gaze speared Edward. "Did you ever meet my niece and nephew? Were you ever at their house?"

Mason jumped in. "That's a question we'll answer in a minute. For now, if Mr. Baas has nothing else to say, I think we've used enough of his time."

That was the politest "get lost" line Jen had ever heard.

Edward stood. "I hope you will allow me to become friends. With both of you." He gestured to Colin and Jen. "I feel as if I know you from everything Caribbean told me. I'd like to get to know her better through you."

Jen spoke her mind. "You are welcome to get acquainted with me ... since I'll be the only one here for a while." The remark struck a nerve but didn't pierce as before. "However, it will be out for coffee or at Lilac Lanes. Until I get to know Edward. No more Ned."

Colin came around the table, ostensibly to show the other man out.

Edward shook his hand. "I'm hoping to move in the near future. I'll be in contact. You look so much like your sister."

His mouth thinned to a grim line. "I miss her, terribly. But not as much as I'm sure you do." With that, he escorted himself to the door.

Colin sat back down. "Something tells me I need to keep an eye out for that guy."

"Keep your friends close and your enemies closer, eh? Smart." Mason seemed pleased with his plan. "Now that he's out of the way ... he wasn't Caribbean's stalker."

Oz took over. "Cari was right. It was her ex. The twins' father."

"But I thought there wasn't any proof." Jen leaned forward.

"Your friend, Ethan, sends his regards." Oz took a dramatic sip of her coffee. "He followed your advice and came to the station. Smart man, he documented everything he felt could be fraudulent activity—which was finally verified this morning—regarding one Bart Golden. Except there's no such person in the system."

"There is however your Gilbartson Bartholomew Guildane, III." Mason supplied with a touch of glee. "But his usual aliases are Gill-B or G.B. Guildane, who has quite the rap sheet. Mostly misdemeanors from when he was young, but a couple bigger charges." She consulted her notes. "B and Es. Domestic assault. That type of thing. And driving while under the influence, causing bodily harm."

"Putting his brother, August, in a wheelchair." Although Jen didn't know the man, if he had been important to Cari, her heart hurt for the younger brother.

"We know of August Guildane's request that his best friend, Richard ... or Ricky, or whoever he is ... watch over the children for him. In my professional opinion, a paternity test would be in good order, to prove whether this Gill-B joker is indeed their father." She glanced at Melissa who remained quiet.

Mason gestured to Oz, got up and walked to the kitchen. "Melissa, could you come here a second?" The child advocate joined her and the sound of tap water running in the sink soon followed.

Oz leaned toward Jen and Colin. "Let me make this quick. With the break-in, stalking, violating multiple restraining orders—at least one requested by Cari—plus other offenses, you two may want to keep on top of Cari's intruder case and collect any information you come across about this guy. It could give you ammunition down the road. I'm just saying." She leaned back and crossed her arms.

Mason and Melissa returned to the dining room, neither with a glass of water.

"So, if this guy has such a long criminal record, why isn't he in jail?" Colin's nostrils flared. "Richy-rich parents?"

"No. They actually tried to get him some help." Oz grunted. "It was the granddad. Seems the first Gilbart doesn't want his fancy-pants name besmirched. He always bails the kid out. Never does them any good."

"*Golden Boy* was arrested this morning." Mason barely succeeded in hiding her smile. "Innocent until proven and all that, but your friend Ethan's testimony will help." She jabbed her pen at her notes. "Plus, we got the fingerprints back from Caribbean's apartment. His were on one item. I won't elaborate more now."

Jen looked around the table. "So ... that explains Edward and the Golden guy, which explains why you two are here." She pointed at the detectives. "No offense, Melissa, but why are *you* here?"

The advocate grinned from ear to ear. "Mostly for moral support. And because a lot of this affects Ree and Auggie at a peripheral level. I need to know this to move forward."

"Care to share?" Jen asked.

Melissa's eyes twinkled. "Not yet. I won't do anything of consequence without consulting you two first. But I don't want to get anyone's hopes up—least of all my own."

Later that afternoon, Jen was ready to melt in her lounge chair from the warmth of the indoor pool area. Her curls shriveled from the humidity. Mom and Dad were making good on their pool promise to the twins before the evening crowd appeared. The detectives and Melissa couldn't make it, as Ree had asked, but they'd invited Gretchen and Toby Millbrook to share in the fun.

Their mom, Georgia, hiked her slouch bag over her shoulder. "Well, I best be going. Thanks for asking the kids to come play. They needed to get out of the house. When do you want me to pick them up?" She waved at her kids, blowing them a kiss.

The men stood to say their goodbyes, while Elaine reached out to clasp the younger woman's hand. "It was so good to meet you, Georgia. I hope we'll see more of you soon."

"I 'spect so." Her southern accent dripped like honey. "Gretchen would be lost without Ree."

Those in the know turned to Jen. Her shoulders tensed. Great, more sadness to deliver. "We should be here a couple more hours. Do you have time for a chat?" She gestured to a table in the corner. "It'll be a little quieter over here."

"Why?" Georgia's lips pressed together.

Jen raised her hands in surrender. "Nothing horrific. I promise."

"Sorry. That's a habit I need to lose." She shook her head, as if to relieve it of cobwebs. "Whenever Bennett had bad news, we needed to *chat*." She air quoted, then followed Jen.

"Nothing like that." She hoped her smile would ease the tension. "How's the job search going?"

Georgia's sassiness deteriorated. "Not good. Either I don't have enough experience, or I have too much." Frustration puffed out her cheeks. "No one wants to hire me until my training's finished, but they can't keep the jobs open. And nights and weekends don't work for me, at least not until my two are older. Bennett suggested daycare. Some people have no choice. I do. Over his dead body is a sitter going to raise my kids." She glanced at the twins and turned apple red. "Sorry. I didn't mean to be so flippant."

"No worries." Jen leaned back in her chair. "How far did you get in your Fashion Merchandising classes?"

"Pfft." Georgia waved her hand in the air. "That was so long ago—"

The same dismissive note Cari used to give. Jen's heart leaped. "I'm serious. I'd like to know."

"I left college prior to my senior year ... so about twelve credits shy. Give or take."

"What did you do for your husband's office?"

Georgia cocked her head. "I'm curious. Why the twenty questions?"

"Humor me?"

"What didn't I do for that man? Whenever one of his *oweffice* gals—" She poured on the drawl, a habit Jen already equated with her wicked sense of humor. "If they were too busy to come to work, I had to drop everything and fill in. You're lookin' at receptionist, errand boy, bookkeeper, and gift-giver—all rolled into one perky, middle-aged mom." She flashed a self-deprecating grin.

"And your southern drawl? Was it a tad more pronounced on those days?" Jen chuckled at the twinkle in the green eyes staring back at her.

"Lil ol' me? Why, bless your heart." Georgia batted her lashes. "What's a girl gotta do to get these highfalutin female clients of his to start talkin' to the little ol' wifey?" All pretense and the heavy accent dropped. "Not much, let me tell you."

Bubbles of laughter erupted from Jen.

Georgia covered her mouth with her manicured fingers. "I better watch my tongue. My snarky attitude is having a bit too much fun." She patted her hair. "Again, if you please. Why the interest in my past?"

"Cari's gone, and I'm definitely not ready for another intern right now." She swallowed a moment of fear at the thought. "One way or another, I need help at the showroom. I'd rather it be someone I know, even a little, and who loves the business." Did she see a spark of hope in Georgia's eyes? "At least think about it."

Jen glanced at the kids in the pool. One. Two. Three. Four. All accounted for. She turned back to Georgia. "Maybe a trial run. A couple mornings a week—while your kids are in school—and learn the office side, at least at first." Jen put on her business face. "Plus ... you'd have to pass muster with the rest of my crew. They're all hurting. I won't put them through someone who doesn't mesh with us."

"Seems reasonable."

"The two you'd be working with the closest, besides me, are Eva and her more-than-boyfriend, Richard. He's our sound tech—if he decides to stay."

Georgia's eyebrows raised in question.

"Long story. Anyway, there are some other players but those are the main two. I won't kid you, there's a lot to learn."

"Wouldn't I hinder you? I'm sure everything I learned is outdated."

"Some has changed, I'm sure. But probably not much. And I expect you learn fast."

Georgia's shoulders sagged. "The hours sound more than what I can give. Especially with summer coming up. I need to be with my kids."

"Do you need to be *with* them or have them nearby and know what they're up to?"

Confusion clouded the other woman's eyes.

"Have you been backstage at Lilac?"

"Gretchen's been there with Ree. She said the kids draw a lot. Toby wouldn't sit still for long."

"*Ree* draws a lot. Which is probably why Gretchen thinks the other kids do. The rest of them have a gazillion things to keep themselves occupied at the showroom. Listen ... why don't you come by and—"

"I'm interested. But I reckon I need to finish this training. I'd want to bring some solid skills to the table for you. And I don't quit on my commitments." Her chin hiked a notch.

"How long?"

"I took the extended course. I have a couple more weeks to go. Can you wait?"

"Would you be able to meet some of the crew, maybe Monday afternoon?" It would help keep her mind off the airport visit that day too.

"There's something you're not saying. I noticed the looks between y'all back there. Seemed a family thing ... but maybe not so much?"

"I have some bad news." She lowered her voice. "And I'm afraid you're the one who has to deliver it. I'm sorry."

Georgia bent toward her.

"Ree and Auggie won't be at the showroom. At least for the next three months, probably."

"Whyever not? Where are they going? Not to a foster home, surely? They have you."

"Custody was awarded to Colin." She glanced in his direction.

He spoke with her parents, but his eyes tracked the four kids. He was a good guardian.

Georgia's eyes were pools of water. "Sorry, I'm a sloppy mess lately. Bless y'all's hearts." She gasped. "Gretchen's going to be crushed."

Jen's heart pinched. She watched the girls whispering in the corner of the pool.

"I don't mean to be selfish." Georgia dug around in her jacket pocket and pulled out a tissue. "I'm sure y'all are devastated. I wondered why Ree didn't seem her usual cheerful self."

"We have someone working on the case to hopefully get a more equitable ruling."

"I'm surprised he filed for sole custody." Lips pursed, Georgia scowled at Colin.

"It's not his doing, it was the judge's. I'll let you know when Gretchen can call Ree."

"Whatever helps the girls stay in touch. It looks as if Toby and Auggie are going to need some phone calling too." She pointed at the boys.

Jen turned in time to get a face full of water squirted from a pool noodle.

Colin clamped his lips shut on a laugh.

"Tobias Milbrook! Young man, what have we been talkin' about? Squirting someone is not being respectful."

Jen choked on her laughter. "We need a Toby around the office."

CHAPTER 29

The air hung heavy around the check-in counter while Dallas Fort Worth International came fully awake. Jen hugged Mom tightly. "I'm glad you'll be back soon. I've missed having you near." Though her eyes were watery, she smiled her cheeriest grin. The weekend had flown by with so much planning and packing for everyone.

"Don't keep yourself so busy you don't have time to think while we're gone." Mom choked on the last two words. She hugged Jen with the ferocity of a lioness. "Give yourself permission to grieve. Tears are okay."

Jen glossed over the advice. "I see two sad kids waiting for hugs."

Ree and Auggie rushed to their grandmother.

Mom gave the kids enough loving to last them three months. "When you and Uncle Colin video call on the weekends, we can have breakfast together. Won't that be fun? You'll have to tell me about the fish ladder and the big red sculpture. I haven't seen them in years."

The twins clung to her, quiet little caricatures of themselves.

Jen wasn't entirely sure Auggie understood everything happening. But tears often meant sadness to him, and there were a lot of those going around today. They both snuggled in closer.

Jen's pride pricked a little. If she was honest with herself—and she was trying to be more so—their clinging to her mother stung a little. But Gramma was a neutral party and had nothing to do with their current upheaval. It was almost as if they entwined their hearts around hers—lifelines for all three.

Dad helped Mom from the floor and kneeled for his own hugs, with an eye swipe or two mixed in. He stood and glanced at the departure board. "We'd better get through TSA. International flights, early arrival and all that stuff, you know."

"You have ten more minutes, Grampa." Auggie informed him.

"Well, so we do."

It seemed he'd forgotten about Auggie's fascination with all things aviation. But Jen understood. Dad needed a break from the strong emotions. "Grampa wants a cup of coffee while they wait, hon. The lines might be long."

Moments later, the little band of four waved until they could no longer see them over the TSA divider screens. Auggie tugged on her sleeve. "Will you tell me when they land? My knower isn't working again."

She'd wondered if his uncanny travel sense would function this time, with everyone going in different directions on the same day. "Grampa went over their schedule with you. They have a couple layovers. It'll be late when they get in." She pulled the timetable from his backpack to remind him. "I'll text Uncle Colin, and he'll tell you in the morning. You can rest easy tonight. They'll be fine."

Auggie studied the flight panels, peered at his watch, then out at the sunshiny Texas morning. "Yes, they will."

Hours later, she and the Marshall family stood near the entrance to the domestic flight's security line. They'd driven offsite to grab an early lunch, so Colin wouldn't be traveling with hungry children. The emotional tangles started all over again. Auggie leaned against his uncle, staring into space. Colin appeared stricken.

Lord Jesus. Please don't let our boy retreat. This trip is going to be hard enough on all of them. I ask this with all the faith I have left right now.

Ree approached her. She bent to give the girl a hug but was kept at arm's length.

"Are we really leaving? I prayed this was all a bad dream. Can't you come with us?"

Jen's heart pulverized. "I'm sorry, you really do have to go. I'll watch until you're through the lines, then I'm going to Lilac and see if we forgot to pack anything for you."

"But I prayed, Engine."

Could a person's heart break again if it was already shattered?

"Aww, sweetheart. Remember what we talked about before? Sometimes, what we pray isn't what God has in store for us. Or we have to wait." She took Ree's hands in hers. "And once in a while, we have to wade through some really hard stuff to get to the good parts."

The girl's eyes brimmed, but she nodded.

"I think this might be one of those wading times." Jen pulled the girl to her, personal space or not. "I have no worries you will help Uncle Colin," she whispered. "But you, my girl, need to take care of yourself too. Not too much mothering either one of them. Deal?"

Ree pulled away, and they walked over to Colin and Auggie. Ree grabbed her brother's hand. He turned to her, questioning. *Thank you, Jesus. He hasn't entirely disappeared.*

Colin ruffled Auggie's hair. "Next week, we'll get some cards and postage stamps. You can send them to Engine, Gramma and Grampa, Toby and Gretchen, and your friends at Lilac."

"Cards are 'spensive. Engine says so."

Colin chuckled. "She's right, but we'll go to my favorite store. We can get a bunch."

"He must know about the dollar store too." Ree whispered to her.

Their light banter glued a couple pieces of Jen's heart back together. They'd be okay. Not great for a while. But they'd all survive.

"Collie Dog." Auggie studied his watch. "We need to get to our gate. We don't want them to leave without us."

"Yes, we do." Ree muttered.

With a flurry of tall hugs and short kisses, Jen watched as the Marshall trio wheeled their carry-ons through the security line maze. Just before they entered the shielded area, Auggie bobbed up and down and waved at her. All she could see of Ree was the top of her curly ponytail. Colin sent Jen a grim smile, then turned and ushered his two young charges forward.

And *poof*, her heart and soul were gone.

Jen left the building and found the van she'd rented to shuttle everyone to the airport. She got in and locked the doors. Anxiety pressed at the edges of her thoughts. She bowed her head, hugged the steering wheel, and concentrated on calming her racing pulse. Sometime later, a tap sounded on her window, causing her to jump. A safety officer stood next to the vehicle, the lights on his truck flashing behind the van. She rolled the glass down enough to talk to him.

"You okay, ma'am?"

"Yes." She blew her nose. "Thank you for checking on me. I'll take off now."

"Only if you can drive safely."

She attempted a smile to reassure him.

"Take care." He gave a short salute and turned away.

Father, thank you for sending me a lifeline.

After an hour's drive through heavier than normal Dallas traffic, Jen unlocked the front doors of Lilac Lane and walked inside. She turned the deadbolt, more for privacy than any danger. The threat was gone.

The foyer loomed dark as her mood. She opened the blackout curtains and raised the shades. Sunshine flooded the interior, making the deserted showroom less bleak. In stark contrast, sorrow curled deep in her chest, ready to lash out and drown her at any moment.

She flicked the switch for the spotlight over the sound booth. Walking down the aisle toward it, she thought back to when she stood in this very spot, discussing the crushed microphone with Richard. A lifetime ago.

She swiveled Auggie's chair and eased into it, careful not to disturb anything left behind. She rocked in gentle motion back and forth, like he'd done when he had to wait for Richard's attention. Touching a knob, she could almost hear him. "Not like that, Engine. Richard says to slide it slow and easy. The bass has to be here or the music booms too loud. Richard says—"

A grin played at the corners of her lips. What would they call Auggie's buddy now, Richard or Ricky? And what would he do without his shadow? Eva wasn't into the technical stuff.

Assuming he stayed, now that his personal mission was over, could one of the other kids help? Jen walked around the outside of the booth, running her fingers along the polished wood.

No, this was still Auggie's domain. They'd revisit that question later.

She hiked herself onto the end of the catwalk. It took too much effort to go farther. Sitting cross-legged, hands limp in her lap, she closed her eyes. The workroom could wait.

Voices came to her. Laughter. Music. She squinted through her lashes. No one was there. Shutting her eyes again, she basked in the memory of past shows a moment longer, reliving the sights, sounds, and smells one last time.

You need a hobby. The voice interrupted her reverie. No shaking hands. No trembling fingers. If this was Cari, maybe it was time to let her go. She'd call her former psychiatrist next week for an appointment. Someone to talk to. A real person. Not some disembodied noise in her head.

Time to get to work, ol' girl. The voice bossed.

Jen opened her eyes, but they refused to focus. Her lashes fluttered. The afternoon light intensified, shafts of it shimmering and racing toward the runway. If she imagined hard enough ... was that Cari throwing her a kiss? She blinked. Nothing there. Just some dust caught on a beam from the house lights.

She sighed and pushed herself up from the catwalk, made her way to the back of the stage, and ran her hand over the filmy curtains still hanging there. As the silky panels glided through her fingers, her thoughts careened back to the larger-than-life photographs splashed across them a few days ago. The closing ones she hadn't allowed herself to even think about again, until now. The final two shots of her and Cari together. Forever.

Annie had snapped the set of them that last morning. The first one serious—the perfect image of competent businesswomen in their natural habitat—was currently at the framers in preparation for the portrait to hang in the front of the showroom.

The second one, the one Annie had goaded them into, was silly. Playful. Themselves. The charity show was the only time Jen intended on sharing that photo. It was hers alone.

Cari, bending low to Jen's height, crossing her eyes, and sticking out her tongue. Jen, mugging for the camera, all teeth, her cheeks riding up to hide her eyes.

Thinking of her favorite part of the photo, she choked. Cari's long, manicured fingers formed bunny ears behind Jen's head. She should have guessed from Annie's chuckle that morning. Her best friend could always make people laugh.

She'd never hear that giggle again. Never receive another hug from her. Read sonnets together or be scolded by her. Never—

"Aagghh." A wail tore from her throat. She tugged at the moorings but stopped herself. How could she ruin what the rest of her team had done to support her final vision for Cari? She groped for the opening in the drapes. Why hadn't she let someone know she was coming in today? Anyone to add a little life, an extra heartbeat, a shoulder to cry on. Rushing through the stage curtains, she fled to the sanctuary of her workroom.

CHAPTER 30

Jen scooped the wad of used tissues into the garbage and stared at her blank sketch pad once again. Keys scratching in the backdoor lock broke her reverie. She'd just turned the corner from the office when the door opened to reveal Eva. "Hi, love. We figured you to be here."

Richard cracked his knuckles behind her. "We also have something we want to talk to you about." Eva gave her boyfriend a sidelong glance.

Now what? I can't handle more bad news today. "How about we go in the office where it's more comfortable?"

Jen curled up on the settee. Eva arranged her full skirt around her and tucked her hands beneath it in one of the visitor chairs. Richard kept going through to the workroom.

"Do either of you want anything from the fridge?" He called over his shoulder.

"Water for me." Jen rolled her neck. "On second thought, make it a sparkling water, please."

"Atta girl." Eva winked at her. "Make that two, love."

Jen turned to the model. "I'm trying, but it's hard."

"It gets less painful. I promise."

A soft assurance flowed between them. "Your Nanna?" Jen knew they'd been close. "I've never asked. Did she ever come to the States to see you?"

Eva shook her head. "She wanted to. She raised me up to travel and explore but never left Barbados herself." Her soft accent shifted around her words.

"That's so sad. I wish she could've seen you here." Jen gestured to the whole of Lilac Lane. Sharing in her friend's old grief lifted some of the ache around her own heart.

"She'da loved you. But shush now. It be long past. And looka here, it gave me all of you as my family." Sadness flashed across her face but disappeared as quickly as her heavy dialect. "And it got me Richard." She winked at him as he ambled back into the room, holding the necks of three bottles in one hand and a half-eaten sandwich in the other. "My always ravenous Richard."

"Hey. A guy's gotta eat when he can." His ears flamed.

Jen stifled a giggle. He was cute when he was flustered, which was often around Eva. She'd be good for him. "Well, now. What did you two want to talk about?"

Richard plopped into the chair next to his girlfriend. "It can wait." He stretched his long legs in front of him.

"You let the proverbial cat out of that bag, love. You might as well get on with it."

He shoved the rest of his sandwich in his mouth and chewed.

Eva seemed content to play along and stayed quiet.

He swallowed. "Well, I uh ... I was hoping you wouldn't ... you know."

"Nope, I don't." Jen had a tough time keeping the mirth from her voice.

"I was, um, hoping you wouldn't fire me."

Time to put the poor guy out of his misery. "I thought about it, but I have no intention of letting you go. The question is, why would you want to stay here? I'll never be able to compete with your Keane Intelliware salary."

He waved a dismissive hand. "I'm good with sound engineer at Lilac, as long as you don't mind me disappearing once in a while, when the Keane crew needs me."

"If you're agreeable to it, I'd like to make you facilities manager." She chuckled at his ear-to-ear grin. "Don't look so surprised. Once your motives for being here were clear, you earned everyone's trust back in a heartbeat."

His face went through the mixture of emotions Auggie swore his buddy possessed.

"If you take it, you'll have to work with Harold to find another maintenance lead. He's retiring. But he said he'll stay on to help until someone else is found, as long as it's with you." She let that news sink in. "You'd oversee maintaining the showroom, keeping the technology running smoothly, setting up transportation to outside shows ... things like that. As for you disappearing sometimes, let me know, and we'll work something out."

He rocked forward, almost upsetting his chair. "I don't know what to say. Except yes."

"Don't you want to know the pay?"

Eva giggled.

"We can talk about it later. I accept."

She hadn't forgotten about his well-heeled background from his early technological developments. She guessed he'd likely work for what she paid him now, just to stay near Eva, but she'd compensate him with what she could.

"Love?" Eva eyed him.

"Oh, yeah. I got a little carried away. So, Jen." He cleared his throat. "Jennifer." His tone turned business-like, but a lopsided grin lit up his face. "That no fraternizing policy we have at Lilac. How firm is it? Like ... does it apply to a husband and wife?"

"What?" She yelped. "You two are ... when ... how ... I don't mean ... but ..." Her words jumbled together. "When's the big day?"

Eva gave a little squeal and held out her hand.

Examining the ring, some of her earlier depression lifted. Excitement hummed through her. The modest-sized stone twinkled. The gorgeous, cushion-cut sapphire, nestled between petite, channel-set diamonds appeared flawless. "It's beautiful."

"Sassy designed it, but she didn't know it was for our engagement." Eva confided. "Richard has a small family, mostly here in Dallas, except for his parents in New York. I have no one other than all of you. We'd like to be married soon, once his best man returns from overseas, and you know more about the kids' future."

Jen left the topic of August Guildane, Richard's friend, and Lilac's fraternization policy hanging in the air for now and took a page from Ethan's book of optimism. "Everything will work out."

"Do you think Colin can bring the twins for a visit? We'll even wait for that stupid three months," Eva spat the words, "if it means they can be here to celebrate with us."

Jen twirled a curl around her finger, thinking. "We'll work on the logistics of the kids coming for the wedding later. But for now, I have a favor to ask."

"Sure. What is it?" Her friends chimed together.

"You probably noticed the police tape gone." She pointed toward Cari's dressing room. "They released the Kingdom. I've been putting it off all afternoon, but I need some time in there, before anyone else. I have to decide what I want to keep for the kids and their future. And I need to say goodbye."

"You sure that's a good thing, love? You want someone with you?"

Jen shook her head. "I need to do this. By myself." She eyed the bottle of sparkling water trembling in her grasp. "But please, don't leave yet."

Eva bobbed her head. "We'll both be here. You need anything, you shout."

They finished their drinks in a comfortable, if thoughtful, silence.

Jen finally stood, fished in her purse for her keys, and clutched them to her chest, the metal digging into her palm. "I'll be back." She turned to leave but spun around and retrieved her cellphone. "In case I get a call from the airport."

Wishful thinking.

Unlocking Cari's Kingdom, easy. Opening it, not so much. Stepping over the threshold, pure torture. Jen shut the door with a soft *whoosh*. The absence of the frieze carpet was the only telltale sign a crime had been committed there. She tiptoed to the dressing table. Placing her keys on the lacquered top, she was careful not to scratch the beloved piece. Her phone trembled in her hand, clutched with white-knuckled tension.

The room was so quiet she could hear the air rush in and out of her lungs. Her chest vibrated with the all-too-familiar warning of an anxiety attack. Maybe this wasn't such a good idea. She sank onto Cari's dressing stool like the last time she was here. Instead of putting her head between her knees—as she'd done then—she bowed it in prayer.

Dear Jesus. Please get me through these next weeks without losing my mind. She usually took vacation this time of year. But where could she go that her broken heart wouldn't follow?

The Bible verse she'd been trying to recall lately played through her memory. She'd learned it as a young girl but hadn't leaned on it enough lately. "Cast all your anxiety on him because he cares for you."

I'm casting everything on you, Lord. Thank you for your love and light and direction. Forgive me if I ask for some concrete notice of your plans for a while, until I get more used to you being in charge without me as a backseat driver. A giggle escaped her. *You know, a phone call or something from heaven would be great.*

Her text notification chirped. She jumped and fumbled for her cell.

Call ASAP. News. Important.

Her heart leaped to her throat, and she sent an appreciative, "Thank you," heavenward.

Melissa answered on the second ring. "Hey, I was trying to catch Colin before he took off but had to leave a message. He should get it when he lands." She sounded out of breath.

"Is everything all right?"

"It's heading that way."

Jen's heartbeat quickened. "How so?"

"I received word from Judge Swanson. He's lightened some of Arbuckle's stipulations."

Melissa's use of her mother's family name was accompanied by a dagger of distaste. *Jesus, please help my friend. She needs you in her corner.* "Can he do that?"

"I may have sicced Dr. Brasil on him to explain the twins' particular needs. The doc did good. Judge Swanson agreed—not in so many words—some of the rulings were plain spiteful, given the unusual circumstances. He's not siding with us as much as I wanted, but more than I'd hoped."

"Is there any chance of shared custody?"

"We didn't get that far. I've got to handle this carefully. I'm going over Arbuckle's head." A pause filled the air. "Something I shouldn't be doing."

Jen's pulse thumped. Would they get Melissa in trouble? "I'm so sorry. If I could think of another way to take care of this—"

"This is my battle to fix, Jennifer. The ruling was directed at me."

"Am I still banned from seeing the kids for three months?"

"Nope. Judge Swanson thinks a visit from their godmother would be a perfect Christmas gift for the twins. But you do have to go there. He doesn't want the kids coming back to Texas until after the New Year for some reason."

"No problem. Christmas in Grand Rapids sounds lovely." Her heart was ready to burst from her chest. "This is good news. Eva and Richard just announced they're getting married. They'd like the twins and Colin at the wedding."

"Excellent. Find out when, and we'll work toward that date for the rest of the details. It's a good reason to get them here for a visit with Judge Swanson too." She giggled. "He'll love them." Melissa cleared her throat. "He originally said they couldn't come back to Dallas until the end of the school year. He didn't want them yanked out again and wasting too much time, but I explained their current hybrid situation. He's going to let the two of you decide what to do regarding their education—*with* court approval. He's willing to oversee this case personally."

"I sense an underlying issue."

"Let's just say he's been a friend of hers for a long time, but he thinks she finally crossed the line of decency—his words. So, the kids stay with Colin for now, you can visit at Christmas, and ... oh yeah, you are allowed to respond to him immediately, in case he has questions. The good judge is certain he will." Melissa chuckled. "We had quite the discussion of bachelors becoming instant fathers with no preparation. He married a single mom himself. Anyway, Colin can get hold of you as soon as he needs to, but he must initiate the call ... in case he wants some space. The judge was adamant about that."

Jen stood and paced the room.

"That's why I was trying to catch him before he left. I'm the messenger. You get to talk to the kids the moment Colin okays it. Judge Swanson originally said two weeks but relented after hearing everything they've been through."

"How can I ever thank you enough? I don't know what to say, other than I am so glad you're on our side."

A weary sigh came through the receiver. "I only hope you and Colin can forgive me for this mess. I would really like to see those kids grow up. It's almost ... somehow it feels like looking into a brand-new mirror from inside a broken one. I don't mean to sound melodramatic, but—"

"I think I understand. As far as being in the kids' lives, we both know that's Colin's department now, but I doubt it will be an issue." Jen looked at her cell. "They should be landing in about half an hour. When you talk to Colin, can you give him a message from me? Tell him ... let him know I'm only a phone call away."

"Will do. Stay in touch, Jennifer."

Peering around the room, Jen's heart was lighter than it had been in days. Eva and Richard would help bring life back to Lilac Lane. There might even be babies learning to toddle through the hallways again. Ree and Auggie would be tickled when they visited in the future.

She turned toward the dressing table and ran her hand over the glass-topped surface. "This may not be the best decision I've ever made, but you're going into my bedroom. I'll ask the guys to move you tomorrow. You're Ree's when she's older. If she wants you."

Swiveling back around, the coordinating white chifforobe caught her attention. "And somehow, I'll figure out where to put you, as well." Auggie would remember the vintage armoire later, she was sure of it. They could always paint it a different color for him.

Other than photos strewn here and there, she didn't feel a pull toward anything else. She would go through the drawers later. Neither child had wanted much when they'd been questioned about it yesterday. Ree requested Cari's fancy barrettes and headbands. And they both asked for their mother's small curio cabinet with their travel mementos. Together, they could recall every country and special trip where each toy or figurine was purchased.

Jen typed the items in her to-do list on her phone. She'd pack them away until the twins' situation was less tenuous. She wasn't quite sure yet about the small selection of gowns that Cari had kept from various events. Into a trunk they would go for now. Everything else, decisions for later.

"Goodbye, Cari. I'm going to miss you." She addressed the stale air. She walked to the door and took hold of the handle. Would she be able to sit across from this room and not continually wait for Cari to emerge from it? Maybe she should take that vacation.

Her phone rang. Surprise registered to see Sassafras's name and new cellphone number. Her jeweler friend was usually in her workroom and unavailable at this time of day.

"Hey, Sassy, I was thinking about getting away. Do you have a burning desire to visit any place special? Want to play hooky with me?"

The other end of the line was silent.

"Sassy?"

Sniffles sounded in her ear.

"Sassafras, what is it?"

"Do you ... could you ... can you come to Seattle?"

"Sure, hon. When were you thinking?"

"Yesterday. Now," Sassy cried. "The sooner the better."

"What's wrong?" Her words were shrill.

"I didn't do it, Jen. I promise. I didn't."

"Didn't what? Sassy! What is going on?"

"They think I killed him."

The End

AN EXTRA TREAT FOR YOU, DEAR READER.

Something Old, Something New, Borrowed and ... Goo?

A true story from my designer days

The beautiful, red-headed bride took sure steps down the aisle toward her groom. Her smile hinted at some delightful news she longed to share. She radiated happiness in her one-of-a-kind gown and headpiece. Whether she'd tucked away the bridal poem necessities symbolizing hope for her future—something old, something new, something borrowed, something blue—was anyone's guess. This dress and headpiece held an extra note of anxiety for my designer's heart. The bride was to join my uncle at the altar and officially become part of our family in a gown I had sewn. And she was doing it with a secret contribution she wouldn't find out about for nearly twenty years.

Several years earlier, loving all things wedding, I started a bridal accessories business. Having already graduated with a Bachelor of Fine Arts, creativity was nothing new to me.

I worked with brides to design their headpieces and bouquets to complement their gowns. Elegant, unusual, colorful, classic, and everything in between. Shoes, gauntlets, and headbands. Embellished and beaded everything.

My husband dared not walk across the carpet barefoot in our spare room for fear of stepping on a straight pin. Spools and spools of ribbon hung from the wall, waiting to adorn the heads of brides throughout Michigan and other locales—even one from New York. Word of mouth worked, but not well. I needed ideas to market this new enterprise, so I enrolled in a Fashion Merchandising program at the local college.

The Garment Construction class culminated with a fashion event. My original design muse—a bride wanting an elegant but simple sheath gown—eloped just weeks before I was to begin the final project. Out of necessity, I accepted an intricate design requiring multiple alterations due to the bride's continual weight loss. The final gown was too delicate to be worn down the runway with other students' work, so our professor isolated it behind velvet stanchions. Showcased but untouchable. Additionally, a bouncing baby boy joined our family that spring and my workroom would serve as his nursery. I figured I had sewn my last bridal costume ever.

My soon-to-be aunt had other ideas and asked me to help plan her gown. Design? Sure. Easy-peasy. Combining bits and pieces of multiple patterns to create the dress of her dreams. Whoever had the privilege of sewing the finished product would produce a gorgeous garment, with unique details, including a heart-shaped cutout across her back.

Then she did the unthinkable and entrusted me to sew it for her as well. Could I? A lowly fashion merchandising student with mid-list sewing experience? The specially ordered satin and lace she chose was even more expensive than the earlier dress I'd made. There was no way I could afford another bolt if I messed up.

But she of the red hair had more faith in me than I did. She assured me there was time, and she would be patient around my new role of motherhood. Which brings us back to the secret.

Our oldest son was born in April of my final semester. Aunt and uncle were to be married in September. During the early summer months, while my husband went overseas for work, I spent hours a day at our not-yet-sold mobile home working on her dress. Baby boy didn't need much in that season. A light blanket, his pop-up crib and diaper bag, and as he got older, his newfound treat of teething cookies. Oh, those messy things. Ooey, gooey, and Maple tree brown. But tasty to a baby boy whose mom didn't always have as much time to play as he wanted.

In the beginning, while he napped, I sewed yards and yards of that buttery soft material into a fitted bodice with a Queen Anne neckline, the heart-shaped cutout in back, and ending with a magnificently draped train. Weeks later came the finishing touches. Good thing, since our home and most furnishings had recently sold. We would soon vacate the premises.

During one of the last days at our house, I plopped on the empty living room floor and turned the dress inside out, spreading it smoothly into a gigantic semi-circle.

Baby boy was only a few feet away on his blanket. He'd been *off* most of the morning, playing with his toes during nursing time and napping fitfully. He wasn't even interested in gumming one of the teething cookies, so I set it aside at the edge of his blanket for later. Finally, he seemed content to lay under his activity gym, batting the rings, squishies, and noisemakers. Happy baby gurgles and my frequent glances ensured his safety. I could settle into my work.

My critical, creative eye inspected every inch of that dress. Did any trim need further tacking? Another pearl? More sequins? Nearing the finish line of the project, everything seemed to be moving along, including the dress ... inching away from my grasp. I looked up to a most satisfied grin adorning my son's chubby cheeks and his little fingers buried deep in the waistband of his soon-to-be great aunt's oh-so-soft satin dress. Cookie goo dribbled from his mouth.

I whisked him to the sink and refused to think of the damage his adorable little digits might have caused the gown. With his sticky fingers and little face washed, he offered a mighty yawn, taxed by his grand adventure across the two feet of blanket. He nursed again, and then I plopped him, peacefully asleep, into his bouncy seat.

I braved a peek at the damage. Brown gooey fingerprints danced along the hem. My mind jumped over the what ifs like a game of hopscotch. Too much water could ruin the material. We were out of time to order more. In a few days, I would lose my space to sew. Seeing no other alternative, I would have to replace the gown. Where was I going to come up with the cash?

In a last-ditch effort, my fingers gently dabbed at the light brown mess. Thankfully, I'd been working with the gown turned inside-out. Even more of a blessed coincidence was that baby boy had found the one section of waist seam I hadn't yet trimmed. I sent up a prayer of thanks that nothing, not one little crumb could be seen from the outside. On the inside, only a tiny smear was visible, deep between layers where the bodice and skirt joined. Nearly invisible, except to this momma who didn't tell a soul for ages.

MURDER MAY I

Years later, I finally gained the nerve to share this story with my aunt. She laughed and glanced at her great nephew, now a tall young man in college, who had uniquely accessorized her bridal poem. Something old, something new, something borrowed, and something goo.

In memory of Nancy Gowell Meyer
Photograph used with permission from Randy Passeno